The Secrets of Summerhayes

BOOKS BY MERRYN ALLINGHAM

The Secrets of Summerhayes

MERRYN ALLINGHAM

bookouture

Published by Bookouture in 2023

An imprint of Storyfire Ltd.
Carmelite House
50 Victoria Embankment
London EC4Y 0DZ

www.bookouture.com

Copyright © Merryn Allingham, 2017, 2023

Merryn Allingham has asserted her right to be identified as the author of this work.

First published as *The Secret of Summerhayes* by HQ in 2017.

All rights reserved. No part of this publication may be reproduced, stored in any retrieval system, or transmitted, in any form or by any means, electronic, mechanical, photocopying, recording or otherwise, without the prior written permission of the publishers.

ISBN: 978-1-80314-768-0
eBook ISBN: 978-1-80314-767-3

This book is a work of fiction. Names, characters, businesses, organizations, places and events other than those clearly in the public domain, are either the product of the author's imagination or are used fictitiously. Any resemblance to actual persons, living or dead, events or locales is entirely coincidental.

1

Something about the scene caught at him, some memory he couldn't grasp. Behind him the tangled mass of alders—they *were* alders, weren't they?—but before his eyes, a landscape he must have read about, or perhaps dreamt. He'd never been here before, that was certain. The last two years had been spent miles away and, though since January his regiment had been moving from camp to camp, this was the furthest west they had come.

Jos Kerrigan pushed past the last few branches and received another scratch to add to all the others. The trees had long ago grown together to form an almost impenetrable barrier. The old fellow who'd given him a lift had heard the word Summerhayes and dropped him at what must have been the rear entrance. He should have stopped at the broken brick columns and found another way in, walked around the perimeter wall until he came to the main driveway. That was probably in the same ramshackle state, but the tanks would have bulldozed a path by now and the going would be easier. Very much easier. He should turn back.

But he didn't. Something made him push on, that dream

perhaps, a misty image he carried with him. Now that he was clear of the trees, he could see more than a few feet ahead. He appeared to be standing on what had once been a paved terrace. Beneath the heaps of dead winter leaves, he glimpsed terracotta. A Mediterranean colour, out of place in an English garden, or even an English wilderness. It appeared to circle what must have once been a lake but was now stagnant water, carpeted from one side to the other with giant water lilies. The air was slightly sour; it smelt of mud, smelt of must. In the centre of the lake, the remains of a statue, broken and chipped, rose strangely from out of the rampant vegetation. It was as though, wounded and maimed, it was trying to escape.

Something about the place held him fast. Jos stood for a long time, feeling his pulse gradually slacken, the rhythm of his heart seeming to align itself to that of the earth. What kind of craziness was that? He shook his head in disbelief and, as quickly as the heavy backpack allowed, made his way to an archway in one corner of the clearing. The exit, he imagined, but it was as overgrown as everything else, its laurel leaves a dense mass.

He looked back before shouldering through this new obstruction. On one side of the lake there had been a small summerhouse, but its roof was smashed and a giant vine had weaved its way through the corpse. Directly across the water, there had been another building, and he could see immediately that it was one built to impressive proportions. Now all that remained of it were two or three shattered columns and the dais they stood upon. It seemed to have been some kind of temple, for the pediment had crashed to the ground and taken several pillars with it. Did English gardens have temples? He supposed they must. In that instant, the sun emerged from a passing cloud and glanced across the remaining pillars, its rays flashing pure crystal. He gave a low whistle. The building was of marble. Once upon a time, this had been a wealthy place.

With some difficulty he pushed through the strangled archway but was immediately brought up short. He was facing what appeared to be an acre of grass and brambles, at least six feet in height, and with no path in sight. Here and there huge palm trees rose out of the oversized meadow, spreading their arms in a riot of tough, sword-like prongs or half-tumbled to the ground, their hairy trunks dank and rotted. Between the palms, gigantic ferns hovered like green spiders inflated to monstrous size. He would never find his way through this, and he was running out of time.

By now everyone would have settled their billets, his men would be waiting for orders and Eddie would be wondering where the hell he'd got to. His pal would be brewing coffee and if he hadn't had to do that damned detour, he'd be drinking alongside him. It had been a waste of time in any case; when he'd got to Aldershot, he'd found the regiment's surplus equipment had already been despatched without any help from him. The logistics of constantly moving were a nightmare and he hoped this was the last camp they'd pitch before the push into Europe.

For months the regiment had been gradually inching along the south coast, practising manoeuvres as they went. It was common knowledge that an invasion this summer was on the cards; he was pretty sure it would be only a matter of weeks. He prayed, they all prayed, there'd be no repeat of the Dieppe debacle. The planners had called it a reconnaissance, his fellow soldiers a disaster. The element of surprise had been lost. A German navy patrol had spotted the Canadians and alerted the batteries on shore. His countrymen had faced murderous fire within a few yards of their landing craft—over three thousand killed, maimed or captured, and fewer than half their number returning to tell their story. Jos had lost friends in that attack and mourned them still.

He pushed on, striking due north in the hope of finding

some sign of men and machines, using his knife to hack a narrow path through grass that grew to the height of a small hut. It was hot and steamy and pungent. The backpack weighed heavier with each minute and, though it was only April, the sun was unusually bright and he was forced to push back the fall of hair from his forehead and wipe a trickle of sweat from his face. After fifteen minutes, he'd progressed just fifty yards. Standing still, he gazed across at the tangle of grass and palms and ferns. He'd had enough.

He turned to go back the way he'd come and it was only then that he became aware he was not alone. Through the long stalks of grass, a pair of eyes peered at him, fixing him in an unnerving gaze. It was as though the grass itself was deciding whether he were friend or foe.

Then a small voice broke the silence. 'Are you lost?'

2

Bethany Merston turned into the drive of Summerhayes and saw the Canadian army had well and truly arrived. The estate had been a military base for years now, the house and grounds requisitioned at the outbreak of war, but this was altogether a far larger invasion. For several days past the clatter of men and trucks had been a noisy backdrop to life. The advance party, she'd guessed, but now it appeared the entire battalion had taken possession of the estate. And the men on either side of the drive—parking jeeps, carrying supplies, marching briskly between temporary shelters—were larger, too. They made the local population look weaklings. Unlike the natives, they'd not endured years of rationing, nor an interwar period of poor nourishment and intermittent work.

This morning, as the first trucks had rolled in, she'd walked to the village for whatever supplies she could forage but returned with little. Neither she nor Alice nor Mr Ripley would get too fat on what her solitary bag contained. But at least she'd managed to buy cocoa powder for Alice's night-time drink. Only a few ounces, and it would have to be sweetened with the honey she'd bartered for last week, but it would keep the old lady going a little longer. If Mrs Summer had cocoa at bedtime, she slept well. Even the drone of German bombers flying low towards London didn't disturb her, and that meant that Beth slept well, too.

She crunched her way along the gravel drive taking care to avoid the whirlwind of activity, but walking as swiftly as she could. If the noise had penetrated to the upstairs apartment, Mrs Summer would be anxious. Her working life, it seemed, had altered little except to exchange the care of thirty small bodies for a single elderly one. Looking after an old lady wasn't that much different from looking after a young child. Both needed reassurance and practical help; both blossomed with kindness.

A few months ago, a stray bomb falling on Quilter Street had obliterated the Bethnal Green school where she worked. It was a miracle it had happened at night and there had been no casualties, but it had left her jobless. Thank goodness, then, for the advert in *The Lady*. Within weeks she'd found the post at Summerhayes, though it was one she had never imagined for herself. But in wartime needs must, and a war spent here was as good as anywhere. The Sussex countryside was beautiful and the estate, though fallen into disrepair, still retained a little of its former glory. Above all, the place was tranquil and, coming from a ravaged London, she was grateful for its peace though now the Canadian army had arrived in force, peace might be a lost treasure.

One or two of the soldiers glanced curiously at her as she made her way to the side door, but she managed to slip into the house without attracting much attention. She slid past the drawing room, catching a brief glimpse of several officers' caps on the mantel shelf, past the dining room where desks were being shifted and typewriters arranged, and then up the stairs to the apartment she shared with Alice, all that was left for the old lady of the magnificent Arts and Crafts mansion she had once inhabited. Almost certainly the senior officers would be billeted in the house, while junior officers and their men were consigned to tents in the grounds. Or maybe this time they would build more permanent structures, though Bethany doubted it. Rumours of invasion were rife and the battalion was unlikely to stay long.

Everyone was aware that the military had increased hugely of late, a steady flow of army units turning into a flood. The whole of Sussex had become a vast, armed camp. Mortars and artillery had long been familiar sounds on the South Downs, along with the screech and clatter of tank tracks in the surrounding villages, but now it was impossible to walk a country lane without being passed by a ten-ton truck or a speeding jeep. On her last visit to the village, she'd had to jump into a ditch to avoid a rogue tank trundling down the narrowest of roads and filling it from hedgerow to hedgerow.

She had reached the cramped staircase to the apartment when the wailing hit her. Mrs Summer! She raced up the remaining stairs, fumbling for the key as she went. The new girl from the village had begun work today and Beth had thought it safe to disappear for an hour and leave her to keep an eye. Molly had been cleaning the small kitchen when she'd left, but when Beth finally burst through the door, the girl was nowhere to be seen. Instead, she found the old lady in the sitting room, hunched into the corner of a wing chair, her body rocking back and forth to the rhythm of her cries.

Beth glanced wildly around and her heart sank. A white envelope. Another letter. Ripley had been told to make sure that no such letters were delivered to his mistress, except via Bethany. But the former butler was an old man, a pensioner now rather than a worker, and he would be laid down on his bed for a morning nap. She had given the same instructions to Molly before she left, but the girl had clearly forgotten.

'Mrs Summer, it's all right, I'm here.'

She flung the bag to the floor, unmindful that their week's rations would be squashed out of recognition, then knelt down at the elderly woman's side and took her in her arms, holding her close and trying to calm the demented rocking. Very gradually, Alice became still and the sobs ceased. Beth stroked the thin, grey hair into place and fished in her pocket for a handkerchief to dab tears from the deeply lined cheeks.

'But it's not all right.' Alice looked up, her eyes pools of sadness. 'It's not all right,' she repeated. 'She isn't coming.'

Beth took the envelope that the old lady was still clasping and extracted a single sheet of paper. With growing anger, she read: *The journey has been difficult but I've arrived in London at last. I will try and get to you soon. You know that is what I want above all else. But I'm feeling so tired that I'm not sure now I can make it as far as Sussex. I will write again when I feel better.*

Someone was playing tricks, Beth was sure. It was cruel beyond belief. The letters were typewritten and never signed, but Mrs Summer had become convinced they came from a daughter who had disappeared thirty years ago. Why the old lady believed this, Bethany wasn't sure. It was perhaps a simple longing for it to be true. Elizabeth Summer, she'd learned, had never contacted her family since the day she'd eloped to marry a man of whom they disapproved. Could a much-loved daughter be so callous as never to have written? Beth thought not. After all these years of silence, it was most likely that the woman was dead.

When Beth had first met her employer, Alice Summer had seemed to agree. But then the letters had started to arrive—as far as Beth knew, none had come earlier—and the old lady had become convinced that Elizabeth was still in the world. It was pointless to argue away her belief. In some corner of Alice's mind she must always have kept her daughter alive. Hadn't May Prendergast said that despite her long-standing opposition,

Mrs Summer had eventually agreed to employ a companion purely because of a name? Bethany, Beth, Elizabeth. The letters must have ignited a long-suppressed desire and given it heart. Beth hadn't told May about the letters, and Mr Ripley and Molly Dumbrell knew only to intercept them. The fewer people who knew of Alice's fantasy, the better.

She took the sheet of paper and folded it back into the envelope. She would destroy it, as she had with the others, and hope Mrs Summer might forget she had ever received it. Still kneeling, she continued to cuddle the meagre frame until she felt Alice relax a little. 'Shall I put the kettle on?' she asked brightly. 'We can talk over tea—I've some news from the village.'

Beth had hoped this might spark interest, but the old lady continued to stare into her lap.

'I met May,' she pursued.

'May Lacey?' Alice lifted her head.

'Her mother sends you her very best wishes. She'd love to come and see you, but May says that she's almost bedbound now.' Mrs Lacey had once been the housekeeper at Summerhayes.

'She was a good worker,' Alice mused, the past as always having the power to animate. 'A trifle sharp at times, but a good worker. And her daughter—she was a bonny girl. She did well for herself, she married the curate—May Prendergast she became—and then she got to be the vicar's wife. Fancy that! It was a shame he died. It's not a happy thing being a widow and this new man at the church—tsk. I'd not give him the time of day. He is far too opinionated, far too sure of himself.'

That was probably what a vicar should be, Beth reflected, but the thought remained unspoken; it was clear that Alice liked her religion vague.

'Mrs Lacey may not be able to visit, but May will come.' She paused at the sitting room door. 'She has a new group of children to settle in the village, but promised to call in later this week. They're evacuees from Brighton. Apparently the house they've been staying in has been declared unsafe.'

Bethany looked forward, as much as her employer, to May's visits. Despite their age difference, the two of them had become good friends in the few months she had been at Summerhayes. It had been May who had placed the advertisement in *The Lady*.

We had the devil's own job to persuade her to get help, May had said. *Me and Mr Ripley between us. She doesn't like change and the thought of someone new in the house sent her frantic. But then she saw your letter—you'd signed it Beth—and that was enough.*

Beth never used her full name if she could possibly help it. Bethany had been her father's choice, a constant reminder of an old shame and of her difference from the new family her mother had created. In this case, though, it had worked to her advantage. A letter signed Beth had won her the job, that and the fact that she was not much older than Elizabeth Summer had been when she had disappeared. Alice must have been thinking of Elizabeth long before the letters arrived. Letters and long-lost daughters, it was an alchemy, but it had given Beth employment when she was desperate for work and desperate to avoid a forced retreat to the home she hated and the family who didn't want her.

'Will Ivy come with her?' Alice asked. 'When May visits?'

'Ivy is married now, remember? That's why May advertised in the magazine. That's why I'm here.'

'I remember. Of course, I remember. Dear Ivy. Such a stalwart girl. And she was Elizabeth's maid before she was mine.'

'I know, Mrs Summer.' Alice must have told her a dozen times already. It was as though the missing girl had come to dominate her mind to the exclusion of all else.

'Yes,' the old lady was saying, 'she and Elizabeth were maid and mistress, but that didn't matter. They grew up together and were the best of friends. Ivy knew all Elizabeth's secrets.' Alice turned to look out of the window. The scene below was one of frenetic activity, but it was clear that she saw none of it. 'All her secrets,' she repeated, 'except where she'd gone. Elizabeth never told her that. She didn't want to get the girl into trouble.'

The old face drooped and a tear formed in the corner of her eye. She looked hopelessly around, then caught sight of the letter still in Beth's grasp. With difficulty she wriggled to the edge of her seat, tensing her feet on the floor, as though she would launch herself forward. Then, with both hands, reached out for the oblong of white paper.

'I'll put it on the mantelpiece for now and make the tea,' Beth said hastily.

3

The kitchen was looking bright and clean. At least Molly knew her job even if she couldn't remember instructions. They rarely drank tea before evening and Beth hoped there would be enough to last them for the next seven days. Standing in the grocer's this morning, it seemed as though the number of coupons in their ration books shrank by the week. She put the kettle to boil and found two clean cups. It was then she became aware that the kitchen table was smothered in flowers: a wonderful bouquet of yellow freesias and white lilies. Molly must have taken delivery of them. There was a card attached and she bent to read. *To dear Aunt Alice. I hope these cheer you. Gilbert.*

Such a kind thought. Gilbert Fitzroy had left home on business but, despite all the rush and bother of departure, he hadn't forgotten his aunt. She hoped Alice would say thank you when he returned, though she couldn't depend on it. Gilbert might be a devoted nephew but his aunt was slow in returning his regard. Whenever he called, it seemed that Alice was too tired to see him, or she was listening to her favourite wireless programme and didn't want to be disturbed, or it was time for lunch or tea or supper. Beth had so far been unable to discover what the problem might be. No doubt the root of the trouble lay in the past since this was where Alice dwelt for most of her waking hours.

Gilbert appeared unfazed by his aunt's evident lack of affection and continued to enquire of her health and, from time to time, send small gifts from the Amberley estate, including today's magnificent flowers filling the small kitchen with their perfume.

She would have noticed them earlier if her nerves had not been so jangled. She must thank Gilbert as soon as he got back, even if his aunt did not. In the meantime, she would do her best to return the favour by teaching his son as much as Ralph was willing to learn. So far, that hadn't proved a great deal; Ralph was not an academic child.

She went back into the sitting room and handed Alice her cup of tea, making sure the old lady had a firm hold of the saucer. Then returned to the kitchen and gathered up the bouquet. 'Look, you have flowers, Mrs Summer. Aren't they splendid? I hope I can find a vase that's big enough. Perhaps the Venetian one?' That was Alice's favourite.

The old lady's face brightened. She loved flowers, loved colour. 'I always had fresh flowers, every few days. Mr Harris— he was the Head Gardener—he'd cut me new blooms and they would fill the house.'

'They must have looked lovely. And smelt lovely, too.'

'They did. The house was very beautiful. I didn't realise how beautiful. I should have enjoyed it more. Now this is all I'm left with.' She waved her hand at the sitting room and the narrow hallway beyond, while Beth jumped to her feet to rescue the tea. Undeterred, Alice went on. 'You see, I was brought up at Amberley, and it was always Amberley where I wanted to be.'

When Beth made no reply, she said, 'Do you know it?'

Amberley was Gilbert Fitzroy's home. 'I know of it. It's the estate that adjoins Summerhayes.'

'It belonged to my parents,' she said fiercely, as though Beth's description had somehow disputed its ownership. 'And then to my brother, Henry.'

'And now to your nephew.'

Alice looked blank. 'Gilbert,' Beth said gently.

'Inheritance knows no distinction,' she muttered.

Beth had no idea what she meant, but she was concerned that at any moment the conversation would lead back to Elizabeth. 'Talking of Amberley, these flowers are from their greenhouse. Gilbert must have asked his gardener to pick them especially for you.'

The old lady sniffed. The subject was evidently closed. 'Can I pour you another cup?' She thought the pot would just about run to it, though the liquid looked more like straw than tea.

'You make a good cup of tea, Bethany. Better than Ivy, she never managed to cope with rationing.'

'Now that she's married to a farmer, it will be less of a problem.'

'But Higson isn't a farmer. Not any longer. He sold the farm —the military paid a good price for it, I believe, and that decided him. He bought a bungalow in Devon, on the coast. A place called Solmouth, Sidton...'

'Sidmouth?'

'That's it. He asked Ivy to marry him before he left. She'd been a good girl to him ever since his wife died.'

'So a happy ending?'

It didn't seem that happy to Alice. She gave a long sigh. 'I miss her. She was with me for so many years. Not that I'm not glad for her. Mr Higson is some compensation. She lost her first love, you know. Poor Miller—such a tragedy. He was our chauffeur, but they found him in the garden at the bottom of the estate. Drowned.'

An uncomfortable tingle started in the nape of Beth's neck and slowly spread the length of her spine. She had walked that way once and been startled by how uneasy she'd felt. There had been a kind of darkness to the place that had sent her scurrying. Afterwards she'd scolded herself for being foolish, but was it possible that the garden still held fast to a bad memory?

'I'm glad for her,' Alice repeated. 'She did well for herself. And May Lacey, too. Girls from humble families. Whereas my daughter threw herself away on an Irishman without a shirt to his back. It's a different world these days.'

Beth agreed, but she'd been only half listening. She should go in search of Ralph. She was already beginning to regret her agreement with Gilbert. The war had closed the boy's school last year and he was woefully behind with his studies. It might have been better if his father had looked for a full-time tutor. Teaching at the same time as caring for Alice was proving a challenge, and she'd had to cancel the last two lessons. Ralph had been happy with the chance to escape since he had far more interesting things to do than sums and composition, but she couldn't let it happen again. Today she'd told herself that she would have at least two hours with him and here was Mrs Summer, trying for an outward calm, but still deeply upset. She could see how disturbed the old lady remained from the way she was holding her cup, rattling it badly in its saucer.

Alice had an inner toughness, Beth had discovered, and she wouldn't like it that she'd been found crying. She was trying hard to put on a brave face, but the letters had caused damage. The first one had arrived a month back, shortly after Beth had come to Summerhayes. She'd been stunned when she'd learned the tragic history of this otherwise unremarkable woman: a husband and son prematurely dead and a daughter who seem-

ingly had disappeared from the face of the earth at just nineteen
years old. That first letter had brought all the sadness that Alice
carried struggling into the light.

The letters were anonymous, but from the beginning they'd
indicated that the writer, whoever they were, was bound for
Summerhayes. The first one had been postmarked Southampton, suggesting a traveller from abroad, but then the second and
third had come from London. In each letter the unknown
writer had claimed to be drawing nearer to Summerhayes,
promising Alice a loving reunion. Until today. Today the
promise had been withdrawn; hence the old lady's cries of
despair.

But if the writer were honest in seeking Alice, why had they
gone to London? Why not travel directly to Summerhayes from
Southampton? But they weren't honest, were they? Otherwise
they would have signed the letters, along with their protesta-
tions of love, and Alice would know for sure who would call and
when.

For a short while, the old lady's iron certainty that the
letters came from her daughter had made Beth question if, in
fact, Alice was right, and that perhaps the writer was an
unstable woman, disturbed enough to contact her mother
anonymously. But there was too much deliberation in the
pattern of the letters; it suggested a calculating mind determined to cause the maximum pain. Alice was being played
with, Beth thought, but why and to what purpose, she couldn't
tell. All she could do was try to protect the poor lady as best she
could.

She rescued the rattling cup and cast around for a way to
soothe her elderly charge. 'Shall I start another illustration?'
Alice loved to watch her draw, no doubt because the lost
daughter had been an artist and in some small way Beth's sketch
pad reminded her of happier days.

With an effort, the old lady agreed. 'That would be nice, my dear. What is it to be?' She pulled herself upright and arranged her face to appear interested.

'Let me see... we'd reached the point where Izzy is lost.' Beth brought her companion up to date with the progress of the story. 'If you remember, she escaped from the cottage when she was told to stay there, and now she can't find her way out of the Tangled Wood.'

Izzy was the naughty heroine who one day, Beth hoped, would entrance a young audience. She found her pad and a handful of sharp pencils, and settled herself in the chair opposite. A forest scene would make an interesting subject. For a while, the only sound in the room was the slight scratching of pencil on paper.

Then Alice spoke into the silence. 'You do know we have an artist's studio here? It's in one of the attics, so the military won't have taken it over.'

Sometimes Alice's mind was as sharp as it must have been twenty years before. She was aware of the army's presence in the building, aware of how much space they occupied. Beth hoped she wasn't aware of the damage several changes of military personnel had caused to the splendid house she had once called home.

'I know about the studio, Mrs Summer, but a sketch pad and pencil is all I need. I'm not a genuine artist— just a writer and illustrator. It's a hobby for me.'

But one day, it might not be. One day, it might be a serious undertaking and earn sufficient money to bring her true independence. In the meantime, it was useful in deflecting Alice from her obsession. Though apparently it wasn't going to deflect her today.

'Elizabeth was an artist,' she announced. 'I have the pictures she painted... somewhere.'

'There's one in your bedroom, I think. And very good it is, too.'

The old lady looked gratified. 'There are others. Lots of them. Maybe in the old studio?'

Beth had been there once and found it a chaotic jumble of mouldering furniture and broken boxes. She'd had to push past thick, furry cobwebs to get into the room and, when she did, had seen immediately that part of the roof must have lost tiles because a steady drip of water had found its way through and was pooling the floorboards. She'd got Mr Ripley to fetch a bucket and asked him to remember to empty it whenever it rained. But she'd said nothing to Alice of the state in which she'd found the place. Fortunately, the old lady never went further than her own few rooms—a sitting room, a bedroom and a bathroom. Beth herself slept in what at a stretch could be described as a box room and Mr Ripley bravely inhabited one of the spare attics.

'Let me see.' Alice leaned forward. 'The trees are beautiful.' She pointed to the tall, slender columns of birch that Beth had drawn, fingering their outline on the page. Their delicate leaves shadowed the winding path that the small girl would tread. 'It is such a pity that you don't paint. Colour would bring the image to life.'

She feared the mention of paint and colour would bring Elizabeth into the conversation once more. 'Shall I draw Izzy into the picture? I think she'll be happy on her adventure—to begin with at least.'

'Yes, do that.' Alice's voice was weary now, her eyes heavy-lidded, and before Beth had finished the illustration, the old lady was breathing steadily.

She fetched a blanket from the bedroom and tucked it around the sleeping woman. She should just have sufficient time to find Ralph and haul him up the stairs for his lesson. He was bound to be in the grounds somewhere, though finding him amid the mayhem of a military arrival could prove difficult. But if she knew the boy, he would most likely be sitting on the largest tank or questioning the gun crew on their stock of ammunition. She edged the front door shut and sped down the stairs.

4

The small boy had emerged from the thicket of grass, but he was inches away before Jos could see his entire person: his hair a thatch of light brown, his smile engaging, and his bare knees scratched and muddied.

'I'm Ralph.' He held out his hand.

'Jos Kerrigan.' They exchanged a solemn handshake. 'You seem to know your way around this wilderness,' Jos said. 'Do you live here?'

'Not here but next door—at Amberley. It's much more fun here though. We don't have any soldiers at Amberley.'

'So can you show me how to get out of this darn place? Or is it all like this?'

Ralph considered the question judiciously. 'This is the worst bit, I think, but the whole estate is pretty run down.' That seemed an understatement to Jos. 'I can take you to the main camp, if you like?'

'I'd like that fine. Do you spend a lot of time there?'

'When I'm allowed to,' the boy said simply. 'There's been a camp for ages, but this week there's been loads going on. And I've made a special friend.'

He was intrigued. 'And who's that?'

'His name is Eddie. Eddie Rich.'

'Is that so? He just happens to be my special friend, too.'

Ralph's grin spread across his face. 'He's the bee's knees, isn't he?'

Jos's deep blue eyes lit with amusement. 'He sure is.'

'It's getting hot out here.' The boy patted several stalks of grass away from his face. 'Shall I take you to him?'

'I'd appreciate that, Ralph.'

'C'mon then.' He turned round and traced a path along what Jos thought must be the thinnest line of flattened grass he'd ever seen, just wide enough for a nine-year-old's feet but way too narrow for his own size twelves.

'I'm crushing a heck of a lot of grass here,' he called to Ralph, a few steps ahead. 'Will it matter?' Why it would, he couldn't imagine.

'It doesn't matter at all. No one comes here except me, and it will make it easier the next time I go to the secret garden. That's what I call it. It's where you came in. It will make it easier for you, too, if you want to go back.'

Jos had no intention of ever returning to this maze of heat and bother. The grass tickled at his nose and infiltrated his ears and, on occasions, he had to sway to one side to avoid a giant fern or be knocked uncomfortably into the rough trunk of a palm tree.

'So why aren't you at school?' he asked conversationally, more to distract himself from the discomfort of the journey, than from any real desire to know.

'My school's been closed. It was just outside London, and they said it was too dangerous for us to stay.'

'You lived at the school?'

'Of course. I was a boarder.'

He'd heard that English families often sent their young children away to school but he'd never really believed it.

'And now?'

'The school moved up to Cheshire. At least, I think it was Cheshire. I don't really know where that is.' Neither did Jos, but it seemed strange that the child hadn't moved with it. He must have felt settled in the school, had friends there. It seemed like a lonely life for him here.

'My father didn't want me to go,' Ralph explained. 'When I was at school near London, I could come back at weekends, you see, but Cheshire was too far. I don't think he wanted to be on his own at Amberley all the time.'

Jos didn't like to ask about the boy's mother, fearing there had been some kind of wartime tragedy, but then Ralph said, 'My mother's a long way away. She's in New York. She's American.'

'So it's just your dad and you?'

'That's right. Well,' Ralph said over his shoulder, 'there are other people. Quite a few actually. There's the butler, and the footman, and the parlour maid, and cook and a kitchen maid, and the gardener and the chauffeur...'

'I get the picture.'

'I could have gone to the village school, but Daddy didn't want me to. He was going to hire a tutor and then Miss Merston came and she's teaching me instead. It's heaps better.'

'And who is Miss Merston?'

The ground had gradually been sloping upwards, but in the last few yards it had taken on an even steeper incline. Beneath the weighty backpack, Jos was beginning to puff slightly and that didn't please him. He'd thought himself fit enough, but he'd need to be a good deal fitter come invasion day.

'Miss Merston is great. She rescued a bird's nest with me last week and I'm helping the eggs to hatch. She's a school-teacher.' Ralph must have sensed a little more explanation was needed. 'She doesn't have a school any more either, and she looks after my father's aunt. That's my great-aunt. Her name is Alice and she's very old.'

They had finally emerged from the jungle of long grass and reached a gravel path. Jos breathed a sigh of pleasure, feeling solid ground beneath his feet again. He allowed himself a short stop and looked around. He was standing in what had once been a vegetable garden, he could see. Vegetable gardens, he corrected himself. The area was immense and bounded to the south by a circular brick wall against which a number of dessicated fruit trees still clung to a semblance of life. Vegetables had not been grown here for many a year; the soil was untilled and broken canes, rotting wooden staves and remnants of netting were strewn across its surface.

In the distance, to the right, stood what was left of a string of greenhouses, their glass long shattered. Nearer to hand, a tarpaulin covered the unknown. He'd bet his life on it being ammunition. It was a dismal picture and made him keen to walk on, but once through the brick arch the view was no improvement. More tarpaulins, more mounds. Several trees had been toppled and lay spreadeagled where the wind had blown them, others had brambles up to ten feet high climbing their trunks. He passed what he thought must be one of the oldest trees in the garden, stoic in its lost grandeur. A fig tree, he was sure of it. Scattered in its branches was shrivelled fruit, unharvested year on year. The gnarled trunk was punctured by bullet marks and, when he looked around, he saw that nearly every surviving tree in this part of the garden was similarly afflicted. Someone had been using them for target practice. Whatever devastation had existed before the war, a succession of military occupations had made it worse.

'This place is in poor shape,' he said.

Ralph looked puzzled. It was evident that for him the Summerhayes estate was fine as it was. 'I s'pose,' he admitted cautiously. 'It used to look different. I saw an old photograph once. But that was a long time ago.'

The boy was still ahead of him, walking beneath the pergola that connected fruit and vegetables with the upper reaches of the garden. The pergola had once been covered by roses and its wooden structure was more or less intact, but what plants remained had grown wild, their thorns a danger to passers-by. Dodging between waving suckers, Jos could see lying ahead another huge open area, once a vast lawn, he presumed. At its far end was a semi-circular flight of steps leading up to a flagged terrace. He could imagine the ladies of the house taking a stroll on that terrace, tripping daintily down the steps to the rolling grass. Now, not a blade was visible. The lawn had been covered in concrete and a row of trucks parked tidily across its expanse.

Noise and bustle were all around. Troops were still arriving, each truckload of men making their way to adjoining farmland where they'd pitch the tents that would be their home. Given the vagaries of the English weather, it wouldn't be a particularly comfortable home, and he hoped that his own billet was nearer to hand—in the gardens, perhaps, despite their dilapidation. The closer he was to the house and offices, the less wading through mud he'd have to do if it rained hard.

Ralph had stopped and was looking back at him. 'Eddie's this way.'

He was a smart kid, Jos thought. It was a new camp with a completely different configuration from the previous one—the forward party had arrived only three days ago—yet the boy already knew his way around. Several young soldiers saluted as they passed and he managed a ragged salute in reply. The back-pack was to blame.

Ralph looked up with another big smile. 'Are you an officer then?'

'A very junior one, kid. Eddie is too.'

'I know. He told me. He's in the outbuildings. We have to go this way. Have you known him long?'

'A fair time. We joined up together when we weren't much older than you—we're both from the Toronto area. That's eastern Canada.'

'I know where it is. I'm good at geography. Well, sometimes,' he added, evidently remembering his problem with Cheshire. 'Have you been together ever since?'

'We've been posted to different regiments in between time, but when Canada joined the war we ended up in the same battalion again.'

'Have you been fighting together as well?' The boy's face sparked with excitement.

'Oh yeah, fighting too.' And that was some fighting. Italy. Monte Cassino. He'd been so very glad to have Eddie alongside.

A young man was shambling towards them, blond hair glinting in the spring sunshine and his gold flecked eyes warm with welcome. 'He's here!' Ralph forgot his dignity and jumped up and down as Eddie came into view.

Eddie Rich wore his uniform as though it were something he'd found by chance while rummaging though a forgotten trunk but, when you looked again, Jos thought, you noticed the straight back, the sinewy arms and an expression that didn't quite disguise a sharp intelligence.

'Well, Ralphie, just look who you've found.'

'He was lost.'

'If he's walked up from the depths, I bet he was.' Eddie put his hands on Jos's shoulders and gave him a quick hug. 'Great to see you, pal. But what were you doing in the badlands?'

'That's what he calls the bottom of the estate,' Ralph explained.

'I was dropped off at what must have been the rear entrance, though I guess it's not been used for a century. I tried walking up from there.'

Eddie pulled down the corners of his mouth, but his eyes laughed. 'Not so great. Ralph to the rescue, eh?'

'Ralph to the rescue,' Jos agreed. 'So when did you get here? How are things going?'

'I came with the advance party, but the rest of the guys arrived today. They made pretty good time from Winchelsea but, as always, it's chaos. You know the drill. How about you? How was that jewel of a town?'

'The same as when we left it four years ago. And a completely wasted journey. Someone—God knows who—had already ordered what was left of our equipment to be sent on here. Has it arrived yet?'

'Not that I know of, but it's early days. So you didn't hang around?'

'We're talking Aldershot, Ed. Mind you, this place doesn't look much better.'

'It's seen grander days, for sure, but it's OK. The house is kinda nice, or it was once. The colonel gets to sleep there, of course. We're over here. I'll show you the way. We've been given the Head Gardener's office, would you believe?'

'No tent? How did you pull that one?'

'Don't get too excited. We're sharing with Wilson and Martel. And the office is twelve by twelve.'

'We've still gone up in the world, I reckon. Lead on!' He turned to Ralph who was looking uncertainly between the two men. 'You better scoot now, but thanks for rescuing me.'

'Before he scoots,' Eddie put in, 'I think a reward is in order, and I might have just the thing.' He fished in one of his trouser pockets and brought out a small bar of chocolate.

'Chocolate,' Ralph breathed ecstatically.

'He can have that later, when he's finished his lessons.' The voice was no nonsense, but vaguely amused.

Jos turned and saw a girl that made his heart falter.

5

'Hi there, Miss Merston,' Eddie said. 'You weren't by any chance intending to bribe this young man with my chocolate?'

'I might, if it gets him to open his books.' She turned towards Ralph. 'Mrs Summer is asleep right now and we can do some work before she wakes.'

The boy pulled a face. 'Must we?'

'Yes, we must. Or I'll have to tell your father that you're not studying as you should, and you know what that means. He'll hire a tutor who'll make sure your nose never leaves the grindstone.'

Ralph looked deflated and seemed ready to leave, but at the last moment tried to delay. 'This is Jos. He's just arrived.'

'Hey, sorry,' Eddie chimed in. 'I should have introduced you guys. This is my buddy, Jos Kerrigan. Jos, this is Bethany Merston, school marm extraordinaire.'

Jos hadn't taken his eyes from the slim figure that stood close by. She wasn't pretty, in the conventional sense, but she had a liveliness that enchanted him. Everything about her shone: her deep brown hair glossy beneath the April sun, soft brown eyes sparkling with a hundred different lights. She wore a faded cotton print, the dress so well-washed and mended, it was a wonder it still held together. He'd seen first-hand the privations suffered by the civilian population, but here they mattered not a jot. Bethany Merston transcended them.

He had to stop. He couldn't think like that. No involvement with the natives, that was his motto. Particularly female natives. Those kind of affairs had been left behind in Canada. It had been work, work, work since he arrived in England. He was a professional soldier with a job to do and he needed no entanglements. Entanglement meant feelings and feelings meant loss and he'd had enough of that to last him a lifetime—however long that proved to be.

'Good to meet you,' he said stiffly.

He didn't sound as though he thought it good. Eddie was looking at him curiously, but the girl merely nodded in reply, a curt little motion of her head. 'Come with me, Ralph, time is precious and we mustn't waste it.'

Slightly bemused, the boy followed after her.

'That wasn't too friendly.' Eddie looked across at him, his forehead puckered. The hazel eyes held a puzzled expression. 'In fact, it was pretty darn rude and not like you, Jos, not like you at all. What's up?'

He felt his shoulders tense involuntarily. He didn't need an interrogation. 'What should be up—other than I'm hot and tired and I've just got back from a wholly useless mission?'

'I know it was a bad call, but still... you didn't have to be quite so abrupt. Bethany Merston is a nice woman, real nice.'

'I'm sure she is, but right now all I want is to offload a kitbag that's breaking my back and get some food. I haven't eaten since six this morning.'

Eddie made no reply but remained where he was, fixing his friend with a hard gaze. It seemed he was trying to puzzle something out.

Finally, he said, 'It's still that woman, isn't it? The one back in Toronto. Sylvie. Wasn't that her name?' His eyes had lost their questioning look and were now shrewd and measuring. 'Gee, that was an age ago. She must really have messed you up. You just don't like women any more.'

Jos felt annoyance grow and tried to subdue it. 'OK. She messed me up—for a while. But now I'm definitely unmessed and that's the way I intend to stay. And I'm fine with women, but we're fighting a war, remember, and they're an unnecessary complication.'

'The women are one of the reasons we're fighting,' Eddie said mildly. 'Anyway, you needn't worry about Beth. We hardly see her. C'mon, we go this way.'

For someone Eddie hardly saw, he appeared remarkably friendly with Beth Merston, but Jos kept this reflection to himself. Eddie's success with women was legendary and it was unlikely Miss Merston would remain immune. Few women did.

'No,' his friend continued, as they started along the gravel path that wound its way to the left of the truck park. 'She's nearly always up there.' He jerked a shoulder towards the house. 'The old lady keeps her busy; she needs a lot of looking after by all accounts.'

He was glad to hear it. Whatever he'd said to Eddie, meeting Bethany Merston had given him a jolt. Something about her had reached down and tugged at his soul, and he needed to stamp on the feeling instantly. Sylvie had led him a merry dance, lying and cheating her way into his life, lying and cheating her way out of her husband's. The husband of whom Jos had had no idea. He was over that, well and truly over it, and Eddie was wrong that Sylvie had soured him. In the end she'd not been so important, a rare stumble in an abiding reluctance to get involved.

But this girl was different. Every instinct was warning him that she was a far greater danger to staying heartwhole than any number of Sylvies. He'd known it the minute he'd looked into her eyes.

His companion stopped outside a line of small buildings. 'This is it. The one in the middle is ours. It's about the only habitable part of the whole caboodle. Next door there's a tool shed and the building at the far end, God knows what that was —it looks like it might have been a john, but primitive isn't the word.'

Jos followed him over the threshold, bending his six-foot frame to get through the doorway. He reached up and tapped the lintel. 'Something to remember.'

'Don't tell me. I must have knocked out half my brains by now.'

'You mean there are some left?'

Eddie punched him good naturedly. 'You're over there.'

There were four camp beds crammed into the small space, two along one wall and two against the wall opposite. The third side of the room boasted a narrow window, whose panes were so small and so badly streaked with dirt that only the dimmest light made its way through. Once the sun disappeared, Jos thought, you'd hardly see a hand in front of you. Several pairs of trousers, one or two serge battledress jackets and the odd shirt were hanging from nails that had been knocked into the supporting beams.

Eddie saw him looking. 'Our wardrobe,' he quipped.

'And these?' Jos pointed to his bulging backpack. 'Do we hang these, too?'

'Stow it under the bed, if you can.'

He did as instructed and sat down heavily on the knobbly mattress. It didn't give an inch. 'Straw,' he guessed. 'Ah well, no doubt we'll be so tired we won't even notice the lumps. But what about a shower? I could do with one before I report to McMasters.'

'When you do, he'll get you to check the camouflage again.

I've done it twice since I got here. The tents are pretty exposed and he's obsessive. Ever since he found out about the Messerschmitts. Did you hear of that? They attacked our guys last week at Cuckmere Haven. That's a few miles down the road and he doesn't want a repeat. The bastards came skimming over the water at sunrise and up the valley.'

'I'm fine with the camouflage. I just need to get a wash first.'

'They're fixing a washroom for us right now. The men have already got theirs, a couple of shower blocks built in the fields.'

'And I guess the colonel's got his. He'll be up at the house washing in luxury.'

'He's billeted there, natch, along with the rest of the senior officers, but I'm not too sure about the luxury. The house is pretty beat up.'

'Who owns it anyway? It looked a sizeable place on my way up here.'

'It's large enough but at one time, I guess, it must have been a good deal larger. Seems there were farms attached. We're camped on one, though I'm not sure who owns it now. The house and gardens belong to a little old lady called Alice Summers.'

'And your friend, Bethany, is her companion?' He didn't want to talk about the girl and he couldn't understand why he was.

'That's it. Beth looks after her. It was Alice's husband who built the place. Some time around the turn of the century. Since then, it's been more or less abandoned—you're looking at thirty years of decay. No one's worked the land or maintained the house. And after all the money the guy must have spent on it! By all accounts, he was real wealthy— made his fortune in buttons, would you believe?'

'So one of the nouveau riche,' Jos joked. 'We should feel at home, the nouveau bit at least.'

'The old man certainly was nouveau, a businessman made

good, but not Alice. She's the real deal. Comes from a local aristo family who own next door. That's where Ralph lives.'

Jos stretched out on the mattress, trying to work his body into the lumps and mould them to his shape. 'He told me. Some place called Amberley.'

'That's the one. His father is the grand seigneur of the village. He's Alice's nephew, by the way. I've never met the guy myself, but Ralph seems fond of him. His Ma is in the States.'

'So he said, though not why.'

'I have a theory.' Eddie flopped down on the far bunk, a grin on his face. 'I reckon she's done a runner. She left when war was declared and never came back.'

'Could be she doesn't like being bombed night and day.'

'I don't think that's it. The raids here are tip and run. Nothing like London. The bombers only let fly on their way back from the city. There's been a direct hit on a cinema or two, but otherwise it's been a breeze. Maybe it's Ralph's Pa—he's not to her fancy any more.'

'Whatever the reason, it's a shame for the boy. He's too young to be motherless.'

Jos knew what it felt like to live without a mother. People could be kind, could be caring, but it wasn't the same. It was like having a spare blanket thrown over you in winter, as you slept; there was always a piece of the blanket didn't cover, a piece that stayed cold.

Eddie yawned. 'Ralph doesn't seem too worried. He's got his father and there's a mountain of servants to look after him. A different world, my friend. But he's a great kid. He likes a bit of fun. Yesterday, we made some pretend footprints in the mud right down in the badlands. Where you came in. They were huge, animal paw prints and he persuaded one of those toffee-nosed footmen at Amberley that there was a jaguar prowling Summerhayes. When the guy came over—he'd been instructed to find out what was going on by the butler—they actually have a butler—it was a gas watching him creep around that stinking lake and then find our clay moulds hidden under a bush. The moulds were Master Ralph's doing. He's clever with his hands.'

Jos remembered other practical jokes Eddie had played, not all of them well received. He was a great friend and a staunch comrade, but sometimes he crossed the line without ever being aware he had.

'I'm surprised the boy is here at all,' was all he said. 'And I think you're wrong about it being a breeze. This far south must be a prime target for the bombers. The coast is vulnerable. I imagine we're close to the sea?'

'Two miles away. Beautiful beaches, some of them, but off limits for sightseeing. Barbed wire fences and every pebble sown with mines. Well, hopefully not every pebble. I reckon that's where we'll be exercising.'

Jos gave a slow nod. 'It's going to be a seaborne invasion all right, but where from? Several battalions have been moved east along the Kent coast, but we've come west.'

'A cunning plan by the great and the good?'

'Most likely. If there's a large force in Dover, the Krauts will be expecting an assault on the Pas de Calais. But I learned from a guy at Aldershot that there's been a big deployment to Scotland, too. That would mean invading through Norway.'

Eddie rustled through an untidy heap on his mattress, looking for a cigarette. 'It's so damned hush hush, we won't be told until the last minute. Are we the deception or the real thing, do you think?'

Jos gave a low whistle. 'If we're the real thing, it means we'll be on our way to Normandy. And that's ambitious, to put it mildly. The Germans are thoroughly dug in there. They look impregnable. It'll take a huge amount of planning to get it right, if it's even possible.'

'Well, my friend, we'll be the ones to find out. Aren't we lucky? And pretty soon. To have any chance, it's gotta be this summer. But hey, no worries. The planning's done and now it's just a simple matter of practice.' He lit his cigarette and puffed contentedly.

'Or not so simple.' Jos rolled off the bed and stretched his tall frame as well as he could beneath the low ceiling. 'Can you imagine the assault—for the infantry, for the crews of the landing craft? How to beach and unbeach. Then the tank crews on how to manoeuvre ashore. You know they've converted the tanks to be amphibious? If we're in the wrong place, or in the wrong order, or if we don't liaise sufficiently with each other or with the air force or the navy... we could be in for a disaster that'll make Dieppe seem like a school outing.'

Eddie looked glumly at him. 'You sure know how to bring a man down.'

The words hung in the air, and both fell silent until Jos remembered his unwashed state. 'I must track down that shower. Coffee would be good when I get back. Then I'll be up to the house to see McMasters and across the fields to find the men. If your guess is right, we're on our way to the beach tomorrow.'

'Looks like it,' Eddie said. 'Tomorrow and the next few tomorrows as well.'

6

Bethany found the next few hours difficult. Ralph was even less willing than usual to buckle down to his studies and she couldn't blame him: synonyms and antonyms had none of the appeal of the military. All the boy wanted was to talk about the tanks and trucks and guns he'd watched trundle into Summerhayes that day and, above all, talk of the new friend he'd made. Eddie Rich had been a splendid addition to his world but evidently Jos Kerrigan was just as splendid.

Jos had made a striking figure, she conceded, but it was a figure she'd no wish to know better. When Eddie had introduced them, the man's face had changed. Quite distinctly. It had become a mask, stonily indifferent. Perhaps he was one of those men who thought women foolish; fripperies with whom to have fun, but an unwanted nuisance in serious matters.

Ralph had taken at least sixty minutes to labour through the two columns of words she'd prepared and was now tapping his pencil against his head and looking longingly towards the kitchen window. A slight stirring from the next room broke the silence. Alice was awake and Beth must attend to her before she took Ralph through his spidery list. The old lady was always a trifle grumpy when she woke, and this afternoon she had been jerked from a deep sleep by the crash of equipment being unloaded just below her window.

As Beth had anticipated, she was fractious and it took a while to settle her into a comfortable chair, bring her a glass of water and switch on the wireless to warm. It was almost two o'clock, time for Alice's favourite—Afternoon Cabaret on the Home Service—though she doubted the old lady understood one in four of Bob Hope's jokes.

Returning to the kitchen, she found Ralph had left his seat and was pressing his forehead against the window, looking wistfully down at the garden. It was a hopeless situation; there was no chance she would get more work from him today.

'You can pack up your books,' she said, admitting defeat, 'but on one condition.'

Ralph whirled around, an overjoyed expression on his face, and started flinging school books into the leather satchel he carried.

'I said on one condition,' she reminded him.

Surprised, he stopped buckling the satchel's straps.

'You're to go straight home. No wandering around the gardens, no talking to the soldiers. Is that understood?'

He looked crestfallen but then nodded his head in agreement.

'*And* you learn the final column of synonyms when you get back to Amberley. I'll test you the next time you come.'

'That's a second condition.'

'Or we can do it right now.'

'No,' he said hastily. 'I'll learn them tonight.'

'Good. I won't see you tomorrow but come the next day, in the morning. Mrs Summer will have a visitor with her and we can work in here while they talk. Come around ten o'clock.'

The boy nodded agreement. 'You're OK, you know, Miss Merston.'

She smiled wryly. 'Thank you for your approval, Master Fitzroy. Now go on, hurry home.'

When he'd gone, she checked on Alice and found her smiling quietly at the wireless. All was well. She would have time to begin supper, such as it was. There was no meat again, but plenty of vegetables. Every garden in the village had its own plot and there was still an abundance of winter stock from which to choose. This morning on her way back from the grocer's, she'd helped herself to a whole bagful from the heap left outside someone's garden gate. She started to peel some carrots. The soldiers would almost certainly be eating a great deal better than this. Their kitchens had gone up several days ago, part of the advance guard that had included Eddie Rich. No doubt he and his friend were enjoying a ration-free meal right now.

Thinking about it annoyed her. Not the rationing; civilians had known for years the sacrifices they must make. It was thinking about Kerrigan that annoyed her. Ralph, it seemed, wasn't the only one who had him on their mind.

When she'd first seen the man, she'd thought him attractive. He had an open face and she'd liked the way that even with a military cut, a shock of hair had fallen across his forehead. His eyes, too, had fascinated—they'd been the blue of deep ocean, a mystical blue in which you could easily lose yourself. But then she'd seen their expression. That had been decidedly unmystical. Decidedly unfriendly. His frosty manner had sent out warning signals. She should forget the attraction she'd felt. Here was a man who could hurt her, and she had no intention of allowing that to happen. She lacked the confidence, the self-belief, to cope with heartache. Her stepfather had seen to that.

Eddie was different. She had known him only a few days but he was as amiable as he was good looking and, though she was unlikely to succumb to his attractions, she enjoyed talking with him. He'd made her a friend almost immediately, but that didn't mean his friends had to be hers. True friendship was rare and true love even rarer. What began as hearts and roses soon became an exercise of power. She'd seen that for herself. And men were not essential for a loving life; if you looked hard enough, love was everywhere.

She'd found it in the job she did and the children she'd taught, and they had repaid her love a hundred-fold. Once this interminable war was over, she would be on her way back to London, to begin again to build a life for herself.

The last of the carrots splashed into the saucepan and she searched around for matches. Jos Kerrigan would take up not a second more of her time than was necessary. She struck the match with force, then waved it towards the gas ring and promptly burnt her fingers.

Two days later, she was clearing Alice's breakfast tray when May Prendergast arrived in the kitchen just after nine o'clock. Her friend was short of breath from climbing the two flights of stairs and made her apologies between gasps.

'Sorry, if I'm putting you out, Beth, but I had to come early. I can't stay as long as I'd hoped either. I've to call on the evacuees as soon as I leave here. We've found places for the children, but there have been a couple of problems settling them in. And guess who's sorting that out?'

She took off her coat and hung it on the back of one of the only two chairs the kitchen possessed, then unpinned her hat. 'How are you anyways?'

'Fine. It's been a trifle noisy with the soldiers arriving *en masse*, but it seems to have calmed now. I imagine they've dug themselves in.'

'Mass is the right word,' May agreed. 'There's certainly plenty of 'em. I walked up from the lodge and there are vehicles and men both sides of the drive, and goodness knows how many in the rest of the gardens and on the farm. But it's the same in the village, mind. Men, tanks, jeeps. You can't move without falling over them.'

Beth filled the kettle while her friend walked across to the window and glanced down. 'Another army camp,' she murmured, looking out across what had once been rolling grassland. 'Old man Summer will be turning in his grave. This place was his pride and glory.'

'Needs must, I suppose.' She tipped a small measure of tea into the pot. 'He was a button maker, wasn't he?'

'That he was—from Birmingham, I heard my mother once say—but buttons or no buttons, he had an eye for beauty, that one.'

'You must have seen the gardens in their heyday. Were they so very beautiful?' She poured the weak liquid into two cups and passed one to May, then sat down opposite.

'They were wonderful, flowers covering the terrace, peacocks on the lawn, and enough fruit and vegetables to feed a town. I was often at Summerhayes in those days, waiting for my mother or doing odd jobs for pocket money. We had a small cottage close by, on the lane leading to the village—so as Ma could look after us, you see, but still be on call at the house twelve hours a day. She was one of the best housekeepers ever.' The words were said with pride. 'It was a hard life, but the cottage came rent free and we ate off the estate. That was important for a family with no father to provide.'

May had never before talked of family, but she must have siblings, Beth thought. Possibly in the village?

'You have brothers and sisters then? Where are they?' And then she wished she hadn't asked.

'Just one brother. Joe.' Her friend's eyes filled with tears. 'He was the nicest brother a young girl could have. He was a gardener here, but then he signed up with the rest of them. The First War,' she said in explanation. 'I remember that day. A black day if ever there was. Every gardener on the estate downed tools together and then, two by two, they walked to Worthing to enlist.' She paused and looked down at her cup. 'He didn't come back. None of them did.'

Beth cast around for something to soften the difficult moment. 'If the gardens were as marvellous as you say, the house too, I can understand why Mrs Summer gets distressed at times.'

'It's a mournful state the place is in,' May agreed. 'Everything crumbled and ruined, and worse now with the army. But then no one wants their house taken over by the military, and knowing that Amberley isn't suffering the same must make it feel worse. The old lady didn't have the money or the connections to keep Summerhayes safe, that's what it was. She didn't go to Eton or Oxford or belong to a gentleman's club. Not like Mr Fitzroy—he could make sure his home stayed untouched.'

As if on cue, they heard footsteps on the uncarpeted staircase and, seconds later, Gilbert Fitzroy appeared at the open door, trailing a somewhat sulky son. Both women jumped to their feet, May's knees bobbing the smallest of curtsies. Old habits die hard, Beth reflected.

'I understood you were in London, Mr Fitzroy.' She was surprised and none too pleased to be entertaining him so early in the morning.

'I got back late last night and thought I'd make myself useful by bringing young Ralph over.'

Beth wasn't sure exactly why he considered this useful, but then she remembered the flowers he'd sent to Alice. Pinning a smile firmly to her lips, she managed to stumble out a proxy thank you.

'I'm glad she liked them.'

He was looking particularly smart, she noticed. He must have bought the clothes in London. New clothing was largely unobtainable now, but if you had money you could probably run to ground anything you wanted.

'I'm sorry to intrude on you both,' he went on, 'but I felt I should make sure Ralph got to his lesson.' His voice was smooth as cream, but he looked genuinely concerned. 'At the moment, I'm not certain he's using your time wisely, Miss Merston. Or would you mind if I called you Bethany? We are working together now—in a manner of speaking—and it seems right not to be so formal.'

She sensed rather than saw May pull a face beside her but, without appearing to notice, Gilbert continued in the same unruffled tone. 'I was hoping I might see my aunt, too.' He must long ago have detected Alice's antipathy, Beth was sure, yet he seemed willing to remain the dutiful nephew.

'I've brought her a new book. Hatchards had it in their window and as soon as I saw it, I thought it was just the thing for her. More flowers, you see, plenty of them.' He flicked through the pages of the brightly coloured volume he carried. Given the rationing of paper, that too would have been expensive. And she would be the one to read it, since Alice's eyesight was failing badly and a daily newspaper was often the most she could manage.

'How kind of you,' she murmured. It was a good job that she liked flowers as much as her employer.

'Do you think I might see her? Just a brief chat, I promise. I like to keep in touch with the old dear.'

His smile was friendly enough, though there seemed a lurking shadow of satisfaction that for some reason made her think of a basking seal. 'I'll see how she is, Mr Fitzroy. She didn't have a good night and may not be up to visitors.' That would be Alice's get-out.

'Gilbert, please call me Gilbert.' He smiled again, this time without guile.

She wasn't sure she wanted to be on first name terms with

him. She had been happy with the professional relationship they'd established, but she found herself returning his smile.

'I'll be back in a moment. And Ralph, find your homework and make sure you're ready for the test we spoke of.'

'Ah, yes,' his father said. 'The test. An excellent idea.'

Alice lowered her magnifying glass when Beth appeared in the doorway. The old lady had begun her painfully slow read through the newspaper and was unhappy with this intrusion into her morning routine but, presented with the fact that her nephew was in the kitchen and had brought her yet another gift, she allowed herself to be persuaded.

'Only a few minutes though,' she grumbled. 'You must come and get him.'

Left alone with May and her pupil, Beth was curious. 'Why did your father bring you today? He's never done that before and you've been coming for several weeks.'

Ralph kicked the table leg with one foot. 'He says I play too much,' he announced moodily. 'And that maybe I should be in school. But I don't want to go away. It's much more exciting here.'

'Then you'd better work hard and prove him wrong. I'm taking Mrs Prendergast into my bedroom to finish our tea, but make sure you know those synonyms inside out by the time I get back. And write me sentences that use the first five words on the list.'

Ralph gave a theatrical sigh but obediently picked up his pencil.

7

'I won't stay more than a few minutes,' May said, when they'd decamped to Beth's bedroom. 'I can see you've got your hands full.' She jerked her head towards the sitting room. 'When he's done, I'll pop in to see Mrs Summer and then I'll be off.'

'He won't be long,' Beth said. She found a nook on the window seat while May took the narrow bed. 'I have strict instructions to rescue her. She seems to have little affection for him.'

'She can be a difficult woman. Not so much nowadays mebbe, but I remember my mother often coming home in a fury about something the mistress had said or done. It wasn't that Mrs Summer was harsh or aggressive—no shouting orders, that kind of thing. She was vague and sort of floaty. You couldn't put your finger on it really, I think that's what got to my mother. Ma never knew what was wrong, just that something was wrong, and the mistress wouldn't be happy until it was put right. Just plain irritating, if you ask me.'

'I think she must have mellowed since then, and I wouldn't have thought she'd give Gilbert Fitzroy problems. It sounds odd, but once or twice these last few weeks when he's come to see her, I've thought him almost scared.'

'Gilbert? Scared? He wouldn't be scared. He's a deep one, though. Mebbe he's just keen to keep on the right side of her and wants to make sure he doesn't put a foot wrong.'

'Why so keen? Alice is a frail old woman. She's no hold over him.'

May pursed her lips. 'You could be wrong there. He's the heir to Summerhayes. He'll want to make sure the place comes to him.'

'But surely it will. She wouldn't disinherit him?'

'Who knows? She's probably too much a daughter of Amberley to do such a thing, but old people get funny ideas in their heads. And she don't like him, so you never can tell. He's probably busy buttering his bread on both sides.'

'He owns Amberley. He surely can't need another estate. What would he want with this wreck of a place?'

May took a long sip of the weak tea. 'There's always been bad blood between the families over Summerhayes. The old man, Henry Fitzroy—he was Gilbert's father—hated the place. He reckoned it was unfairly taken from Amberley.'

'And was it?'

'Not that I know of. Nor anyone else. Alice married Mr Summer and he gave the Fitzroys a lot of money, leastways that was the rumour. In exchange, he got Mrs Summer and a large chunk of the Amberley estate.'

'So if it was all legally tied up, why the problem?'

'The Fitzroys are the problem, my dear. They're some crafty and they've an exaggerated idea of their own importance. Old man Fitzroy never accepted the settlement.'

'Do you think Gilbert feels that way, too?'

'I don't know, but it's bound to rub off, isn't it? In any case, he'll want Summerhayes to prop up his own estate.'

'But Amberley is rich.'

''Tis at the moment,' May said cryptically, raising her eyebrows into two large question marks. 'It's his wife that funds it, leastways that's what people say. She hasn't been near the place since war was declared, and what if she goes for good? There's rumours they don't get on, but he needs her, I reckon. He's overspent on that place something chronic. She's some kind of heiress. American.' May sniffed. 'If she don't come back and her money stays with her, he'll be in a mess. He'll want to make sure of Summerhayes, you'll see. And he'd make a tidy sum on it, even in its present state.'

'Ralph told me his mother was in New York. It's strange she's stayed away so long, but maybe she feels genuinely frightened. The bombing hasn't been anywhere near as bad here as it has in London but still... I wonder why she didn't take her son with her.'

'He wouldn't let her.' May again jerked her head towards the sitting room. 'A bit of a row about it, apparently, but in any case I don't think Ida was too worried. Not exactly mother of the year. And it wasn't just the war to my mind. That was a good excuse for her to pack up and go. Gilbert Fitzroy isn't everyone's choice of a husband.'

'Well, she did choose him,' Beth said stoutly. 'So she must have liked something about him. And he's been good to us. I know the presents for Alice are trivial, she can take them or leave them, but he's gone out of his way to help. He found us a new cleaning woman and that, let me tell you, is worth its weight in gold. If I had to add cleaning to all my other duties, I don't think I'd ever sleep.'

'Molly Dumbrell, isn't it?' May gave a small huff. 'I've heard she's a good enough cleaner but—'

'But what?'

'She's also no better than she should be, if you know what I mean. And Mr Fitzroy recommended her? Well, well.'

Beth was about to probe this cryptic remark when the

opening and closing of the sitting room door halted their conversation. Evidently, Gilbert had been dismissed. Beth, with May following, slipped back into the small hall to meet him and found Ralph by his side.

'Did she like the book?'

Gilbert smiled ruefully. 'I'm not sure she did.'

'Daddy said she put it on the table and didn't even open it.'

'Then I'll try to persuade her to take a look,' May said briskly. 'I'll go in now, if you've finished, Mr Fitzroy.'

'Be my guest. I hope you have better luck than I did.'

Beth was certain her friend would. For the old lady, May was a link to the past, but not such a close link that she brought with her disagreeable memories. Alice would be able to reminisce at will and May could be relied on to say the right things.

'Well now, Master Fitzroy,' she turned to Ralph. 'Time for that test, I believe.'

'Before you begin,' Gilbert cut in, 'I have a proposition.'

Beth was suddenly alert. He was an attractive man with a very obvious brand of charm. Men were best kept at a distance and attractive, charming men even more so. It would certainly be foolish to become embroiled in any proposition.

'I was wondering, Bethany.' He lingered on her name. 'Would you consider coming to Amberley to give Ralph his lessons?'

She was momentarily taken aback. It was the last thing she'd expected, but in the surprised silence Ralph piped up, 'Daddy, no. I'd much rather come here.'

'I know you would and that's the trouble. You're far too interested in the military. And while the army is here, your concentration will be on them rather than on what you should be learning.'

His father was right. Without the distraction of soldiers and tanks, Ralph was bound to give more attention to his lessons.

Gilbert's smile was affable. 'I think it's a sensible idea. By rights, of course, my aunt should be living with us at Amberley. It would certainly make things easier. I've tried to persuade her it would be for the best, but she's incredibly stubborn. Even when a bomb blew her windows out, she refused to move, though one of the Amberley cellars has a first-class shelter. It could house a dozen people. In fact, the whole house has space —and you do seem a trifle cramped here.'

That was putting it tactfully. The apartment had been hastily converted from several of the attics that had once taken up the entire top floor of the house. Summerhayes was large— where Beth came from it would be called a mansion—but even so she and Alice were squashed into a modest sitting room, two small bedrooms, an even smaller kitchen and a miniscule hall. It was good of Gilbert to make the offer and it would be blissful to enjoy space and comfort, but she remained unconvinced. The idea of spending whole mornings at Amberley made her uneasy.

'I couldn't leave Alice for that length of time,' she prevaricated. 'The most I'm ever away is an hour to get to the village and back.'

'Ripley is still living in the house, isn't he? I see precious little sign of him whenever I'm here, but he is a pensioner of the estate. He could sit with my aunt while you're at Amberley. Earn his keep.' It was said with a smile, but the words set Beth's teeth on edge.

When she didn't respond, he said, 'Let me know when you've had time to think it over. I believe it would work well— for all of us.' He patted Ralph on the shoulder. 'See you later, old chap. And mind that you work hard this morning.'

Beth walked with him to the upper staircase and hoped he wouldn't find a reason to loiter. But when he turned to her at the open door, it was to launch yet another surprise.

'There's a dance at the village hall tomorrow night. It's supposedly to welcome our new defenders, but really it's a rare chance for the village to enjoy itself. I thought you might like to go. You need a break and I can always give you a lift if you don't fancy the walk in the dark. The Bentley has just about sufficient petrol. Ripley will do the honours, I'm sure—he'll enjoy an evening with Alice.'

She very much doubted that, but Gilbert had disappeared down the narrow staircase to the first floor before she could respond. She felt ruffled, the peace of the morning destroyed. She didn't want to make decisions about Amberley or about a village dance.

When May emerged pink-faced from the sitting room a few minutes later, she appeared almost as ruffled.

'Phew! The old lady was in quite a taking. Goodness knows what Mr Fitzroy said to her. She's much calmer now, though, and I left her settling down for a nap. I must be off, my love. Time to visit my refugees—and you've a refugee of your own to mind.' She directed a smile towards the kitchen while cramming her hat on her head.

Beth handed over her basket. 'I hope he takes his father's words to heart or I'll feel I'm taking money under false pretences.'

'The boy will either learn or he won't,' her companion said philosophically. 'It's not your problem.'

But something else was.

'May,' she called out, as her friend made her way down the tightly packed stairs. 'Should I go to the dance at the village hall? It's tomorrow evening.'

'That's the best idea you've had for weeks.' May beamed with enthusiasm. 'I'll come and sit with Mrs Summer if you like.'

'I wouldn't ask you to do that. You'll want to go yourself and Mr Ripley will look after Alice, I'm sure.'

'She'd prefer it was me. Why did you want to know?'

'Gilbert Fitzroy mentioned it. He offered me a lift to the village.'

May's eyebrows rose steeply once more, this time forming almost vertical question marks, but she said nothing and made her way down the remaining stairs in silence. It left Beth feeling confused and a little troubled.

They weren't to exercise on the beach after all, but on the east side of the Adur river. When they landed in France, so the briefing went, they'd need to negotiate river crossings where the bridges had been destroyed by a retreating enemy. A Bailey bridge was the answer and all day they'd practised an assault across the river using portable canvas-sided boats, alongside the engineers building the bridge. It had been a long day before the final vehicles had trundled their way across. Jos was tired in mind and body. Depressed, too. The exercise had shown just how difficult it was to move an army through enemy terrain. And it assumed they had actually landed in France.

It was impossible to see how they were ever to get a foothold in that country, let alone storm the fortifications along the coast-line. For soldiers in war, the chance of death was ever present and several times he'd come close to it in Italy, but now it was no longer a chance but a racing certainty. Even as the landing craft ramps were lowered, they would be pummelled by machine gun fire and artillery shells. If they made it to dry land, they would be throwing their frail bodies against concrete and limb-destroying machinery, crawling upwards across an open beach while the Germans sat prettily in their cliff-top bunkers, annihi-lating them from a comfortable distance. It was a mad, mad plan and they would need the devil's own luck to be successful. But he understood that it was the only possibility. They would have to go through with it, risk all, and bear the consequences.

And what, after all, was he leaving behind? Who would

grieve for him? His proxy parents who'd cared for him on and off for most of his childhood? Mostly on, since his own father had so often been incapable. And their children, who had been as near to brothers as he was likely to get. But there was only distance now; their lives had taken them in different directions. For a while, they would mourn a lost cousin but three, four thousand miles away, Jos's death would arrive from another world.

And his father? Unlikely. On good days, he knew his son but there weren't many of those. Jos's visits to the hospital were, for the most part, conducted in silence and he would sit guiltily counting the minutes until he could decently leave. The nurses, of course, were relentlessly upbeat. *Your father is doing really well. Yesterday, he walked in the garden and helped Charlie pick flowers.* Charlie was the ward clerk. *He likes Charlie, he talks to him.* And there was that veiled accusation. He talks to the ward clerk but not to his own son.

Jos didn't return to his billet immediately. All the men with whom he shared would be there, and right now he had no taste for company. Instead he wandered down through the gardens, past the tanks, past the temporary cook and bath houses, and under the pergola of straggling roses to the abandoned vegetable garden. He would go back to that wild place, he decided, the one where young Ralph had found him and led him out. Out of the wilderness. How biblical it sounded. If only his own wilderness were as easy to leave behind.

When he got to the brick archway, he stopped. Glancing through it to the jungle beyond, he saw the narrow pathway that he and the boy had made only days before had disappeared and instead an acre of tall grass and overhanging tree ferns lay before him. Did he want to risk the ignominy of getting lost again? But something was calling him to walk through the morass, to find his way to that enclosed space at the very bottom of the estate. The badlands, Eddie had called it. And he was right. A sour smelling ruin if ever there was, yet the need to return was strong.

It must be the feeling that he'd dreamt the place, a feeling that persisted even though it was utterly illogical. Dreamt it or read about it perhaps. As a child, books had been a sanctuary amid the turmoil of an unhappy home, and he had been a voracious reader. He had loved tales of England, of knights and horses, of palaces and jousts. He must have borrowed a book from the library that mentioned Summerhayes, though he doubted the estate had ever seen a knight or a joust. Horses maybe, before the motor car displaced them.

Reluctantly, he turned back. He had wanted to find the garden again, walk the cracked pathway, circle the stagnant lake and pay homage to its shattered temple. But now was not the time. He had work to do, and he needed a shower and a change of clothes. A day submersed in water meant he smelt of river weed himself.

When he got back to the small brick building, Eddie was just emerging, a towel slung over his shoulder. 'Down to the showers, my friend, we're going dancing.'

'You may be, but not me.'

'Don't be a grouch. It's a hop, a simple village do—they want to welcome us to the bosom of their community.'

'This is community enough. I'm happy here.'

'There'll be a band,' Eddie tempted. 'And you know you love swing.'

'I can imagine what kinda band.'

'It'll be the real thing. A couple of the guys were saying the village has hired a gang from Brighton. That's the local fun palace. It should be good.'

'Then go and enjoy. I've a report to write for McMasters on today's hullabaloo. We avoided disaster by the skin of our teeth and there'll need to be a rethink.'

'You can do it tomorrow. Manoeuvres have been cancelled and we're being stood down.'

'How did that happen?' Jos had been preparing for another day of punishment and was taken aback.

'Our near disasters won't have gone unnoticed. I guess the colonel will be doing his own rethink, so maybe you don't need to write that report after all.'

'Then God knows what'll be in the new plan.'

'You won't know until tomorrow. So, c'mon, spivvy up and let your hair down.'

'Thanks for the invite, Ed, but I'm beat.'

'Me, too, but never too tired to dance.' Eddie looked at him closely. 'Sure it's not because there'll be women there?'

Eddie was closer to the truth than he realised. But it wasn't women he wanted to avoid; it was one particular woman. He hadn't been able to get her face out of his mind. He needed to keep clear of her or she would get under his skin. She had got under his skin. But no further.

'Chicken,' Eddie taunted.

His friend wasn't giving up. And how likely was it that Bethany Merston would be there? She had her old lady to look after. He gave in.

'OK, OK. I'll come.'

8

She was tempted by the dance, Beth couldn't deny it. Whenever she'd had the opportunity, she had loved to dance, but she was unsure of leaving Mrs Summer in Ripley's care. It was true the old lady had seemed more settled in recent days. Elizabeth was no longer a name on her lips and she appeared to have forgotten the letters. Beth had continued to keep a sharp eye out for the postman, collecting any mail from the panelled hall immediately it arrived, but there had been no further alarms. She began to hope that the letters had stopped, though why they should have done was as much a mystery as to why they'd begun in the first place. But although Alice had recovered her placidity, leaving her for an entire evening was a step in the dark and Beth hesitated. Mr Ripley, though, when she talked to him, seemed unfazed by the idea and assured her that he and the mistress would be fine.

'Just put her to bed, Miss Merston, and I'll read to her. Or we'll listen to the wireless together. And I'll make sure she gets her nightcap.'

'I'm not certain when the dance will finish. It could be late.'

'It's no matter. Once she's asleep, I'll leave her in peace and doze in here.' They were in the sitting room. 'You deserve a bit of a break. I know it's not easy.'

'Mrs Summer is no problem.' And to be honest, she wasn't. It was the unvarying nature of their daily routine that could be wearisome.

The old man shook his head knowingly. 'She is and she isn't. It was always the same. Mind you, it was her husband who was the real problem. Old Summer could be a hard man, though a fair enough employer. But Mrs Summer was always fidgeting over the household arrangements, never quite telling you what she wanted. I don't think half the time she knew herself. It fair drove Mrs Lacey and me to distraction.' Since this was very much what May had said, Beth could well believe him. 'But you leave her to me, I can deal with her.'

'I'll think about it,' she promised him.

'Mind you do more than think.'

It was a kind offer but it wasn't only Alice preying on Beth's mind. If she went to the dance, what should she do about Gilbert's offer? Probably accept it. It was just a lift. He could have no personal interest in her; he had a wife for heaven's sake. But when they'd first met, his handshake had lasted just a little too long and, several times since then, she'd surprised him gazing intently at her. She scolded herself; she was allowing her imagination to become lurid. The offer of a lift wasn't a date, and the dance itself was simply to welcome the Canadians to the village.

They were another problem, of course. Why did she keep finding problems? Eddie was certain to be there. He wouldn't be able to resist the fun and he'd take comrades with him. If Jos Kerrigan were one, he most definitely wouldn't be fun, and she didn't fancy dancing her heart out while he scowled from the fringe. She was sure that Eddie would try to persuade his friend into going, but the more she thought of it, the more certain she became that he'd fail—Lieutenant Kerrigan was a man unlikely to enjoy a village hop. And the thought of dancing, of throwing off the dreary pattern of wartime life for just one evening, was intoxicating. She weighed up the arguments.

She would go. She would go and enjoy herself despite the fact that her one best dress had faded slightly in the wash and her second-best pair of shoes were scuffed at the heel. She feared the sole was coming loose, too—all the more reason to give them one last outing. Her frock and shoes were dowdy, but at least she could make something of her hair. Instead of tying its length at the nape of her neck she would pin it up, winding it into soft layers and pulling down a few tendrils to frame her face.

While Alice slept that afternoon, she practised and, after several unsatisfactory attempts, managed something with which she was happy. A puff of powder and a smudge of lipstick and she would be fine. No one would notice her dress. Outside, the blackout reigned and once inside the village hall, the lighting would be mercifully dim. She would dispense with Gilbert's lift, she decided, and walk there by torchlight. That way, she would feel in no way bound to stay with him for the evening.

Her plan went like clockwork. Alice was amenable to being put to bed ahead of time and for once seemed excited by the evening ahead. She had demanded that Ripley bring the pack of playing cards and was looking forward to gin rummy, and to beating her old butler. It was doubtful how accurately either of them would decipher the cards, but Beth was sure they would enjoy the sparring. She laid out the tray for the nightly cocoa, and a small plate of biscuits for them both.

Before she left, she did a last twirl in front of the half mirror that was all her bedroom offered, and thought she looked passable. Her hair was positively elegant. Everything had gone swimmingly, so why was her stomach clenched tight? It must be that she'd become so unused to social occasions that taking herself to one felt as though she were climbing a very high mountain. But climb she did and, flashing her torch from side to side along the country lane, she reached the village without mishap. It was fortunate that all military activity had been suspended that evening. She would have hated to be forced again into a ditch and ruin the one decent outfit she possessed.

From the moment she reached the top of the main street, she could hear the music. A swing band was playing and they were surprisingly good. She found herself walking to the rhythm of the notes, the music growing louder as she made her way down the street and turned left into the narrow alley that led to the village green and the hall at its western edge.

She was brought up short by seeing a sizeable group of soldiers gathered outside the building. All were carefully groomed and pressed, their shoulder flashes bearing the single word *Canada*, and their uniforms barely distinguishable from their British counterparts, except for better material and a more stylish cut. The men were loitering outside the entrance, seeming uncertain whether or not to go in, before the door was flung open and May stood on the threshold. Several young girls in their best frocks appeared in the doorway beside her.

'Bethany, you've come.' Her friend peered through the darkness at her. 'It's good to see you. And you chaps,' she said to the hesitating soldiers, 'do come in.'

'Yes, please come in. We need you to get the dance going,' one of the girls said. And that seemed sufficient invitation for the men to throw away their cigarettes and a trifle sheepishly allow themselves to be escorted inside.

The red, white and blue bunting used on the village green for every Empire Day since the turn of the century had been strung from beam to beam along the walls and across the ceiling. It gave the hall the look of a liner about to set sail. The old-fashioned wall brackets had been draped with branches of forsythia, and the lights shining through the foliage bounced a bright yellow around the walls and splashed the floor with colour. Each floorboard had been brought to sparkling life, every inch of wood diligently polished with beeswax from the local hives. *That must have hurt a few knees*, was Beth's first thought.

May pressed a glass of homemade lemonade into her hand. 'Nothing stronger, I'm afraid. Not at the moment. The men are sure to produce something more exciting once they relax.'

'They do seem a little stiff.'

'Shy, would you believe? But the lasses will untie their tongues.'

She wondered what else would be untied during the evening. Already several of the young women wore flushed faces and one of them sported a blouse half unbuttoned from her exertions.

'Great to see you, Miss Merston. I hoped you'd come.'

It was Eddie Rich, freshly laundered, and looking as handsome as a Greek god. She glanced in the direction from which he'd come and saw Jos Kerrigan standing in the shadow of a supporting pillar, his face devoid of expression.

Eddie took hold of her hand. 'And you're tapping your feet already. Definitely time to dance.'

She was reluctant to agree; it was just as she'd feared, having to dance beneath an unfriendly gaze. But before she could refuse, Eddie had propelled her onto the dance floor where the band had changed rhythm and was playing a quickstep. For several seconds, she felt her feet fumbling for the steps, but he was an excellent dancer and it took only a short while for her to be skimming smoothly across the polished floor.

'Hey, you're a real shincracker, Miss Merston.'

'A good dancer? I've a very good partner. And please call me Beth. Miss Merston is beginning to sound odd.'

'Beth it is,' he said, steering her around the curve of the dance floor and narrowly missing a frowning Jos. She looked up at her partner and smiled. In this light, Eddie's eyes were almost

golden. He was impossibly good looking, but he posed no threat
to her peace of mind and she felt herself relax into his friendly
clasp.

'I hoped you'd find time to come tonight,' she said. 'It's nice
to see a familiar face.'

'I'll always find time for dancing.'

'Even after today's exercise?'

'It was tiring, sure, but we're pretty well settled at Summerhayes now. It's beginning to feel like home. But you didn't bring
Ralph with you and I was looking forward to seeing him.'

'I didn't mention the dance to him, but in any case I doubt
he'd be allowed to come.'

'That's a pity, but it won't stop us. And if my ear is tuned
right, the fun's just beginning. It's the jitterbug.'

'You dance that?'

'Don't I just. And if you don't know it, I'll teach you.'

And when the band began to play, Beth found herself being
pushed this way and that, twisting and turning to the beat, so
that in a short time she was completely breathless. 'I shall be
begging for mercy any moment,' she said, tipping her head back
and laughing aloud.

'No mercy. Not from this guy.' Eddie, too, was laughing.

But when the jitterbug music faded and the band segued
into a foxtrot, Eddie whirled her towards the side of the room.
Only fair, she thought. There must be plenty of girls he wanted
to dance with, and she couldn't cling to him as her one and only
friend of the evening.

Small groups of soldiers were gathered around the edge of
the dance hall, talking, smoking, some drinking. She noticed
that several bottles of whisky had made their appearance alongside the lemonade. The evening could be heading towards
rowdiness, and that would be the time to leave.

Skilfully, Eddie weaved a path through the slow-moving
couples, pivoting her across miraculously opened spaces to the

very edge of the dance floor. With one last twirl, he bumped her to the side of the room and into Jos Kerrigan. Kerrigan's face remained impassive, his features moving not a jot, even when a warm Beth was spun into his arms. But, instinctively, he put out his hands to catch her.

9

'Go, guy. Enjoy the dance,' was Eddie's parting injunction, as he cut across the floor towards the glamorous redhead he must have spied earlier.

Bethany tried to disentangle herself, growing hotter by the second. 'I'm sorry. Eddie is...'

'Eddie is a menace.' His tone was surprisingly gentle. 'But he's set us up to dance, so why don't we?'

She could think of several reasons but she liked the way he was holding her. And liked his fresh tangy scent. Slightly dazed, she nodded agreement and together they slipped back into the mingle of dancers. The rhythms of a slow foxtrot allowed her to catch her breath, though not for long. Dancing with Jos Kerrigan, she found, was not conducive to a stable pulse. Whereas Eddie had been fun, flinging her this way and that but never once losing the beat, Jos held her close, as though she were something precious. And while she danced with him, she felt she was. The slow, sensual rhythm gradually entwined them, their warmth seeping into each other. It was the oddest feeling, as though their individual bodies had become a single entity, wrapped and enclosed within the strains of the music. She daren't look at him to discover whether he felt it too, but instinct told her he must.

They were coming to the end of the dance; the music faded and the band readied themselves for a new number. He still held her close and, shamefully, she wanted nothing more than to stay right where she was. But a disturbance behind them made both turn. A man was pushing his way across the dance floor to reach them.

'I thought it was you, Bethany. I spotted you from the doorway. Sorry I'm a bit late, a last-minute hitch, but why didn't you telephone? You should have let me call for you.' Gilbert nodded briskly at Jos, as though he had only just noticed him.

Jos allowed his arms to drop and she felt the coldness they left behind. She wanted to say something, something to rescue the moment, but her mind was empty. In the awkward pause, Gilbert took his chance and reached for her hand. 'Shall we?'

She looked for Jos, but he had turned on his heels and was lost once more among the smokers and whisky drinkers.

'A waltz,' Gilbert said. 'How traditional, but very enjoyable.'

She had to acknowledge that he was a decent dancer, but the magic of the evening had gone. Fatigue was setting in and growing by the minute and when, after two consecutive dances, he proposed finding a drink, she braced herself to say goodbye.

'To be honest, Gilbert, I think I should go home. Mr Ripley is minding Alice, but I'm reluctant to leave him too long. He's no longer a young man. He'll be tired and he'll want to get to bed.'

She saw a shadow of annoyance pass across his face. 'You must go, of course.' There was a false heartiness in his voice. 'But I insist on driving you.'

'There's really no need. I've a powerful torch and I can easily find my way. And you've hardly danced. Stay and enjoy the rest of the evening.'

'I've danced enough to satisfy the village. The old *noblesse oblige* thing, you know. And I wouldn't dream of letting you walk home alone at this hour.' She wondered what he imagined might happen to her along a quiet country lane. 'In any case, it's my fault for turning up so late.'

Beth would have preferred to go home alone, but his insistence made escape difficult—unless she was prepared to make a scene. And she wasn't.

'I'll get my coat,' she said.

'Good. The Bentley is parked in the High Street. I'll meet you there.'

The night air gave her a shock, but after the cloying thickness of the hall, it felt invigorating. A group of young soldiers stood to one side of the door enjoying the freshness of the evening. She heard a scuffling and saw several couples shrink from sight into the bushes opposite. Pulling her coat tightly around her, she brushed past a tall figure standing to one side of the group. She knew, even in the darkness, that it was Jos. He stiffened as she walked past, but he said not a word.

'Over here,' Gilbert called, waving to her from the junction. The car was parked a few paces away, its silver bodywork gleaming beneath a moon that, for the first time that evening, had swum free of the clouds.

Within minutes they had left the village behind. Gilbert drove fast but expertly along the lane she had walked earlier.

'I hope you won't find that my aunt has been difficult.' He half turned his head to check her response. He wanted to talk, and she felt she owed him that at least since she'd brought him away from the dance far too early.

'I'm sure she's been fine—as long as she's won. I left her playing cards with Mr Ripley,' she said in explanation.

In the driving mirror, she saw him give a wry smile. 'The butler playing cards with the mistress? What a topsy-turvy world we live in.'

'I don't think Mrs Summer thinks of him as her butler any more. He's just Ripley, an old man who shares her house.'

'Aunt Alice doesn't think much at all, does she? I don't like to say this, Bethany, but it's struck me recently that she isn't all there up top, if you know what I mean.'

She was startled and hastened to reassure him. 'She's a little vague, I know, but that's just her way. Her mind is fine. If ever she's confused, I think it's because she finds life at Summerhayes so different now.'

'I imagine she does. Who wouldn't? The other day when I called, I had a good look around the house and it's a mess. The panelling is scratched, the floors are ruined—when I was a boy, they were a brilliant golden oak. The shine on them could outdo the sun and as for the decorative glass! Young boys don't usually notice these things, but I do remember the way those glass panels threw amazing colour into every room.'

'Then I'm glad she can't see what the house has become.'

'No, indeed. Best she stay within her own four walls. I reckon some of the furniture is missing, too, and that would upset her greatly.'

'I wouldn't know. The house is much the same as when I came in January, except that Mrs Summer has sold some of the paintings.' *But not Elizabeth's*, was her unspoken thought. 'Perhaps it's the pictures you've missed rather than the furniture.'

'I was thinking more of the huge sofa that used to be in the drawing room. It was upholstered in the best velvet. And the ladder back chairs in the dining room. They were designed by Philip Webb and would cost a fortune now.'

He took the final bend at speed but was quick to correct the car. 'I suppose we should be glad there's still furniture left and that the panelling hasn't been torn down for firewood. My aunt's husband was a modern man, but even he didn't manage central heating and these old houses are cold.'

'Tear the panelling down?' She looked nonplussed. 'Who would do such a thing?'

'Plenty, or so I hear. Military men don't like being cold.'

She gave a little puff of breath. 'Thank goodness it's April then and we needn't worry. Not for a few months at least.'

'If rumour has it right, we can forget worrying for longer than that. A grand invasion is on the cards in the not-too-distant future and our Canadian friends will be in the thick of it.'

Her heart flinched. An image of Jos Kerrigan lying dead on a French beach had her squeezing her eyes shut, trying to erase the picture.

Gilbert swept the car off the lane and brought it to a halt at the lodge gate. He rolled his window down as the sentry approached. 'Just taking this young lady home, soldier.' There was a satisfaction in his voice that she didn't like.

The sentry flashed a torch into the darkness of the car and, recognising Beth's face, waved them through. As soon as they drew up at the front entrance of the house, she had the car door open and was clambering out. She'd no wish to dally.

'Thank you for the lift, Gilbert. It's kind of you to go out of your way.'

He cut her thanks short. 'I hope you'll be coming to Amberley, as I suggested. I've had a room made ready and Ralph has moved all his books and papers there.'

He was putting her on the spot and he knew it. When she hesitated, he pressed further. 'At least give it a chance. If you don't think the arrangement works, there's no harm done.'

It was all so reasonable there was little she could do but agree.

'Tomorrow then. I'll call for you. Around ten o'clock, shall we say?'

'There's really no need, Gilbert. I'm happy to walk.'

. . .

Before she reached the top of the stairs, she saw that the door of the apartment stood wide open. Her stomach gave an involuntary lurch. She ran up the last few stairs and into the tiny hall. An eerie quiet blanketed the apartment. Where was Mr Ripley? She tiptoed into the sitting room, thinking that perhaps he had fallen asleep and forgotten to lock the front door. It was always kept locked. There were too many people on the move in and out of the estate, and in the general confusion anyone could evade the duty sentry by climbing over the perimeter wall and walking into the house unnoticed and unchallenged.

But the sitting room was empty. Had Mr Ripley returned to his attic room and left the door temporarily ajar? It was unlikely and her stomach tightened. She must make sure that Mrs Summer was safely asleep. But when she pushed open the door to Alice's bedroom, she saw immediately, even in the near dark, that the bed was empty. Panic clawed at her. The elderly woman had gone. Somehow she must have opened the front door and crawled down the stairs to the ground floor. Even now she must be wandering the gardens with poor Ripley in pursuit. Why ever had she gone to the dance? It was the stupidest thing she could have done.

As Beth stood there, she heard a noise. It was coming from the far corner and she pushed the bedroom door further ajar so that the light from the hall fell diagonally across the floor. Then she saw her—and nearly fainted with shock.

Alice was at the window. The curtains had been drawn back, the blackout rolled up, and light blazed across the concrete below, an open invitation to any passing German plane. The old lady's hands were splayed across the glass as though she were trying to thrust her way through its panes. Periodically she beat her forehead against the window, all the time emitting a barely audible moan. Now Beth's ears were attuned, she shivered at the sound; it was like that of a small, wounded animal. Had Gilbert been right when he'd suggested, just minutes ago, that his aunt's mind was as fragile as her body?

As softly as she could, she walked over to the half prostrate figure and took her by a night-gowned arm. 'Mrs Summer, it's me, Bethany. You must come back to bed.'

But Alice refused to move. She was surprisingly strong, and her figure grew more rigid with Beth's attempts to loosen her clasp on the window. And all the time she continued the soft moan, though it had grown noticeably harsher the minute she'd felt the touch of a hand. It was the most dreadful sound and Beth could feel her scalp spiking with fear.

'Mrs Summer,' she repeated. 'You will get cold if you stay out of bed. Let me help you back.'

This time Alice must have heard her because she twitched her head and breathed heavily, opening and shutting her mouth, as though she were suffocating. Struggling to get words out, but finding it impossible.

Beth stayed holding her fast, until finally the elderly body collapsed against her and Alice found the words she'd been seeking.

'They're there,' she said, and then kept on saying, 'They're there, they're there. I can't get to them. But I must.'

Beth was seriously alarmed. Gilbert's prophecy seemed to be coming true before her eyes. 'Please come away from the window,' she pleaded.

'I can't,' Alice said simply. 'I have to get to them. I have to get to Elizabeth.'

The letters may have stopped, at least temporarily, but it was clear that Alice had not forgotten. The desire to be reunited with her daughter still burned bright.

'Elizabeth isn't there,' Beth said softly.

'Yes, yes. She's there,' Alice insisted. 'She'll be with Joe, you'll see, she'll be with the others.'

Somehow she had to get the old lady safely back into her

bed. She would need to use cunning. 'You can't reach them through the window so why don't we wait for them indoors? They've seen you now and they'll come. You can wait for them in bed. You'll be warmer there.'

Alice turned and stared at her for what seemed like minutes. Then she let go of the glass and allowed herself to be led towards the bed. With difficulty Beth steered the tired figure onto the mattress and covered her gently with sheet and quilt, then strode back to the window and reeled down the blackout, pulling the curtains smartly closed.

'Rest a while, and I'll make you a hot drink,' she told her. 'You'll feel much better for it.' Alice lay back on the pillows and closed her eyes.

It would have to be cocoa again, which meant three cups in one day and their ration was dwindling fast. But there was no help for it. She must lull the poor woman to sleep and hope that slumber would clear her mind, and that by morning she'd realise whatever she'd seen had been imaginary.

The kettle had reached a brisk boil when Mr Ripley staggered through the still open front door. Beneath the naked electric light, his face was an unhealthy crimson. His few strands of hair were impossibly tangled and the old cardigan he wore was scattered with small pieces of broken twigs and odd leaves. He tottered towards her, leaving muddy footprints on the kitchen floor.

Beth felt immense relief. 'Thank goodness you're back. But whatever's happened?'

His breath was coming in great heaves and when he was finally able to speak, his voice rattled in his chest. 'She saw a ghost, Miss Merston, on the lawn. She didn't call it a ghost, mind. She said he was real.'

A distorted imagination, as she'd thought, but she still found herself asking, 'Did Mrs Summer say who it was that she saw?'

'Oh yes, it was Joe Lacey. She was certain of it.'

'May Prendergast's brother?'

Ripley nodded. His breathing was gradually returning to normal. 'He had his gardening apron on, and twine around his trousers and she said he was wearing his old felt hat. She reckons they've come back, the gardeners that is. All of 'em. And they've brought Elizabeth with them.'

Somehow, that made things worse. 'And you went to investigate?'

Again, Ripley nodded. 'I had to. She was fair beside herself. I thought if I looked as though I was doing something, it would calm her down.'

'And was there anyone there?' She felt stupid even asking the question.

'No. Not a thing. I searched what's left of the lawn and the rest that's under concrete, just in case. Then I went round every bush and every tree that she can see from her window.'

That explained his dishevelled appearance. He'd had no torch and must have felt his way in total darkness. He was well over seventy and she dreaded to think what harm he might have come to.

'You did your very best. You must sit down and rest.'

She'd been tardy in offering him a chair but, still bewildered from the encounter with Alice, she wasn't thinking clearly. The sight of the old lady in that long white nightgown, trying to push her way through the window, had been terrifying. She was realising now just how terrifying. They had managed to avoid a major calamity, but only just.

She left Mr Ripley slumped in the kitchen chair and went back to Alice to check on her. At the door, she saw the old lady had drifted into a deep sleep. A mercy. And one cup of cocoa was going spare.

'Here,' she said to Ripley when she returned to the kitchen. 'You should drink this.'

'That's kind of you, Miss Merston. I'm feeling a bit shook

up, I have to say. I'm not as young as I was, not for midnight rambles.'

'Indeed not, and you must never do that again. But I know you wanted to help her and I appreciate what you were trying to do.' She reached out and clasped his hand.

'I didn't like to see her in such a state. I went back to collect my book, you see—I'd left it on her bedside table—and then I found her, out of bed and trying to get through the window. Leastways, that's how it looked. It gave me a real turn. I thought if I went down to the garden to investigate, it would pacify her, but it didn't.'

Beth shook her head, remembering the scene all too vividly. 'I doubt anything would have pacified her—except perhaps sleep. What do you think actually happened?'

'I don't rightly know. Perhaps she heard a noise and got out of bed to look. She might have caught sight of something blowing across the garden. The soldiers leave so much rubbish around, and there's been a wind getting up these last few hours. Mebbe she thought it was a figure, a real person.'

'And decided it must be the one person she wanted to see.'

He shook his head sadly. 'Miss Elizabeth must be dead. At least, I reckon so. She's been gone thirty years and not a word. I knew that girl since she was so high, and if she was alive, I know she'd have written. But the mistress never would believe it. Master William afore he died tried to make her see sense. He'd waited for his sister for years, but in the end he decided she wasn't coming back. It made no difference. His Ma kept saying that Elizabeth *was* alive and that she would come back—to her mother.'

He paused and rubbed a hand across his chin. 'It's funny really. The old lady was always closest to her son, or so it seemed to all of us. But it's her daughter she misses most.'

Beth thought about it. 'Maybe she can accept her son's death more easily. She knows for certain that he's gone. She buried him after all. But Elizabeth is different. She doesn't know what happened, so her daughter remains tantalisingly alive for her.'

Ripley rubbed his chin again. This was a little too whimsical for him and Bethany brought the discussion back to earth again. 'Why did she decide it was Joe Lacey she saw?'

'I thought of that,' he said proudly. 'I reckon it was Mrs Prendergast coming here the other day. It reminded her of Joe and all the men who worked with him in the gardens.'

'So if all these people from the past were coming back to see her, it must follow that Elizabeth would be among them?'

'I reckon so. Hallucination they call it, don't they?' The cocoa was working wonders.

'They do, Mr Ripley,' Beth said sadly. 'They do.'

10

The following day Gilbert was at the front door of the apartment before she'd had time to wave Molly Dumbrell off the premises and talk to Mr Ripley about the morning ahead. Beth felt flustered and irritated. It was a kind gesture to drive over from Amberley, but it had been unnecessary. The walk there was two miles at most and she had little to carry, but here he was already, under her feet and pacing the worn hall carpet.

He was in the way of Molly and her brush and the two of them did a small dance around each other. The girl had turned an unusually bright shade of red and, for a moment, May's unfathomable remark seemed to make sense. But in another, Beth had dismissed it. Village gossip, she thought, and rushed into her bedroom to collect handbag and hairbrush. Through the window, she saw the Bentley parked on the front drive, its silver bodywork gleaming in the morning sun.

'Ralph can't wait to get started,' Gilbert threw at her as she ran back into the hall. 'He's already at his desk. Seems happier now that he's on home territory.' The joviality was edged with impatience.

Knowing Ralph as a most reluctant scholar, Bethany

thought it unlikely but stopped herself from saying so—having his son ensconced at Amberley must mean a good deal to Gilbert. Instead, she sped past him into the kitchen and hurriedly packed away the breakfast dishes. Ripley had followed her and stood in the doorway.

'Mrs Summer has had her pills,' she told him, 'but could you put the bottle back?' She handed him the Veronal tablets. 'Top shelf of the bathroom cabinet. And don't worry about lunch. I'll be home in good time.'

'You mustn't concern yourself, Miss Merston. I'll manage the mistress fine,' Ripley called out, perambulating towards the bathroom.

'Of course he will,' Gilbert put in genially.

She'd noticed how pale and tired Mr Ripley was looking this morning, and hoped they were both right. Beth's nerves were still frayed from the previous evening and here she was, only twelve hours later, asking the poor old man to stand guard once more.

Once in the car, she tried to put Summerhayes out of her mind and relax into the Bentley's leather cocoon for the short journey to Amberley. Gilbert maintained an easy flow of conversation, pointing out land on either side of the road that was farmed by his tenants, and regaling her with a history of the Fitzroy family and their ancient country seat. She was grateful that he seemed to require little in the way of response. Her mind was disobedient, skittering here and there but returning always to the problem of Alice and her hallucinations.

By rights she should divulge last night's events. Gilbert was Alice's nearest relative and if anything should go really wrong, he would at least have been warned. And it looked as though something could go really wrong; if that happened, her employer would need more than Veronal. It still terrified her to think of the old lady battering herself against the window, unknowing of where she was, unaware of the fantasy she'd created.

Nevertheless, Beth felt herself holding back. It would complicate matters to tell Gilbert and, if she were being truthful, complicate matters for herself in particular. It meant that he would have another reason to call at Summerhayes regularly, to consult her as his aunt's companion. And though she liked him well enough—there was little to dislike, he was attentive, courteous, willing to help—a small niggle within her insisted she remain as uninvolved as possible. She wouldn't mention last night, she decided, as they pulled up outside the large oak door of Amberley, but if anything untoward were to happen again she would have to tell him.

The house had once been beautiful. Mullioned casements, a red roof of weathered tiles, and on either side of the studded oak door, griffins sitting proudly atop their pedestals. The April sun bathed the scene in a mellow glow. But look to one side of the house and mellowness was lost. An ugly modern building had been partially attached. It was jarring, dislocating. A building that lacked all sensitivity to its surroundings, that constantly challenged the old to a fight and just as constantly won.

'My new office block,' Gilbert said proudly. 'I couldn't work in the house—it's big enough but not functional. The minute I moved to the new office, I felt efficient.'

'It's certainly efficient looking,' she murmured.

The large, square hall was a complete contrast: baronial and dark panelled and hung with a dozen family portraits, most of them, she saw from a passing glance, of formidable personages. But she was given no time to dawdle even if she'd been inclined. Gilbert was already bounding up the grand staircase to the first floor and she followed meekly in his wake. But not so meekly that she was unaware of every inch of her surroundings.

The stair carpet bristled with newness, the curtains hanging at tall windows had barely found their creases, and everything shone with an abrasive veneer. It was well tended, well curated, but it didn't work. Like the office block outside, the aggressive newness jarred with what had gone before and, though immaculately maintained by what must be an army of servants, it remained soulless.

Climbing the stairs, she passed row after row of ancient oils; they did little to lift the spirits. There were no flowers, no photographs, no bric-a-brac. If you were to venture to a living room she was sure there'd be no magazine out of place, no book left lying, nor a spread of toys on the carpet. No jumble of family life.

Ralph was waiting for her in one of the first-floor rooms. It was bright and airy and completely bare of distraction. Two desks had been placed opposite each other and a blackboard positioned behind the desk she took to be hers. There was a table to one side on which several piles of reference books had been stacked, along with a plentiful supply of paper and a variety of pens and pencils. Where had Gilbert obtained all this stuff, she wondered? Paper had been rationed for the last four years; wrapping paper for most goods was prohibited and newspapers seemed to grow thinner with every month. Even school textbooks were not being reprinted.

He beamed at her from the doorway. 'Well, what do you think?'

'It's very—efficient.'

'Splendid. I'm glad you like it. I hoped you would. Now, if you'll forgive me, I've several things piling up in the office downstairs so I'll leave you two to get on with it.' He waved his hand towards a surprisingly old-fashioned bell pull on the far wall. 'Do ring if you need anything.'

When the door had closed behind him, Ralph said, 'You don't like the room, do you Miss Merston?'

She was shocked to realise he'd read her thoughts so accurately and tried to allay his concern. 'It's bright and cheerful, and we have everything to hand. What more could we want?'

'But still...' he began.

'Ralph, we're here because your father feels you'll work better in your own home. So let's make sure we don't disappoint him.' Her tone was rallying.

Over the next few hours, the boy tried. He tried very hard, Beth gave him that, but if ever a child were unsuited to academic work, it was Ralph. Each sentence he wrote drew a heavy sigh, each sum he finished was smudged with sweat. After a particularly tortuous tussle with fractions, she decided they both needed a drink. Things might go better after some refreshment. She eyed the bell and ruled against it. She was wondering if she dared suggest to Ralph that they slip down to the kitchen for a glass of milk when the door opened and Gilbert stood on the threshold.

'I was wondering if you fancied a little food.'

'I don't think there'll be time to eat,' she was quick to say, 'but a drink would be welcome.'

'It's just a small snack that Cook has prepared. It's in the dining room. I'm sure you could do with something. You both look famished.'

Beth had been up very early that morning to make sure Alice was settled before she left and had missed having breakfast. She could certainly do with that something.

'I can't stay long though,' she warned. 'I need to get back to Summerhayes to relieve Mr Ripley.'

'You must. And I'm most grateful for you coming here. It's an awkward business—my aunt in one house and us in the other. Years ago, of course, we wouldn't have had the problem. The two estates were one, did you know? Summerhayes was a part of Amberley and my family owned the whole.' He bathed her in a warm smile. 'But the past is the past and it's the future we must think of. Ralph's future. We must build on your morning's efforts. I suggest you set him work to do this evening, and then pick it up with him again tomorrow.'

'But—' she started to say.

He wasn't listening and had disappeared down the main staircase. All she could do was to follow him, with Ralph trotting alongside like a puppy released from its chain.

When Gilbert had first broached the subject of his son's education, she had offered to teach Ralph for nothing. It would keep her teaching skills up to scratch, she'd reasoned, yet put her under no obligation. Gilbert, though, had insisted she take a fee and reluctantly she'd agreed. It was a small tie but one she hadn't wanted. Mindful of the care she owed Alice, she'd made clear from the outset that her teaching must take place in any time she had spare, and never two days in a row. Gilbert appeared to have forgotten this.

Across the hall they went and into a dining room that overlooked the gravelled turning circle beyond. The corner of the hideous office block was just in sight, but if she angled her gaze a little differently, Beth could cut it from view completely. She couldn't cut from view the feast that awaited, spread across the long rectangle of a Jacobean table. Apart from lettuce and tomatoes picked from the greenhouse, there was a platter of assorted cheeses, a large plate of ham and one of tongue, and a beautifully fresh loaf with a wedge of butter so large it made her blink. And then there was the cake, a round delicious confection of eggs and even more butter and, beside it, a huge bowl of tinned fruit and a jug of cream. How had Gilbert managed to get hold of such food?

The same way, she imagined, as he'd thwarted the rationing on new clothes and on paper. Money and connections still counted. She felt guilty at sitting down to such a magnificent spread when others, Alice and Mr Ripley and May, had so little. But Gilbert was pulling out a chair and she took her seat obediently. She wouldn't eat much, she told herself, she would leave in a few minutes, stay just long enough to be polite. But in the end temptation proved too great and she cleared a full plate, with a large slice of cake to follow, while her host looked on approvingly.

'That should help,' he said. She looked enquiringly at him. 'You're very thin, I hope you don't mind my saying.'

'We're all very thin, we've had rationing for the last four years,' she said a trifle tartly and then wished she hadn't. She had just wolfed food that must have cost him a fortune.

'All the more reason to feed you up when we can,' he said complacently. 'Ida is thin, too.'

Her mind skipped. 'My wife,' he helped her out. 'She is exceptionally thin, even without rationing. But then that's American women for you. And she smokes.' He was disparaging. 'That depresses the appetite, you know, apart from being a filthy habit. You don't smoke, Bethany, I suppose?'

'No,' she said, wondering where the conversation was going.

Ralph got up from the table, encountered a glare from his father, and slipped back on to his chair. 'Please, Daddy, may I leave the table?'

'You may, but don't make too much noise. I don't want to be disturbed.'

The house was a tomb, silence stretching from floor to ceiling, and she couldn't imagine how Ralph could ever make sufficient noise to disturb. No wonder he preferred the hustle of the Summerhayes estate. This was an unnatural environment for a nine-year-old.

The boy wandered out of the room and Gilbert relaxed back into his chair. She'd been hoping he would suggest she take her leave, but he seemed in no hurry to see her go and, having eaten her way through enough of his food to last a week, she felt obligated to stay, if only for a short while.

'Ida is in America, did I tell you?'

'I believe Ralph mentioned it.'

'She took off shortly after war was declared. No stomach for it, you see. I can't say I blame her. The Sussex coast was starting to look like a war zone even then. And see what's happened to it since. Brighton used to be a beautiful town, but now... Have you been there yet?' She shook her head. 'Then I wouldn't bother. It's fenced with enough barbed wire to cover the country and huge barricades of anti-tank blocks, dragon's teeth, all along the sea front. It's grim. But *I* couldn't leave. This is my home. I've too much at stake here.'

'And Ralph? Didn't he want to go?' From the outset, Beth had felt strongly that the child's place was with his mother.

'Ida would have been willing to take him, but I thought it best he stay in England. This is where he belongs.'

A mother willing to take him. It was as though Ralph was a burden to be negotiated between reluctant adults.

'I expect Ralph will get his mother back as soon as we've won the war,' she said brightly. 'Let's hope that's not too distant.'

'Let's hope not. But I doubt it. Ida coming back, I mean. England never suited her. Sussex really. She loved London— that's where I met her, the year after my father died. She was spending the summer with people she'd known in New York. They'd taken an apartment in Bayswater. She was fine with London, but Sussex proved a little too provincial.'

'London is a wonderful city. Does your wife enjoy art? And the theatre perhaps?'

'She enjoys spending money and there's not much opportunity for that here. She's an heiress. Filthy rich. Dozens of hangers-on, too.' She hoped he'd say no more, but he wasn't stopping. 'Her old man was a railway tycoon. He made a fortune running a line somewhere or other across the States. Left Ida every penny he had.'

Beth fidgeted in her chair, thinking that surely she could go soon.

'It's funny, isn't it?' He leant forward, a conspirator across the table. 'All that money and she wasn't happy—ever. She missed him. That was it. Missed her father and couldn't get on without him.' His wife's feeling for family appeared to surprise him. 'She tried several other chaps before me,' he said confidingly, 'but the engagements fell by the wayside. They weren't Papa, I suspect.'

'And you were?' She tried not to sound incredulous.

He gave a loud crow of laughter. 'Absolutely not. Just the opposite. For one thing I'm ten years younger than Ida. And for another, I'm nothing like her father. Nothing like the Yankee poker player either, the one she was engaged to before me. I expect that was the reason for my success.'

The marriage, it seemed, was no love match and there was unlikely now to be a sibling for Ralph. Nine years was a large gap. 'How nice,' she said, for want of anything sensible to say.

'Not really. It turned out that she was a fish out of water. Didn't belong here. Doesn't belong.'

This was what May had said, that there was trouble in the marriage, but Beth had no wish to hear more.

'Not like you, Bethany. As soon as I saw you at Summerhayes, I could see you fitted the life here like a glove. And you're wonderful with children. That's certainly not true of all women.'

'How good of you to say so.' She felt herself flush a bright pink. The conversation had turned uncomfortable to say the least. 'But this glove had better be getting back.'

'Of course.' He made no attempt to detain her. 'I'll drive you home straight away.'

'Again, there's really no need.'

'I'd like to. To show my appreciation for your hard work with Ralph. He's not the easiest of fellows.'

'He's nine years old,' she said simply.

'You're very understanding. And with your help, I know he'll make great strides. Now, about tomorrow?'

'I teach him every other day,' she reminded him.

'I do remember our agreement, don't think I don't, and I feel bad asking you for another favour. But Ralph seems to have made better progress this morning, don't you agree? And I'm keen to capitalise on it.'

'I'm not sure—' she began to say but was immediately overruled.

'I'll ensure he does the work you've set him and if you *could* come tomorrow, it would mean a lot. But if not, is it possible to squeeze us in for just one extra day this week?'

He had beautiful manners and a good deal of charm. Moreover, she had eaten his delicious lunch and was being chauffeured back and forth in the most comfortable car she'd ever sat in. It was impossible to refuse.

They were halfway back to Summerhayes when they heard it, a low flying aircraft emitting sharp cracking sounds. Gilbert glanced behind him, then up at the sky, and immediately swerved the car towards the nearest hedge. It was fortunate he'd found a field with its gate partially opened and was able to nose the vehicle almost off the road and into a space well-sheltered by spring greenery.

The plane was now virtually overhead, brushing the tops of the trees, and she realised that the cracking sounds—skip, skip, skip—were gunfire, as the gunner on the plane strafed the road beneath. The machine thundered over them, its black swastika menacing even in bright sunlight, and the hail of its bullets missing the wing of the car by inches.

Her hands were gripping the seat so fiercely that her knuckles turned white. It had been a perilously close escape.

Gilbert reached towards her. 'It's OK, we're OK.'

She felt his body closing in and his hand tighten on hers and instantly forgot her fear. This was not where she wanted to be.

'I'm sorry,' she said, wriggling free. 'That came out of the blue—literally. We haven't had much in the way of raids lately.'

He made no reply but steered the car back onto the road. Its entire length was pockmarked with a trace of bullets, until finally it seemed the ammunition had run out. They saw the plane in the distance, climbing high in the sky and disappearing out to sea. She wondered if the pilot would make it to the French coast.

As they came to a halt in front of the Summerhayes house, it was clear the Canadians had not witnessed the attack. The regiment must have only just returned from another long exercise and the soldiers were in a bustle of activity, eager to stand down once they had finished the unloading of trucks and support vehicles. By the look of the troops, muddy and worn, they had spent the entire day tramping the South Downs. It wouldn't have been easy.

She looked over the heads of the men closest to them and saw Jos. She couldn't be sure, but he seemed deliberately to look away. It was stupid to be disturbed by a man she hardly knew— but she was. The beginnings of a bond had blossomed between them as they'd danced, a bond that Gilbert Fitzroy, in a rare display of boorishness, had fractured. And now it had ruptured further. Despite Bethany's vow to keep her distance, she hated the thought they could be enemies. Surely not. Yet she had an uneasy sense that they could.

11

Eddie's talk of a day without manoeuvres had proved a myth and they had spent the last ten hours tramping the South Downs in various degrees of discomfort. The exercise had not gone well. Though recent days had been fine, there had been rain most nights, with the result that many of the trucks and Bren gun carriers had become stuck in churned mud before they'd managed to scale even the smallest slope. It had been a hard slog to reach their destination, though with support from the heavy artillery guys they'd eventually managed to loose trench mortars and machine guns roughly in the right direction, the shells whistling overhead like rockets. Villagers for miles around must have followed the sound—thirty seconds between gunfire and explosion—no doubt expecting their windows to fall in at any moment, even their houses to crumble.

Jos supposed it had been some kind of success to get the machinery in place and firing, but he felt tired and dispirited, nevertheless. However you looked at it, the future was bleak. It wouldn't be just a case of moving heavy guns onto beaches strewn with barbed wire and anti-tank devices. Nor of confronting a superior German force, shielded by mile after mile of concrete bunkers and machine gun nests, and heaven knew what other fortifications designed to obstruct an invading army.

There was also the small matter of getting a five thousand vessel armada, stretching as far as the eye could see, across a hundred miles of unpredictable and dangerous English Channel. Jos had read somewhere that an invading army hadn't crossed that stretch of water since 1688. He hadn't gone on to read what had happened to them, and he didn't think he would.

'Let's make a break for it.' Eddie slapped him encouragingly on the back. 'We'll wash up and trot down to the village. The food sucks but the beer ain't bad, if you can cope with it warm.'

'I don't think so, Ed.'

'Why not? It's been a pig of a day. Sorrows need drowning.'

'I'd rather stay on base. I've a hundred hammers in my head beating a tattoo. Noise is the last thing I need.'

'Hair of the dog, Jos, hair of the dog. The pub will work magic.'

He managed a faint smile but shook his head. 'Thanks, but I'll take the garden.'

It was Eddie's turn to shake his head. 'No accounting for tastes. And there are some tastes in the village I could really get to like.'

'I'm sure there are. But don't land yourself in trouble.'

Eddie had already escaped that kind of trouble by the skin of his teeth. It was a well-worn joke between them that in signing up for the army he'd put himself in danger but saved himself from a greater one.

'Once bitten... you can depend on me.'

Jos wasn't sure he could. When his mood was wicked, Eddie could get himself into the most difficult of scrapes. But his friend was a grown man and must look after himself. No, a slow stroll in the evening air was what Jos needed; it should stop his head from bursting its seams.

Until now, the humiliation of getting lost on that first day
had made him reluctant to walk much further than the
vegetable and fruit gardens. He hadn't known the layout of the
place at the time, and he'd been tired. Hot as well, and confused
by the garden's seeming familiarity. He was thinking of that
now, as he traced a zigzag path through massive grasses and tree
ferns. Not this part of the garden so much, nor the vegetable
plots and greenhouses, and certainly not the house and terrace.
It was the garden at the very bottom of the estate, a good mile
and a half away—Ralph's secret garden—that had fazed him. It
was a fair distance, but he would go there. With limbs aching
from what had been an endless day, it would be good to stretch
them with a decent walk.

He pushed his way through the untamed stretch of palms
and head-high grass, still tumid from the day's heat, not fighting
it this time but bending himself to accommodate its eccentrici-
ties. The laurel hedge, when he reached it, needed greater force.
At one time there had clearly been an archway here, marking
the entrance to this final part of the garden, but now it was so
heavily overgrown that only the faintest outline of the earlier
shape remained. The space beyond was completely still. Behind
what was left of the temple, the trees moved not an inch and
from the sluggish water, covered in water lilies and choking
weeds, there was only an occasional burble.

The sun had almost set and the moon not yet risen, but
there was light enough for him to pick his way around the oval
of water. This part of the garden was too distant for most of the
men to venture and, as a result, had been left untouched.
Undamaged by heavy vehicles, by heavy boots, by stray
gunshots. But for all that, it remained a wasteland.

A pathway had once circled the lake, he could see. He
scraped one foot against the broken stones and in the low beam
of sunlight that pierced the trees, glimpsed a glittering piece of
mosaic amid the shattered terracotta. This had been an orna-

mental path, a thing of beauty, but now in fragments. He picked up a shard and brushed the mud from its surface—its aquamarine was bright and true. He felt the edges and was surprised to find them sharp. Sharp enough to cut a finger. This wasn't the result of a gradual dissolution then. The pathway appeared to have been hacked to pieces by a jagged instrument. But when and why?

He stood and looked across at the other side of the lake. The marble pillars still standing were stained by verdigris, and in the half-light they seemed to have developed large cracks into which ivy had poured itself in gratitude. The portico, too, was badly damaged. It wouldn't take too many years before the whole edifice crumbled to the ground.

What must this place have been like in its heyday, he wondered? Magnificent was the answer. He couldn't have dreamt this garden or read of it in a story book, he decided. That was just a fancy. It was far more likely he'd seen an image of the garden or something very like it in a magazine. One of his father's old magazines, perhaps, when the guy was more or less still managing to work.

Whatever the memory, it was strong enough to make him hanker to restore the garden to its former beauty. And that was ridiculous. Almost as ridiculous as imagining one man could make any impression on such desolation—particularly now, when any day he might be under orders and with the slenderest chance of ever coming back. Yet something called to him to tend this ground, to nurture it, to make it whole again.

It would at least give him something to think about, other than how dire his future and how miserable his present. He'd seen Bethany Merston return this afternoon and clearly she'd allied herself to this Fitzroy character. It shouldn't matter a fig. For one dance he'd held her close and that was it, so what was he bellyaching about? He was here to work, he reminded himself. In any case, he shouldn't be surprised. His lips twisted at the thought. The man was wealthy, had a large estate and a flashy car. There was a wife somewhere but, hey, this was wartime and such considerations were petty. Loyalty no longer counted. He'd thought the girl might be different but, as always, he'd misjudged. She wasn't any different and he should forget her.

Beth had made it clear to Gilbert that from now on she would get herself to and from Amberley, and would not be staying for lunch. As soon as she'd agreed to teach Ralph for a second day, she'd regretted it, and was scrambling to mark some kind of boundary—and it was important that she did. Important for others, too, that she was not pulled unwillingly into Amberley's orbit. She'd felt bad asking Mr Ripley to spend another morning on Alice duties, but he'd smiled in his wintry way and said that, yes, of course he would help out.

'Though I am feeling a little downpin this morning, Miss Merston,' he'd said. 'I think I may have a cold coming.'

That made her feel guiltier than ever. 'You can stay in your room and rest for most of the time,' she offered, aware that it was hardly an enticement. 'But if you could look in on her once an hour and make her a hot drink mid-morning, I'd be very grateful.'

'I'll do that gladly,' he said, attempting to stifle a cough.

At least Molly had come and gone, whisking through the apartment and turning it into a small, shining palace. Intent on keeping the old lady on an even keel, Beth hadn't wanted to leave the girl on her own in case it might upset Mrs Summer. Nothing out of the ordinary had happened these past few days and she was hopeful that Alice might have forgotten the events of that dreadful night.

Today it was almost as quick on foot to Amberley as it was by car since a general mobilisation seemed underway. Regiments moving camp, she wondered? Several convoys of heavy Churchill tanks, interspersed with gun carriers, rumbled past her in succession. They were escorted by outriders on motorcycles and the occasional policeman on his regulation bike. Talk in the village had sharpened. It was reckoned now that an Allied invasion was a certainty in the next few weeks, if not days, and the continuing build-up of troops, the long ribbons of tanks trundling through the byways of Sussex, suggested the village was right.

Amberley's massive oak door was opened to her by a footman. At least, she supposed he was a footman, but this was a foreign world to her. Without waiting for him to announce her arrival, she made her way up the broad staircase to the first-floor room she and Ralph had occupied the previous morning. Today there was little sun, but stepping from the shadow-laden stairway with its dark panelling and disapproving Fitzroy ancestors, the room appeared bright and welcoming. She stopped at the doorway. Ralph was at his desk and already working.

'My word, you are an early bird!'

'Hallo, Miss Merston. I didn't manage all the stuff you set yesterday, but Daddy said that if I did it before you came and finished everything you gave me this morning, then he'd take me up on the Downs after lunch. There's lots going on. We might find a military exercise there—though I don't s'pose we'll be allowed to see much.'

Bribery always succeeded, she thought wryly, but if it encouraged Ralph to work, it was forgivable.

'Let me have a look.' She skimmed the top sheet of the two pages of long division he'd completed; most of them appeared correct. 'You've done well, but I'll mark them properly this afternoon when I'm back at Summerhayes. Finish the sum you're doing and we'll move on to writing. I thought this morning we'd concentrate on description. Amberley is very old and very beautiful, so think of as many adjectives as you can that describe the house and the gardens. Then decide what you'd like visitors to see, and plan a route for them around the estate, using some of the words you've listed.'

Behind her a scuffing from the doorway signalled that Gilbert Fitzroy had arrived and had evidently been listening in. 'Good morning, Bethany. What a splendid idea!' His greeting resonated around the near-empty room. 'It means Ralph can practise on you.'

'I'm sorry, I don't understand.'

She couldn't prevent herself from sounding terse. His interruption was unwelcome and, though she understood how important Ralph was to his father, she needed to be left alone to get on with the job for which she'd been hired.

'*You're* one of the visitors to Amberley,' he explained. 'You can be Ralph's guinea pig. But before he drags you around the house and gardens, I've something to show you.'

'I don't intend Ralph to move from his desk, and we've only just begun the lesson.'

Her severity should have put him off, but it didn't. 'I won't keep you more than a few minutes, but I'd welcome your opinion on something new that I'm trying in the garden. Ralph can remain chained to his desk, if you prefer. I'm sure he can get on for a short while without you.'

Beth wondered why, if Ralph could get on without her so easily, she'd walked the mile or so to Amberley. But she could see they would have no peace until she agreed.

'I'll be back shortly,' she said, 'and by then I'll want to see several lists completed.' The boy's forehead puckered with worry. 'Think of the house first,' she suggested. 'Try going round it in your head and write down the words you think best describe each room.'

Ralph reached for a clean sheet of paper and, brow still furrowed, bent himself to the task, while she followed his father back down the staircase, fuming at this cavalier treatment of their lessons and struggling to govern her temper. Once they reached the hall, Gilbert turned left along a wide flagged passage to an outer door. On the way they passed the kitchen, a stainless-steel monstrosity, so out of place in the ancient building it was ludicrous. He saw the look she gave it.

'I know.' He was laughing. 'But Ida insisted. She thought the old kitchen unhygienic. A place fit only for the bugs,' he drawled in a mock-American accent. 'So we had this horror installed and guess what, she never went near it. It's Cook's domain and *she* never tires of grumbling. She says it doesn't work like the old kitchen, but she still manages to produce some pretty good meals.'

I bet she does, Beth thought, particularly if she isn't hampered by the shortage of food. He opened the door for her, and she passed through it and into the overcast day. Without the sun, the garden felt chilly and her arms beneath the thin cardigan dimpled with cold. He saw her shiver slightly.

'Here, this should help.' He peeled off his jacket and, before she could protest, draped it around her shoulders.

'Thank you,' she murmured. A familiar unease took hold and replaced her anger.

'The least I can do,' he said gallantly. 'We're just along here. I want to show you the new rose garden. Actually, I want to show you the statue I commissioned. There—'

He stood back to allow her to walk through the crumbling stone arch that led to what, at one time, must have been an extensive rose arbour. New borders had been constructed, and the old hedges that had once partitioned the garden had been cut back and left to die behind recent planting.

'It wasn't like this in my father's time. We've had to make the arbour a good deal smaller. Pity, but there it is. It was just too damned big, and you can't get sufficient staff these days. Not when I've all these acres to maintain.' He waved his hand to indicate the grasslands that sloped into the distance. 'So what do you think of her?'

He meant the statue in the middle of a newly constructed stone circle. The sculpture, around four feet in height, dazzled in white marble, its subject the goddess Diana with a pair of hounds at her feet.

'It's beautiful,' she assured him.

It *was* beautiful but somehow the image grated. A rose garden was a place of peace, of soft petals and warm scents. She imagined the old arbour had been such a place; a classical goddess on her way to the hunt seemed an ill fit.

'Ralph's description can give it pride of place,' he said cheerfully. 'And I'm so glad you like it. I wasn't sure at first whether I'd made the right choice.'

Minerva, goddess of wisdom, or Venus, goddess of love, might have been better, but Beth wasn't about to set herself up as his artistic adviser. She was here only to mentor his son. With that in mind, she turned to go back to the school room.

He stopped her with a light hand on her shoulder. 'How about this rose I've recently acquired?' He pointed to a bush in full flower that nestled in the lee of the archway. 'It was developed four or five years ago—in Germany, of course—but with the war, it's taken a while to arrive here. It's called Martha Lambert. A fantastic red, don't you think?'

He seemed determined not to let her go, but she was equally determined to cut the encounter short. 'I don't know much about roses, I'm afraid. In fact, I know very little of gardening.'

'Did you never have your own patch as a child?'

She shook her head. The house in the countryside beyond Nottingham had boasted a long, narrow plot to the rear. There had been a small space at its very end, sitting beneath the shadow of the boundary wall, reserved for the children of the house. But reserved for her siblings alone.

'Ida never had a garden either,' he said conversationally. 'She was brought up in Chicago, a city of towers, then spent most of her time in New York or in one or other European capital. Gardens were a closed book to her, but she seemed to like the challenge—at least at first.'

It was becoming a pattern. Whenever she was with Gilbert, he seemed intent on talking of his absent wife and it made her uncomfortable. She had come here to help Ralph, that was the whole idea of the extra day's tuition, and now his father was taking up precious minutes to regale her with details of a woman she had never met and had no interest in meeting.

'In fact,' he went on, oblivious to her mood, 'she didn't much like Amberley at all. Once the initial novelty had worn off, she found the place inconvenient. I let her have her way with the kitchen, but when it came to tearing out the panelling and opening up the downstairs rooms and getting rid of every painting in the house, I had to put my foot down. You don't blame me, do you?'

'No,' she stuttered, though in truth she had no idea whether she should blame him or not.

'I thought you wouldn't. You're a reasonable woman, Bethany. Not like Ida. She'd been indulged all her life, of course, thanks to J P Rochford the Third. When he died, she looked for someone else to keep up the good work, but husbands have their limits.'

Beth made a strenuous dive for the stone archway, hoping this might end his monologue, but he continued to talk as he followed in her wake.

'Ida tried to fit in, I suppose, but she never managed it. Once she'd stripped the kitchen out and flirted with the garden, she'd had enough. By then, Ralph had arrived. You'd think that would have settled her, but no. A baby irked her even more and she started spending time in London. More and more of it. I think she felt she'd produced the necessary son and heir and could go her own way. She liked the drinking and the dancing. Liked the bright lights.'

'Who doesn't?' Beth said lightly.

'There's liking and liking.'

She longed for him to stop talking. The one-sided conversation had become discomfitingly intimate. Compelled to get away, she almost raced for the side door, at the same time freeing herself of his jacket.

`When they were once more in the dark panelled hall and her foot was on the first stair, he stopped her again. 'I'm sorry, I've embarrassed you.'

'No.' She tried to brush it off but didn't quite succeed. 'Well, perhaps a little.'

'Then I apologise again. I don't have the chance to talk much. You can't say these kind of things to servants, though I'm pretty certain they all know the score. It's ghastly.' His voice dropped to a murmur. 'Ida didn't just like the bright lights, she liked all that went with them—there were men, you see.'

She knew her face must be crimson by now. 'I'm sorry,' was her feeble response.

He reached up and lifted her hand from where it rested on the bannister and squeezed it tightly. 'I know you are and that's why I'm telling you. You're a kindred spirit, Bethany, so different from... but that will all be sorted.'

She wondered what he meant, but then he left her in no doubt. 'The Americans are accustomed to divorce. It won't come as a complete shock.'

Bethany had heard enough and fled up the stairs and into the room where Ralph was anxiously chewing on his pencil.

12

On her walk back to Summerhayes, Beth made a decision. She would not be returning to Amberley. She would go down to the regimental office this afternoon and ask to use the telephone. It was a cowardly way of imparting the news, but Gilbert Fitzroy was too adept at getting his own way for her to trust herself to tell him face-to-face. He would pile pressure on her to come back to Amberley—every day, if he had his way. And then what?

She had a lively vision of his next move. The clasp of his hand, the warmth of his gaze, had been warning enough. When he'd spoken of his wife, he seemed to be inviting her to step into the benighted Ida's shoes. She could be wrong, Beth conceded; she could be allowing her imagination to rip. But it was a chance she wouldn't take. He was a pleasant enough man, but a man who was used to having his own way, and for peace of mind she must keep clear of Amberley. If Gilbert wanted his son to continue lessons, then Ralph must study in the Summerhayes kitchen. It would be less comfortable for the boy, but a great deal more comfortable for her.

And she couldn't continue to ask Mr Ripley to deputise. It

was unfair. This morning she'd made herself ignore his watery eyes, his hacking cough and the audible sniffs, but that couldn't happen again and as soon as she reached Summerhayes, she went to his room, wanting to reassure him that his duties for the day were over. She found him asleep in his armchair, snoring rhythmically, and tiptoed away. Quickly, she walked along the landing to the front door of the apartment. This time the door was locked as it should be.

She went first to her bedroom, discarding the thin cardigan she wore and kicking off her shoes. Her body ached from head to toe and she stretched her arms high to the ceiling, trying to find relief. It had been a tense morning and she had come away from Amberley filled with a sense of things being awry. She would make lunch, she decided, looking around for her house shoes. It was a little early but the simple task would distract her and she could work undisturbed while Alice, too, slept soundly.

But when she crossed the small landing to the kitchen, she heard a shuffling from the direction of the sitting room. Then what sounded like a low moan followed by a definite groan, and then another low moan.

She rushed down the hall. The sitting room door was ajar and she pushed it wide. At first, she saw only an empty room. Then she heard the shuffling again, much louder now.

'Bethany?' The old voice cracked.

'Mrs Summer, what's happened?' These days she seemed always to be saying that.

She scurried across to the old lady's side. Alice was curled in a heap on the floor between the room's two fireside chairs that stood, not by the fire but on either side of the window. The window again. She must have tried to get to it and tripped and fallen. The visions were still working then, still vivid. Alice hadn't forgotten.

'I'll have you up in a jiffy.' She got her hands beneath the elderly woman's arms, the bony shoulders digging into her legs, and pulled hard. The only result was a painful groan that set her teeth on edge.

'I'm so sorry, Mrs Summer. I'll try not to hurt you, but you're well and truly wedged. Do you think you could untangle your legs?'

Alice's limbs seemed to have fallen like a marionette's, the legs bent at an impossible angle, with one on top of the other. The old lady shook her head and her face was filled with pain. Bethany repositioned herself, trying to take more of the woman's weight in her arms and shoulders. This time the crumpled figure moved very slightly, but not enough. With every attempt Beth made to lift her, Alice grimaced pitifully, biting down on her lip to prevent herself from crying out. It was clear she could stand little more of this manhandling.

There was no alternative, Beth thought, she would have to get aid. A stronger pair of arms was needed. Definitely not Mr Ripley's, but surely in this army camp of thousands, she could find a willing soldier.

'I'll have to get help. I'll be as quick as I can,' she promised.

She tumbled down the two flights of stairs to the ground floor and looked anxiously into one room after another: the communications office, the planning suite, the library. You would have thought there'd be an officer when you needed one. But clearly there wasn't. From an open window, a burst of loud cheering reached her. There was some kind of match going on —football, baseball—whatever the Canadian equivalent. Even the old dining room which served as a general office was empty. The men must be watching the match, and that's where she had to go. She rushed along the passage past the kitchen where the cooks, too, had gone absent, out of the side door and on to the terrace, only to crash full tilt into a mud-splattered Jos Kerrigan.

He put out his hands, whether to keep her from the mud or to ward her off, she wasn't sure.

'Sorry, I've an emergency,' she panted. 'Alice, Mrs Summer. She's had a fall and I can't lift her.'

He stood looking at her for what seemed a ridiculous amount of time, but could only have been seconds, while he processed the information.

'Can you help?' she demanded, impatient and very worried.

He held up two mud strewn hands.

'We do have a bathroom,' she snapped.

'You'd better lead on then.'

She did, and within minutes he'd scrubbed himself clean and was trying to keep his trousers from dirtying the carpet— and from dirtying Alice.

'Don't worry about the mud,' she urged. 'It's Mrs Summer that matters.'

Jos had broad shoulders and a lot of strength, which was just as well, as Alice was firmly fastened between the two chairs. 'If you can,' he instructed, 'uncurl her legs as I lift. I'll give you the signal.'

On the count of three, he bent down and scooped up the elderly woman from behind, while at the same time Beth tried to liberate the sprawled limbs. Both of them were red-faced from the effort, but somehow they managed to pull the poor, tired figure free and half carry, half drag her onto one of the offending chairs.

'Thank you,' Beth said crisply. She could feel him wanting to get away as soon as possible.

'I guess you'll want to get her to bed.'

'I will, but I can manage now.'

His eyebrows lifted. 'Really?'

'If I have trouble, I can wake Mr Ripley and he'll help me.'

'Ripley? The old guy? It might be better if I stuck around some. Let the lady get her breath and then we'll get her into bed.'

It wasn't a case of 'we', she had to acknowledge. It was Jos alone who once more gathered Alice into his arms and carried her into the bedroom, settling her on top of the mattress. Beth had already pulled back the counterpane and now covered her employer with its quilted warmth.

'I'll get you a drink, Mrs Summer,' she said. The older woman's eyes were closed. She seemed too relieved by her rescue to want to speak.

'Can I get you some tea, Mr Kerrigan?' It was the barest courtesy.

'Lieutenant Kerrigan. Or just Jos.'

'Which do you prefer?' she challenged.

'Which do you?'

'Can I get you some tea, Jos?'

'Thank you, I'd like that.' He'd won the tussle and was magnanimous in victory.

She warmed some milk for Alice and made two cups of weak tea. 'I'm sorry,' she said, after she'd returned from delivering the milk. 'Our tea ration has taken a hit this week.'

Jos looked down at his cup. 'It's a novel colour.'

'Not to us.' She sounded belligerent though she hadn't meant to.

He was just feet away and his closeness was filling her with a mix of sensations—excitement, fear, annoyance even—but when she spoke again, she made a conscious effort to keep her voice even. 'Tea has been rationed here for years—two ounces a week each. By the end of the seven days, we're down to little more than hot water.'

He said nothing but sipped the liquid without complaint, and Beth felt a strong compulsion to fill the silence. 'I might have a couple of biscuits in the tin, though I wouldn't swear to it.'

'No cookies, thanks. That would be too much largess for such a small act.'

'Not such a small act. I was getting panicked. I tried to lift her but I couldn't move her an inch.'

'You seemed a little panicked.' He appeared to savour the thought.

'You seemed a little muddy.' He wasn't going to have it all his own way. 'What on earth had you been doing?'

It was his turn to be on the back foot. He cleared his throat. 'I'd been gardening.'

It was so unexpected that she couldn't stop a peal of laughter. 'Gardening? At Summerhayes? You'll certainly have your work cut out.'

He didn't take offence, as she thought he might, but gave a sad shake of his head. 'You're right, but now I've started on it, I'm kinda hooked.'

'What made you start in the first place?' She still found the idea extraordinary.

He looked across the table at her, a puzzled look in his eyes. 'I wish I could answer that. I guess it was because this must once have been a magnificent estate and it felt sad to see it so beat up. I suppose I wanted to make things better, even if it was just one small corner.'

'That's very noble of you,' she teased. The antagonism between them was dwindling fast.

He gave a half smile. 'Nobility is something I can't claim. It's a selfish pleasure—I find the work satisfying. I thought I might.' He put his cup down and pushed to one side a strand of hair that had fallen across his forehead. She noticed that he'd been brave enough to finish the unappetising drink. 'It must be real painful for Mrs Summer to see her home in such a bad state,' he said.

Beth was touched by his sensitivity. 'She doesn't say a lot, but it's fortunate she's not strong enough to walk much further than this apartment. When she does speak of the gardens, it's always in the past. The way it used to be.'

'That's understandable. The place where I've been working
—that would have been some garden.'

She was intrigued. 'Whereabouts is it?'

'At the bottom of the estate. Have you been there?'

'I did go once, if it's where I'm thinking.'

'You should take another look. I think it must have been
some kind of showpiece. It's enclosed, virtually cut off from the
rest, but I reckon in its heyday it would have been stunning. It
has a lake—that's not much more than silt now—and a summerhouse and a classical temple, both destroyed.'

'I remember. I thought it a sad place.' More than sad, but
she wouldn't confess to the disquiet she'd felt.

'I doubt many people have seen it. It's a fair walk downhill.
Well over a mile, I reckon. The garden is a complete ruin but,
even so, it has its own beauty.'

He was an interesting man, one who clearly felt deeply. But
she'd known that. It was one of the things that had scared her
from the outset and, if she were at all sensible, she'd be walking
him to the door right now. But Bethany didn't feel sensible. She
felt as though she wanted to know him, to find out everything
about him.

'Are you a gardener by trade? Before you joined up, I
mean?'

That made him smile. 'I never had the time to learn a trade.
I joined the army when I was seventeen.' He swivelled round in
his seat and stretched out a pair of long legs. 'But I always
wanted to work outdoors, with nature. To create something
special—in the same way my old man did with bricks and
mortar.'

She wanted to press him, but his eyes had lost their light
and she could see that he'd retreated to another place. Then,
seeming to realise it, he snapped out of his thoughts to ask,
'How about you? Do you have green fingers?'

'Not in the least. The nearest I've come is helping my

Quilter Street pupils grow marigolds. But that was before the war destroyed the marigolds—and the classrooms with them.'

'Quilter Street?'

'I worked at a school in Bethnal Green. In East London.'

'A city lady. Were you a city child, too?'

She wasn't sure she wanted to answer. Her response to questions about her childhood was always to bat them away. It was a part of her life that had gone, and good riddance to it. But he had let his guard down just a little and she would match him.

'I grew up in the countryside,' she admitted.

'And you didn't have your own garden? I thought all country kids had their own small patch.'

Her lips barely moved. 'Not in my family,' she said thinly.

He must have got the message because he didn't push her to say more. Instead, he reached out for the sketch pad she'd rammed to the back of the table. She was always careful to squirrel it away, but this morning she'd had no time before she'd hurried out.

Before she could stop him, Jos had the pad in his hands and was riffling through its pages. 'You may not have been a gardener, but you sure can draw countryside.'

'Illustrating is a hobby of mine.'

'A pretty professional hobby, by the look of it. And you don't just do nature well—the drawing of the little girl is great, too.'

'She is part of a story. I used to write stories for my pupils and can't seem to get out of the habit.' She wished he would put the pad down. Seeing him studying her drawings made her feel exposed, as though she were being stripped of an essential covering.

'You're good, very good. Why don't you try for a publisher?'

'I might if there were any books being published.' Now she was over the first blow of having her work discovered, irritation had taken hold. But not for long. There was that half smile again and it was disarming.

'OK. I get it. The paper shortage. But after the war...'

'After the war is all we seem to say these days.'

'It will come, that's for certain.'

He laid the sketch pad down and gathered their cups together, carrying them over to the large Belfast sink. She watched him as he scrubbed them, her gaze taking in his sturdy hands, the solid shoulders, the thick copper hair that defied a regulation trim.

'And how was Amberley?' he asked, his back still turned to her. 'I saw you coming back yesterday.'

'I thought you might have.' Saw me and turned away, she kept herself from saying. 'I was teaching Ralph. The school room there is everything this kitchen isn't.'

'So the change of scene was worth it?'

He turned then and his eyes were fixed on her. 'I shan't be going again,' she blurted out, and then scrambled for an airy tone. 'It's too difficult to leave Mrs Summer. You can see what happens when I do.' He didn't need to know how ill-at-ease Gilbert Fitzroy had made her feel.

An awkward silence fell. It was the moment to say goodbye but neither of them seemed to want to. 'I best be off then,' he said eventually. 'The match will be over by now—time to get back to work.'

'And your gardening?'

'That will keep.'

'You'll go again though?'

'Definitely. I'm starting to feel possessive about it and I've made progress, even in one morning. Tamped down the broken path and cleared at least two feet of border. And tomorrow, I can spend the whole day there.'

She walked ahead of him and opened the front door. 'How's that?'

'We've been given some free time. The high command must think we need freshening up. They've suspended exercises for a couple of days. There's been a rumour they would, but the grand moment has actually arrived.'

'Then Eddie will be free, too. Will he be joining you? Somehow, I don't see him as a son of the soil.'

His face lit with pure pleasure. 'Eddie gardening would be something to see. But he's already made his plans. He's off to check out the bright lights—in Worthing?'

'If you want some extra help in the garden, I could maybe manage a few hours,' she offered. Then wondering where the words had come from, she was quick to add, 'If Alice recovers well, that is, and Mr Ripley doesn't mind. He'll be around—it's his morning for cleaning what's left of the silver.'

She was casting around for excuses, excuses to visit a part of the garden that for weeks she'd avoided, even on her longest walks. She wanted to be near him, that was the truth. Wanted to hear him talk, to see him smile. It was an unwilling admission, but it didn't surprise. She'd felt the connection before: when they'd first met, on the night they had danced together. It seemed to exist almost in spite of themselves and, though it had been broken by Gilbert's intrusion and by Jos himself, this last hour—the tea, the talk, the mutual effort of rescuing Alice had restored it. Warning bells sounded, but she was choosing to ignore them. She wanted that connection.

And so, it seemed, did Jos. 'I'd like that,' he said. 'Any time you have spare, I can always find an extra trowel. There's a whole shed of tools.'

He was almost out of the door when he remembered he'd left his haversack in the sitting room and made off down the hall. But he didn't return immediately, and she wondered what could be keeping him.

'Hey, you need to see this,' she heard him call out.

Beth found him kneeling on the floor between the two fire-side chairs. 'What's going on?'

'This,' he said, and held up his hand. A length of dark cord was threaded through his fingers.

'Whatever is it?'

'It's twine, thin enough not to be noticed and dark enough to blend into the carpet.'

He got to his feet while she stood immobile and confused. 'Twine?'

'Yep. I take it that it wasn't you who tied it between the chair legs?' Her mouth fell open in horror. 'My guess is that Mrs Summer went to the window for something—was called to the window perhaps—and caught her foot in the twine and fell. But who the hell would do such a thing?'

Called to the window for something. Called by voices that Alice alone heard for a precious sighting of Elizabeth.

Bethany swallowed hard. 'I don't know who, but I'm convinced that someone is trying to hurt her.' And throwing caution aside, she described the scene she'd returned to on the night of the dance.

'You say someone in the garden called her to come to the window?'

She nodded dumbly. 'Not just come to the window either. She was almost out of it that night. Banging her fists against the glass as though she would break through to the other side.'

'And cut herself to shreds in the process.'

'Yes,' she breathed. White-faced, she was slowly realising the implications of what Jos had found. 'Today the twine was to make sure it happened.'

'Except it didn't work.'

'Thank God.' Beth was trembling as she said it.

'Thank God indeed.'

13

She woke feeling uncertain. In promising to meet Jos, she'd broken a fundamental rule and broken it badly: don't get involved, stay free, stay safe. Over the years the rule had served her well and she'd never for one moment doubted its truth. She'd seen the way a man could destroy a life, change a woman until she was hardly recognisable. It had taken several years of marriage, but slowly and surely Thomas Marshall had colonised her mother, leached the life blood from her, until a poor facsimile took the place of the loving woman Beth had known. Her mother had been stolen from her at an early age. It was a salutary lesson and one she'd never forgotten—until now.

From their first meeting, she'd known instinctively that Jos would pose a challenge and dealt with it at first by manufacturing an antagonism she hadn't truly felt. For a while it had worked, but now the impulse to know him had become impossibly strong.

She could still save herself. She could make her apologies if later she were to see him in the house or around the camp, pretend that today she'd been too busy with Mrs Summer to think of gardening. Alice appeared completely recovered, but the need to care for her after the fall was a more than adequate reason for Beth to stay home. Not that she'd need a reason very soon. Within weeks, Jos would have gone from Summerhayes. *And that's why you should go to him*, a small voice whispered traitorously.

Even so it was well past ten o'clock before she squeezed through the laurel hedge. It had been a long walk through the estate, and a difficult one. By the time she'd traversed the abandoned vegetable gardens and waded through grass as tall as herself, she was feeling hot and scratchy. But the sight of him, kneeling uncomfortably on the broken pathway and digging furiously with an ancient trowel, made her feel a good deal better, though she refused to think why. It was evident he'd been hard at work for some time—a stack of weeds was piled high in one corner and a spread of earth, three-foot square, looked turned and fresh. Scattered across the border several lone plants were beginning to raise their heads to the morning sun.

'Sorry to be late reporting for duty.'

He turned his head at the sound of her voice, then leaned back on his knees. 'Better late...'

She came to stand beside him. 'Mrs Summer is well but she's been a mite unsettled this morning. She's remembered some of what happened yesterday and it's troubling her.'

'I'm not surprised, especially if she has an inkling of what's behind it.'

'I wish *I* had an inkling.' She pulled a floppy sunhat from the bag she carried and dropped down beside him. His clean fresh scent mixed with the earthiness of the garden.

'You've no idea?'

'I'm bemused. I tried to think how that cord could have been rigged without my seeing. It had to have been yesterday morning before I left for Amberley. If it had been earlier, I would have tripped over it myself when I drew the curtains.

And the only other person in the flat yesterday morning, apart from Alice and myself, was the cleaner. It seems mad to blame her, but it couldn't have been anyone else.'

'So...'

'I telephoned May Prendergast this morning—she's a friend from the village—and asked her to tell Molly not to come again. It may be unfair, but I have to protect Mrs Summer. I made an excuse that she was too unwell to be disturbed. In a few weeks I'll ask May to look out for another cleaner. She'll be happy enough to do it, I'm sure—she's most disapproving of Molly. Apparently the girl is the village flirt. But if it *was* Molly, why? She had the opportunity, but why on earth would she want to hurt Alice? And risk her job in doing so.'

'A grudge?'

'It must be an inherited grudge then. Molly is barely eighteen.'

He pulled a long trail of weed clear and grunted with satis-faction. Where his collar had pulled to one side, she noticed the tanned skin of his face meeting paler skin below.

'I did some thinking, too,' he said. 'It's either a prankster—but what kind of prankster would risk hurting a frail woman in her eighties?—or a deliberate attempt to harm her.'

'I think we got that far yesterday.' She was abrupt, unsettled by his closeness, then reached out and grabbed a spare trowel and began digging fiercely.

'Why have you saved those?' She pointed to the one or two green splashes that had survived his onslaught.

'Those are plants, Bethany, not weeds. Be careful where you dig! OK, so it must be deliberate which raises the question we didn't ask. What if Alice's fall had been lethal? What if she'd died? Who would benefit?'

She looked at him hard from beneath the brim of her hat, her trowel suspended in mid-air. 'You mean who would inherit? As far as I know, Gilbert Fitzroy is the heir. He seems to be her only living relative, apart from Ralph. But I can't point the finger at him. There would be no earthly reason for him to do such a dreadful thing. Alice is an old lady, she's unlikely to live for much longer, then Summerhayes will be his. At its most basic, why would he risk his reputation, not to mention a prison sentence—or even the gallows?'

Jos had no answer and returned to his digging. 'Look at this.' He pointed to a drooping cluster of green. 'You know what I reckon this is? An elderflower orchid. Look at its small, sword-shaped leaves. I saw them when I was in Italy. Old Man Summer must have imported plants all the way from Europe.'

Beth hardly heard him; she was still following her thoughts. 'In any case, I don't believe Gilbert would do such a thing. He's fond of his aunt, though she gives him precious little affection in return. He's always concerned for her welfare, remembers small treats, that kind of thing. He's a good nephew.' She paused for an instant. 'And yesterday when whoever pulled this stupid trick was making free of our apartment, Gilbert was at Amberley. I was with him.'

He ignored whatever provocation the words held. 'So who does that leave?'

'No one. At least, no one I know of. And you can see what a poor condition the estate is in. Whoever inherits, it won't be a honeyfall.'

'Did Alice have no children?'

'She had two, a boy and a girl, but they're no longer here.'

'Poor lady. What happened to them?'

'She hardly talks of William. But May—she was a schoolgirl here at the time—told me that his health was always fragile. He died young of a heart attack.'

'And the daughter?'

'She disappeared and no one knows where.'

He moved the rough piece of sacking he was kneeling on several paces to the right and went on digging.

It was a while before she spoke again. 'Mrs Summer is convinced the girl is still alive.'

'She'd be a middle-aged woman by now, I guess. If she is alive, what's stopping her from getting in touch? God, I must stretch my legs. Kneeling is a killer.' He got to his feet and added the newly dug pile of weeds to what was already a tottering heap.

'Ripley, who was the family's butler, is adamant that Elizabeth would have contacted her mother if she were able to. He seems certain the girl is dead.'

'How about you?'

'I think Ripley's probably right. But Alice is stubborn and believes she'll turn up.'

'I can understand that. It's the strongest of bonds, the one between mother and child. The last one to let go.'

She could see that he spoke from the heart, but it was a good deal more complicated than he imagined. 'The letters haven't helped.' She needed to tell someone about them, and Jos was that someone.

He was about to drop to his knees again, but this stopped him in his tracks. 'What letters?'

'Supposedly they're from the missing daughter, telling her mother she's on her way back to Summerhayes.'

He screwed up his eyes against the sun. He seemed to be searching her face for a clue as to how serious she was.

'I'm not making it up,' she said stoutly. 'The letters came. First from Southampton and then London. They're very calculating in their effect. The latest one said the writer wasn't sure after all that she could make it to Summerhayes. It caused Mrs Summer enormous heartache. The letters are why she was so eager to get to the window the night of the dance. She thought her daughter had arrived. There were voices encouraging her to beat her way through the glass.'

'That's kinda crazy. And what do voices have to do with the letters?'

'They were the gardeners' voices—the ones who worked here.'

His face was expressionless. 'And?'

'They're all dead. They died in Flanders thirty years ago. But Mrs Summer was certain they were there beneath her window calling to her, and that they had Elizabeth with them. She thought the letters had come true after all.'

He gave a low whistle and resumed his weeding. 'She's seeing stuff. Shouldn't you be telling someone?'

Beth was nagged by the fear that she should, but still prickled at the implied criticism. 'Who would you suggest? The police maybe? They're currently down to two bobbies on bikes, having to patrol three villages and two towns. Or the local doctor or hospital perhaps? They're run off their feet patching up bodies broken from whatever bomb has fallen. No one is going to listen to me. They'll think I'm as batty as Alice.'

'And is she batty?'

'At times her mind can be confused, but at others it's as clear as crystal. Which is another reason I don't want to tell tales. I'd feel I'd betrayed her.'

'I get it.' He said it with a heaviness that surprised her. 'Once you bring the authorities in, it's downhill all the way.'

'But you said—'

'Forget what I said. I'm sure you and the old guy can keep her safe.'

'I hope so.' She couldn't prevent a sigh, and when she turned back to the soil, her efforts were lacklustre.

'The earth's rock solid. It'll need more buzz than that.' His smile took the sting out of the words. 'Here, have a drink. It's thirsty work.' He rummaged in his haversack and brought out a bottle of soda.

'I don't deserve this. I've barely started.' She was glad, though, to take a long draught of the cool liquid.

'You're not a gardener, that's for sure. But then I don't think looking after old ladies is exactly your thing either.'

'It isn't, but my school was bombed to smithereens. A night raid, thank goodness, so the children were safe, but I lost my job and this one turned up at just the right time. I like it here. The place is run down but Mrs Summer is a sweetie. I could have done a lot worse.'

'A lot better, too, I guess.'

'I couldn't be choosy.' She wasn't sure why she was telling him this.

'How about your family? Couldn't they have helped out?'

She could feel her mouth tighten in familiar fashion. 'I don't see my family.'

He'd started back with his trowel, but at this he stopped. 'Why not?' He was nothing if not direct.

'They're not my real family. They're a step-family. My father died when I was very young and my mother remarried.'

'Did you know him? Your father?' Something in Jos's voice told her that the question was important to him.

'I can't remember a thing about him. I know he was a lace worker in Nottingham—a twist hand, my mother told me. That's the elite of lace workers. But he had an accident with one of the machines and died, and my mother had to go back to work in the factory to support us. It was where she and my father had met.' She paused for a moment. 'It was where she met her second husband, too. He was the boss.'

'And the boss didn't want the bother of another man's child,' he hazarded.

'He didn't like me,' she said baldly. 'But he had his reasons.' She wondered why she was bothering to defend her stepfather.

'What kind of reasons?' Jos was evidently a man who didn't let things go.

Bethany had never spoken of her family to anyone, and she didn't want to now, but his deep blue eyes were fixed on her and his smile was kindly. A smile to invite confession.

'For one thing, I was born just shy of nine months and in a small community that meant gossip. My mother had been an illegitimate child herself, so the rumours were even more salacious.'

'The rumours don't seem to have deterred her boss.'

'Apparently not. He married her two years after my father died. I imagine he told himself he was making an honest woman of her.' She couldn't control the bitterness in her voice.

'You really don't like him, do you?'

'I was never given the chance to like him. In his eyes I was the product of sin, even though my parents married before I was born. His Christian duty meant he had to feed and house me— he's a strict evangelical—but it didn't mean he had to have anything to do with me.'

'Jeez. I thought my family was bad enough. And you were the only child?'

'Oh no, I have two half-sisters and a half-brother—and, before you ask, I've no problem with them. But we were treated very differently. My own father had been a worker, a highly paid one, but still a worker. I remember my mother telling me that sometimes he could come home as black as a miner from the graphite used on the machines. Marshall didn't like being reminded that he'd married the widow of a working man, and I was a constant reminder of it. My brother and sisters were given the new toys, the new clothes, allowed to have friends to tea. And I wasn't.'

'I bet they had their own patch of garden, too.'

'And you'd be right.'

His understanding smoothed the sharpness of memory and after that there seemed no reason to talk more. For a long while they worked in silence, side by side. She'd confessed the pain she carried to a man who was almost a stranger. It was a startling thought, difficult to believe. But she had, and in an odd way Bethany felt cleansed—scrubbed clean of hurt, of resentment. As though by speaking at last, she'd shared an impossible burden, and one that he recognised.

He'd said little of his own family, but she guessed it had been no happier than hers. The casual damage inflicted on children! Angered by the thought, she thrust her trowel hard into the earth and there it stuck fast. Waggling the tool this way and that to loosen it, she caught sight of her watch and jumped to her feet in a panic.

'I have to go, Jos. Mrs Summer will be expecting her lunch. She likes to eat early.' She nudged at the trowel with her foot. 'Can you move this thing?'

'That's right, leave the tough stuff to me.' He grasped the tool and wrenched it to one side. It flew free, sending a shower of earth sailing through the air.

'What a man!' she teased.

'Give thanks for him,' he teased back.

14

MAY 1944

Jos had hoped to return to the garden the next day, but it was a while before he found his way back to it. The interval between manoeuvres turned out to be brief, and only days later he was immersed in the largest military exercise yet. They were lucky with the weather; the fourth of May turned out to be a perfect day on which to launch the final rehearsal for invasion. A huge force—Canadian and British troops, together with commando and armoured units—set sail from Portsmouth, from Southampton too, he believed, with orders to mount a full assault on a stretch of 'enemy' coastline running between Little-hampton and East Head.

Organisation was meticulous, the logistics long planned: vehicles had been matched to landing craft, their loading order decided, and their position on board carefully calculated to maintain the boat's trim. The landings had gone smoothly, their craft unmolested by any U-boat flotilla patrolling the Channel. Mock battles had followed all along the coast and they had gone well, too. And though the fighting had been short lived, it had been complicated enough for them to rehearse the tactics they would very soon be using in earnest.

They'd arrived back at Summerhayes early that morning, exhausted by the fighting and deafened by the clamour of battle. Jos found he had no stomach for breakfast and, after he'd showered and changed uniforms, he left Eddie tucking enthusiastically into ham and eggs and walked the length of the gardens. He needed a respite and knew where he'd find it.

Thanks to a pair of rusty clippers, the archway once carved into the laurel hedge had assumed some of its original shape, and he was easily able to brush past its branches and into the space beyond. He was stunned to see Beth. Stunned, but happy.

It was barely seven o'clock in the morning, yet there she was sitting on a pile of broken Sussex flint. A sketch pad was on her lap and in her hands, a bundle of pencils. She looked as though she were posing for a picture herself, so bright and luminous, that he allowed himself to look at her for far too long. At the sound of his footfall, she flew up, the pad and pencils scattering across the broken pathway.

He picked up the pad and saw that the story he'd glimpsed earlier had progressed a few pages. Apparently Izzy had now discovered a summerhouse in the wood, one that looked remarkably like the building opposite when it had first seen the light of day.

'Sorry, did I scare you?'

'Just a little.' He thought that an understatement. Her face had paled beneath the light tan she'd acquired these last few weeks.

'This place can be creepy,' she said defensively. 'I always feel there might be something wrong here.'

He looked around. The sun was beginning to climb over the alder trees, its rays touching the iridescent marble of the temple in bright, glinting patches and then gliding across the still lake to the tumbled stones of the summerhouse.

'In what way wrong?' He was puzzled. He could see little that was sinister in the scene.

'It's just a feeling. I was silly to come, but I thought I'd do some drawing while the garden was quiet.'

She sounded embarrassed and he didn't want her to be. 'You've sure started work early.'

'Alice is still asleep and Mr Ripley is eating his breakfast in the kitchen. I thought it safe to go absent for half an hour. And I can't call it work.'

'I remember, it's just a hobby.' He walked towards the mound of masonry at the far side of the garden and sat down beside her, feeling the warmth of her slender figure and trying not to think of it. 'Are you still finding the place creepy?'

'Not so much now.'

'I must have the magic touch.'

'Or the sun has come up and the shadows disappeared.'

She wasn't going to admit she liked him being there, he could see. They sat for some minutes without speaking, but then she broke the silence with a question she was evidently longing to ask. 'Are you allowed to tell me where you've been?'

'I guess I can. We've had a full-scale rehearsal for invasion. The final one. We sailed out to sea and sailed back again, and then we attacked the English coast. All in all, they were two darn good days.'

'I'm glad it went well.'

'It did. A big relief. The possibility of things going wrong was substantial.'

She put her head on one side. She always did that when she was thinking something through, and he found the gesture endearing. 'How could it have gone wrong? You were on home territory.'

'How about U-boats lurking off the coast? They could have spotted us and done their worst. And then there's friendly fire. That disaster last month at Slapton Sands, for instance.'

'I hadn't heard.'

'No one has. Or no one outside a small circle. It's been hushed up to spare morale. It was American troops who caught it that time. There was a live firing exercise to acclimatise the guys to a naval bombardment—the sights and sounds they'd hear.'

'Battle conditions, you mean?'

'Yeah, that's it. A British cruiser was to shell the beach with live ammunition for half an hour, then the beachmasters would have another half hour to inspect the beach and declare it safe before the men landed. But some of the ships were delayed and the officer in charge decided to postpone the start of the exercise for sixty minutes. The trouble was, not all the landing craft got the message, and there were troops on the beach when the bombardment was going on. Result? One heap of bodies.'

'That's truly terrible.'

'War is terrible. But Fabius went okay. No disasters, thank the Lord.' He got up from the pile of stones and brushed the dust from the seat of his trousers. 'There's a flint sticking in just the wrong bit of me.'

'Where would the right bit be?' The quip slipped out before she'd had time to censor herself. She gave a hasty glance at her watch and jumped up to join him on the pathway.

'I should be walking back. In fact, I should be back right now. Mrs Summer won't like it if Ripley brings her tea while she's still in bed with her hair uncombed. Not the thing at all!'

Despite the seeming urgency, they travelled a slow path through the stretch of wilderness. The traffic of recent weeks had made the going easier, but he wasn't in any hurry to say goodbye and he didn't think she was either.

'You seem very matter of fact about war,' she said over her shoulder. 'Was your father a soldier, too? I've heard that often there's a military connection in families.'

'I'm matter of fact because that's the only way to survive. But as far as I know, I'm the first Kerrigan soldier.'

They'd come out into the huge acreage that had once been the vegetable and fruit gardens and stopped to get their breath. It was a fair pull from the bottom of the estate. The quiet beauty of the morning had gone and clouds, some dark and thunderous, had begun to pile across the sky.

He glanced up at the fast-moving panorama. 'We better find shelter. I've had enough of getting soaked.'

They walked on more quickly side by side, crunching across the cruciform of gravel that bisected the garden. 'How about your family?' he asked. 'Do you have anyone with a row of medals?'

'I wouldn't know. My mother has no relations living and I haven't a clue who my father's family were. May Prendergast said that with my name, it's likely they came from Merston—that's a small village to the west of here. If they were poor, and it's a good bet they were, there'd have been precious little work for my father except as a farm labourer. He probably moved north for that reason. He got himself an apprenticeship in Nottingham.'

'He did well. That can't have been easy. Lace making must be a tough business, but I guess he could have had it tougher—signing up as a lowly foot soldier, for instance.'

'You mean you? You can't be that lowly, Jos. You're an officer.'

'Now I am, but it's taken time and I'm still at the bottom of the heap.'

'I'm sure your family is proud of what you've achieved—your father especially. If you asked him, you might discover you've an ancestor who had a glorious military career.'

He hated talking of his father, but he felt he owed her an answer. 'I hardly know him. And I know nothing of my wider family, so maybe you're right and there's a hidden general in there somewhere.'

She looked expectantly at him; he knew she wanted him to say more. 'My mother died a few days after I was born,' he found himself telling her, 'and I was more or less raised by my father's cousin and his wife. They were kind souls, but I guess there's no real substitute for your own family.'

She didn't speak, but he could see from her face that she felt his sadness. 'They gave me a good home,' he said bracingly. 'And their sons became my close friends. The two of them joined the Canadian railways and were keen for me to follow suit. They were sure there'd be a great future for me there. But I didn't want to settle for being a railway clerk. Too restless, I guess. And I didn't want to be a burden on them, I'd been that for years. As soon I could, I signed up.'

'You said you were seventeen when you went into the army. Was that legal?'

'It was if you had your parent's written consent.'

'And did you?'

'Nope. I forged my father's signature.'

She gave a gurgle of laughter. 'You're an enterprising man, Jos Kerrigan. I hope it's been worth it.'

It had been and ten times over. The army had been the best choice he could have made. It had given him another family— still not the real thing, but almost as good. He wasn't about to make that confession though. 'It gave me the excitement I wanted, for sure. There were a few quiet years in Ontario, but then the regiment went off to Iceland for training and the adventures began.'

'And from Iceland to here?'

'Via a little place called Monte Cassino. That's in Italy.'

She came to a halt, her face solemn. 'I know where it is. I've read about it. It was an horrendous battle. And you were there?'

His hand chafed roughly against his forehead, as though if

he rubbed hard enough, he'd rub away the memory. 'I was. We didn't all come through, but Ed and I made it. Whether we'll make it through the next show is another matter.'

'The invasion?'

'Sssh. It's top secret.'

She giggled again. 'Of course it is. Sussex is one vast military camp, the whole area is cut off from the rest of England. We have checkpoints on every road and piles of supplies and equipment waiting in just about every village. And this morning you wrapped up the final rehearsal. But naturally the invasion is secret.'

He felt his face crease into a wide smile at her laughter. That hadn't happened for a very long time. He was thinking of a retort to keep her laughing when he saw a rounded figure making its way down the stone staircase from the terrace, one careful step at a time.

'Sorry to interrupt, Beth.' The woman was slightly out of breath from her efforts. 'But Mr Ripley asked me to find you.' Her gaze swung interestedly from one to the other of them and he saw Beth's cheeks tinge a delicate pink.

'What's happened, May?' So this was May Prendergast.

'I called in to leave you a few rashers of bacon—I can't abide bacon. I don't know why, but there it is. But that was all the butcher had today and if I didn't buy it, I'd have lost the points. He didn't have much, but I thought you could use it.'

'I can and thank you. But what's happened?'

'It's Mr Ripley. He's having a bit of trouble upstairs. He wondered if you could come and sort the old lady out.'

'Sort her out?' Beth was sounding alarmed.

'It's her wireless. It's broken.' May's voice had taken on a sepulchral tone.

'Now that does sound serious,' Jos put in. He couldn't prevent the taunt.

'It *is* serious.' Beth turned on him. 'You have no idea.'

'Then I'll leave the matter in your capable hands. I can manage old ladies who've taken a tumble, but a broken wireless is beyond me.'

He jumped up the steps to the terrace and disappeared through the side entrance. The buzz from the general office hit him immediately—typewriters clacking, telephones ringing. At least someone was finding work to do. With the final rehearsal over, he wondered how everyone else would spend the time until they did it for real.

'What did he mean old ladies who've taken a tumble?'

'It doesn't matter,' Beth said distractedly. 'Can we get the wireless mended?'

'There's Mr Sanderson—he's in the cottage by the pub. He's retired now, but he used to run an electrical shop in Worthing. Perhaps he can help.'

'I'll take it to him. Straight away.'

'He won't be hurried,' May warned. 'He was never a quick one and now he's retired, well... I mebbe could find a gramophone for you in the meantime. That might amuse her.'

'You could?'

'Mr Prendergast liked his classical music, but when he died, I packed the gramophone away. Didn't have the heart for it any longer. I think I put it under the spare bed, and there's plenty of records.'

Beth could feel her face droop. 'That might be a problem— the classical music. I don't think it will be to Mrs Summer's taste.'

May gave a yelp of laughter. 'Bless your heart, I didn't mean Mr Prendergast's records. I meant mine. I bought quite a few though I never told him. Gracie Fields and George Formby and the Andrews Sisters. I used to play them when he was out doing the parish rounds.'

Beth perked up. 'They sound just the thing. Thank you, May. I can come by tomorrow after I've seen Mr Sanderson.'

They turned to walk back to the house and she felt her friend looking at her. 'You're getting to be quite the belle of the village,' May said. 'First Mr Fitzroy, now your soldier.'

Beth wished she hadn't blushed earlier. 'He's not my soldier,' she said, deliberately indifferent. 'He simply helped me with Mrs Summer when I needed it.'

May was having none of it. 'If he's not your soldier, I'll eat my hat. I saw the way he looked at you.'

'You haven't got a spare hat to eat.'

'I can find one.'

'Better still, find the gramophone. Damn, it's beginning to rain and I'm nearly out of groceries. The bacon will be wonderful, but it won't feed the three of us for long.'

'Did I hear groceries?' It was Eddie Rich, looking tired but smiling, as always.

'How are you?' she felt duty bound to ask, though Jos had said enough for her to realise how punishing the last two days had been.

'Absolutely fine, princess, but if you'd like a ride to the village, I'm going that way myself. The Colonel needs his whisky. Half a crate of it. It's lucky for him that Scotland's still making malt.'

May was looking shocked and about to make her feelings known when the heavens opened and an almost vertical sheet of water descended on them. All three rushed for the door and tumbled into the passageway, wet and breathless. Eddie wiped a shirt sleeve across his forehead. 'English weather is kinda quirky. You'll need that ride to the village.'

'I'd love to take up the offer, Eddie, but I don't think I can leave Mrs Summer again.'

'I can stay,' May said, casting another meaningful look at Bethany. 'You get her settled and I'll sit with her.'

'See you around eleven then?' Eddie slouched off in the direction of the general office.

'Well,' May smirked, 'it's just as I said. The belle of the village. Two soldiers now *and* Gilbert Fitzroy.'

15

Alice needed some persuading that a gramophone could in any way substitute for her beloved wireless. But once Bethany had promised faithfully to consult the electrical genius living in the village, she subsided into only occasional grunts of annoyance. It was lucky that May was here. Her friend offered distraction, promising to regale Alice with the latest news from the village; her comfortable figure was even now busy in the kitchen, setting up a tray for the old lady's mid-morning snack. Outside the rain still fell in torrents. Beth pressed her face against the streaming window and gave thanks for Eddie's jeep. And for May.

'I'm sorry you're having to stay,' she apologised. 'But I'll be back as soon as I can.'

'It's no trouble, my love. I've the morning free. Vicar dropped me at the gate and he'll call in on his way back to see if I need a lift. He's over at Merston this morning. Pity you couldn't have gone with him. You might have found a relative or two in that graveyard.'

It was more than likely. Her father could easily have moved from here to Nottingham for work, but Beth would never know. She'd been told so little about him and had been too

young to gather memories of her own. Their house had
contained no mention of him, no letters, no photographs. Once,
in an unguarded moment, her mother had said that Bethany
looked like him; no doubt that had fed her stepfather's resentment. And though she was a townie through and through,
Gilbert had been right when he'd said that rural life fitted her
like a glove. Her ancestors could well have been country
people.

She glanced at the kitchen clock. Almost eleven. 'I think I'll
give Alice her tablets before I leave, then you'll be guaranteed a
peaceful morning.'

'Give them to her by all means but she'll be fine without.'
May dried the few dishes left on the draining board. 'Now go
and get ready.'

Bethany gathered her purse and shopping bags, then
hunted through the dresser for their ration books. She felt guilty
about Mr Ripley. The old man ate hardly anything, yet will-
ingly gave her his coupons for them all to use. Next week he
was to go to his daughter. Meg had invited him for a long holiday, and he'd be taking his ration book with him. She had better
fill the cupboards today as best she could.

'It's lucky you were home when I called,' May said, pouring
warm milk into a large cup. 'I thought you might have gone to
Amberley. I was sure it was one of your teaching days today, but
Mr Ripley said no.'

'It was, but I'm not seeing Ralph.'

May looked surprised. 'Don't say the little tinker has fallen
sick?'

'Nothing like that.' She decided to be honest. 'I rang
Amberley and told Gilbert I wouldn't be coming, but that
Ralph was welcome to continue his lessons here.'

'And how did he take it?'

'Not well.'

'I can imagine. You don't gainsay the lord and master.'

'He's not *my* lord and master,' she said sharply. 'And our arrangement was that I teach Ralph here.'

'Of course it was, my dear. But still... I did hear they'd set up a schoolroom for you over at Amberley, all neat and proper.'

How on earth did the village learn these things? Any item of news was a small explosion that travelled underground at the rate of knots, then thrust itself to the surface, cottage by cottage.

With an effort she kept her voice level. 'It was good of Gilbert to go to so much trouble, but in the end I decided that going to Amberley on a regular basis was too difficult.'

'In what way difficult?' Her companion plumped herself down on one of the hard kitchen chairs, forgetting the milk and forgetting Alice.

'It was getting a little too personal.' It was a limp response, but it seemed impossible to put her worries into words.

Her friend looked disconcerted, and she said quickly, 'He didn't make a pass at me. Nothing as dramatic as that, but I felt I was being coerced into a friendship I didn't particularly want. It was as though he'd decided something in his mind and was manoeuvring me to fit into it.'

Unexpectedly, May nodded. 'That makes sense. He's attracted to you, anyone can see that. I watched his face when you were dancing together—he was like he'd won the main prize.'

'But he's a married man.'

'Don't make no difference, my dear, not with a man like Gilbert Fitzroy. If he sets his eyes on something he wants, he'll get it.'

'Well, he won't get me,' she said forcefully.

'You be careful, Beth. He's not a man you'd want to cross.'

'I've no wish to cross him. I just want him to remember that he has a wife. I wish she was in England. By the sound of it, she's pretty cute and she'd put a stop to any nonsense.'

'No doubt she's got her reasons for staying away. There's a

rumour going round.' May spoke so softly that Beth had to strain to hear. 'I don't know how true 'tis, but Charlie at the pub heard from one of the Amberley men that Ida wants a divorce. He saw a letter lying around.'

'Saw a letter lying around? You mean the man deliberately spied on his employer?' She felt a stab of sympathy for Gilbert. Being the focus of so much tittle-tattle was unenviable.

May shrugged her shoulders. 'You can't blame him. It's his livelihood. If Ida pulls out of the marriage, no one knows what Gilbert will be left with. Those Americans—I reckon her lawyers will have tied up her fortune right and tight.'

'Even so, he has Amberley.'

'An estate that swallows money by the minute, and if there isn't money...'

Beth's mind was busy with the conundrum. If what May said were true and the village grapevine was right—and so far she'd found it infallible—then within the next year Gilbert Fitzroy would once again be a single man. He'd hinted as much but she hadn't taken him seriously. Is that why he'd thought his advances would be acceptable? But if he needed to marry money again, she had virtually none, and no chance of adding to it. Whatever small sum she possessed had been won by her own labour. Her stepfather had done her that favour at least: his callousness had taught her independence from an early age.

She was still puzzling over why Gilbert should be so keen to win her favour, when he walked into the kitchen. She'd forgotten to shut the apartment door after they'd arrived wet and dishevelled, and he simply walked in. Marched in, rather.

'Wasn't my schoolroom good enough for you?' he demanded. May jumped up from her seat, a startled look on her face.

'I beg your pardon.' Beth couldn't stop herself stammering. Their telephone conversation had been uncomfortable enough, but it seemed he'd saved his real fury for later.

'The room I set up for you at Amberley. The room you said was perfect.'

'It was perfect, Gilbert, but as I tried to explain to you on the telephone, I'm finding it difficult to get away from Summerhayes for any length of time. If you remember, our agreement was that I teach Ralph here—'

'You know why I want him to study at Amberley. You know there are good reasons, but you've completely discounted my concerns.'

She'd been prepared to be conciliatory but his hectoring tone was making her seethe. 'I understand your concerns, but mine have to come first and they are for the lady I'm employed to care for. I can't be looking after her when I'm two miles away.'

'My aunt can be left to Ripley. She doesn't need to be mollycoddled in this fashion.'

'I must surely be the best judge of that.'

He marched right up to her then and towered over her. Inwardly, she flinched but held her ground.

'You are mistaken, Miss Merston. You've been here a matter of months and think you know everything there is to know about my aunt. In fact, you have no idea and worse, you set your judgement above that of someone who does. My aunt may pay you, but I am her closest relative. Why, for example, wasn't I told that she had received anonymous letters? Why wasn't I told of her fall? How dare you keep such things from me and then tell me you know best!'

The grapevine apparently had been busy again, or at least a small part of it. Beth struggled to defend herself. 'You can be sure that I'll keep your aunt safe and if anything untoward should happen, I promise to let you know.'

'How untoward does it have to get? When she falls down the stairs, or out of the window?'

'I give you my word, Mr Fitzroy, that if your aunt deteriorates in any way, you will be the first to know.' He had been coldly formal and so would she.

He ignored her. 'Mrs Summer shouldn't be living here—not in this place.' He waved a disparaging hand at the small, shabby kitchen. 'I've tried to make my aunt's life easier, no thanks to you. I found someone to clean, didn't I, a perfectly fine girl, but *she* wasn't good enough for you either.' His scowl deepened as he brooded on this further iniquity, causing Beth to wonder again just what Molly Dumbrell meant to him. Then he seemed to recover himself and resumed his attack. 'My aunt should be properly looked after. At Amberley. I shall speak to the doctor— I'll do it this morning—and make the necessary arrangements. A scrubby schoolgirl should not be in charge of anyone.'

He seemed to loom even larger and Bethany had never felt so small. May had moved towards her, but it was Eddie coming through the still open door, who rode to her rescue.

'Hey,' he said. 'The jeep is on the drive and raring to go.' He looked from Gilbert to Bethany and seemed immediately to grasp the situation. Sliding between their two erect figures, he took hold of Beth's arm. 'We should go now or the shelves will be empty.'

'We haven't finished our conversation yet,' Gilbert almost barked. 'Please leave us.'

'Sorry mister, this lady and I have business to do.' He steered Bethany towards the kitchen door. 'Go pick up your raincoat. You're going to need it.'

Gilbert lunged forward and placed a heavy hand on Eddie's shoulders. 'You appear not to have heard me,' he said in a loud voice.

The soldier spun round, wresting the hand away. 'I heard you, pal. You don't seem to have heard me, though. Miss Merston and I are going shopping.'

Gilbert bunched his fists together. His face was blotched and his lips were moving uncontrollably. Beth seemed stranded in the doorway and May, open-mouthed, stood motionless, tray in hand but going nowhere.

Eddie walked up to the bellicose figure, so close that their chests were almost touching, and said in the softest of voices, 'I really wouldn't think of doing that.'

His antagonist was now redder than a turkey cock, bunching and unbunching his hands, while Eddie turned his back on him and pushed Bethany through the doorway into the hall, unlooping her coat from its hook as he did so.

'C'mon girl, we've wasted enough time already.'

She climbed into the jeep, hardly noticing what she was doing. She had been thoroughly shocked by Gilbert's outburst and terrified that he and Eddie would come to blows. Alice was close by, just yards away in the sitting room, and she dared not think how upsetting the old lady would have found a brawl, particularly when one of the combatants was her own nephew.

'The guy's a creep,' Eddie muttered, driving fast along the narrow lane. 'You should tell him to get the hell out.'

'That could be difficult.' Her voice dragged. She was reeling from the attack but trying to be fair. Gilbert had not been himself, at least not the self she had known since she'd come to Summerhayes. 'I can't stop him visiting his aunt—and I wouldn't want to. At least now I'm no longer teaching Ralph, he can't make that an excuse to call.'

'He doesn't deserve the boy.' Eddie had made up his mind about Gilbert Fitzroy and he wasn't about to unmake it. He swept the vehicle around the last narrow bend only to come to a screeching halt. A long line of trucks filled most of the lane; it was impossible to edge the jeep past and their speed dropped to a snail's pace.

'This is going to take a while, Lady B. Seems like they're moving ammo.'

If the trucks were collecting ammunition, they had a lot of travelling to do and a long day ahead. There were huge dumps in every town and village; the one on the green had already wreaked its havoc. May had told her days ago that there'd been an accident, an explosion, with half the village hall reduced to rubble and, when they finally reached the green and she saw it for herself, her eyes filled with tears. Thankfully, Eddie was too busy parking the jeep to notice.

Beth was remembering the night she'd danced there with Jos. The hall was gone now, swept from the world as though it had never existed. That's what history did, and mashed up your heart in the process. The morning she'd picked her way through the ruins of her school was still vivid in her mind. She had grown to love that building, feel it was her home, and suddenly there was nothing left: no children's drawings, no carefully preserved notebooks, none of the animals they'd nurtured. All blown to scrap. At that moment, she'd been ready to pack her small suitcase and walk out of London for ever, except that she'd had nowhere to go.

Not back to Nottingham, for sure. There'd have been smiles from her siblings, she knew, and maybe a wary welcome from her mother. But from Thomas Marshall, only animosity. Not that she'd ever been physically attacked, or even verbally abused. Her stepfather's morality was of too high an order for such crude tactics. He would simply make her feel unloved, as he always had. More than that—he would make her feel a non-person all over again.

'A penny for them.' Eddie had shifted in his seat and was turned towards her, looking concerned. She couldn't stop a large tear from trickling down one cheek. There was no hiding it.

'Sorry for being weepy,' she snuffled.

He handed her a large white handkerchief. 'Weep away, princess, if it makes you feel better.'

'Those trucks—the ammunition. It brings it home, how close the invasion is. No wonder I'm crying.' It was a half-truth but it would have to do.

'Hey, you're to stop right now. No worrying about France. I'll come back in one piece *and* I'll bring Jos with me.'

She felt his gaze intent on her, as though he were hoping for a confession, but she kept her face empty of emotion. She didn't want to talk about Jos. She didn't want to think about his not coming back.

'I'd feel better if I knew what to expect, and when to expect it.'

'Can't help you there, Beth. At some point, our great military machine will crank into action and throw us across the Channel, but when they're going to throw us and where...' He shrugged his shoulders and climbed out of the jeep, then ducked his head back in at the open door. 'Hey, maybe we could ask Hitchcock. He's good at mysteries.'

'Are you never serious?'

'Jos does serious, not me.'

'And that's why you're friends?'

'The best of. Since we joined up together. Escapees both.'

'What made *you* enlist so young?'

'Sssh! We don't talk about it.' He grinned at her and walked around to her side of the jeep. 'But if we're going to... it was a scandal. What else? But it worked out OK. I found I enjoyed being a soldier.'

'A scandal of your own making?' She thought it another of his jokes and leaned over to grab her shopping bags from the back of the jeep.

'Afraid so but see, it's difficult. Women can sometimes give me a problem. And that time it was a real bad'un. Her father was blowing a fuse and wielding a shotgun.'

She had the jeep's door half open, but at that she stayed sitting. Her mouth formed an O.

'You get the picture?'

'I think so. You're a rascal, Eddie Rich.'

'But a charming one, you have to admit.'

'Utterly charming.' She laughed, knowing her heart was safe from him at least.

16

Beth was not allowed to call on Mr Sanderson the next day, as she'd planned. Alice remained stubbornly reluctant to let the wireless out of her sight, insisting that Ripley take it to pieces and look inside for broken wires that could be mended. When his search proved futile, she'd spent several restless hours, the wireless on her lap, turning every knob and pressing every button she could get her hand on. After that, it was the electric plug that was the problem and had to be changed immediately.

It took many hours before Beth could persuade her that if the wireless were ever to work again, it would have to leave Summerhayes and, in the meantime, a gramophone could provide entertainment. May had telephoned and left a message with the regimental duty clerk that she'd found the turntable just where she'd expected, under the spare bed, and she'd put aside a dozen records to accompany it. Alice was unimpressed, but eventually allowed Bethany to walk to the village with the wireless tucked safely in her shopping basket.

The final rehearsal might be over, but there seemed little decrease in military activity. Several low-flying aircraft sporting the black and white invasion stripes passed overhead and, if anything, there seemed to be more men and machines than ever, filling the lanes and spilling across every green verge. Rounding the final bend into the village, Bethany met a line of armoured vehicles choking the narrow main street. The tanks were only able to follow a single line and, at each bend, the swivel action of their tracks was pitting the road surface. A gang of council workmen chugged after the convoy, shovelling back into holes what each tank had churned out.

After she'd delivered the wireless to a ponderous Mr Sanderson, and swallowed a swift cup of tea in May's kitchen, Beth started back to Summerhayes, weighed down on one side by a shopping bag filled with a dozen heavy records and on the other, an equally heavy gramophone. She'd walked less than half a mile when its serrated handle began to cut into her fingers.

Another convoy passed her, a much smaller one this time; three or four trucks overflowing with soldiers, all of them singing at the top of their voices. Several jeeps brought up the rear, one of them limping and on tow. Then she saw Jos. He was on the back of a motorcycle that swerved to a halt a few yards ahead. The helmeted rider continued on his way, but Jos walked back to meet her.

'You look as though you're struggling. Let me help.'

She was hot and sticky, her dress was creased and she was wearing her shabbiest shoes. The last person she wanted to see was Jos Kerrigan. It was at least satisfying that he looked almost as rumpled. Attractively rumpled. Whatever the latest exercise, it had been another challenge.

'I'm out of practice.' She looped a strand of damp hair behind her ear. 'Teaching rarely involves being a beast of burden.'

He took the gramophone from her with one easy swing of his hand. 'Say no more. You've found yourself a beast.' Then he reached for the shopping bag.

'I'll carry the records,' she said firmly, unwilling to play the helpless woman. 'But shouldn't you stay with them?' She pointed to the rear of the convoy disappearing around the next bend.

'It's a day off, or should be. Our reward after Fabius. Eddie plumped for the movies, but the detachment picking up equipment and ammo from the Downs was an officer short, so I volunteered.'

'You see, you *are* noble!'

He shook his head. 'The truth isn't at all noble. I was in the garden all day yesterday and planning to go back today. But when I got out of bed this morning, I couldn't bend an inch. Gardening was out of the question. I'm not sure it was worth the pain either. If I cleared a few yards, I'd be surprised. I could have done with you behind a trowel.'

'Sorry, I was mending a wireless. Or rather, I was trying to persuade Mrs Summer that I couldn't. But why the motorcycle?'

'The jeep gave up the ghost a few miles down the road, so I hitched a lift on the bike rather than walk. But now I'll walk.'

They began a slow stroll back to Summerhayes through lanes festooned with flowers. The banks on either side were a blaze of yellow—primroses, iris, trumpets of cowslips— and beneath the white hawthorn, clumps of bluebells showed a shy face and smelt their sweetest. Only a few vehicles passed them; it was peaceful enough to hear a thrush somewhere repeat its three-note song. Walking silently beside Jos, she felt herself deeply happy—until a stray thought, flashing across her mind, had sudden fear crowd her chest.

'All the activity this afternoon in one small village. There's a reason, isn't there? It's coming. Today, tomorrow?'

His eyes softened, but his expression was hard to read. 'The sooner the better, don't you think?'

'I suppose your cousins in Canada know where you are?' It

suddenly seemed very important. If he wasn't coming back from France, his family should know. 'You're still in touch with them?'

'On and off. Their sons are fighting somewhere, too. They may even be in England for all I know.'

He sounded indifferent but she thought he probably wasn't. And knowing the raw patches of life were better left alone, she said no more. Then, almost brutally, he turned the tables on her.

'When was the last time you were in touch with *your* family?' The golden daze they'd been walking in crumbled.

'When I left home.'

'And that was?'

'Three years ago.'

'I'm guessing around the time you qualified as a teacher?'

'Yes,' she said reluctantly. 'I trained locally in Nottingham. Goldsmiths College was evacuated there which was a real piece of luck. Afterwards I went to London.' Now she'd begun talking, it felt easier. 'My fees were paid by the council in London, otherwise I could never have afforded to train. I had to promise to work for them for two years, but that was easy enough. The school they sent me to was in the East End, and the children were lovely.'

'It still sounds a tough life. Maybe you wouldn't have gone, if things had been different at home.' She swallowed hard, unable to answer. 'Did your mother never fight for you?'

'She tried, but she married a man who domineered—everything and everybody. In the end, it was she who had to spend her life with him and I didn't. She did what she could, but it wasn't much. I was glad to go as soon as I was able.'

'You were way too young to leave home.'

'You were even younger. And I was lucky to have a mother to wave me goodbye. She seemed genuinely upset to see me go. For a while, she was almost the woman I used to know.'

She glanced across at him, wondering if she'd been insensitive, and saw his face change. He looked older and more care-worn. 'I didn't know my mother, it's true, but I'm sure she was beautiful, all ways round.' His smile wavered a little. 'That's how most men think of their mothers, I guess.'

'Do you have a photograph?'

He shook his head and there was silence again between them while they walked the last few yards to the Summerhayes entrance.

'I do have one thing.' He stopped, and from a small pocket inside his shirt, he brought out a tiny velvet pouch and handed it to her. 'Take a look.'

The gesture restored an intimacy that had gone missing. Curious, she opened the pouch and brought out a single earring. It was a drop pearl but set within a most distinctive design. The round pearl was held in an open heart of diamonds, clasping the jewel to its centre, and then fanning out to a small rectangular bar of more diamonds. She ran a finger lightly over the pearl. In the sunshine, it glowed warm and translucent.

'It's very beautiful,' she said softly. 'And very elegant. Expensive, too, by the look of it. But why only one?'

He took the earring back from her and tucked it once more into its velvet pouch. 'I've no idea what happened to the other. For some reason, my father gave me this. I was about ten years old at the time—and I've kept it close ever since.'

'A good luck charm,' she said, as a thunderous noise ripped the heavens apart. They looked upwards, shielding their eyes from the sun's glare. A plane had punched a huge hole in the sky. Black smoke plumed from its tail and its cockpit was red with fire. Shards of metal were falling at different speeds to the ground, spreading themselves over a wide area. The silhouettes of two figures slumped across the windshield, were clearly visible against the flames.

Jos almost flung the gramophone onto the grass verge. 'I've gotta go. They'll need help.'

'Yes, go!' she said hastily. 'But take care. Please.' Watching him run towards the burning wreckage, she was punctured by fear again. And that, she knew, was the price of feeling.

He dashed back along the empty lane, acrid smoke already filling his lungs. A gang of soldiers came racing out of the Summerhayes drive towards him and stood for an instant watching the ominous cloud of grey ash and fumes spread like an ever-growing plant on the other side of the hedge. It took a while for them to push their way through, and some of their number fell into the deep ditch that ran alongside.

Jos had shouldered through broken twigs and leaves, his face and hands scratched, when he heard a familiar voice. 'Another fine mess, Ollie.'

Eddie had hitched a lift from Worthing and the driver had pushed him out into the lane. The man was civil defence and needed to get home and collect his equipment.

'Did you see what happened?' Jos asked him.

'No idea. My manic driver saw the smoke and dumped me. It looks bad though.'

They were into the field now and running through rows of carefully tended crops. The farmer would wince at the damage, but two lives were at stake—the lives of enemy pilots. That became clear when the black swastika on the tail of the plane came into view. Jos and Eddie were within twenty yards of the stricken aircraft when there was an enormous explosion and two balls of fire, like giant incandescent twins, shot into the sky. They fell to the ground shielding their eyes and covering their heads with their arms. Eddie had fallen on top of his friend.

When they emerged, he panted a sorry. 'Not as sorry as those poor guys.' Jos pointed to the plane which was now little more than incinerated metal.

Eddie grimaced. 'Nothing more we can do. Best leave the

clear-up to civil defence. My friendly maniac and his buddies will be along soon.'

Another struggle through razor-edged branches, a leap across the water-filled ditch, and they were back in the safety of Summerhayes.

'So, how was Worthing?' Jos was anxious to forget the tragedy they'd just witnessed. It didn't do to dwell on these things.

'A gas. You should have come. I met Len Capilano in the Horse and Groom and we managed a vat or two of warm beer, plus some choice fish and chips—not rationed, think of it—then we went to the movies. *Two Girls and a Sailor*. The film was rubbish, but Joanie was something else.'

'Joanie?' Jos queried wearily.

'One of the usherettes. A real good looker.'

'So that's why you're so late back.'

'You've got to live a little, Jos. We had fun.'

'I bet you did.'

'I put on her cap. You know one of those pill box things the girls wear in the movie theatre, and her frilly apron, and took hold of her tray. She'd been moaning how heavy it was. I couldn't see how—she didn't have much to sell—but when I strapped it on, it *was* pretty heavy. Anyway I sold every one of her stale cookies, and for a little bit extra, too.'

'What do you mean, extra?'

'A small surcharge. The guys got something additional—me serving them—so it was only right they paid a little more for the goods. Joanie was delighted. The profit she made will buy her a pair of nylons.'

'And then you said goodbye?' It was unlikely, he thought. 'Or did Joan repay you for your ingenuity?'

'Well, you know how it is.' Eddie grinned. 'When I try, I'm irresistible.'

'And even when you don't try, apparently.'

'So what's with you? Don't tell me you spent the day going over plan number one hundred and eight, or were you the crazy guy who volunteered for the hustle on the Downs?'

'What happened? Is anyone hurt?' Beth had given up guarding the gramophone and was now carrying it as fast as she could towards them.

Jos tried hard not to look at her. He'd give himself away and he knew Eddie too damned well to do that. 'Afraid so,' he said. 'The airmen are beyond help.'

His friend gazed slowly from Jos to Beth and smiled delight-edly. 'I guess plan number one hundred and eight had to wait.'

Bethany frowned. 'Hallo Eddie, how are you?'

'Well. And you, too, it seems?' His eyes danced with mischief as his glance moved between them. Jos looked stoically ahead.

It was clear that Eddie wasn't going away any time soon and Beth must have realised it. He heard her take a deep breath before she plunged in. 'Jos, I've just remembered. I don't know how I forgot to give you the message, but this morning Mrs Summer asked to see you.'

'Why me?' He had to look at her directly now and hoped that Eddie's eyes were elsewhere.

'It's all right,' she reassured him. 'You're not in trouble. Just the opposite. She wanted to thank you for coming to her rescue the other day. Do you think you could call in to see her—maybe after supper this evening? She won't keep you long, but she's decided she must thank you personally. It's important to her that she does.'

'Then I'll come. You can leave the gramophone with me. I'll bring it along.'

When Beth had gone, Eddie dug him in the ribs. 'You're a sly fox. Carrying on with the delectable Miss Merston, and without a word to Eddie.'

'I haven't been carrying on with anyone, as you so delicately put it. Mrs Summer had a bad fall and Miss Merston, Bethany, couldn't lift her. I helped, that's all.'

'And today?'

'Today I met her on the road carrying way too much.' He tried to sound as prosaic as possible.

'And helped her again. Quite the white knight, aren't you, fella!'

He wouldn't tell his friend about the hours he'd spent with her. They were too special.

When Beth had bundled into him on his way back from the garden, he'd not wanted to be involved. He'd been trying to forget the dance they'd had together and how good it had felt, but she'd been in such obvious panic over Mrs Summer that he'd had to do what he could. Later, as they'd talked over cups of the weakest tea he'd ever drunk, the coldness he'd intended to foster had slowly slipped away, the barriers dismantled. Since then, their time together had seen the unrolling of the smoothest of carpets on which to walk. To walk and to talk. And, as they'd talked, he'd felt as though her life had become his and his life hers.

Was the closeness of their experience why he felt such a pull towards her? Maybe, among other things—like a striking face, a lovely figure, a fierce spirit. He wondered if she'd ever been in love and what that felt like. Did it feel like this, he wondered? But he couldn't ask her. Of course he couldn't. At least she hadn't fallen for Gilbert Fitzroy, as he'd suspected. The man wasn't even a favourite, and his heart exulted at the thought.

17

Alice insisted on changing her dress before they sat down to supper and, once their plates were cleared, asked Beth to bring a hairbrush.

'We have a visitor tonight,' she said. 'I must look tidy.'

Beth glided the brush through thinning locks before arranging a shawl around the gaunt shoulders. She wondered if Alice might ask for a long-forgotten lipstick, but the old lady seemed happy that she'd done all she could to be a good hostess.

When Jos arrived, he seemed to fill the apartment. She hadn't noticed that before, but then the last time he'd been here, she'd summoned him in a moment of panic and had been thinking only of rescuing poor Alice from the floor. Now his tall figure was blocking the sitting room doorway and she had to slide past him, acutely aware of skimming his body as she did.

'Mrs Summer, this is Jos Kerrigan.' She rushed to make the introductions. 'He was the kind man who helped us after your fall.'

'I must thank you so very much, Mr Kerrigan.' Alice's voice was surprisingly strong. 'I am much obliged to you. And Bethany is much obliged, too.'

He was beginning to push aside her thanks when Alice continued. 'Jos is short for Jocelyn, I suppose. A good English name.'

'I don't think so,' he said gently. 'I'm just Jos.'

She blinked at him, trying with failing eyesight to make out his figure in the room's dim light. He understood her predicament and walked forward to kneel by the side of her chair. His face was now level with hers and even in the muted lamplight his lineaments must have been clear to her. She took some time to look at him and Beth wondered if he was unnerved by this protracted stare. He didn't seem to be, holding out his hand to the old lady and saying in a quiet voice, 'I'm real pleased to meet you, Mrs Summer.'

His words seemed to wake Alice from her reverie. She took her hand from between his and cupped his face with it, her fingers stroking his cheek. It was as though she were memorising every line and every hollow. Beth stared at her in amazement.

'You've come.' There was wonder in her voice.

He looked around, seeking guidance, but Beth had none to give. It was evident this moment meant a great deal to Alice Summer, but neither Jos nor she had any understanding of why.

'I hope you don't mind, but I've been working on your garden,' he said easily. That seemed to break the tension.

'There's a lot of garden,' Alice said flatly. 'And most of it ruined, I daresay.'

'It's not in a good state,' he admitted. 'But the patch I've been working on is small enough to clear—with a bit of luck.'

Beth translated for herself: he might finish it before his regiment was summoned to France and, if he were lucky, might survive and return to do more.

'And where is your patch?' Tonight, Alice's mind was clear and uncluttered.

'At the bottom of the estate. It's surrounded by a very high hedge—I think it's laurel, though I'm no expert—and there's still

the trace of an original entrance. The archway is badly overgrown, but you can push through the gap I've made. Once
you're in, it's an enclosed space with a lake and what looks like
the remains of a temple. Do you know where I mean?'

She gave a cackle. Half enjoyment, half bitterness. Beth had
never heard her laugh before but it wasn't a sound you could
enjoy.

'I know it well. It was called the Italian Garden. At least,
that was what my husband called it. It was his project. All the
garden was—except the vegetables and the cut flowers and the
herbs and the fruit. They were Mr Harris's domain. He was the
Head Gardener, you know. Long dead now. But the Italian
Garden was my husband's grandest project.'

'I can see why he called it that. The building must have
been a replica of a classical temple. I guess the place was
beautiful.'

'No doubt, but it brought us anything but beauty.'

Beth could see Jos's expression. Perplexed and uncertain.
'Would you prefer that I stop working on it?' he hazarded.

'It matters not. It's all finished, all gone. Everyone from that
time has gone.' Her head sank into a melancholic droop, but as
Jos got to his feet she looked up and said in a strangely bright
voice. 'Our gardens were the most beautiful in Sussex.'

'I imagine they were.'

'I have photographs. You must see them. It's right you
should, and they will help you. Bethany, there are photographs.
Where are the photographs?'

Beth crossed the room to her, concerned the old lady was
becoming agitated. 'I'm afraid I haven't seen them. Can you
remember where they might be?'

There was a long pause. Jos and Bethany looked at each
other. It seemed their hostess might have fallen asleep. But then
she spoke a single word. 'Wardrobe.'

'Your wardrobe?'

'Of course, *my* wardrobe.'

'I'll look,' Beth said hastily.

It took some time to find them. In the end, she put her hand beneath a pile of crocheted blankets on the top shelf and felt a photograph's thin edge. There were more behind. Some had been pushed to the very back of the shelf so that she had to get a chair to reach them. She thought of asking Jos to use his height, but then decided he was best employed keeping Alice happy.

He seemed to have done that, for when she returned to the sitting room, he'd drawn up a chair beside his hostess and was explaining the hideous noise that had woken Alice from her nap that afternoon. She hadn't asked Beth about the burning plane and Beth hadn't volunteered details.

There were a dozen photographs in all, most of them black and white, a few sepia- coloured. Beth spread them out across the small table on which Alice sometimes played cards. The old lady looked at them, one by one, then handed them first to Jos and then on to Beth.

Even with a restricted colour palette, it was clear that Summerhayes in its heyday had been a magnificent place. There were pictures of the vast lawn, pictures of flaunting peacocks, of a pergola weighed down by rose heads and a flagged terrace filled with enormous urns overflowing with flowers. Then image after image of a truly immense vegetable garden, and the south facing brick wall, circular in shape, and bearing every fruit possible.

'You must have fed the entire estate from those gardens,' Jos said.

'We did.' Alice was proud. 'The food wasn't just for our kitchens, but for every family of every worker at Summerhayes.'

'That's amazing.' He was genuinely impressed.

'It's what estates did,' she said simply. 'It was different then. But here is the garden that you're working on. The Italian Garden, a few days after it was completed.'

Beth moved nearer and looked down with Jos at the image of a shimmering lake, caught beneath bright sunlight; at a magnificent temple, its marble seeming to glisten through the very surface of the photograph; and bed after bed of what looked like new planting.

'This is an ornamental path, isn't it?' He traced his finger along the mosaic which ran around the oval of the lake, making no mention of its current plight. 'And this a summerhouse?'

Beth was pleased. The sketch she'd completed had come close to realising the original, though there was now only the slightest vestige of what had once been a charming building.

'The garden was truly beautiful.' He returned the photograph to the pile.

'It was cursed,' Alice said with finality.

Beth had thought herself fanciful in sensing a darkness there, but now Alice was suggesting she might have been right. Seeing Jos looking dumbfounded, she hastened to smooth things over, saying quickly, 'The gardens appear to be empty, apart from one or two of the gardeners.'

'My husband didn't want people in his photographs. He couldn't do much about the gardeners. They were always there —they had work to do. But he didn't want any of us cluttering up his pictures. We were painted instead.'

'You have paintings of the family?' Beth had long been curious to see likenesses of the children, but had never dared ask.

'Dozens of them, my dear. All by Elizabeth, of course. She is a brilliant artist. But you know that.'

Beth sighed inwardly. The problem was not going away. Alice refused to accept that it was unlikely Elizabeth would ever return; for her, the girl was still alive.

'I do know, Mrs Summer, but I've never seen the paintings.'

Alice started forward. 'Then you must see them. Mr Kerrigan, too. I can show you. I think they must be in Elizabeth's studio, next to Ripley's room. We must go and find them.'

'Tomorrow, perhaps,' she suggested, wondering if, on second thoughts, it was best that Alice forget the paintings. The sight of Elizabeth's work was bound to stir hurtful memories.

'Yes, tomorrow.' The elderly woman lay back in her chair, her eyes closed. 'I am very tired now.' But then as Jos was tiptoeing to the door, she opened them again. 'I've enjoyed meeting you, Mr Kerrigan. Or should I say, Captain Kerrigan?'

'Lieutenant Kerrigan, in fact.' He smiled at her. 'I'm still making my way up the ladder.'

'The military is always welcome at Summerhayes. You must come again. For drinks next time.' Alice had sunk back into the past and was the grand hostess issuing her invitations.

'I'd be delighted,' Jos said gallantly, allowing Beth to shepherd him out of the sitting room and into the small hall.

'Thank you for being so understanding,' she said. 'Alice tends to come and go between the past and the present. I know it can be disconcerting.'

'It's not Mrs Summer that troubles me.' For a moment, the blue eyes were intent, then his gaze slackened. 'I'd like to see those portraits, though—if you can find them.'

It didn't take long for Beth to settle her charge that night. Since Jos's departure, Alice had said little but she sensed his visit had done the elderly woman good. She'd tucked her into bed, laid out clothes for the following day and filled a night glass with water when, out of the blue, Alice said, 'That friend of William's did it.'

Beth was used to sudden changes of conversation, but this had her confounded. 'Which friend is that?'

'It was years ago now. The boy came to stay with us that summer. The summer war was declared. It was very hot and he stayed for weeks. He died later in France, I believe. He would still have been a schoolboy, but we heard he'd volunteered to fight. He was a courageous boy, I'll give him that. But he was dangerous, too.'

Beth sat down by the bedside. 'Why dangerous?' She was intrigued.

'All sorts of reasons,' Alice murmured vaguely. 'But it was he who destroyed the garden. The Italian Garden. The one your friend is trying to put to rights.'

'Why on earth would the boy have wanted to wreck the garden?'

The old lady gave a long painful sigh. 'He loved William. Loved him far too much. And William got into great trouble for helping his sister.' She sat musing for several minutes, then turned her head and looked directly at Beth. 'So many bad things happened that summer. Poor William. And now they're happening again.'

Beth was startled. What bad things did Alice mean? A war that had raged these past five years? The invasion of Europe, so close at hand? Beth had a dreadful premonition that she didn't mean either, that the old lady had realised the presence of a different kind of trouble. The presence of a threat to herself.

'What kind of things?' She asked the question without wanting to know.

'Bad things,' Alice repeated. 'Accidents. Not to William this time—the poor boy is no longer with us. He had a weak heart, you know. No, bad things happening to me.'

There was a stricken silence. 'Did you not know?' the old lady went on. 'My mind can be confused at times, but at others I see very clearly. I know that Summerhayes is threatened again, just as it was all those years ago.'

Beth had no notion of the past; it was the present with which she must deal. And it was horrifying to think that Alice was conscious of the threats made against her. Had she seen the twine? Did she realise the 'ghosts' had meant her harm? She put her arms around the old lady and held her tight.

'I'll keep you safe,' she promised.

'You and Jos,' Alice said.

Jos had felt pulled towards Alice Summer in a way he couldn't explain. He'd wanted to put things right for her, to restore the beautiful gardens she'd known and make this dilapidated house a home again. It was ridiculous. There was no possibility of his doing either and he was in danger of allowing himself to become even more involved than he was already. He was glad to have helped the old lady after her fall, but that should have been the end of it. His tinkering in her garden—for a moment he'd been spooked when she'd pronounced it cursed—was just tinkering. He would be better to let things cool, allow his connection with Alice and the garden to peter out. The paintings could stay hidden.

Bethany Merston was another matter entirely. Whenever they met, he found himself wanting more. He'd never felt so vulnerable, and he didn't like it. A fair number of women had passed through his life, but they'd barely ruffled a feather. Sylvie had come close, but it was more anger he'd felt at her deception when he found her out, than any feeling of loss. Perhaps he'd known what she was all the time. A married woman, a relationship that could go nowhere. Subconsciously he must have chosen her for that very reason. He'd been safe with her.

But not with Beth. He had to step back and step back now, for both their sakes. He was bound to see her from time to time, he couldn't prevent it, but as much as possible he'd try to keep out of her way until the order came to mobilise.

For several days he did exactly what he'd promised himself and felt good about it. It was for the best, not just for him but for

Beth, too. He was not the right man for her. His future was uncertain and his past even more so; he couldn't impose that on her. But then the days began to drag, and every morning he found himself longing to be with her.

Once or twice, he'd caught sight of her neat figure as she passed through the house to go shopping or run errands of one sort or another, and he'd wanted to run after her, pull her back, look into those sparkling brown eyes and tell her how much he was missing her. But he kept his vow.

Until one evening, after a long, wearying day, he cut supper and instead showered and changed and at seven o'clock, knocked at her door. He didn't know why he was doing it, why he couldn't keep his pledge; he just knew he couldn't.

18

The meeting with Alice had gone well, and it was natural to believe that Jos would call again. Every day Beth had expected him, but he hadn't come and, on the few occasions she glimpsed him in the house, he'd been hurrying from office to office, a stack of files under his arm and with no more than a brief glance in her direction. She tried not to mind and kept herself determinedly busy. She should be grateful he was keeping away; it had helped break the spell she'd been falling under. Except that it hadn't, and she felt chafed and unwanted. And that was exceptionally stupid since he'd only come to the apartment at Alice's request. He hadn't come to see her. There had never been anything more to his interest.

The end of the week came at last. Friday evening and beneath her window she could hear the voices of soldiers as they streamed out of the base on their way to the village. They would be making their way to the Horse and Groom for a relaxing evening. Mr Ripley had gone as well, to meet his old cronies, and Alice was in the sitting room listening to the wireless.

Feeling something of a forgotten Cinderella, Beth tore a

sheet from her notebook and sat down at the kitchen table to plan the week's menu. She'd managed a good haul on her last shop—no eggs but small amounts of butter, cheese and tea, a few slices of ham and two lamb chops, plus two large bags of vegetables. But how to feed all three of them for seven days was stretching her imagination.

When she heard the knock at the door, she was in two minds whether or not to go. She had an uncomfortable feeling that it could be Gilbert Fitzroy. May had been right when she'd said he would get what he wanted, come what may. Beth had been appalled when his smoothly polished manner had disappeared and a bullying, blustering individual had taken its place. It seemed wholly uncharacteristic and she hoped that when they next met, he would once again be the person she'd known.

But she had to admit that she'd felt threatened. And felt Alice to be threatened, too. There had been no more said of Gilbert's proposal to move the old lady to Amberley, but Beth knew she would fight it whenever it came. Mrs Summer belonged at Summerhayes.

She opened the apartment door a few inches and there was Jos, smiling at her from the stairway.

'I thought I'd call by—see how Mrs Summer was doing. I hope you don't mind.' He seemed awkward, as though he wasn't sure he should be there. Beth wished she didn't feel so happy seeing him again.

'Come in. I'm fighting a battle over meals at the moment, and losing.'

'Eddie said you weren't able to buy over much in the village when he took you.'

'That particular trip I came home with a great deal more than usual. Eddie has a smile that charms the sausages from under the counter. Still no coffee, I'm afraid.'

He followed her back into the kitchen and perched on one

of the unforgiving chairs. 'Tea will be fine. Ed mentioned you had a bit of trouble that day. It seems he had a busy time.'

She flushed slightly. 'Eddie turned up at the right moment.'

'He told me. What was it about?'

She filled the kettle and banged it down on the stove with rather too much force. 'I told Mr Fitzroy that I couldn't teach his son at Amberley, and he didn't like it. He didn't like it either that I hadn't told him about the letters Alice received or the fall she'd had. Luckily, he doesn't seem to have heard of the ghosts. I dread to think what he would have made of that.'

'He has a point. Not about your teaching at Amberley,' he added swiftly, 'but not being told about his aunt. He's her only relative, after all. Why didn't you tell him?'

She passed over a cup of beige liquid, a minor improvement on the last drink she'd offered him. 'I don't know. I was wary, I suppose. I'd decided I would say something if anything bad happened in future, or if she became more confused. But since her fall, things have been quiet. And I was right to be wary. Now that he knows, he's threatening to move her to Amberley. He says I'm not a fit person to look after her.'

'He can't do that, can he? Move her, I mean.'

'I think he might,' she said miserably. 'He's her next of kin and spoke of talking to her doctor. If he gets the doctor on side...'

Neither spoke for a moment and then she said in a low voice, 'If Alice is made to leave Summerhayes, it could kill her.' Tears started in her eyes and she tried ineffectually to brush them away.

He jumped up and walked around the table. Without thinking, it seemed, he put his arms around her and kissed the top of her head. 'You can fight him. I'll help you.'

She put out her hand and touched his. 'I'm sorry, Jos. I'm not normally such a cry baby, but the thought of poor Mrs Summer being dragged to Amberley against her will is awful. Her brother tried to get her to move after her husband died, but she refused, and there must have been a reason for that. After all, it's her old family home. She doesn't like Gilbert any more than she liked his father, and she'd be wretchedly miserable there.'

'She's not the only one who doesn't like Fitzroy,' he remarked wryly, 'though I reckon Eddie enjoyed his turn up with the guy.'

'Eddie was magnificent. I don't know what got into Gilbert. I've never seen him so unpleasant. He was a different man from the one I've known all these weeks. A chameleon.'

Jos shrugged and walked back to his chair, though she would have liked him to stay. 'Appearances can deceive.'

'And I've been naïve, I suppose.'

'You've been trusting, and why the hell not? Forget the guy, he's nothing.'

She wasn't sure that was true, and not sure that she could forget Gilbert's livid face, his raised voice, his clenched fists, but she would try if only for her employer's sake. Jos was here and it felt good to have him close by. When he'd said they would defend Alice together, she knew he would.

'How is Mrs Summer?' he asked.

'She's fine. Her wireless is back, thank the Lord, but for days she's been playing the gramophone. I suppose I should be grateful to the Andrews Sisters for keeping her happy. Mr Sanderson certainly took his time. And grateful that she didn't hear the altercation with Gilbert. He hasn't been back since.'

'From what you say, she won't miss him. Any case, she seems happy enough with just you and the old guy for company. She was certainly on good form the night I was here. I enjoyed looking at those old photographs, by the way. The Italian Garden was a beautiful space. I've been wondering if it would ever be possible to return it to the way it once looked. Could be worth a try, I guess—if I didn't have to take a trip to France meantime.'

There was an uneasy silence, but Beth forced herself to speak cheerfully. 'There may be other photographs—there are plenty of spare attics. Only half of them were converted to make our apartment and there's stuff everywhere. Maybe we could find some photographs that showed the garden before it was finished. They'd be more help to you—when you get back.'

His smile was grateful. It was clear Jos wanted to think of the future as little as she. 'What are we waiting for? Why don't we look now?'

'We could try the room next to Mr Ripley's. That was Elizabeth's studio. I spoke to him today and he said that all her surviving paintings are stored there, so why not more photographs?'

'I guess if we can't find them, we can gorge on the paintings instead.'

She led the way out of the front door, leaving it open in case Alice called, and then along the corridor to a set of rooms on the east side of the building. 'I've never looked in any of these,' she said as they passed each door. 'Except Mr Ripley's, of course. There's never been time.'

'Now that you've lost your pupil, you might get more of your life back.'

'That's true, but I'm sorry about Ralph. He's struggling with his school work and needs help.' She came to a halt outside a dusty oak door. 'This was Elizabeth's studio. I've been here once before and found the roof leaking, but I didn't see any paintings.'

The attic room was large but dark, a single light bulb illuminating the considerable floor space. A blackout curtain had evidently been erected when hostilities first broke out, since even in the dimmest of lights she could see it was caked with dust. A bucket, half empty, had been positioned beneath one of the eaves.

'No one ever comes here,' she said unnecessarily.

Jos threaded his way around the scatter of boxes, moving the odd mirror, the odd lamp, and pulling several blankets from stray pieces of furniture. 'No photographs by the look of it, but...' He strode towards one of the few empty spaces. 'Quite a few paintings.' He'd located a stack of canvases almost hidden in one of the room's dark corners. 'And all by the long-lost daughter, I imagine.'

'They must have been painted by Elizabeth—she was the only artist in the family. I didn't spot them when I was here before.'

He turned to her, his face expectant. 'Shall we take a look?'

'By all means. But I don't think I'll mention to Alice that we've found them. I want her to forget about her daughter as much as possible. When she frets over Elizabeth, it makes her more confused.'

'These are good. Come and see.'

He was surveying a pair of landscapes: a beach scene in which the sun shone and the sand glistened. A small group of children were playing cricket to one side of the picture and several boats were drawn up onto the furthest reaches of the beach.

'It looks like East Dean.' She peered closely at it. 'I went there a few days after I arrived at Summerhayes. It was a church outing and May persuaded me to go. Not that we could get onto the beach, it was barricaded off by razor wire, but the village was lovely. We went on to Chichester for tea afterwards.'

'Here it is again. Or maybe this is another part of the coast? It looks like the area we used for Fabius.'

'She is good, isn't she?' Beth stared at the canvases. 'Good enough to be professional. And there are plenty of paintings of the gardens. Let's see if we can find one of the Italian Garden.'

She flicked through the stack. 'Yes, look, here's one. I'm pretty sure this is it. Yes, it must be. There's no temple in this one but that must be the summer house—the one that's just a

pile of rubble now. Wasn't it attractive? It would be wonderful
to see the garden restored to something like its old self.'

She'd been prattling on without realising that her
companion had become completely still. She glanced across at
him and saw that his face was washed white, every vestige of
colour fled. His eyes were staring blankly down at the pile of
canvases.

'What's the matter?'

He pointed to the stack of paintings. 'There.'

She shook her head, not understanding. Jos sprang forward
and skimmed through the canvases again, one by one, beach
scene following garden scene, until a picture came into view
that was completely different. She had missed it on her swift
passage through the stack. It was a portrait, the face and shoulders of a young woman.

'That must be Elizabeth. It's a self-portrait. Thank goodness
we found it. I don't want Alice to see.'

After his dash forward, Jos hadn't moved. He seemed frozen
to the spot.

'What's the matter?' she asked again. He was making her
scared.

'Look at the face. Isn't it familiar?'

She had only glanced at the portrait, seeing a young woman
and assuming it was Elizabeth. Now she bent down and studied
it as closely as the dim light allowed. The eyes, the mouth, the
hair. Yes, she knew them from somewhere.

'And look at this.' Very carefully, with one extended finger,
he touched the canvas. He was pointing at the girl's ears—no, at
her earrings. They were pearl drops with a heart-shaped clasp
of diamonds flowing into a small wedge-shaped fan of brilliant
stones. She recognised the earrings, but where had she seen
them?

In answer to her unspoken question, he undid the top two
buttons of his shirt and fumbled in an inside pocket. The small

velvet pouch he had shown her in the lane was in his hand. He shook it and one beautiful pearl drop, an exact match to the earring in the painting, tumbled into his palm.

'Coincidence, surely,' she stuttered. 'Those earrings must have been very fashionable for someone in Canada to buy them.'

'Perhaps they were never for sale in Canada. Perhaps this,' and he patted the velvet pouch, 'came from England. Came from here.'

He was staring at the portrait, an expression half bewildered, half aglow, spreading across his face. She was struggling to understand and he helped her.

'Look at my face, Bethany.'

She straightened up and looked at him. Really looked at him. The eyes, the lips, the hair. She put her hand to her mouth. It couldn't be.

'That's some coincidence,' she said shakily.

'Isn't it just.' His voice was rough, filled with emotion.

'Sometimes people look similar,' she gabbled, 'people who have no relation to each other. It can't be what you're thinking.'

'I think it may be.'

'But your mother's dead.'

'Well? Don't people think that of Elizabeth?'

'But wasn't your mother from Canada?'

He shook his head. 'She was English, or so my father told me, though he told me little else.'

'But her name?'

'He said her name was Ellen. But once or twice, when I was a young kid, I remember his cousin mentioning an Elizabeth. Then he said he'd made a mistake and not to worry. I thought he was talking about someone else he knew, someone I didn't.'

'But why would your father have told you a lie?'

'I can only guess. He was an Irishman who travelled to

Canada to avoid being interned, that's all I know. Maybe he changed his name because of that. Maybe he changed hers.'

'Interned in the First War, you mean?'

He nodded. '1914.'

She gasped. 'The year that Elizabeth disappeared.'

'It seems that way.' He'd regained his calm, but she could see from the deeply etched lines on his face that he was struggling to believe what he was looking at.

'It could still be an extraordinary coincidence. It's hardly credible that if this is your mother, you should find your way to her old home after all these years.'

He sat down on an old packing case. 'I knew the place,' he said flatly.

'What do you mean?'

'I knew the place. The first day I came here. I went to the wrong entrance—the rear entrance that's been closed off, except that the stones have crumbled and you can push your way through. I squeezed in, then walked through the trees and came out in the Italian Garden. And I knew the place. It was uncanny.'

'But you'd never been here before.'

'No.'

She took a seat beside him on the packing case. 'Had you seen pictures of Summerhayes?'

'I thought maybe that was it. That I'd seen photographs in one of my father's magazines. He was an architect until—anyway, I'm sure I hadn't. But I still don't understand why it felt so familiar. Do you think it's possible to transfer feelings in the womb? Or memories?'

Her laugh was uncertain. 'It's a theory, though a pretty tenuous one. But if you're right about Elizabeth—Jos, if you were right, Alice is your grandmother. And not just that. If she's your grandmother, it means you'd inherit this place. Summerhayes would one day be yours.'

His face relaxed. 'Why do you think I'm so keen to restore the garden?'

'I'm serious, Jos.'

'I am, too. Just trying to cope.' He pushed the hair back from his forehead in a gesture she was growing to love. 'Whatever the truth, we can't say anything to Alice. It would disturb her too much. She might gain a grandson, but for how long? Better leave it unsaid.'

They sat silently for some while, Beth thinking hard, trying to retrieve a moment she sensed had been significant. Then it was there in front of her. 'I think she's already said it. Do you remember, the other evening when you came to see her, you knelt beside her and she stroked your face and said, *'You've come.'*

'I thought she meant I'd come because she'd asked to see me.'

'So did I, but what if she knew you, what if she saw your resemblance to Elizabeth? That it was you who'd arrived rather than her daughter?'

It was his turn to look startled. 'She couldn't have.'

'I think she could. At times, she sees deeply—sees in a way that most people don't. And this is her own flesh and blood. It could be that womb thing again.'

'Well, we'll never know. We daren't mention it—not now.' Beth knew he was thinking of the fight that lay ahead.

She packed the canvases back into a pile, making sure the portrait was well-hidden. She noticed that Jos gave it a lingering look and wondered if she should suggest he take it with him. But she couldn't be sure what he claimed was true. It was too astounding to believe. She would make enquiries. It was always possible the earrings had been on general sale and another young woman had bought them to travel to Canada. Coincidences happened all the time. In fact, it was far more possible than Jos's own explanation.

'We should go,' she murmured. 'When you come back from France, we'll do some digging. Find out about the earrings. We can ask Alice.'

'Ask Alice what?'

They wheeled around like tops at the end of a spinning string. Alice Summer stood silhouetted in the doorway.

19

'We were coming to find you, Mrs Summer.' Beth's nervousness made her jerk out the words. 'We've found the paintings you told us about. Paintings of the gardens. Jos thinks they'll be useful.'

Alice's smile was serene. 'Elizabeth loved the gardens. William loved them, too. He kept the paintings safe while he waited for her to come back. And he kept a picture of her, too. It was the only self-portrait she ever did, but he saved it along with the others. I've no idea where it might be—he had to hide it away. From his father.'

'We must try and find it.' Beth was picking her way through what had suddenly become a minefield.

'Yes, do dear. I want it hanging on the wall when Elizabeth arrives.'

It was then that Beth noticed the white envelope Alice carried and her heart sank. At least three weeks had passed since the last letter, and she had dared to believe it really was the last, and that whoever had sent them had tired of the game. She had put the letters out of her mind and fervently hoped that Mrs Summer had, too.

But now, out of the blue, another one. Why now? Could it be that Elizabeth was alive after all and near to Summerhayes? Was Alice about to be proved right? Or was this a new attempt to hurt the old lady? The 'ghosts' on the lawn, the twine tied between chairs, had failed, so had the unknown writer regressed to earlier tactics?

Perhaps there were two people involved. The ghosts and the twine were crude attempts to harm, but the letters had a psychological subtlety designed to disturb a woman who was already confused. The old lady had known such sadness in her life that she was bound to grasp at the small piece of happiness the letters offered, and then be driven to madness if that offer melted to nothingness.

'Shall I take that for you?' Beth held out her hand, meaning to remove the letter from sight as quickly as possible.

The fragile figure made no answer, but backed out of the doorway and shuffled along the corridor to the apartment and the open door. For an instant, Beth was too surprised to move, but then rushed to follow, catching up with Alice on the threshold.

'You best settle her,' Jos said, coming up behind. 'I'll call when I can.' And disappeared.

Jos walked back to the billet without realising where he was going. His mind was chasing phantoms from his past, snatching at half-remembered conversations, trying to make sense of what had happened this evening. His mother had lived here. His mother was Alice Summer's daughter. It verged on the inconceivable. He'd been bold in his assertions to Beth, but now his brain teemed with doubts.

How could this have happened? He could accept that his father might have been here. As a young man training as an architect, what better project than Summerhayes, with its new house and new garden? He could imagine how his father might have met Elizabeth, fallen in love, even eloped with her across the Atlantic. He knew little family history, but there was one thing he did know and that had always rung true. Once war was declared in 1914, an Irishman with brothers fighting the British in Ireland, would have faced internment. An escape to Canada seemed perfectly logical. The story was exotic, certainly out of the ordinary, but credible. What strained belief was that he, Jos, should have arrived in the very place his mother and father had met. That took some swallowing.

When the regiment returned to England after the fighting in Italy, they'd gone first to Kent, and then gradually moved westwards along the coast. The plan, as he'd understood it, would see them ending in Hampshire or Dorset, but once they'd reached the western edge of Sussex, the orders had changed. They were to stop where they were. And so he had come to Summerhayes. An unbelievable coincidence.

His rational mind told him it *was* unbelievable. That maybe those earrings weren't unique. Or if they were, they had been lost or stolen and somehow his father had bought them for his mother. That, maybe, his likeness to the woman in the portrait was imagined. But it wasn't, was it? Even Beth, sceptical though she was, had acknowledged the fact.

When he'd first seen the portrait, he'd had a visceral reaction. He'd looked at the eyes, the hair, the shape of the nose, and known the features instantly. He had been looking at himself. More than that, he'd known the inner essence of the painting, if that weren't too extravagant. He'd known the expression, the gaze. It was his.

And then there was the familiarity of Summerhayes, a place he'd never visited, never seen. His father had not possessed one photograph of his earlier life, and the idea that his son knew the garden from an image in a magazine had simply been a feeble attempt to explain the strange affinity he'd felt with the place.

He couldn't have seen it, yet the instant he'd stepped into the garden he'd felt that he belonged there. He'd known it in every atom of his body.

If he were right, and he couldn't yet bring himself to feel certainty, it meant that he had a family beyond his father, a man who had ceased being a father many years ago. A family that consisted of one very old lady, who had known him the moment she had looked into his face. His father had told him that every one of his grandparents was dead, but then his father had told him a legion of lies, so why not that? If Jos's instincts tonight had rung true, he had a grandmother—and a new home. Summerhayes.

He stopped outside the old Head Gardener's office, unable to walk through the door and join the casual chatter inside. A tempest raged within him, a mixture of wild excitement and apprehension. And it wasn't his discovery of the painting alone that was to blame. It was Bethany, too.

Despite all his caution, she had inched her way into his heart. She was there, right now. Tonight, he'd come closer to her than ever. He'd hated to see her so upset, so fervent to save an old lady from an unhappy end. He'd wanted to reach out and comfort her, to fold her in his arms and kiss her happy.

She had breeched his heart without even trying, but he couldn't tell her. Better for him to go to war and leave only the gentlest of regrets behind. She didn't know him, not the real Jos, didn't know his family or what there was of it, and he couldn't tell her. The past never truly died, that was the harsh truth. It reinhabited the present and brought its guilt with it. He had no right to burden her with the necessity of rejecting him. And she would reject him when she knew the worst. What woman wouldn't?

Through the narrow gap between blackout curtain and window frame, he saw the light go out in the billet. It was safe to go in.

. . .

Beth helped Mrs Summer into a nightgown and into bed without saying a word about the letter. When she returned with the old lady's cocoa, the sheet of white paper was lying on top of the counterpane, the envelope fallen to the floor. Alice appeared unperturbed by what she'd been reading and that was strange. It gave Beth time to think how best to deal with the situation and, while she whisked around the room tidying underwear, sorting playing cards, stacking newspapers, her mind was busy with just how that letter had arrived.

She had been in the apartment all day, apart from an hour this afternoon when she'd dashed to the village to retrieve the wireless from Mr Sanderson. But May had been here, packing away the gramophone and the records, ready to return them to her spare bedroom. And her friend had had strict instructions that any post that arrived was to be kept from Alice.

Tuck it behind the mirror in the hall, she'd told May. There had been two envelopes when she got back: one an invoice and the other a letter from the village committee asking for help in accommodating another group of evacuees. It could go unanswered; Summerhayes was already overwhelmed. But that had been the sum total of mail, so where had the message come from and why had Mrs Summer not told her of it?

She gazed at the letter lying on the bed.

'If you wish, you can read the letter, Bethany,' Alice said.

Unwillingly, she took up the single sheet of paper and read: *I'm coming. Tomorrow, look out of your sitting room window. I'll be waiting for you on the terrace. Elizabeth.*

The name was typewritten, but it was the first time the sender had identified herself. The stakes had just increased, and this was going to be one very difficult letter to deal with. From the moment Beth had learned Elizabeth's story, she'd thought it likely the woman had died and, if by the remotest chance Jos was correct, his history made it certain. She dipped down and picked up the envelope, giving it a surreptitious glance. It was postmarked Horsham, a town not twenty miles away. If Alice had seen that postmark, she would need no more convincing that Elizabeth was nearly home. This could be a cruel, cruel joke, and Beth had no idea how she was to comfort her employer if it were.

'When did the letter come, Mrs Summer? Was it when May was here?'

'Yes, my dear. May was here and the cleaning girl, too—I don't remember her name. She called in for her wages and she brought it to me. May didn't know anything about the wages and neither did I, and then one of the soldiers came up from downstairs and said that May was wanted on the telephone and she went to answer it. I knew she wouldn't like me to open the letter, so I hid it. Did I do wrong?'

'It's your letter,' Beth said hopelessly. 'But who was on the telephone?' It seemed important to know. 'Who did May speak to?'

'No one. There was no one there when May got to the office. She was very cross. Two flights of stairs for nothing.'

So she'd been right about the girl. It had been her who'd given Alice the earlier letter. At the time, Beth had put it down to forgetfulness and had only grown suspicious after Alice's fall. It seemed now that she'd had good cause. Almost certainly it was Molly Dumbrell who had tied twine between the chairs.

But why was Molly doing things to hurt an old lady she must hardly know? At least, Beth supposed that to be the case. May hadn't liked her, she'd made that clear from the outset, so perhaps there was a past history, bad blood of some kind. That was the trouble with a place like Summerhayes: too much history. Layer after layer of individual stories with no one ever knowing the full picture, not even May. And now, after Jos's discovery, heaven knew what the full picture was.

Beth had been right as well about there being two people involved. It wasn't the girl alone in this heartless crusade. She had to have had an accomplice, the person who had made the telephone call to distract May's attention.

'She's coming, you see.' Alice raised a bony finger to point at the letter. 'And I want to be ready.'

Beth didn't know how best to respond and made a fuss plumping the pillows.

'Elizabeth was such a wonderful artist, but her father wouldn't have her work on the walls, not after she left us.' Alice was roving the past and wanted to talk. 'He took down all the paintings she ever did—even the one of him that he was so proud of. It hung in the hall between the tiffany lamps. William managed to save some canvases, but his father burnt all the others. There's a portrait of Elizabeth somewhere. I told you, didn't I?'

'You did.'

'Tomorrow you must look for it. Then you must bring it to me.'

And with those words, Beth was dismissed for the night.

For hours she battled with her conscience. Should she tell Alice that the portrait of Elizabeth was among those she and Jos had found in the attic? Or should she pretend that she'd looked hard but had no success, that perhaps the painting had made its way onto Mr Summer's bonfire after all? It was a wearisome tussle, but in the end she found she couldn't tell a lie that meant so much to the old lady.

Immediately she'd made breakfast, Beth returned to the studio and the stack of canvases. Viewing the portrait again in the much brighter light of the kitchen, she could see that Elizabeth's face was unmistakeably Jos's. But was there perhaps another explanation, a distant relationship they knew nothing about? A meeting of family trees way back in the past?

When she returned to the sitting room, her employer was where she had left her, propped against cushions and sitting in her favourite chair.

'I think this is the painting you meant.' She leaned the self-portrait against the far wall.

Alice craned forward. 'That's it! That's the painting. She was a beautiful girl, wasn't she?'

Beth noted the past tense and was quick to agree. And Alice was right. The chestnut hair was thick and lustrous, falling across her forehead in a movement that was familiar. Her eyes were blue, as deep a blue as Jos's, and the mouth was the same too, wide and generous. But surely he had to be mistaken. It was too improbable.

'The earrings are unusual,' she ventured.

'Her father had them made especially,' Alice said contentedly. 'It was a most important event when Elizabeth went to court. She was presented to the king and queen, you know. Imagine! She wore the most beautiful dress for the occasion. I can see it now. But she left it behind—the dress. She left all her dresses behind.' Her voice had grown wistful. 'All her clothes, all her jewellery.'

'All her jewellery?' Beth asked eagerly.

'All except those earrings. She took those. There was a matching necklace and she gave that to her maid. Ivy confessed to me years later that Elizabeth had given her the necklace as a going away present, though at the time the girl didn't realise that's what it was. It was the earrings that Elizabeth kept. They'd cost a fortune, but I don't think that was the reason. I believe it was because she still kept some small part of her heart for her father.'

'The earrings were unique then. No one else had a pair like them?'

Alice looked bemused. 'No one. Mr Summer designed them himself. He had a great flair for design. He might only have been a button maker, but he had an artist's eye for beauty. That's where Elizabeth got her talent.'

The old lady suddenly abandoned her cushions and sat bolt upright, her eyes bright and enquiring. 'Why do you ask, Bethany?'

She supposed she should confess, but she was troubled how she could do so without causing Alice more suffering. If the old lady came to accept Jos as her grandson, she must also accept that Elizabeth was dead.

'It's silly really,' she began. 'The other day, I saw an identical earring. It belonged to Jos's mother. Now I'm wondering how it came into her possession, if there were only one such pair in the whole world. I suppose the earrings must have been lost or stolen. Perhaps Jos's parents bought them—in good faith, of course. It's an amazing coincidence, though, isn't it?'

She hoped her voice sounded unconcerned and bent to retrieve the old lady's slippers. Alice grasped a handful of her skirt. 'Not a coincidence, my dear.'

'Mrs Summer...' she said uncertainly.

'If Jos has an earring, it belongs to my daughter. He is her son. You have only to study his face.'

'How can you know that?' She'd said as much to Jos, but hearing it from Alice herself was incredible.

'I know,' Alice asserted. 'I knew when I first saw him. When I saw his face. It was Elizabeth's.'

'But his name,' she stammered. 'You didn't recognise it.'

'It's not the same name, but it's still Irish, I believe. His father was an Irishman. Kellaway, that was his name.'

'He changed it?'

'You would, wouldn't you?' Alice said placidly. 'If you had eloped and didn't want to be found?'

Had Jos's father changed his surname? Told Jos a false

name for his mother? Their discovery last night was beginning, unbelievably, to seem a possibility.

'Ask your young man if he comes from Toronto. Elizabeth went with that man to Toronto—William told me, years later. He knew where they'd gone, but he never said a word at the time. He wanted to protect his sister.'

Beth ignored the assumption that Jos was her young man and thought hard about Toronto. Jos had never told her where in Canada he came from, but he'd soldiered in Ontario and she didn't need her childhood geography lessons to know that Toronto was in that same province.

'We tried to find her,' Alice went on. 'Her father put a notice in all the national newspapers. Discreetly, you understand, but there was no response. It was hardly surprising.' Her face wore a look of grim satisfaction. 'We had no idea where she'd gone and even if we had, it seems she was travelling under a false name.' There was the smallest of pauses and her face slumped. 'I wonder why she didn't write. She said she would. I believed she would. William, too. We waited and waited, but no letter came.'

Beth took a deep breath. She was terrified at how Alice would respond to what she must say. 'If Elizabeth *is* Jos's mother, maybe she intended to write when he was born. I'm sure she would have wanted you to know you were a grand-mother. Perhaps in the end, she couldn't.' Alice's eyes were intent on her and Beth struggled on. 'Jos's mother died in childbirth.'

'Ahh.' A whisper containing all the sadness of the world echoed around the room. Then there was silence. For a long time, the old lady remained staring straight ahead, her eyes filmed with tears and her figure stiff and unbending, as though if she were to make a move, it would break her in two. Beth's anxiety mounted. Had she done the right thing?

But then the elderly shoulders softened and the eyes, still

blurred by tears, focussed on Beth's face. 'And the letter from Elizabeth?' she asked. 'The one I had yesterday saying she would be here?'

'I believe it was a trick, Mrs Summer. To make you unhappy. I checked a few minutes ago and there is nobody on the terrace. But that's no surprise. We know now that it couldn't have been Elizabeth who sent the letter, and whoever did is too cowardly to appear in broad daylight.'

'And the other letters?'

'They were a trick, too. I don't understand why anyone would do such a thing.' Beth was surer than ever they'd been a hoax designed to unsettle the old lady's mind completely, though she would never say it aloud.

Alice clasped and unclasped her hands. 'I see.' There was another long pause while she thought this over. 'But she did come back, didn't she?'

Beth's spirits plummeted. Were there to be more frantic imaginings?

'She came back to me through Jos. Yes,' Alice repeated happily, 'she came back. We must hang the painting. Over there, I think.' She pointed to the empty wall facing her.

Beth picked up the breakfast tray. That was something practical she could do. 'I'll find a hammer,' she promised. 'In the meantime, it might be best not to speak of this to anyone. It's a complicated business and there's bound to be legal stuff to arrange. As soon as the war is over, the lawyers can investigate Jos's claim properly.'

'I don't need a lawyer to know my own.'

'I know,' she soothed, 'but it could land Jos into difficulty if word got around.' She was thinking of Gilbert Fitzroy.

'I'll say nothing. And Bethany,' Mrs Summer called to her as she reached the door. 'Jos isn't for Jocelyn, is it? It's for Joshua. Joshua Summer. There *was* a piece of her heart that Elizabeth kept for her father.'

20

EARLY JUNE 1944

The long spell of fine spring weather had come to an end. Throughout most of May one sunny day had followed another, but the first of June brought low, grey cloud and a spitting rain. For the troops anchored in their camps, it meant enforced idleness. A month had passed since the final rehearsal and there was still no sign that they were on the move. There could only be so much polishing of boots and cap badges, so much checking of ammunition and equipment, so much running over the lessons learned from Operation Fabius.

Along with his fellow officers, Jos had been trucked to Lavington House for a meeting that day. The briefing had been lengthy and comprehensive, suggesting that the signal to go was at last imminent. They'd pored over detailed diagrams and relief models of enemy fortifications, along with a large number of aerial photographs collected over the previous months. The models and photographs were effective in showing the layout of the French coast and pinpointing the most important landmarks —houses, church spires, headlands—and every officer left the meeting aware of his objectives and what awaited him and his men.

But the precise location of the landing beaches remained a mystery, the names of towns and villages known only by their code. *The far shore* was the phrase that was constantly repeated, and was all they were to know of their exact destination until the last moment.

It had been a hard, crowded day but, at the end of it, Jos felt more cheerful than he had for weeks. He was now privy to a wealth of information, everything from instructions on marshalling and embarkation to a knowledge of the relevant security and wireless networks. The complexity of bringing together infantry, artillery, air power and special forces from a welter of different countries was mind boggling, his own part one very small cog in the whole. But he had a part and he was proud of it. The operation was still fraught with mischance and danger—the vast majority of men going ashore with him had no combat experience—but he had come away from Lavington believing he had a sporting chance of survival.

And there was a reason now to survive. A month ago, he wouldn't have cared over-much. He might almost have welcomed the opportunity to die in battle. But if his fantastical guess proved right, a new life had appeared. It was there for his grasping and, with it, a new family. His world could change, and change dramatically. He need not be the Jos of old.

The jeep came to a halt on the Summerhayes drive and he jumped down, seeing Eddie emerge from one of the vehicles bringing up the rear. His friend's feet had barely touched the ground when out of nowhere a saloon car tore down the drive and skidded to a halt outside the front entrance of the house, churning the gravel beneath its thick tyres and narrowly missing the line of jeeps disgorging their cargo. Gilbert Fitzroy had arrived and it seemed he was irate. Jos watched the man yank open the driver's door and wondered if he should intervene. Fitzroy might be making for the second-floor apartment, intent again on haranguing Bethany.

'This doesn't look good.' Eddie was beside him. 'Not good at all.'

Before Jos realised what was happening, his friend had grabbed a bundle of camouflage netting from the stack that sat on one side of the drive and kicked it so that it unrolled across the gravel. It stretched as far as the Bentley, the strong wind spreading it wide and as Gilbert stepped out of the car, his feet became enmeshed in the netting, and he stumbled and fell. Several of the soldiers nearest him couldn't prevent a guffaw, but one of them stepped forward and offered his hand. Ill-temperedly, Gilbert pushed him away.

'Tut tut,' Eddie said. 'No gratitude.'

Jos grabbed his friend's arm. 'It looks as if he's mad at something, and you've just made him a whole lot madder. You shouldn't have done that.'

'Who shouldn't?' Eddie was pugnacious.

'I reckon he's a bully and bullies go for the weakest, in this case Beth and Mrs Summer. I'm pretty sure that's where he's headed.'

'He might intimidate the old lady, but not Beth. That girl's a fighter.'

'She'll need to be. It looks like he's in full battle mode.'

They watched as Gilbert strode towards the front entrance. It was clear there was only one place he was going.

'Let's leave him a little present.' Eddie pulled his service revolver from its holster. He twisted the gun several times in his hand and then his finger found the trigger and a bullet made its unerring way into one of the Bentley's back tyres.

At the sound of the pistol, Gilbert's head shot up and he half ran back towards his car, but not before the gun went off again and another bullet found a home in the nearside tyre.

'God darn it,' Eddie said, unable to keep his face straight. 'I was never good with guns.'

Jos shook his head. 'That's a trick for a rookie.'

'It worked a treat when I *was* a rookie, so why not now?' his friend said cheerfully. 'The guy's a pain and needs a lesson. He's going to find a swish getaway a teensy bit more difficult now.'

There was the sound of thudding feet and Gilbert arrived in front of them, his cheeks an unhealthy red. 'What the hell have you done, you stupid oaf?' he shouted. 'It was you, wasn't it, Rich? Your name *is* Rich?'

'Rich in name, but not in pocket,' Eddie quipped.

His nonchalance enraged Gilbert even more. 'What kind of stupid trick is it to fire bullets at a man's car? We're in a war, for Godsake. Don't you have anything better to do?'

'Lots to do, old chap,' he said in an exaggerated English accent. 'But as for being in the war, how's it playing with you? By the look of it, fine and dandy. But if ever you fancy joining us in France, we'd be delighted to have you. You couldn't take the Bentley, of course.'

Gilbert's wrathful gaze swivelled round to fix on his car as both tyres subsided gracefully onto their hubs. His face was screwed into an angry red ball. Jos thought that at any moment Fitzroy would explode into a pillar of fire.

'You'll be sorry for this,' he spat out.

'I already am, old chap, really, I am.' Eddie ran a casual hand through his bright blond hair. 'But it's these pistols, you see. They're unpredictable. Canadian war office issue, I'm afraid. A false economy in my view.'

Gilbert turned on his heel, muttering incoherently, and stormed back to the front entrance of the house. Eddie stayed just where he was, a wide grin on his face.

'You didn't need to do that, Ed. The guy has a lesson coming to him anyway.'

'Oh yeah, and who's teaching him?'

'C'mon, let's drop these packs. I've something to tell you. The darndest thing has happened.'

'Tell on!' Eddie looked eager.

They walked around the side of the house and once they'd reached the terrace, Jos said, 'I made a discovery last night. A pretty big discovery, but you have to stay dumb about it.'

'Go on,' his friend urged.

'I found out my mother once lived at Summerhayes.'

Eddie stopped walking. His mouth dropped open. 'Here? You gotta be kidding.'

'I know it sounds crazy but I've seen a painting of her. It's among a stack in one of the attics. She looks like me, Ed, and she's wearing earrings that are the same as the one I carry, the one that belonged to my mother. This one. You remember it?' And he withdrew the pouch once more from his inside pocket and showed his friend.

'Yeah, I remember. I always thought it looked special.'

'It could have been copied, I guess, but I don't think so. It's just too individual.'

Eddie thought this over. 'And you say the portrait looks like you. Who is she?'

'Elizabeth Summer, the daughter of the house.'

'Beth said a girl disappeared way back. Is that the one?'

'The same. She eloped to Canada. And I believe she eloped with my father.'

Amazement coupled with disbelief chased across Eddie's face. 'You gotta be kidding,' he said again.

'I'm not. C'mon, we need to get back to the billet and change for dinner.'

They were crossing the concreted lawn towards the Head Gardener's office when Jos said, 'I wish you'd be more careful around Gilbert Fitzroy. The guy won't take kindly to being made a fool.'

'He's a knucklehead.'

'Maybe, but knuckleheads can be dangerous. And I don't like the look of him.'

'Who does? Though I guess someone must. It's crazy, but I hear the guy's a big noise around here.'

'It could get crazier. He might not stay a big noise.'

'Now what are you talking about?'

'Think about it, Eddie. If Elizabeth Summer is my mother, then Alice is my grandmother. And if Alice is my grandmother, I'm her direct descendant—not a mere nephew like Gilbert. I'd be the one to inherit Summerhayes.'

Once more Eddie stopped abruptly. 'Jeez. So Gilbert would be stuffed?'

'Pretty much. That's why we need to be careful.'

'Why be careful if you're sure?'

'I'm not a hundred per cent certain,' Jos admitted. 'But I don't want to see his reaction if even a suggestion of this reaches him. One day I could be declared the legal heir and he'll be stymied. Until then I'm worried he might lash out if he suspects what's going on. If he does, it will be Beth and Alice who are in the firing line. I might need your help in protecting them—I don't know what state I'll be in after France. If I come back at all.'

'We'll both come back, fella, and in one piece. But hell, the guy's got his own place. Why should it worry him?'

'Summerhayes could be valuable. It doesn't look much, but the land must be worth a good deal. The house, too, if the damage were made good. And then there's the farm where the men are camping.'

'So the guy is greedy. He's not content with acres of his own, but wants this place, too.'

'He may have acres, but rumour says what he doesn't have is money. It's his wife that has the lettuce and she's decamped to the States. May Prendergast, she's a good friend of Beth's— you've met her?—told Beth that our pal Gilbert could be in for a divorce. That could leave him high and dry, money-wise.'

'Couldn't be better. Let's hope the rumour is true. He

deserves all he gets. And anything I can do to pile on the misery, let me know.' He ducked his head to escape the low lintel.

Jos gave up and followed him in. He'd confided his astonishing news out of worry that one day he might need Eddie's help. But perhaps it had been unwise. To Eddie, Gilbert was a pantomime villain, but Bethany took the man seriously and Jos wasn't sure that he didn't agree with her.

When Gilbert appeared at her door, dishevelled and with a high colour, Beth wasn't sure how to react. She hadn't seen him for several weeks and his last words to her had been distinctly unfriendly. She wondered if she were about to suffer another harangue but, before he'd even walked over the threshold, he began apologising. She was surprised at how remorseful he seemed and, in something of a dream, led him into the empty sitting room. He followed her docilely enough, but refused to take a seat. He seemed unable to keep still, fidgeting first with the knot of his tie, then his jacket sleeves and finally plunging his hands in his pockets.

'I won't stay, Bethany. I won't disturb your routine, but I had to come.' His face wore a sheepish expression. 'I haven't been able to settle to anything since we quarrelled. I wanted to come earlier, but I was worried you'd throw me out. And quite right, too. I behaved like a complete cad. Anyway, I screwed up my courage today and I've come to offer you an abject apology.'

'That's generous of you.'

She couldn't resist the churlish thought that it seemed to have taken him an extraordinary amount of time to decide to apologise. Had he really lacked the courage to pay her an earlier visit? Still, now he was here, the least she could do was be conciliatory.

'I'm sorry we had words. I've no wish to fall out. You've

been kind to me and you're always most thoughtful to Mrs Summer.'

'It's good of you to say so. I've no reason not to be kind. You're doing a splendid job with my aunt—forget my stupid words. I said the first thing that came into my head, and they *were* stupid.'

He appeared genuinely upset and she felt warmer towards him than she had for days. If she were honest, she hadn't been blameless herself. She'd kept information from him that he'd had every right to know.

'Won't you stay for a cup of tea?'

'Thank you. I'd like that.' He followed her into the kitchen and watched in silence as she set out cups and saucers.

'The truth is that I'm worried about Alice,' he said after a few minutes. 'My father always said there was something wrong with his sister, and I'm fearful that whatever mental incapacity she suffered from previously has become a great deal worse in old age. There's no telling what she might do.'

'I don't think you should worry about Mrs Summer. She does have confused moments, but nothing that I can't deal with. Her fall was the kind of accident any elderly person might have.' She excused herself the lie. If Gilbert were sincere in his concern, she'd no wish to cause more anxiety.

He drank down his cup in a few gulps and tapped his fingers on the kitchen table. 'I suppose I'm jumpy as well because of this whole invasion thing hanging over us. They'll be going any moment now, I reckon. And it could mean a lot of trouble—retaliatory bombing or, even worse, a German invasion along this coast. It's not just Alice that could be a problem if the worst happens. It's Ralph, too. I should have sent him away somewhere safer instead of keeping him at Amberley.'

'I'm sure he's been a good deal happier living with you. And if you're anxious, it can't be too late for him to leave.'

'Perhaps not. But it takes time to make arrangements, and it doesn't look as though we've got much left.'

'We've coped with the bombing so far,' she tried to reassure him. 'And I doubt we'll be invaded any time soon, even if the attack on Europe isn't successful. There'll be a chance to sort something out for Ralph.'

He slumped back into the chair, his face glum. Inwardly, she was urging him to go since Alice would be waking soon and she was wary of what the old lady might say to her nephew in an unguarded moment. For the time being, it would be best by far that Jos's discovery remained a secret. She'd seen how unpredictable Gilbert's reactions could be and if May were right and Summerhayes was so important to him...

When the silence looked to be never-ending, she felt impelled to offer him another drink, hoping he'd refuse. She was grateful when he did.

'I must be off. I came only to tell you how sorry I was—and to ask if you might consider continuing to teach Ralph. Just until I've a chance to make those arrangements. Teach him here, of course. I understand your difficulties in coming to Amberley.'

'Thank you, Gilbert. It is much better that I'm here for your aunt.' She was beginning to understand why he'd come. She was to keep Ralph out of mischief while his father went about his business. But she wouldn't refuse. She would meet him halfway.

'And better, too, that village gossip is silenced. I know how pernicious it can be.'

She felt her eyebrows travelling skywards. Here was a novel suggestion.

'They'll be talking,' he went on. 'You can be sure of that. A single woman visiting a married man's house while his wife is absent.'

'But Ralph—'

He cut her short. 'Oh, that won't wash. They have minds that can scour the bottom of a milk pail.'

She wasn't sure who 'they' were. Certainly not May or Mr Ripley and his old drinking pals.

'They'll come up with something scurrilous you can be sure, and I wouldn't want you to have to face that every time you visit the village.'

'No, indeed,' she said faintly. 'Particularly as they'd be very wrong. In this case, there's no fire behind the smoke and whoever spreads rumours must see that.'

'But that's the point. The fire *is* there—you and I both know it.'

'I'm sorry, I don't understand.' She wondered if he were suffering from the same confusion as his aunt.

He got up and walked around to her chair, placing his hands on both her shoulders and bending his head so that his face was within inches of hers. 'I don't know if you realise—I've tried dropping a hint or two but you're such an innocent, I don't think you understood me—but I'm likely to get a divorce very soon.'

His warm breath fanned her cheek and she felt a fierce urge to push him away.

'I didn't realise,' she murmured. She would play the innocent he thought her. 'I'm sorry to hear it.'

'My wife, if you can call her a wife, has bought herself a great many admirers over the years, but this time she's allowed one to come a little too close.' His tone was acrid.

He straightened up then and she was thankful to see him walk back to his seat. 'There's only so much a chap can take, even for his son's sake.'

He seemed to sink back into melancholy, and she wondered if she should collect the cups and rattle them into the sink. But within seconds he'd roused himself. 'I'm off to London tomorrow—or at least I was—to see my lawyers.'

'And you're not now?'

'I've no car. That fool—Rich, I think his name is—decided to shoot up the Bentley's tyres.'

'What!?'

'Exactly. The man is an aggressive little nobody. He uses military swagger to browbeat.'

That didn't sound at all like the person Beth knew; she must be sure to ask Eddie what lay behind this new enmity.

'I'll try to get the tyres mended,' Gilbert said heavily. 'One of my men can go to Tattons—the garage, you know—but I'm almost sure I'll be braving the train service tomorrow. And these days it's anything but reliable. I suppose you wouldn't mind if I walked through the estate and used the rear entrance. It's the quickest route home and I need to get a mechanic here as soon as possible.'

'I think it must be closed off.' If she had a choice, she'd rather not have Gilbert coming and going at will.

'It was, but several of the stone blocks have crumbled and there's just sufficient space to squeeze through.'

'I'm sure your aunt wouldn't mind in the least.' She was forced to be diplomatic but relieved that, at last, he'd risen from his chair.

'I imagine I'll be gone for a few days,' he said at the open door. 'The boy will be looked after at Amberley, but I'm delighted you're happy to teach him again.'

'I've missed seeing Ralph,' she said truthfully, 'and we can carry on with our lessons where we left off.'

'Wonderful. Will it be all right if he comes tomorrow?'

'I'll look forward to it.'

She was quick to agree, willing him to leave and watching with relief as he made his way down the narrow staircase and disappeared from view.

21

Beth was finishing stuffing a marrow with whatever vegetables were spare when Mr Ripley returned from the village, late and empty-handed. Since Alice's fall, he'd been more subdued than ever, blaming himself for not keeping a better watch on his old mistress. He'd even suggested he cancel the visit to his daughter, and Beth had had considerable trouble in persuading him to go. He was due to leave the next day and had walked to the village in the hope of buying a present.

'I tried, Miss Merston,' he said morosely. 'But there was nothing in the grocer's, nothing in the baker's, nothing in the paper shop. And I wanted to take Meg at least a little something.' He collapsed unhappily into a chair.

Beth went on chopping a parsnip, her knife slowing as she thought. 'What about a present that comes free? Flowers perhaps? It's June and there must be some on the estate. I know for a fact roses are growing along the pergola. They may be a trifle wild by now, but they'd still make a beautiful bouquet. We'll pick some first thing in the morning. There'll be time before you leave.'

He brightened. 'Roses could be just the thing—I'd be glad of your help, miss. Mind you, I might not even get to travel.' He relapsed into his earlier gloom.

'Why ever not? The buses are running, aren't they?'

'They might not be tomorrow,' he pronounced. 'They've been to a meeting today.' He cocked his head towards the lower floors. 'Been away for hours.'

Jos must have gone to that meeting, though she couldn't be sure. She hadn't seen him for several days, not since the night they'd discovered the painting together. He'd slipped away while she was occupied with Alice and since then he'd been too busy to call. Or that's what she told herself. Whenever she'd ventured to the ground floor, she'd been met by a roar of voices and the jangle of ringing bells, but part of her wondered if he hadn't called because he'd taken fright. There had been a strange intimacy to their discovery of the portrait. She'd felt it strongly and he must have, too; it could be reason enough for him to retreat into the hard shell he'd first worn.

'All day, at Lavington House,' Ripley repeated. 'It's the invasion they've been talking about. It'll be here tomorrow, mark my words. Then there'll be no buses.'

She didn't follow his logic, but it wasn't the availability of buses that was uppermost in her mind. The old man's conviction and Gilbert's words this afternoon were pointing in one direction alone, and it sent her stomach somersaulting. It shouldn't have done; she'd been waiting an age for this moment. They all had.

Jos came at eight o'clock that evening and the minute he stepped through the door she felt the difference in him. He wasn't unfriendly. He wasn't even distant. It was more a reluctance, as though he felt an obligation to come but would much rather have stayed away. Mr Ripley had retired to his room and Alice was tucked into her favourite chair. Since she and Beth had spoken of the painting, the old lady had said nothing of the grandson she'd acquired, except that she hoped he would visit again soon.

'Alice is looking forward to seeing you,' was Beth's greeting, when Jos's tall figure appeared in the doorway.

His smile was a little off-centre. 'Does she know yet what we found?'

'She does. But she already knew.'

His forehead creased into small lines. 'How come? Unless she was at the door longer than we realised.'

Beth shook her head. 'I don't think so but, in any case, she didn't need to overhear. She knew who you were. It was as I said—she recognised your face.'

'And that was enough?'

'There's not a shadow of doubt in her mind that you're her daughter's son.' And it was true. Alice Summer seemed to have a knowledge that went deeper than any surface reality. 'And you? Are you still sure?'

He shuffled his hands in his pocket, clinking together what sounded like keys. 'That night I was certain, but ...' She was taken aback. They seemed to have moved in opposite directions. She'd been the one to have doubts until Alice had convinced her otherwise. Perhaps his uncertainty was producing this strange mood.

'...I still *feel* it's true, but hard evidence is what matters.'

They'd moved no further than the cramped hall, and she was sure that at any moment Mrs Summer would hear their voices and call out. She should put his mind at rest before he saw his grandmother.

'It might help if I told you the earrings in the portrait *are* unique. Alice is adamant about that. There was only one pair ever produced and they were made for Elizabeth Summer's court presentation in 1913. Her father designed them himself, especially for the occasion. They were the only piece of jewellery she took with her when she eloped.'

Disbelief flitted across his face, then delight, then simple amazement.

'So it must be true!'

'It's convinced me. Alice didn't need convincing, of course. She knew immediately. One of the earrings must have been mislaid, maybe on the journey out to Canada, and that left just the one for your father to give you. Perhaps it was the only token he had of your mother.'

Jos smiled then, for the first time that evening, and she found herself bathing in its sudden warmth. Found herself remembering his caress and wanting it again. But she wouldn't allow herself to follow that thought, and was quick to usher him into the sitting room where Alice was propped against her bank of cushions and waiting.

The old lady glanced up as the door jamb squeaked, then patted the chair nearest to her.

'Move the lamp, Bethany, please,' she commanded. 'I want to see his face again.'

Beth did as she was asked and for a long time Alice sat and looked at the young man, studying every contour, every line and crevice of his face. Then she reached out and touched the lock of copper hair that flopped defiantly across his forehead. She breathed a sigh of satisfaction.

'You have her hair and her eyes.'

'I'll have to take your word for it. I've never seen an image of my mother. Not until the other night.'

She nodded. 'You saw the portrait. Elizabeth painted it when she returned from London—after she was presented at court. She painted it for her father. They'd had a falling out. That wasn't unusual, they were both such strong characters, but that time it was a serious disagreement.'

'What was it about?' He sounded eager to learn more of the mother he'd never known.

'Elizabeth had turned down two marriage proposals while she was in London and her father was very unhappy.' Whenever she talked of the past, Alice's mind was sharp and certain. 'That was what the Season was all about, you see—finding a husband. And she had found one, two in fact, but they didn't suit her. Joshua was infuriated. He'd spent a great deal of money so that Elizabeth could meet and marry a suitable man.'

'And who would that be?'

'A man who was well connected. Someone with a title maybe. But they weren't the kind of men Elizabeth liked, and she was always such a headstrong girl. Too headstrong.'

Beth saw Jos's shoulders stiffen. He didn't like the criticism and she couldn't blame him. The whole idea of the Season and its marriage market rang as false to her as it did to him.

'And she painted the portrait to make amends?' he asked.

'In a way. Not for rejecting the marriage proposals. She was unapologetic about that. But she'd made things worse when she got back by saying she would never marry. She would live independently. Support herself as a painter. It upset Joshua greatly.'

'And that was wrong?' Jos sounded uncertain. Faced with a world so foreign, he seemed adrift.

'Wrong then, my dear,' Alice explained in a kindly voice. 'Young ladies like Elizabeth, girls from good homes, did not work, and they certainly did not become professional artists. It was not the thing, not in the least.' She shuddered. For Alice, it seemed, times had changed little.

'I guess she never became a professional artist, but she didn't stay single either. She married in the end.'

'Evidently.' Alice looked vacantly down at her lap, her mind years away. 'The letter she left said they would marry, though Joshua thought it a false pledge.'

'You mean he believed my father would renege on his promise?' Beth could see Jos stiffen again. Meeting the past was proving uncomfortable.

Alice looked contrite. 'For myself, I wasn't sure. Mr Kellaway was an honest man, at least I thought so. But he was just starting out in his profession and marriage could only be a burden. Joshua was convinced that his daughter had thrown her life away.' She twisted her hands in the blanket that covered her lap. 'I don't think we ever understood how she felt, though I tried.'

'The letter she left said they were eloping?' Jos was pushing, hungry for information.

'It did, but it didn't say where they were going.'

His face lightened. 'They went to Toronto, but I guess you know that. My father's cousin and his family lived there, they still do. They're real nice people and they made your daughter welcome.'

'That is good to know. But she didn't write and she said she would.' Alice's hands began twisting and turning, the veins thick blue ropes beneath the milky skin. 'Why didn't she?' There was a note of anguish in her voice.

'I can't rightly say why that was,' Jos said gently. 'My father never spoke of it. For that matter, he hardly ever spoke of my mother, which is why I'd no idea who she was and where she'd come from. When she died, the world seemed to finish for him. He died too—in spirit at least.'

Beth was struck by the dramatic image. What had happened to Jos's father for his son to describe him in that way?

Her grandson took hold of Alice's twisting hands and held them in his own firm clasp. 'I think she must have meant to write, but she fell pregnant almost immediately and I know from my cousin that she was unwell for a lot of the time. Perhaps that's why she delayed writing and decided to wait until the baby arrived safely and she felt less ill. Maybe she thought it would help if she could tell you that you had a grandchild. If you were still angry with her, it could have made things better.'

'I wasn't angry. William wasn't angry. We were heartbroken. And so was Joshua, though he would never admit it. He died the following year, you know. Once the men went to war, the gardens lost their beauty and when Elizabeth stayed away, Joshua fell ill. I had to employ a nurse, but it didn't help. He was incensed all the time. He hated being bedridden, hated being made to eat what he called pap. He was devastated that he'd lost the daughter he loved. In the end, his heart really did break. If only she'd written.'

Jos's smooth brown fingers circled hers. 'I'm sorry I can't bring you the news you wanted.'

They remained like that for a long time, but when Alice looked up again, her face had cleared. 'You've brought me the next best thing—a grandson.'

He smiled. 'That's for sure. And I'll make certain I'm the best grandson ever.'

She smiled back and nestled into her cushions, closing her eyes. Jos took the hint and got up from his chair and followed Beth into the kitchen.

'That was difficult for you,' she said, once they were out of earshot.

'I'm sorry she knows for certain that her daughter is dead. It's sad for me, but I never knew my mother. She was Alice's girl, though, and it must be hard after all these years of hoping and waiting.'

'The hope has gone but, in a way, I think it's a relief. She no longer has to wait. And she has you, and that's something she could never have imagined.'

'And I'm such a prize,' he mocked.

'She thinks so.'

'And do you?' He seemed to fling out the question unthinkingly.

She didn't answer him but turned away to put china into the cupboard. He came up beside her and put his hands around her waist. His voice was in her ear, his face against her hair.

'I had to see Alice or I wouldn't have come. I shouldn't have come. But if I don't return, look after her and look after yourself.'

She dropped the plate she'd picked up and twisted around in his arms. 'Don't say things like that.'

He pulled her so close that her face was buried in his chest. 'We danced like this, do you remember?'

'I remember,' she said in a stifled voice.

'But I never got to kiss you.'

He bent his head and his lips found hers. She didn't want this, her mind was yelling, even as her heart beat out a different message. She didn't want it, it was wrong, utterly and completely wrong. He was going to fight. He could return to Summerhayes in a shroud. Or maybe not at all. And then she gave up the uneven struggle, and stood on her tiptoes to kiss him in a way she had never kissed anyone before.

22

Bethany was awake before dawn. In fact, she doubted she'd even slept. She had tossed, she had turned, she'd punched pillows and flung herself from one side of the bed to the other, but sleep had eluded her. Last night she'd ignored every vow she'd ever made, and she was angry—with herself, and with Jos. He hadn't wanted to come, he'd said, and his reluctance had been evident from the moment she'd opened the door to him. She understood it now. He hadn't wanted to come because he feared what might happen between them. And it had. He hadn't been able to stop himself from kissing her, from making that commitment. And she had let it happen.

As soon as the first chink of light edged itself around the blackout curtain, she clambered out of bed; every muscle in her body ached and she needed to move. She would slip into the gardens and cut the roses for Mr Ripley's daughter.

Before she left, she checked that Alice was still asleep, then donned raincoat and hat, and grabbed a pair of scissors from the kitchen drawer. The high winds of yesterday had moderated a little, but when she slipped out of the side entrance, the chill dank of storm filled the air and made her shiver. The bushes still wore a dress of raindrops, their branches sending droplets tumbling as she brushed past.

When she reached the old wooden pergola, she found the plants drenched. But though bedraggled, there were roses aplenty, their colour rich and their scent strong. She walked to the far end of the living archway and began snipping, the sound of her scissors echoing in the damp air. For the first time, she became conscious of an unusual stillness. Summerhayes was uncannily quiet and she wondered why. By this hour, the soldiers would normally be on the move, but this morning she appeared to be alone in the world. It suited her. She'd no wish to meet anyone; in particular, she'd no wish to meet Jos. At some haunted hour of the night, she had decided she would not see him again, would not even think of him. But with every snip of the scissors, she contradicted herself—and thought of him.

He was not a Thomas Marshall, thank goodness, he never would be, and Beth wasn't stupid enough to think so. But he was a man with a past of which she knew little and a future hanging in the balance. It was too late to save herself from loving him but, if she put an end to it now, it would make forgetting—and she had to forget—a small degree less painful.

Within half an hour she'd picked a respectable bouquet and started back to the apartment, hoping her luck would hold and Summerhayes would continue to slumber. She hurried across the terrace and had almost made the side entrance of the house when Eddie appeared, shrugging on his battledress jacket against the morning's cold.

'Off to a wedding?' He pointed at the roses. In the circumstances, it wasn't the most sympathetic remark, though he could have no idea how unfeeling it sounded.

'These are for Mr Ripley,' she explained. 'He's leaving this morning to stay with his daughter.'

He nodded. 'Better that he goes today.'

The old man's worries had not been unfounded then; the

possibility of a disrupted journey could mean only one thing.
Her hands, grown cold while picking the roses, turned unpleas-
antly clammy.

'The camp is so quiet this morning. Is something happening?' In her heart Beth knew the worst, but still felt compelled
to ask.

'Confined to barracks,' he said cheerfully. 'And waiting.
The weather could still defeat us. Right up to zero hour. The
meteorological team are just about the best, but English
weather, who knows?'

'I suppose that once the decision is made, there's no going
back.'

'Got it in one, princess.'

Yesterday's meeting at Lavington House had to have been
the final briefing, and the regiment would know now where
they were bound. No soldier would be allowed to leave
Summerhayes until the signal was given.

Beth looked up at a sky bruised and dark. 'It doesn't look
good,' she managed to say.

'I'm not so sure. The rain's eased and the wind's already
dropping, so let's hope.'

Let's hope, she thought, climbing the stairs to the apartment. Hope for what—success, glory, death? Jos walking into
death, that was the mantra ringing in her ears. She had fallen
under the spell of a man who was walking into death.

'Miss Merston, thank you.' Mr Ripley was in the kitchen,
smartly dressed, and with a small bag by his side. 'The flowers
are beautiful. My girl will love them.'

She tried to shake off the dread that had taken hold and
focus instead on bundling the flowers into a single sheet of
brown paper. It was the last piece of wrapping in the house and
she'd been saving it for months.

'Make sure you wear your overcoat,' she told him. 'It may be

June, but it's miserably cold and Meg won't want a sick father on her hands.'

'She won't that,' he chuckled. 'But you look after yourself, too, miss. And Mrs Summer—'

'Mrs Summer will be fine. Go now or you'll miss your bus.'

Bethany shooed him out of the door but, once he'd gone, she felt oddly vulnerable. He was an old man, slow and creaking in his movements, but he was company and, more importantly, he knew Alice and her ways. But she would cope with the old lady. She always did. And there were far greater worries ahead: once the weather cleared, the regiment would be gone, and the invasion begun.

She couldn't think of it. Ralph was coming this morning and, if she were to be of any help to him, she must empty her mind of this gnawing fear. She would make breakfast for Alice and then go in search of her school bag. It was a while since she'd needed it, but they would be using several of the textbooks she kept there.

When she finally located the bag on the window seat of Alice's bedroom, she saw the young boy already making his way across the gardens. Mrs Summer's room overlooked the concrete standing that now housed row after row of jeeps and trucks and tanks. Ralph had stopped there and was talking to a soldier. She saw the man reach into his pocket and draw out a large document. Pressing her forehead hard against the window, she recognised him. It was Eddie, and was that a map he was flourishing? A map of France perhaps, though she was too far away to see clearly, and she couldn't imagine he would be divulging invasion plans to a small boy. It made her smile, seeing Ralph's serious young face as Eddie jabbed his finger this way and that around the map.

She'd turned to make her way back to the kitchen when she saw Gilbert Fitzroy at the far side of the vehicle park. He'd evidently followed his son through the gardens to the house.

Both father and son were making liberal use of a supposedly blocked entrance. It was unnerving to think that people could come and go without her knowing—and without the military knowing, for that matter.

Beth stared hard at the three figures. Gilbert had now drawn level with Eddie and his son and, if she were not mistaken, there appeared to be a confrontation brewing. Gilbert's figure was stiff, his face turning the mottled red that signalled a growing anger while, as always, Eddie was relaxed. Insultingly relaxed. She must go down immediately, prevent whatever trouble was in the offing.

Making sure that Alice was immersed in the morning paper, she ran down the two flights of stairs, in her haste tripping on the bottom step, along the hall, through the drawing room, and out on to the terrace. From here she could see and hear that the confrontation was no longer brewing, but had arrived.

'The boy has to go to his lessons,' Gilbert barked. 'And you're in the way, Rich.'

'You think I'm stopping him? He can leave any time.' Eddie waggled his hand, making a grand gesture in the direction of the house. 'Go forth, young man.'

'I can go in a minute.' Ralph's young voice carried to her on the damp air. 'I'm early and Miss Merston won't be ready for me yet.'

Gilbert looked down at his son, impatience melding with anger. 'You're to go now, Ralph. And you,' he was facing Eddie again, 'you are to stop interfering. This isn't the first time you've encouraged my son to disobey me. I'm sure preening yourself in front of a child is a boost to your ego, but Ralph is at Summerhayes to learn, not to mix with a halfwit in uniform.'

Eddie assumed a hurt expression. 'How very cruel! I am stricken to the core.' And he thumped a hand hard across his chest. But the playacting wasn't enough, it seemed.

'Seriously, fella, you should get to know your boy. These last few weeks he's learnt a thing or two and still got to his lessons.'

'What could he possibly have learned from a common soldier?'

'A lot more than from a common hick.'

For a moment Gilbert look bewildered, unsure if this was some kind of stupid joke, then evidently decided to take him seriously.

'Before you use words like hick, you should know who you're talking to.'

'I guess I do know,' Eddie drawled. 'You're the guy with the bankrupt estate.'

Bethany had remained on the terrace, hoping the situation would resolve itself. It wasn't about to, and she had a bad sense of where this was going. Jos had agreed that keeping his identity quiet for the moment was important. Could he have told his friend of his astonishing discovery? And, more disturbingly, was Eddie about to use it to taunt his enemy?

'You know nothing of my affairs,' Gilbert growled.

'Enough to know that it's your old lady who has the dough—and I guess that means your place is going down the pan. Such a shame you won't be getting Summerhayes any time soon. No siree. No help there.'

'How dare you!'

'I dare all right. *I'll* be the one sitting pretty. Right here, where my mother was born.'

Beth felt her breath catch. What on earth was Eddie playing at? Mocking the man for his arrogance was one thing. Making Jos's story his own simply to annoy Gilbert was quite another. Surely—hopefully—Gilbert would not take him seriously.

'You're mad.' Fitzroy turned away in disgust, grabbing at his son's arm.

'Meet the new grandson and heir, fresh from Toronto,'

Eddie called after them. 'The letter arrived this very morning, would you believe? The one from the legal guys in London. What a coincidence, eh, me being posted here of all places. Breaks you up, don't it?'

He slouched off then, a wide smile on his face, while Bethany stood as though carved from stone.

At that instant Gilbert caught sight of her. 'Miss Merston is here, Ralph. Go indoors and get your books ready,' he ordered, trying to rearrange his features into something approaching agreeable.

'I'm off to London this morning,' he said awkwardly when he reached her. 'One of my men will collect Ralph at lunchtime, but on no account is he to wander in the gardens.'

'Don't worry. I'll keep him busy until your footman arrives.'

'I'm much obliged.' He gave her a thin, tight smile. 'I must be off. I'm catching the train and Richards is giving me a lift to the station. He should be here by now delivering his bread.'

'I wish you luck with the train.'

'I'll need it.' His voice had a barbed edge. 'The garage has the Bentley. They couldn't do anything with the tyres and it will be at least a fortnight before replacements arrive. If they can get any, that is. All thanks to that moron.'

It seemed that he'd taken Eddie's mockery to heart, and she tried to temper the damage. 'You shouldn't let Lieutenant Rich trouble you.'

'I don't.' The smile got thinner. 'I don't let rubbish trouble me.'

She was about to protest at his words when Ralph, who'd stayed behind despite his father's injunction, tugged at her hand. On reflection it was best to leave the matter there. Gilbert was seriously ruffled and no wonder. Eddie's taunts had been far from amusing.

'Go and get your desk set up,' she said to the boy. 'The front door is open.'

Ralph bade a brief goodbye to his father and ran ahead, while she followed in his footsteps more slowly. Slowly enough to meet Jos in the doorway.

A dawning smile spread across his face, the blue eyes warm and beguiling. Her sole defence against his charm had been to avoid a meeting, and now she saw how foolish that had been.

'Bethany?' His smile was a little dented. 'Are you OK?'

She tried hard not to look at him. 'I'm fine, just some bother between Eddie and Gilbert Fitzroy. I didn't know what to do.'

He leaned casually against the door jamb. 'Nothing is the answer. Do nothing. Let them lock antlers and stand well clear.'

He didn't know how inflammatory Eddie's taunts had been, but Beth wasn't about to go into detail. His friend would regale him later with news of the quarrel; her priority was to disappear as swiftly as she could.

She tried to stretch her mouth into the semblance of a smile but failed. 'Thanks for the advice,' she said hurriedly. 'I'm afraid I can't stop to talk. Ralph is here.'

'I know. I just saw him. He told me he was on his way to the apartment.' Jos's eyes were still fixed on her and she felt herself naked beneath their keenness. 'There's something else wrong, isn't there? What is it? What's happened?'

'Really, nothing,' she lied, her voice deliberately carefree. 'I'm not feeling too wonderful this morning, that's all. I had a disturbed night.' And still she could not bring herself to meet his eyes.

'With Alice?'

'Yes.' She grabbed at the excuse, no longer caring how many untruths she told. 'She couldn't sleep for more than an hour or so—I think she ate supper too late—though she's perfectly well this morning.'

He was frowning hard, as though he were trying to make himself believe that a disturbed night was all that ailed her. She was clearly a rotten liar. Convinced or not, he continued, 'I'm

glad we met up this morning. I didn't expect to. But once the
weather puts on a better face... well, let's just say I'm not likely
to have time to say a proper goodbye.'

He was standing close to her, far too close, and she could
feel the heat of his body and smell the freshness of his cologne.
This encounter was worse than anything she'd anticipated.

'Eddie mentioned it,' she stumbled. 'The weather ... just as
well we said our goodbyes last night. Alice too.' She swallowed
hard, hoping the mention of Alice would destroy any lingering
romance.

Jos's expression grew more uncertain and his eyes more
searching. Almost instinctively he lifted his arms as though to
embrace her, then dropped them to his side. She could see he
was floundering. Trying to make sense of a girl who last night
had kissed him so thoroughly, yet now was treating him to the
coldest of shoulders. Beth looked fixedly down at her feet for
what seemed like minutes, all the time conscious of a gaze that
never wavered.

When at last he spoke, it was to say a simple 'I see.' And in
that small phrase, she knew, was contained a world of feeling.
'Well, I won't keep you. You obviously have a busy morning. It
seems like Fitzroy is back on the scene—and you'll need to keep
him happy.'

'I'm teaching Ralph, that's all,' she said stiffly. It was
perverse of her, but she couldn't bear that he might think her a
heartless flirt.

'Of course you are.' His words were clipped of all
expression.

'It's not what you think...' her voice trailed off.

'It's OK, Beth. Really. There's no need for explanations.
Better not, in fact. I'm used to the treatment. The only mystery
is how I could have thought you were different.'

He pushed past her and walked out into the garden,
whistling to himself.

23

Three hours of simple fractions should have put Jos out of her mind, but they didn't. She sat at one side of the kitchen table with Ralph at the other, reassuring him when he took a wrong direction, praising him when he was successful. But her thoughts were elsewhere, looping, coiling, circling. Relentlessly. So much so that at times her breathing became irregular and her heartbeat almost audible. Ralph was a nine-year-old boy and not the most observant of beings, but even he cast her a few puzzled looks.

'Are you all right, Miss Merston?' he asked at one point. 'You've gone a funny colour.' If only going a funny colour was all that was wrong with her.

The clock ticked on, the day mercilessly slow in passing. Once she'd seen Ralph off to Amberley and cleared away their small lunch, she went to sit with Alice. The old lady rarely asked her to read aloud, preferring to pick her own slow path through the newspaper and an occasional book, but today her eyes were rimmed red and sore.

'It's those replacement glasses,' she complained. 'I told the man at the time they weren't right, but he wouldn't listen. Medical men always think they know best.'

Beth was fairly sure there was nothing wrong with the spectacles, but she had no wish to be at odds. It was peace she craved. 'We could ask him to call again.'

'We should. And soon. Even reading a newspaper for an hour is uncomfortable. And I've a new book arrived. The mobile library delivered it this morning.'

'Would you like me to read it to you?' It wasn't what she wanted to do but hoped the offer would put an end to the old lady's complaints.

Alice nodded and lay back in her chair, waiting for Beth to begin. She listened contentedly to the opening chapters of *Friday's Child*—Georgette Heyer was one of her favourite authors—but before an hour had elapsed, she'd fallen into a doze and from a doze into a deep sleep. Beth wasn't sure whether to be glad or sorry. Reading had been a trial, but not reading was even more of one. It was crucial that she keep herself busy, yet it was too early to make supper and she'd already marked the work Ralph had brought with him from Amberley.

She went to her room and threw herself onto the bed, pushing her sketchbook aside. Drawing had lost its attraction, and poor Izzy seemed consigned to stay forever in her wood. For a long time she lay staring vacantly at the ceiling, but in her mind saying all the things she'd wanted to say to Jos but hadn't. From their earliest meeting, she'd known him for a fellow spirit, and these last few weeks had taught her how right her first unthinking reaction had been. The two of them were so much alike it was laughable. But she wasn't laughing now.

Her decision to walk away had been the most painful thing she'd ever done, but how much worse if she'd allowed the affair to continue? In the short time they had left together, they would become lovers. It was inevitable. All the longing, the pent-up desire that over the years she'd dammed so successfully, would overflow into love for him.

And then what? Her future to be decided by the turn of the weather. And if by chance he should survive the coming ordeal, what possibility was there of a life together? His world was one of soldiering, of constant disruption and danger. He might be the heir to Summerhayes, but he wouldn't stay. His inheritance could take years to prove and in the meantime he would go from Summerhayes—within an hour, a week, a month—and she would never see him again.

The evening, when it came, was no better. She spent it with Alice in the sitting room, and was glad to have the wireless fill the silence. There were several hours of music and comedy with Alice chuckling over ITMA while Beth tried to join in the laughter at the right places. She was immensely thankful when the old lady brought the evening to an early close, saying she was tired and asking Beth to bring a cup of cocoa to her bedside.

Beth wasn't sure how truly tired she was. From time to time that evening, she'd been aware of her employer watching her. Mrs Summer would say nothing—it would be anathema for a woman of her class and generation to raise a personal matter—but Beth wondered if the older woman, with a lifetime of experience, had discerned something of what she was feeling, and this was her way of showing sympathy. When finally she regained the sanctuary of her room, she was so utterly weary that she was almost asleep on her feet. The quickest of visits to a cold bathroom, the next day's jumble of clothes pulled from her wardrobe, and then into bed. Surely she must sleep.

She would push away the day's events, cast them as far from her mind as possible. Think instead of London, of the school she'd loved, the children she'd loved. But it wasn't laughter and fun that her mind saw, but the burnt wreck of a building, the scattered lives, the destroyed hopes. She hadn't cried for years, not since her mother had left her lost and flailing. But now sobs rose in her throat and tears burst through the flimsy blockade she'd built. Her pillow turned wet with grief—for a lost childhood, for the world she'd tried to build in its stead. And excoriating grief for a love she was too fearful to embrace. They were desperate feelings.

Despite her anguish, or perhaps because of it, she fell into a deep sleep. It wasn't until she woke at seven the next morning that she realised the thudding, banging, grinding she'd heard in the night were not part of a dream, as she'd thought. She stumbled into the kitchen and pulled the curtains, and there it was—an empty terrace, an empty and vast spread of concrete and beyond, an empty garden. The army had gone.

Alice had only to look out of her window to see the overnight evacuation for herself but, after giving it some thought, Beth decided to stay silent and follow their familiar routine as though nothing had happened. The old lady was more tranquil these days, no longer worried that 'bad things' were happening at Summerhayes and feeling, perhaps, that she had found Elizabeth at last in the shape of Elizabeth's son. The news that he was on his way to France to face days and weeks of extreme danger could wait a while.

Having settled her with her newspaper, Beth spent an hour tidying the apartment before she set about preparing for Ralph. She missed Molly's cleaning expertise and wondered if she should recall her, even though she distrusted the girl. There had been no threat to her employer for several weeks. She would wait a while longer, Beth decided, and then speak to May.

The boy arrived promptly at nine thirty, accompanied by a footman from Amberley. On the surface he appeared unconcerned that he'd been left alone in a very large house—if you could call it alone when a dozen servants lived beneath the same roof—but his enthusiasm for study had waned even further and Beth wondered if he were missing his father.

'Have you had news from London?' she asked encouragingly.

Ralph looked vacant.

'Your father,' she prompted.

He shook his head. 'Daddy never telephones while he's away.' He didn't seem unduly worried by this. 'The men have gone to France, haven't they?'

So that was why he was so listless. 'Yes, they must have left during the night.'

'And Eddie was with them?'

'He was.' And Jos, too, her treacherous mind murmured. 'I'm sure we'll be hearing great things of them very soon.' Somehow she managed to sound as though she meant it.

Ralph beamed at her across the table. 'I know we will and, when Eddie gets back, he's going to tell me all about it. A blow-by-blow account, he said.'

'That's something to look forward to,' she agreed. 'But right now you need to finish the leaflet you were writing for visitors to Amberley.'

He gave a long sigh and obediently bent his head, but by halfway through the morning he'd managed only one small paragraph and was struggling. Fate, however, was about to be kind. Constable Harris knocked at the apartment door and as soon as the policeman's tall figure appeared in the kitchen doorway, Ralph's listlessness vanished.

Their visitor took off his helmet and laid it carefully on the table. 'I thought I'd drop in now that the military's gone, Miss Merston. Make sure you ladies are nice and secure.'

'We're fine,' she hastened to assure him. 'It was a shock this morning, though, when we woke to an empty estate.'

'It's the same everywhere—they're all gone,' he said with satisfaction. 'I've been cycling the roads since dawn, my colleagues too. It's the same story. Petworth, Lavington, Wyke-hurst Park in the north, Firle in the east.' He wiped a hand across his brow. 'Never seen anything like it. Just vanished, all of 'em.'

'I know they've gone to France, but where exactly?' Ralph fixed the constable with an expectant stare.

'No one knows precisely, lad. Top secret, you know. Evidently somewheres on the coast first—Portsmouth or Newhaven mebbe. They'll be waiting to embark.'

Ralph looked disappointed. 'What are they waiting for?'

'For the weather. Weather's got to be right, hasn't it?'

Beth could feel a tight spiral somewhere beneath her chest. How unbearable to be waiting hour after hour. How unbearable for Jos.

'I thought there'd be fighting by now,' Ralph said gloomily, when Constable Harris had disappeared. He'd gone back to toying with his pencil, turning it this way and that between his fingers, occasionally dropping it on the table, but writing very little. Beth had just decided she must be severe with him when they faced a second interruption. This time it was May Pren-dergast.

Her friend dumped a basket on the kitchen table in the spot vacated by the constable's helmet. 'My hens have been proper lively this week. It's been quiet, you see. No explosions or guns firing off. Anyways, I've brought you a few eggs. Mrs Summer always liked a boiled egg for breakfast, if I remember rightly.'

'Eggs! How wonderful. You're so kind, May. I can pack the egg powder away for a week.'

'That's what neighbours are for. Leastways in the country-side. I can't get used to this quiet, though. The silence is that strange. Them tanks opposite my house, the ones tucked into the woods, they're all gone. It's good they've gone, I suppose. Might bring us one step nearer the end of this dratted war. But then... I keep thinking how awful it will be if it's like the first do.

I keep thinking of Joe and all those boys. What if these poor lads face the same? And what if it don't work? The Luftwaffe will be back here in force.'

Bethany wanted her to stop talking, but out of politeness asked, 'Will you stay?'

'No, my dear. I can see how you're busy and I won't interrupt the good work.' She smiled down at Ralph. 'How's it going, young man?'

The reluctant scholar pulled a face. 'OK, I s'pose.'

May walked over to the window and peered through the glass at the garden below. 'You know it's hard to believe, but I reckon Summerhayes without them looks even more desolate.'

Ralph looked up from the smudged page in front of him. 'I know it looks bad now, Mrs Prendergast, but it won't always be that way. When the war's over, Daddy and I will put it to rights. When Summerhayes belongs to us.'

Bethany and May stared at him, then Beth found her voice. 'What are you talking about, Ralph?'

'Summerhayes. Mrs Prendergast said it looked desolate. I think that means it doesn't look good. But it won't always be that way,' he said confidentially. 'When my great-aunt dies, it will belong to us again and then my father will make it good. It won't be long now.'

Bethany was too shocked to say anything, but May was sharper. 'Is your Pa still in London?'

'Yes, Mrs Prendergast, but he'll be back soon.'

'Then you better make sure you get some work done to show him,' she said brusquely, picking up her basket. 'I'll be off now, Beth dear.'

Beth walked with her into the hall, closing the kitchen door behind her.

'That boy's following in his family's footsteps,' May said in a lowered voice.

'That was a dreadful thing for a child to say.'

'I daresay his father is feeding him the same lies as he was fed.'

Beth stared at her. 'What lies?'

'That Summerhayes was taken from the Fitzroys. T'aint true. Old Joshua Summer bought it fair and square, like he bought his wife, but Henry Fitzroy always maintained it was stolen from them. I told you, didn't I? He was happy enough to have Summer's money, but he didn't like keeping his side of the bargain. Especially not when Joshua gave Summerhayes the loveliest gardens in Sussex. Put Amberley in the shade, that did.'

Ralph's blithe mention of his great aunt's death was horrifying, but Beth couldn't believe that Gilbert would speak so to his son. If his own father had fed him lies, he would surely want to protect Ralph from the same ugliness.

'What kind of man was Gilbert's father?' she felt impelled to ask.

'All charm and bonhomie—leastways to them that mattered —but a nasty, cruel man beneath. His wife left him and no wonder. Not that she was much better. No one liked Louisa, but they liked Henry even less.'

'Gilbert's mother left? When?'

'He'd be about nine or ten, I guess. Up and went one night, ran off with the doctor, would you believe? It gave the village a great laugh, the doctor not being exactly top drawer. Pricked Henry's pride something rotten.'

'It couldn't have been funny for Gilbert.' She felt sadness for the small boy who had faced such upheaval, and with no one to care a jot.

'He was away at school when it happened, and Louisa Fitzroy wasn't a great mother. I daresay he didn't miss her over much.'

Beth doubted that things were as black and white as village

opinion would have, but May's words had given her pause. 'It's as though history is repeating itself,' she said slowly.

'I dunno about that. There's rumours for sure but they might not be right. Ralph's Ma could come back when the war's over.'

Beth shook her head, and said in a quiet voice, 'Gilbert has gone to London to settle the divorce.'

Her companion's expression changed to one of alarm. 'He actually told you that?' She gave her head a quick shake. 'You be careful, my dear. Don't you go trusting him.'

Bethany bridled. 'The divorce has nothing to do with me. I hope you know that, May. And as for being untrustworthy, I've never had cause to doubt him. He's always been perfectly pleasant—most of the time,' she amended, 'and very kind to Mrs Summer.' She felt an obscure need to defend Gilbert.

'You said he made you feel uncomfortable.' May was reaching back into memory.

'For a while he did, but once he realised I wasn't interested, he stepped back. I don't have any fears in that direction.'

May looked at her keenly, her sharp eyes probing. Then she sighed. 'No, I reckon not. Likely your fears run in a different direction entirely.'

24

The first few days of June unfolded so slowly that at times it seemed to Beth she was living in a dream, that the army, that Jos, had never been at Summerhayes. Each morning she scanned the sky as though she were a farmer in the fields or a sailor on the ocean. As though her life depended on it, though in truth it was other lives that did. The worst of the storms had subsided, but the sky was still a mass of grey and the wind continued to blow. She'd read somewhere that airborne troops could not be dropped if the wind was stronger than a force three. What a force three felt like she had little idea, but the complete absence of news was ominous. It must mean the plans for invasion had fallen into serious doubt.

The fourth of June saw the return of high winds and thick cloud. When the postman called later that day, it was on his way back from Lancing.

'Seas like mountains,' he reported. 'All along the front. Not much chance of launching them landing craft in that. Flat bottomed, you see.'

'The army has been waiting for days and there must come a

time when they give up. If they do, will the regiment come back here, do you think?' She was a mix of fear and longing.

'I reckon they might, unless there's a change in the weather pretty soon. Sod's law, in't it? All Spring we've had fine days and now look at it.'

Bethany looked at it and felt despair, even when on the following evening the cloud cover lessened and, for fleeting moments, she could see a full moon through her bedroom window. But the wind was blowing as hard as ever, and she went to bed wretched. Some time during the night she heard the heavy drone of aircraft and shuffled irritably to the other side of the bed. *A stray German bomber*, she thought, *let him do his worst*. It was when she rose the next morning, unrefreshed from a restless night, that the thunderbolt struck.

When she took Alice her morning tea, the old lady was sitting up in bed and nursing a humming wireless. Beth was taken aback; her employer had evidently tottered out of bed and grappled with the electrics. But there was more to follow.

'It's started,' Alice said simply.

'The invasion?' She was incredulous.

'Of course, the invasion. There were planes in the night—a procession of them—didn't you hear? I listened for hours. Every one of them filled with airborne troops. We've been waiting so long for this to happen.'

They had. And for the first time she realised how thoroughly tense everyone had been. Not just her, but Alice and May, the postman, the policeman, even Ralph, who despite his lacklustre studies continued to come to Summerhayes every day.

'It was on the wireless when I woke,' Mrs Summer said. 'There was moonlight last night and they could drop the men with their parachutes. And the other planes could see to bomb.' The elderly face was lit with excitement. 'The announcer said there was a rising tide at dawn—that's for the landing craft. If they hadn't gone last night, the weather man was convinced they'd have had to wait another fortnight.'

Beth had remained immobile while Alice regaled her with what she'd learned. She'd barely understood what the old lady was saying, but now she put down the cup she was carrying, her hand shaking in an odd fashion and slopping tea into the saucer. After the initial surge of relief that at last the invasion had begun, she was gripped with foreboding.

'What has actually happened?' Her voice was as shaky as her hand. Paratroopers and bombers were one thing, but it was the infantry who would bear the brunt of the fighting. The old lady couldn't have connected the news to Jos, she thought, to the grandson she'd only just found, or she wouldn't speak so cheerfully.

'I've told you what's happened, my dear. And do sit down, you're fidgeting me. The eight o'clock news will be on in a few minutes. We'll listen together.'

But Frederick Allen reading the BBC news had little more to tell them than Alice had already related. They had to wait another hour and a half for the first official announcement.

This is London, the announcer began. *London calling in the Home, Overseas and European services of the BBC, and this is John Snagge speaking. Under the command of General Eisenhower, Allied naval forces, supported by strong air forces, began landing Allied armies this morning on the northern coast of France.*

'But he hasn't said what's going on.' Beth bounced up from her chair. 'Why hasn't he said which regiments are involved? Or what's happened to the men they've landed?'

'He's telling us all they know,' Alice said calmly. 'We'll learn more as the morning goes on. I'll have one of May's eggs for my breakfast. I feel I can eat something.'

Eating was the last thing Beth could contemplate, but she was in danger of losing herself in panic. She needed to learn from Alice. Her employer had been through this before, thirty years ago, and she had as much to lose as Beth. More, in fact. It wasn't too dramatic to say that the future of Summerhayes could be at stake. Jos was its heir, even if he chose to remain a soldier.

At ten o'clock John Snagge was back, but with little to add. *D-Day has come. Early this morning the Allies began the assault on the north-western face of Hitler's European fortress.*

That's it? she murmured to herself despairingly. They had to wait until midday before they learned more, this time from Winston Churchill who was addressing the House of Commons. Alice walked from the sitting room to the kitchen carrying the wireless. Beth had never seen her move so confidently and Ralph, who was bent over an intractable passage of French, looked up amazed at seeing his great-aunt so animated.

An immense armada of upwards of four thousand ships, together with several thousand smaller craft, crossed the Channel, Churchill intoned. *Massed airborne landings have been successfully effected behind the enemy lines, and landings on the beaches are proceeding at various points... The fire of the shore batteries has been largely quelled. The obstacles that were constructed in the sea have not proved so difficult as was apprehended... So far the Commanders who are engaged report that everything is proceeding according to plan... Fighting is in progress at various points.*

What fighting? her heart thumped out. *Who is fighting? Where are they?*

And then words that made her grasp the kitchen sink so hard that she almost tore it from the wall. *But all this, although a very valuable first step, gives no indication of what may be the course of the battle in the next days and weeks... heavy fighting will soon begin and will continue without end... It is, therefore, a most serious time that we enter upon.*

'Miss Merston?' Ralph was looking anxiously at her. 'It will be all right, you know,' he comforted. 'Our men are the very best.'

She smiled at him, watery-eyed. 'I know. Never mind me. I'm sure things are going exactly to plan as Mr Churchill has said.'

'You must have faith,' Alice remonstrated, and tottered back to the sitting room, still clasping the wireless to her chest.

Once Ralph had returned to Amberley, though, whatever faith Beth had managed to conjure dwindled rapidly. She was all too aware of how strongly those beaches were defended. It seemed the Allies had enjoyed the advantage of surprise. There had been some kind of deception going on, the Germans believing the invasion would come from Dover or even Scotland. But surprise could last only so long. As the Prime Minister had said, the Allies were entering a most serious time.

The gravity of the situation nagged at her and a terrible restlessness took hold. It picked her up and tossed her from room to room, leaving her frantic to escape the apartment, if only for a short while. It seemed safe enough to do so. The threats to Alice appeared finally to have ended, along with the letters. If it had been Molly behind the attacks, she supposed the girl and her accomplice too busy now to bother with an old lady, no matter what the grudge.

Alice had foregone her usual afternoon nap and was listening avidly to whatever bulletin was broadcast, though there was no real news and the same few lines were being endlessly recycled. But she was content to stay listening, with a promise from Beth that she would be back very soon.

Out of earshot of the wireless, the house sat in silence. Beth walked swiftly down the stairs and through the empty rooms, registering every creak of the staircase, every rasp of the floorboards. What a sad sight it was. The beautiful oak panelling scratched and dented, the coloured glass above the oak front door now dull and nondescript, and wooden floors that had once been golden, scuffed and seemingly scarred beyond repair.

She was glad to leave the house behind and walk out onto the terrace. The damage was not so evident here but, once down the semicircle of steps, the huge swathe of concrete, stark and empty, stared her in the face. Beneath its weight an expanse of lawn lay dead.

The wind had calmed since the morning and a weak sun shone fitfully through patchy cloud. She picked up her pace, glad to feel her limbs in motion and her breath sharp in her chest. Soon she'd made her way through the deserted vegetable garden, then past the circular brick wall with its sad reminders of bountiful fruit, and into the wildest part of the estate. She hadn't ventured this way since she'd been here with Jos and it didn't feel good.

The wilderness was tough to penetrate and she was out of breath by the time she reached the laurel hedge. Together they'd cut back its branches to reveal the tall archway that had once been an entrance to this secret space, but even in the short time that had elapsed, the hedge had grown back with vigour and Beth had to use considerable force to battle her way through the gap that remained. She emerged scratched and dishevelled, and saw immediately that the one flower bed they'd cleared was already filling with weeds. Weeds paid no heed of a month that had been unseasonably chilly.

Idly, she yanked at one or two of the tallest then, straightening up, looked around her and listened to the silence. The spirit of the place had changed. She could feel it. No longer welcoming as it had been when she and Jos had worked together but filled once more with that sense of disquiet. The garden carried a sadness that seeped into her heart—but it was more than sadness, wasn't it? There was something dark here, something malignant.

She gave her shoulders an impatient shake. Too vivid an imagination again, but no, there was something definitely wrong —a brooding presence that melted into shadow whenever Jos was around. Was that because he signalled a new beginning for Summerhayes and could wash the garden clean of past sins, banish whatever evil there had been? It sounded foolish if you said the words aloud, but in Beth's mind they rang true. With him by her side, she'd felt the possibility of beauty; here, alone, she sensed only darkness.

They had managed to make good a tiny part of this once beautiful space, but it was a mere dent in the widespread devastation. The lake lay still and fetid, the temple sad and broken. Putting this garden to rights would be a labour of love and she wondered if it would ever be restored to its former glory. It needed an owner. It needed Jos. She felt the tears welling and fought them back furiously. She shouldn't be feeling this bad. She was being feeble, she told herself, because he was a friend and he wasn't safe. But she knew it was more. Far more. It was a gut need to have him again in her arms, to kiss his mouth, to feel him close. To stop this dreadful feeling of emptiness.

25

When she arrived back at the house, she was astonished to find Gilbert Fitzroy waiting for her. He stood at the bottom of the sweeping staircase that led to the first floor, a large bouquet of white roses in his hands. An expensive bouquet, by the look of it.

'How nice to see you.'

It was said automatically, a cover for her confusion, and then she realised she *was* pleased to see him. She needed to talk to someone of what was happening just a few miles away. Gilbert's contacts in London might know more—where the fighting was worst and which regiments were involved. The wireless bulletins had so far been annoyingly anodyne and told her nothing. And she couldn't discuss her fears with Alice. The old lady appeared to have forgotten she had a grandson involved in the conflict and Beth thought it best to avoid any such mention.

'I'll take the flowers into Mrs Summer,' she said, as they mounted the stairs together.

'No, don't do that.' He stopped her with a light hand on her arm. 'They're not for Alice, they're for you.'

May's warning reverberated in her ear: *Gilbert Fitzroy isn't all he seems.* But Beth already knew that. She'd seen his suave manner turn to anger, seen his temper at work. He'd apologised profusely, though, and apart from that one solitary instance, had been a pleasant and agreeable neighbour.

He must have felt her arm tense beneath his hand because he said, 'A small gift only, Bethany. For all the work you've done with Ralph. I've just seen the young blighter back at Amberley, and looked at his books. He's come on well and that's entirely down to you.'

She wasn't sure which books he had scanned, but she'd no wish to argue with his good opinion. 'It's nice of you to say so. And to bring these wonderful flowers.'

They'd mounted the second staircase and stood outside the apartment door, recovering their breath. 'I bought them because I thought you might need cheering up. The world is pretty chaotic at the moment.'

She did need cheering, and things could not be more chaotic. Gilbert knew nothing of her feelings for Jos, but it was a difficult time for all of them and he had sensed her unhappiness.

'I'll put these in water and get us a drink.'

'Not for me, thanks. I must be getting back—lots to do at Amberley, you understand. And it's best that I don't bother my aunt right now. I imagine news of the invasion is upsetting her. It's bound to bring back memories of the First War.'

'If it does, she seems not to mind. Just the opposite, in fact. She's glued to the wireless for most of the day or has her head buried in a newspaper. This morning she waded through the front page of the *Daily Telegraph*, despite swearing her glasses don't work. The headline got her very excited—that Allied troops are now several miles into France.'

'And you? Are you excited?'

Before she answered she finished arranging the roses in the

biggest vase she could find. 'I can't say I am. I've listened to one or two of the BBC bulletins, but I missed the King's speech last night. I think it's best not to dwell on what's happening until there's a clearer picture.' In truth, she'd done little else *but* dwell on it and was amazed at how fluent a liar she'd become.

'That's very sensible. After all, there's nothing we can do to affect the outcome. We must just sit tight and wait.'

Gilbert was right. It was the helplessness that was getting to her. 'How was London? Still depressing?' She needed to change the subject.

'A little. There seem more bombsites each time I visit, but people are incredibly resilient. Defiant, I think I'd call it. And my own news, I'm glad to say, is anything but depressing.'

She positioned the enormous vase of flowers in the middle of the kitchen table. The pure white of their blossoms appeared to cast light into every corner of the small room. 'They look magnificent,' she said. 'Thank you so much.'

'It's a pleasure. I felt I wanted to celebrate in some way.'

'What are you celebrating?' She was genuinely interested.

'The news from the legal chaps. Ida wants the whole thing wrapped up as swiftly as possible. The divorce, I mean. That's the way she does things. But I'm not complaining. It means I'll be a free man in record time.'

It was difficult to know what to say. She had never encountered divorce before and felt awkward talking of it. But her silence didn't appear to worry Gilbert; he seemed newly energised at the thought of his coming freedom.

'And that's not all,' he went on. 'The finances are fine, too. She's prepared to settle a fair amount on Amberley.'

Beth was beginning to feel uneasy again. She had no need to know any of this.

'Sorry, I shouldn't be boring you in this fashion.' He'd guessed at her discomfort. 'It's just relief. I was pretty confident it would work out, but you never know. And then Ida just falling in with my wishes so easily, well it was a real gift. I'm still feeling euphoric.'

'I'm pleased things went well for you,' she murmured, then made haste to change the subject once more. 'Were you able to make arrangements for Ralph while you were in town?' He looked at a loss. 'To move him somewhere safer,' she reminded him.

'Oh, that. I'm thinking now that it may not be necessary. The troops are already making their way into France. The invasion appears to be on target so the news is good as far as it goes.'

'As far as it goes...' she trailed off.

He was standing close to her and, hearing the catch in her voice, reached out and gave her a quick hug. She didn't shrug him away. 'It's not like you to be despondent, Bethany.'

Really, he could be very nice, she thought, and tried to smile. 'I'm going to have to buck up, I know. Everyone else is coping.' Though not everyone else had someone for whom they cared so deeply.

'How about coming over to Amberley for dinner one evening? Would that help?'

The suggestion unnerved her. She was glad to have him as a friend, but if she agreed to dinner, it might say a whole lot more.

'Thank you for the invitation.' She would be as tactful as she could. 'But at the moment, I'd rather stay close to home— until we know more.'

It was a silly thing to say. How could staying in the apartment help with anything or anybody? Yet she felt the need, a compulsion even, to remain within the confines of Summerhayes, just in case. Just in case of what though?

The day finally dragged to its close. For the remaining hours, she'd tried but failed to keep herself busy, while Alice had taken it in turns to doze or to listen to whatever snippet of news she could find on the wireless. The BBC had broadcast nothing of any substance and the day's newspaper had contained little more.

Beth had read as much of it as she could bear, studying closely the map it had reprinted of the sixty miles of Normandy coastline. Each of the five beaches involved in the invasion—Utah, Omaha, Gold, Juno and Sword were their code names—had been marked for the paper's readers with a dispassionate cross. She'd learned that Juno beach was where the division of Canadian soldiers was headed, but that was all she knew. No precise details of the fighting had been given and there had been no mention of casualties. What *was* happening to the men she knew? To the man she knew? It was news of Jos for which she yearned. When Alice tuned in to hear the nine o'clock news that evening, Beth was drawn moth-like to the wireless.

All the landing beaches are now cleared of the enemy. Reinforcements and supplies are getting across safely. More airborne landings were made during the night... Heavy armoured fighting has started inland.

Only a little more forthcoming but hinting at the ominous. Is that where Jos was now, clear of the beach and fighting his way through Normandy? The news the next day appeared to confirm it. It was another brief bulletin, but Alice cranked the volume to a point where Bethany, working in the kitchen, could hear every word. Stuart Hibberd's smooth voice filled the apartment.

Allied troops have captured Bayeux, five miles inland on the road to Caen...Now that we've cleared all the beaches of the enemy, our troops are coming into heavier fighting.

Towns captured, heavier fighting, it was a catalogue of fear. And what if Jos weren't in that heavy fighting, what if he were lying cold on a beach or in a makeshift mortuary? She was so agitated that she cleaned the bathroom twice without realising she had done so. Her limbs seemed to have a mind of their own, unable to be still, yet unable to do anything purposeful. She would have to walk again. She would walk to the village and back while Alice took her afternoon nap. She wouldn't be able to shop—they'd used the last of their coupons earlier this week—but, in any case, it was unlikely there would be much to buy.

She set a brisk pace there and back and, an hour later when she walked through the door of Summerhayes and climbed the stairs, she felt refreshed. Until she walked into the kitchen and saw Alice raising a glass to her lips, a glass filled with a ruby red liquid.

'Don't drink that, Mrs Summer!' She bounded forward and snatched the glass from Alice's hand.

The old lady took a step back, her eyes blinking in confusion. 'Why ever not?'

Beth couldn't answer. She had no idea why she'd stopped Alice from drinking. Instinct, perhaps, the need to protect her from anything unfamiliar. She was being overly suspicious but, in the light of recent events, could hardly be blamed. Keeping a firm hand on the glass, she picked up the bottle and squinted at the label. It read *Domaine de Dionysus, Côtes de Rhône Villages*. She knew little about wine, but the label appeared authentic.

'I don't recognise the bottle,' she said a trifle lamely.

'Of course, you don't, dear. I found it outside the door. I heard a knock and thought you might have forgotten your key, so I came to look. And there it was!'

Instinct might have been right. Beth's suspicions increased. Why had that bottle been left on the doorstep and why no note with it?

'One of my neighbours must have left it,' Alice answered her unspoken question. 'Wasn't that kind of them? A little treat, and we don't get many of them. It seems years ago that I drank wine.' Her face wore a faraway look; for a moment she was walking in the past. Then she brightened and said, 'I didn't even have to open the bottle, the cork was loose and waiting for me, just when I needed a little something to boost my spirits. The Germans say that Rommel has started his counter-attack.'

Beth didn't know what to be most worried about—the appearance on the battlefield of the legendary general or the strange red liquid Alice had been about to pour down her throat. A brief ponder and she decided in favour of the wine. But she would have to be subtle. Alice could be stubborn when she chose and there was nothing to suggest there was anything wrong with the drink. She picked up the bottle again and turned it towards the window.

'It looks a little muddy, past its best, whatever that was.'

'It can't be past its best, silly girl. It's red wine and the longer you leave it, the better it tastes. Ripley told me that and, if he were here, he'd tell you too. He knows a great deal about wine.'

'I don't, but I do know it doesn't look good. Maybe whoever gave it has stored it wrongly.'

It was Alice's turn to look concerned. Bethany had made a sensible point, it seemed. 'We should smell it perhaps?' she suggested, and, when Alice nodded, she lifted the glass to her nose. It smelt of red wine certainly, not that she'd had much acquaintance with the drink, but there was a slightly sour odour that lay just below the surface, and she didn't like that at all.

She cast around for a way of dissuading her employer. 'Let me take it down to the village tomorrow—to the Horse and Groom—and ask the barman. He'll know for sure.'

'But what if it was him that gave it to me?'

'Then I'll simply tell him your thanks and ask his advice on how best to drink it.'

This seemed to find favour and once she'd settled Alice with a cup of strong tea, a substitute treat, she stored the bottle at the very back of the cupboard beneath the sink. With luck, Mrs Summer would forget about it, and in a day or two she could pour it down the drain where it surely belonged.

.   .   .

Beth had intended to go to her room after supper and pick up her drawing again. Days ago, she'd lost all inclination to continue Izzy's story, but she needed distraction and working on a half-finished illustration was the best she could do. By nine o'clock that evening, though, she found herself once more in the sitting room, in the seat next to Alice and with the wireless between them.

Our troops are now pushing on beyond the Norman town of Bayeux and are in contact with enemy armour, the voice intoned. *In tonight's war report, listeners will hear the voices of some of our fighting men wounded in action and now safe in hospital.*

As one man after another told his story, Alice nodded approval, occasionally interjecting a comment of her own. The men who spoke had been badly wounded, some of them hardly able to gasp out the words they wanted to say. For Beth, the broadcast was torture. She clasped her hands in her lap to prevent their shaking, knotting them together so fiercely that it looked unlikely they would ever come undone. *How many men had been wounded? Who were they? Were their wounds all as serious?*

'Jos won't be one of them, you know,' Alice said out of the blue.

The casual remark caught her off-guard. The old lady had appeared to forget she had a grandson caught up in the turmoil that was northern France. But appearances had lied.

'How can you be sure?' Try as she might, Beth could not keep her voice stable. She pulled her fingers violently apart, bruising them as she did.

'He'll be doing well,' Alice said complacently. 'You mustn't worry.'

For a moment she had an intense desire to jump up and

shake the old lady, scream at her even, but instead she asked as calmly as she could, 'Aren't you at all fearful for him?'

'Why would I be? Elizabeth is with him. She'll see he comes to no harm.'

'Elizabeth?'

'He carries a part of Elizabeth with him, don't you remember? In his pocket.'

Beth grappled with this for an instant and then realisation dawned. *The earring, she means the earring. His mother's jewellery is going to keep him safe?* She wondered whether this peculiar reasoning was a manifestation of old age, but no, she imagined it was Alice's own brand of logic, the way she had always thought. A fey kind of logic.

If only she were right. It could be weeks before they knew Jos's fate, months perhaps— unless the worst had already happened. They'd know about that, she guessed. Eventually, there'd be a list of those who had died. By then she would not have a fingernail left. She wasn't pretending to herself any longer. She loved the man and she hated that she hadn't been honest. Hated that she had sent him to war, without telling him the truth.

26

Four days later the trucks began to arrive back. Ralph was at the kitchen table, labouring over yet another composition, when the sound of engines and the heavy tread of tyres on gravel reached them through the open window. For the first time in days the weather had cleared sufficiently for them to enjoy the morning air.

The boy had arrived an hour earlier, accompanied by an Amberley footman rather than his father. Beth had been disappointed that Gilbert hadn't come; she was hoping he might have learned more of the fighting. Instead, she'd had Ralph's opinions relayed to her in the gap between each laborious sentence. He was excited by stories of the Allies' march through Normandy, and longing to see Eddie again.

'I want to hear all of his adventures, Miss Merston. Where he went, what happened, if he met any Germans. He's my best friend, you know.'

She had to work hard to stop her mind painting a very different picture to the rosy outcome that was all Ralph could envisage. For a child, death was inconceivable. The deep growl of the trucks' engines brought him bouncing from his seat, his face aglow.

'Can we go and see?'

She hesitated. If she went, she might hear the worst possible news from the men who'd returned. How would she bear it? But if she didn't go and left Ralph to discover all, how could she bear that?

'We'll go,' she said at last, and threw a jacket over her light dress. The weather might be greatly improved but flaming June was a long way off. At the apartment door, she stopped.

'Just a minute, Ralph.' She'd remembered the red wine or whatever was festering beneath the sink. She couldn't leave it and Alice alone together in the apartment. She pulled the bottle from its hiding place and lifted the cork. The sour smell was more potent now. Ralph leaned over and took a look.

'Phew, that stinks. It's kind of the same colour as the wine at home, but it smells awful.'

'Then let's get rid of it.'

Pouring the noxious liquid down the sink, she washed the last sign of it away. The empty bottle went into the small dustbin; she hoped that Alice wouldn't come looking while she was out, but she would be gone a few minutes only.

It *was* only a few minutes. Half a dozen trucks had reclaimed their space on the concrete parking lot, and a handful of soldiers were milling around, unloading what looked like boxes of supplies though she couldn't be sure. Elsewhere men were being helped from the trucks, various parts of their bodies bandaged and several on crutches. These were the walking wounded, she imagined. She didn't recognise any of them and neither did a disappointed small boy. Should she ask for information, she wondered? She could pretend she was enquiring on Ralph's behalf.

But he beat her to it, only to return to her side a few seconds later. 'The men aren't from Eddie's battalion,' he said despondently. 'Though they were on Juno beach. They said the fighting was tremendous.' His eyes were saucer-shaped.

'We best not bother them any more. Come on, you have a composition to finish.'

'Must I?'

'Yes, you must. Let's go.'

They were walking across the flagged terrace when Gilbert Fitzroy appeared around the corner. She felt embarrassed to be discovered here with Ralph, when his father had explicitly requested that he be kept away from all things military, but he cut her apologies short with a wave of his hand.

'I heard some of the men had returned. I thought I'd pop over and see for myself.'

The village grapevine, she presumed. But why Gilbert should find it interesting enough to drive from Amberley, she had no idea.

'Has anyone you know come back?'

She thought it an odd question and shook her head. 'Most of the regiment is fighting its way across Normandy, isn't it? These men are the wounded—those well enough to leave hospital, I guess.'

'There's no one we know, Daddy,' Ralph put in. 'I thought Eddie might be here, but he's still fighting.'

At the mention of Eddie's name, Gilbert's lips tightened to a thin line. 'Time to go back, Ralph,' Beth said briskly, hoping the boy would say no more. 'We've work to finish.'

'Yes, do as Miss Merston says,' his father reiterated. Ralph looked from one to the other, then thought better of arguing and walked towards the house.

'To tell you the truth,' Gilbert said, when his son had vanished through the side entrance, 'I don't want to encourage the boy's friendship with this Rich fellow.'

'I know the two of you don't see eye to eye,' she said cautiously.

Gilbert's words had been mild, but she could see that his feelings were anything but. He had been so determined to keep his son from Eddie, that he'd driven from Amberley to make sure the soldier was not one of those who had returned.

'It's far more concerning than not seeing eye to eye.' Gilbert fixed her with an anxious gaze. 'I think the man is seriously unhinged and I worry about Ralph keeping company with him.'

She had to protest. 'I'm sure you're wrong. Eddie is a prankster, I know, but he's quite sane. He couldn't keep his job if he weren't.'

Gilbert made a noise that sounded like a snort. Of derision, perhaps. 'He seemed as mad as a hatter to me. Do you know that he actually claimed to be the heir to this place? To be Elizabeth's son? I was a small boy when my cousin left, and I hardly remember her or her paramour. But the suggestion is utterly crazy.'

Beth had been stunned by Eddie's mischief making that day on the terrace, and now it had become even more unsettling. However much Gilbert might protest, it was clear he was taking the story seriously.

'I think you'll find Eddie was trying to be annoying.'

'He doesn't have to try,' Gilbert said heavily. 'I've never heard such balderdash. A stream of nonsense about a painting and an earring and a letter from his lawyers.'

The mention of a painting was new. When had Eddie dropped that bombshell? She wondered how much she hadn't overheard, how much of Jos's secret his friend had revealed. Deliberately, she slowed her breath. She must throw Gilbert off the scent, and keep him there for as long as Jos was absent.

'I hadn't heard about a letter. But the picture and the earrings—I know why Eddie mentioned them. He saw a painting of Alice's daughter when he was helping me clear a pile of jumble,' she lied. 'He took a shine to the earrings she was wearing in the portrait. I think you'll find he concocted the whole fantasy around that, hoping to make you angry.'

Her companion pulled himself up to his full height. 'I'm glad to say that he didn't succeed.' Now who's lying, she thought. 'But, in any case, he's not a fit person for Ralph to associate with. If he should return here, I hope you'll make sure the boy doesn't talk to him.'

'I'll do my best, of course. But I don't think you need worry. About his coming back. I doubt that Eddie or any of his battalion will be returning here.'

He looked at her closely. 'That sounds severe. Do you have bad news?'

'I've no news,' she was quick to say. 'But they're likely to be fighting for months in France and when it's all over—if it ever is —I imagine they'll be posted elsewhere.'

'You're probably right.' He looked pleased with the idea.

'I should be going. I need to drag the requisite number of words from Ralph before I send him home.'

'I don't envy you.' He was smiling easily now. 'But all work, you know... really, Bethany, you can't stay confined to Summerhayes for months. I hope you've not forgotten my invitation.'

'I haven't and thank you.'

'Shall we say next Tuesday then? That should give you time to find help. I'm sure May Prendergast would be willing to sit with my aunt.'

She was still reeling from the revelation of how risky Eddie's taunts had been and her tired brain was slow to summon a suitable excuse. 'I'll ask her,' she said.

'Splendid. I'll drive you, of course.'

Bethany sat through an early supper that evening, tasting nothing and hearing little of Alice's conversation. Her mind was bedevilled. She had committed herself to going to Amberley, the very thing she'd wanted to avoid. Accepting Gilbert's invitation to dinner presaged a slow slide towards something more than friendship. It was Eddie's fault, she told herself, stabbing angrily at a round of carrot. Eddie's game playing. The shock at his dangerous mockery had left her vulnerable to pressure. Not that there'd been much pressure. That thought weighed more heavily than all the rest. She'd agreed to Gilbert's invitation as meekly as any lamb. And what did that say about her feelings for Jos?

Nothing, she decided, after mentally tearing herself into small pieces. It meant nothing, and was it any wonder she had made a bad decision? For days, fear had tossed her every which way, while she'd had to pretend a detachment she was far from feeling.

She was thankful when supper came to an end and she could clear the table. She was still washing the dishes when Mrs Summer called to her from the sitting room, inviting her to listen to the latest bulletin from the BBC. She put the tablet of soap to one side and hurriedly dried her hands.

'Would you mind if I took a short walk instead?'

Alice seemed surprised, but happy enough to be alone with her wireless. Beth snatched her cardigan from the chair before she could find herself drawn once more to a news that was no news, and ran out of the apartment and down the stairs.

The June evenings were long, but it was darker in the garden than she'd expected. They must have sat over supper far longer than she'd realised. The moon, a slice of white, was already riding high in the heavens, with a sprinkling of stars faint but discernible. Enough light to walk by, for the moment at least, but when she studied the sky more thoroughly, she saw a skein of cloud begin to chase the moon. It would have to be the short walk she'd promised Alice since she carried no torch.

Across the terrace and swiftly down the steps to circle the trucks that had returned that morning. There was no sign of the men who had returned with them. She didn't know what happened to the wounded after they'd been shipped back to England. Perhaps they were left in camp to recuperate and wait for new orders.

Strolling the length of the pergola, she thought of Mr Ripley and hoped he was enjoying his stay with his daughter. Meg, it seemed, had had the best of the roses. Most of the flowers were now brown-edged, their petals crinkled by wind and rain and their stems untamed and overgrown, reaching out to catch at her cardigan and enclose her in a thorny embrace. With difficulty, Beth freed herself and walked on.

The roses were sad. The entire garden was sad. It had once been a place of great beauty, she'd seen that from Elizabeth's paintings: Summerhayes in its full glory. It still had a kind of magnificence, she thought, walking through the arch of warm brick into the long-abandoned vegetable garden. Even in decay, the estate was magisterial.

The sky had grown darker now, just as she'd feared, cloaking the landscape in a veil of mystery. She had never before ventured out so late. It was only the threat of another empty news flash that had prompted her to walk at all. *And* the tormenting knowledge that she had burnt at least one boat in agreeing to go to Amberley.

She would walk to the wildest part of the garden, and then turn back. The wilderness, as she'd named it, would be impossible in the dark. What pathway there was, bent and twisted in its meanderings, was overtopped by straggling palms and grasses six feet high. A deep frustration took hold that she could go no further; her mind and her body wanted to keep walking. To walk on and on, until she could leave behind the mess she'd made of her life. But that was something she couldn't do. There was no escape and she must stay strong—for herself, for Alice. For Jos. One day he might come back and she had to believe that.

She had reached the wilderness now and stood immobile, looking out over trees and bushes keeping their silent guard. A rustle in the grass, a waving of palm fronds. Yet there was no breeze—since she left the house, the air had been unwavering in its stillness. Her eyes picked out a dark form some distance away... so grass and palms had been moving to the rhythm of a man. He was walking slowly, as though utterly fatigued and, as he drew nearer, she saw that he had his left arm plastered and resting in a sling. Hanging from his right shoulder was a large backpack.

He was obviously one of the wounded and she wondered why he hadn't come with the rest of the men. She was going to turn in her tracks, not wishing him to know he'd been observed, when something about the way the man walked, even in extreme weariness, made her pause. Her heart pinched. And then pinched some more. Her breath caught in her throat. Hallucination, that was what it was.

The man was all the time drawing nearer, all the time growing more visible. It wasn't a fantasy. She wasn't going mad. It was him. It was Jos. With a wild yell of delight, she ran forward, tripping, stumbling, every so often losing the path, until she stood face to face with him.

He dropped the backpack onto the ground and looked at her. For what seemed a long time, he stood and looked at her.

'Jos?' she said uncertainly, wondering now if indeed this was a fantasy. Was he dead and this was his ghost she was seeing?

She put out a tentative hand and touched his fingers. They were warm with life. No ghost this man.

'Jos!' She flung her arms around his body and clutched him tight. Very slowly his right arm encircled her shoulders.

'You're safe,' she sobbed.

'I'm safe,' he agreed.

They walked back up the garden in complete silence. From

time to time she stole a sideways glance, hardly able to believe he was there walking beside her. The moon had floated clear of cloud and in its crystalline light he looked immensely tired. Deep lines were edged either side of his mouth and his eyes, empty of expression, were fixed on the path ahead. He seemed hardly to have the energy to put one foot in front of another and no energy at all for talking.

Apart from that reluctant arm around her shoulders, he'd shown little pleasure in seeing her. He must be in pain as well as fatigued, she reasoned, aware of the awkward angle at which he held his injured arm. Or perhaps, an insidious voice murmured, you killed his feelings for you the day you rejected him. Not that it made any difference to the way she felt. And she must tell him how she felt, whether he wanted to hear it or not.

At the door to the Head Gardener's office, he turned and vouchsafed her a brief nod before ducking his head beneath the lintel.

'Shall I tell Alice that you've returned?' she asked, before he disappeared.

He ducked back out again and for the first time met her eyes directly. 'I'll tell her myself. Tomorrow.'

Then without another word he walked through the doorway and out of sight.

27

He came, as promised, the next morning. Beth had endured a night of sleeplessness but comforted herself with the thought that when she saw him again things might be different. After a long rest, he might again be the Jos she'd known. He would treat her as a friend, if nothing more. But when he arrived at the apartment door, freshly shaved and in a neatly pressed uniform, his greeting was curt.

'How is she? In good health, I hope?'

He was here only to see his grandmother, he was making that plain. Inwardly, her soul shrivelled. 'She's well but will be even better for seeing you.'

'No more ghosts or letters then?'

'The threats appear to have stopped, though I can't be sure they won't come back.'

She wouldn't mention the wine. In her mind, that was still a worry needing an answer. It could easily have been a well-wisher delivering a bottle, she conceded, one they'd had too long in the kitchen cupboard, and it would probably be wise to forget the matter.

'I'll go in now if that's OK.' He was edging his way towards the sitting room, ill at ease and wanting to escape from her as soon as possible. 'I won't stay long. I don't want to tire the old lady.'

'I think you'll find it will take a lot to tire her. She'll want to hear all that's happened to you.'

For the first time he managed the glimmer of a smile. 'Then I better tell a good story.'

When he walked through the doorway, Alice put down the newspaper she was reading.

'You're back,' she said simply, not seeming at all surprised.

'I am, and very pleased to see you looking so well.' He bent to kiss her cheek, then took a seat beside her.

'*You're* not looking so well.' She pointed at his arm.

'A little inconvenience, that's all.'

'Not half as inconvenient as the Germans are finding it.' There was the hint of laughter in her voice.

'We gave them a shock, didn't we?' He stretched his long legs in front of him and laid back in the chair, perfectly relaxed. 'They thought we'd go for the shortest distance across the Channel, but what do you know, it turned out to be Normandy.'

'And they never guessed?' Alice's face was alight.

He shook his head 'Nope. Their high command was caught completely unawares. The weather helped, I guess. It was pretty bad and being a logical people, the Germans reckoned we'd never chance it. Rommel was actually back in Germany celebrating his wife's birthday. Did you hear that?'

The old lady laughed out loud. 'I did. Serves him right. But we also heard on the wireless that he'd travelled back to France in a pother.'

'Driven back at high speed. What was priceless—and you'll enjoy this—was the Field Marshal commanding the German army in France. The story going round is that he heard reports there was fighting in Normandy but carried on believing the invasion was aimed at the Pas-de-Calais. He could have mobilised a Panzer Division as a precaution, but didn't like to wake Hitler to check if he should. And Hitler went on thinking the news from Normandy was excellent, that whatever fighting there was, was just a cover for the real invasion further up the coast.'

Alice snorted. 'The man is a fool.'

'I wish he were but, in this instance, we had the better of him.'

She shifted in her chair so that she was half facing him. 'Tell me what happened to you. When did you leave for France? Not the same day as you left Summerhayes, I'll be bound.'

'It took a while to get there, for sure. After we left here, we trundled over to Wykehurst Park. That was a Marshalling Camp for the troops embarking from Shoreham.'

'You sailed from Shoreham,' Alice said wonderingly. 'So close.'

'That's right. From Wykehurst we went to an assembly area near the port and waited there for last instructions. Then, finally we were off—in the early hours of what turned out to be D-Day. Ship after ship of us. You'd think the whole allied army was being taken across in one night. We landed shortly after sunrise, but the navy had been busy beforehand bombarding the beaches. We were a bit late landing, the sea was so rough.'

Beth had remained standing by the door. She might as well not be in the room, she decided, then pushed away the ungenerous thought. The two of them were talking like old friends and she should be glad of it.

'The crossing was bad then?' Alice asked.

'Afraid so. Most of the men were seasick and even some of the boat crew. I can tell you we were glad to get ashore, whatever was waiting for us.'

The old lady's expression changed. Her face lost its excitement and folded into furrows. 'And what was waiting?'

Jos leaned towards her, giving her his whole attention. 'It

was odd. There was a big swell and our landing craft was banging into the ship's hull. You were scared of falling into the water before you even got to the beach. We'd done all those waist-high training exercises, but the tide was high and the naval officer in charge of our craft ran it so far up the beach, I didn't even get my boots wet. I just walked ashore onto dry sand.'

'I don't suppose it stayed that easy.'

'You're right, it didn't. The water was rough and there were enemy mines beneath the sea and across the beach. Some of the landing craft were sunk, but far more made it through. The beach master was an army sergeant and he did a brilliant job keeping us away from the spots he thought dangerous. He managed to find us a safe avenue through the sand dunes. If I hadn't been hit right then, I'd have been off with the rest of them, across the beach and onto the roads beyond.'

'What about the German fortifications? The newspapers have been full of how strong they were.'

'Their coastal defences put up a stiff resistance, it's true, but within half an hour we'd managed to silence their machine guns.'

'And then what?' Alice was enthralled.

'And then it was the open road, according to the guys who made it off the beach. I talked to some of them in the field hospital. Tanks and men beginning their march through Normandy.'

'So a success?'

'Certainly more than we could have hoped for.' He smiled encouragingly. 'We didn't make our particular objective—that was Caen—but by the end of the day, we'd gained a secure foothold.'

Alice breathed a long sigh. 'That is good, Jos. And so very good that you are home again.'

She took up the newspaper she'd abandoned and proceeded very slowly to fold it into a smaller and smaller square. She seemed to be lost in the activity and, when Jos looked across the room at Beth, there was a question in his eyes.

Beth turned and walked into the hall, and he followed her.

'I'm glad you didn't tell her the worst,' she said quietly.

'How could I?'

'Was it very bad?'

'Pretty bloody, in all senses of the word.'

'Tell me.'

'It doesn't make for pretty listening.'

'Maybe not, but I want to hear.' She had to know what he had gone through.

'A good third of our landing craft hit mines. There were hundreds of guys in the water washing around in the shallows, poor devils. They'd been training for months and they barely made the shore. And those that did make it often had to wade chest-high through the sea and dodge bullets as best they could.'

'Did you really not get your boots wet?'

'That was true. Our captain was pretty tricky.'

'And the fortifications?'

'That wasn't so true. The German machine gunners had a field day, firing from seaside houses and bunkers. They cut the men down in droves and the beach was a mass of bodies. Awash with blood. The first hour was just brutal. I reckon the leading assault teams must have suffered a fifty per cent casualty rate. Most of our men were youngsters with no battle experience, and the gunners picked them off one by one. But a lot of them got through. They were brave guys, very brave.'

His voice had grown husky with memory and instinctively she reached out for his hand. He didn't take it away.

'And your arm? What happened?'

'A bullet smashed the humerus into pieces. Not a clean break, but the guy who fired did me a favour. He hit me above the elbow which means I've got movement in my left hand, even though wearing a sling I can't use it much.'

'And you travelled back from France with just a sling for support?'

'There was no alternative. They dosed me up with morphine and once we'd landed, I was shuffled off to a hospital in Chichester—St Richards? A surgeon operated the next day and stuck me back together with a metal plate.'

It sounded fearsome and she wondered if he'd be permanently disabled. 'You'll be able to use your arm?' she asked tentatively.

'Six weeks minimum and I should be raring to go.'

'Back to France?'

'Back to France. There's a lot to do.'

'You told Alice the Allies had a secure foothold now.'

'And they have, but we're still vulnerable. News was going round the hospital that a Panzer division had mounted several counter attacks. They gained no ground apparently, but they did inflict heavy casualties. And there's a nasty rumour that they murdered the Canadian soldiers they took prisoner.'

'How terrible!'

'What's ahead is likely to be more terrible. Weeks of tough fighting to get to Caen and beyond. A whole summer of it.'

'A whole summer before Europe is liberated.' She turned the words over in her mind and felt her heart weigh heavy.

'It will be though—eventually. Sheer force of numbers will win it for us.'

While they'd been speaking, Jos had moved closer. He seemed to have forgotten that yesterday he'd wanted to keep her at arms' length, and she thought that maybe now was the time to tell him how wonderful it was to have him back, tell him that she never wanted to lose him again, that she'd been so wrong to build a barrier between them.

She'd steadied herself to speak when there was a knock at the apartment door. Gilbert Fitzroy appeared on the threshold, a bright smile on his face. When he saw Jos, the smile turned to a heavy frown and he stood staring at him, a pained look on his face, as though the soldier's presence was in some way a personal insult. It was seconds before he regained his usual smooth manner.

'I hope you don't mind, Beth, but I haven't seen my aunt for a while and I thought today might be a good time to call. Just a small chat, you know. I've bought her a little treat from London.' He waggled a small bar of chocolate in the air. 'Do you think she'll like it? It's the real thing.'

'I'm sure she will.' Beth bit back her frustration. 'She hasn't seen proper chocolate for at least four years.'

'Good, good,' he murmured, and stepped fully into the hall.

For a moment her attention was deflected, and it was then that Jos slipped out of the door. She heard his footsteps on the stairs and could have cried with vexation. She hadn't managed to say the things she wanted so badly to say and worse, he would draw his own conclusions from Gilbert's presence in the apartment, conclusions that would be utterly wrong.

As calmly as she could, she led her second visitor back into the sitting room, determined he would suspect nothing amiss.

'Mrs Summer?' Alice opened one eye. 'Mrs Summer, your nephew is here to see you.'

Alice grumbled beneath her breath. She'd evidently had sufficient visitors for the day and Gilbert was never a favourite.

'I won't stay long,' he said hurriedly. 'I've brought you a small present from London.'

'What is it?' Her tone verged on rudeness.

He placed the brown-wrapped bar of Hershey's in her lap. 'Chocolate. And not ration chocolate either,' he assured her. 'I thought you'd like it.'

'It is a treat, isn't it?' Beth tried to sound enthusiastic. After all, Gilbert had gone to the trouble of finding real chocolate, an elusive item these days.

'I hope it's better than the wine someone left me.' Alice was unremitting in her grumpiness.

'Someone left you wine? My goodness.' He looked surprised by the news.

'Such a shame it had gone sour,' Beth put in. 'I think it must have been stored badly.'

'Bethany had to throw it away,' the old lady muttered.

'That was a shame, but I'm pretty sure you won't find a problem with the chocolate.' He spoke to her as though humouring a child. 'Anyway, do enjoy it, aunt. I'll be off now and leave you in peace.'

Alice made no reply and Beth walked with him to the apartment door. 'She's a little tired at the moment, but when she's feeling better she'll love it,' she assured him.

'It's fine. You can relax,' he said easily. 'I'm inured to my aunt's moods. In any case, I've something far more important on my mind. I hope you haven't forgotten.'

'Forgotten what?' Her question suggested that she had.

'You're having dinner at Amberley tomorrow evening. That's a far greater treat than any chocolate bar. At least for me!'

28

Alice loved the chocolate a little too much. When Beth brought her morning tea, she found her employer wide awake and nursing her stomach.

'Are you sick, Mrs Summer?'

'A little,' the old lady confessed. 'I think it's the Hershey bar that my nephew brought.'

'Something was wrong with the chocolate?' She found that difficult to believe. 'Shall I try a piece to test it?'

'You can't,' Alice said, slightly shamefaced. 'I've eaten it.' She laid back and closed her eyes. But a second later had opened them again and was mounting a vigorous defence. 'I woke up early, you see, and I was hungry. I didn't want to disturb you, so I ate the chocolate.' Her face twisted as another spasm struck.

'You ate it all?'

'It was only a very small bar,' she protested. 'And I didn't think you would want any.'

'You've not been used to anything as rich for years. Even a small bar can upset you.'

'It has,' she said flatly. 'I've been foolish.'

'Should I call the doctor?'

'Definitely not. The pain will pass and I don't want that old fusspot here.'

'Dr Mallory is a good physician, you know that.'

'Hmm. He might have been at one time, but not now.'

The doctor was the family's medical man but an ancient foe as well, and Mrs Summer was not about to modify her opinion of him.

'If you're absolutely sure.' Beth had to accede to the old lady's wishes, but she was concerned. Alice's pale complexion was this morning tinged with grey.

'I am sure. I don't require any breakfast thank you, but if I feel I'm about to be ill, I will call you.'

The sickness had put going to Amberley out of the question. That, at least, was a relief.

'I need to go downstairs to the general office and make a telephone call,' Beth told the frail figure propped against a mountain of pillows. 'I'll only be a few minutes, but shall I leave you a basin?'

Alice looked appalled at the thought of such indignity.

'On second thoughts, perhaps not.'

Beth flew down the two staircases. For days, an eerie quiet had pervaded the rooms on the ground floor and this morning was no different. In the hall a ray of sun slanted through the beautifully patterned glass above the front door, possibly the only part of the house left untouched, splashing clusters of dusty colour across the black and white tiles. She walked across the hall into what had once been the dining room. At one end of the main office a solitary uniformed figure sat at a typewriter, and beneath the window a sprinkling of injured soldiers had gathered around a long table and were studying the printed sheets spread across its surface. She wondered if the men had been given new orders.

The man at the typewriter rose and limped towards her. 'Miss Merston, isn't it? I think we've met before. Captain Salito.'

She vaguely remembered him on one of her rare visits to this part of the house. 'Yes, of course. How are you, Captain?'

'Not so bad. A bit of a problem with the leg that's all—but it will mend.'

She was about to ask if she could use the telephone when bad luck struck. The worst possible. Jos had entered the house through the side door, walked along the tiled passage, and arrived in the office at completely the wrong moment. If there was one person Beth didn't want in the room while she spoke to Gilbert, it was Jos Kerrigan.

He barely acknowledged her before he made his way to a desk covered with rolls of maps on the far side of the room.

She almost turned tail and fled back to the apartment, but she had no option but to make this call. Captain Salito had resumed his typing and it was Jos she must ask.

'I'd like to telephone. Is that all right?'

'Help yourself,' he said offhandedly.

She went to the nearest piece of black bakelite and asked the operator to put her through to Amberley, aware that Jos would hear every word she spoke.

Gilbert answered. Good mornings were exchanged and then she had to break the news. 'I'm well,' she said, responding to his enquiry, 'but I'm afraid Mrs Summer isn't. She liked your chocolate rather too much. Her stomach isn't used to such rich food and she's not feeling quite the thing. I'll need to be here today—I'm afraid I'll have to cancel dinner.'

There was an annoyed response at the other end, and she waited for a moment to say, 'I hope she's better by this evening, too, but even if she is, I won't want to leave her with anyone else.'

Another burst of irritated comment flowed down the line. Out of the corner of her eye, she saw that Jos was fidgeting with the maps, unrolling and then rolling them up again. She knew he was listening intently.

'I'm sorry to let you down,' Beth said in a sharpened tone, when finally she managed to interrupt Gilbert's monologue. She was becoming as irritated as he; he seemed to think his aunt's illness was a deliberate ploy to spite him. 'Perhaps another day,' she suggested, hoping that might find favour.

It didn't, and she was forced once more onto the back foot. 'I didn't know you had to go to London again. Well, maybe when you get back.' Without waiting for the next barrage of complaint, she replaced the receiver.

'Love's path not running smoothly then?' Jos had been unable to resist. There was an ill-natured glint in his eyes. She ignored him and went to walk out of the room, but before she got to the door, he demanded, 'Is Alice ill?'

She glared at him. 'She's suffering from being a little too greedy.'

'Shouldn't you ring for a doctor? There's a Dr Mallory somewhere in the village. I can do it, if you like.' Despite her vexation, she was touched by his concern.

'Thank you, but no,' she said in a level voice. 'Alice doesn't want to see him, and I'm sure she'll be fine. She just needs watching over.'

'Pity about your dinner party, though.' His voice was filled with malicious enjoyment.

'No, it isn't,' she said tersely, and walked away without another word.

Jos watched her walk out of the office, his gaze fixed on the door through which she'd left. Then, sensing Salito's eyes on him, he turned and fumbled again with the documents on his desk. He couldn't think and he couldn't concentrate. She'd rejected him, hadn't she, just when he was embarking on the fight of his life and in a manner that left no doubt? She couldn't have made it plainer if she'd written the words on a large banner and hung it from her window.

So why the other night had she run to him? When he'd first recognised the figure carving a path through the tall grass, his heart had banged so hard it could have leapt from his body. The throbbing in his arm, the fatigue in every limb, the wretched memories of the past few days had crumbled, and he'd felt a desperate need to scoop her into his arms— into his one arm, at least. But then he'd remembered and had stopped himself.

He must think of her no more. His job was to get fit, fit enough to fight again. His claim that he'd be raring to go in a mere six weeks had been little more than bravado. He'd been hit by a single bullet, but it had done terrible damage. The bone would grow again, would wind its way around the steel bar holding his shattered arm together, but how long that would take he had no idea. He couldn't think that far into the future; for now, he was where he wanted to be.

From the moment the sniper's bullet had smashed his arm to pieces, he'd been desperate to return to Summerhayes. The twenty-four hours he'd lain prone in that field hospital, slugging water and drowsing in morphine, Summerhayes had been his star, shimmering a welcome, showing him the path home. As soon as he could walk, he'd left Chateau de Beaussy and bagged a berth on a landing craft back to England. He'd been lucky. Transport had been waiting at Southampton to take him to Chichester and an operation that same night.

Once he was able to stumble from his hospital bed and, in some fashion, dress himself, he'd signed his discharge. Then grabbed a lift from a friendly nurse going off duty and asked his benefactor to drop him at the bottom of the estate. He'd wanted to walk through the gardens as he'd done when he first arrived, to know again its damaged beauty, to feel that he was coming back to a place he could call home—to a grandmother he could love and a house that might one day be his. It was only Beth that was wrong, a black mark on an otherwise white page.

Or so it had seemed. But when yesterday he'd visited the apartment, she had reached out to him for the second time. She had wanted to know the truth of D-Day, wanted to share its horrors with him. Was that to compensate for her earlier rejection? Did she hope empathy would heal the wound? He hadn't known. All he'd known was that he needed that healing very badly.

Until, that is, Fitzroy had arrived on the scene. Then suddenly the situation had become clear, as transparent as a newly formed sheet of ice. She had reached out to him because she felt guilty. Guilty that she'd led him to believe her feelings went far deeper than they did. And guilty that she intended to throw her lot in with Gilbert Fitzroy.

He had wealth, a large house, a large estate. Whatever stories were told in the village, the man showed no sign of imminent penury, and Jos would wager a large bet that in the end they were just stories. So who could blame her for making that choice? What did love ever offer? He should know better than to ask.

It was evident she had been going to dinner at Amberley this evening, no doubt to seal whatever devil's pact she'd made with the man, but his grandmother's sickness had put paid to it. Now that he knew Alice was not seriously ill, he could feel a twisted satisfaction that things were going awry. From what he'd gathered of the conversation, Gilbert had not reacted in a lover-like fashion. Bethany would need to learn deference if their liaison were to prosper, and Jos couldn't see that happening. But he must drive them both from his mind.

And Summerhayes, too. No matter what his feelings for the place, he must forget them. His grandmother was at the end of her life, but he was a soldier on the move. Maybe, one day it would be different, but the possibility of owning Summerhayes was far distant. There would be all kinds of legal hurdles which he had neither the time nor the money to surmount.

For a brief moment, he'd been given a new world, had become a new person—someone with roots, with a family and, most prized of all, a girl he loved. But it had been a moment only, a will o' the wisp. He could see now that it was a dream too far. In reality, his world had not changed, and he must face his old life as best he could.

29

Bethany was relieved to find her employer a great deal better the next day, though far more restless than was usual. She wondered if the improved weather was making the old lady fidgety. Gentle sunshine and a soft breeze offered a perfect morning on which to walk, yet Alice remained trapped in the upper reaches of the house. Beth would have loved to take her for a short stroll on the terrace, but the upper staircase from the apartment to the first floor was steep and the stairs so narrow there was insufficient space for a companion to walk alongside and lend a helping hand. She dared not allow the elderly figure to navigate the stairs alone. If only there was a lift, but the house had been built at a time when Joshua Summer and his wife had no need of such an aid.

'What does the clock say?' Alice asked for perhaps the third time that morning.

'Just after ten. It will soon be time for your drink.'

She hadn't meant to sound patronising, but it was clear she had. 'You don't have to humour me,' the old lady snapped.

'I don't mean to, but I can see you're unhappy and I'm not sure how to help.'

'You can find Jos,' she said to Beth's surprise.

'Jos?'

'You remember—my secret grandson! I want to speak to him. I'd like you to bring him here.'

Beth was still smarting from yesterday's encounter and had hoped for time before she had to meet Jos Kerrigan again. It looked as though she wouldn't be getting it.

'He'll be working,' she prevaricated.

'I need to speak to him. I've something on my mind and it won't go away. He won't object to giving me a few minutes of his day, I'm sure. I won't keep him long.'

Mrs Summer's face had settled into a mulish expression and Beth could see that if she were to have any kind of peace today, she would have to find Jos.

'I'll go and look for him,' she said reluctantly.

'Yes, do. And don't be too long about it.'

She had never known Alice so exacting. The 'something' that was on her mind was evidently bothering her greatly, and the old lady was likely to stay exacting until it was settled.

Bethany let herself out of the door and down the narrow staircase to the first floor. The same emptiness reigned here as elsewhere in the house. The bedrooms were unoccupied except, she imagined, Captain Salito's. Before the regiment left for France, she'd rarely bumped into anyone on her way out of the house, but still there had been signs of life everywhere—a towel flung over the bannister, shoes lined up for polishing, a pile of papers on the landing console. Now it was a space for ghosts.

On the ground floor she retraced yesterday's steps across the hall and into the office. If Jos were at work, he'd be here. But he wasn't. Only the Captain was in residence.

'Jos?' He wrinkled his forehead. 'I told him to lose himself for a few hours. There's not a lot to do today.' He spread his hands wide to indicate a clear desk. 'Tomorrow will be different. We've another convoy of wounded coming in, but today is playtime.' He gave her a faint grin.

'And where is he playing exactly?'

'That I'm not sure of. He might be in his billet or—I think he mentioned something about the garden. Maybe he's walking in the gardens.'

'Thank you. I'll look there.'

She was soon outside the old Head Gardener's office and put her head around the open door. The room was empty. She was taken aback by how small it was. Despite its size, she saw it housed four camp beds, only one of which was being used. There was something eerie about that, too. Where were the men who'd slept here? Where, in particular, was Eddie? And how had he fared in the invasion? She'd thought of him every day, but so far had kept herself from asking Jos for news. If he knew Eddie's fate, it was clear he wasn't ready to share it.

She walked on down through the gardens. She knew now where Jos would be. As she pushed through the archway of laurel, she saw him bending over the earth they'd only recently cleared and, with his free hand, upending the odd weed. He straightened up when he heard the rustle of leaves.

'It's a constant battle, isn't it?' She indicated the green shoots scattered across the flower bed. It seemed a neutral enough topic to begin the conversation.

'And by the look of it, not one you wanted to wage. Too busy, I guess.'

There was a sour tinge to his voice. Beth had been wrong. It wasn't a neutral topic and she knew exactly what he was implying. But she'd wouldn't let it pass, she couldn't let it pass. He was going to know the truth.

'Too upset would be more accurate. I did come once while you were away, but I hadn't the heart to do anything.'

'Oh?'

She took a breath and plunged in. 'I've been sick with worry over you, Jos. I haven't been able to do more than just get through each day.'

'You are talking to the right person?'

She went up to him then and clasped his good hand. 'I am talking to the right person. And you have to listen. I can see you feel differently now and I understand why. I want to say I'm sorry for what I said, for the way I behaved—before you left.'

'It's water under the bridge. Best we say nothing more.'

'No, it's not best.' The passion in her voice had him cast a baffled look at her. 'I was scared, that's why I behaved the way I did. Terrified that I'd got too close to you, scared I'd be hurt. I've never let anyone get close, not for years.'

He looked away, but did not loose her hand. His eyes were half closed and his mouth downturned. The muscles of his face seemed to jump and jerk. He was waging some kind of inner war, she could see. Was he fighting against a desire to believe her?

'So why tell me now?' he said at last. Struggle had become confusion.

'Why now? Because since you left, I've been through every kind of torment, and nothing could be more painful than these last few days. I realise you no longer feel the same, but it doesn't matter. I still have to tell you. I love you.'

That turned his head. He looked down at her, his gaze half wondering, half incredulous. 'You realise I no longer feel the same? How is that?'

'You hardly look at me. You don't want to touch me. You don't want to kiss me. Isn't that enough?'

She felt her hand gripped more tightly. Then he bent his head towards her and very gently brushed her lips with his. 'Looks like you could be wrong,' he said softly.

Tears pricked at her eyes, but she wasn't about to waste this moment crying. She laced her arms around his neck and pulled him close, kissing him so long and hard that he had to steady himself against her, flinching as he did.

'Your arm—I'm so sorry.'

'The kiss was worth it,' he said, and kissed her again.

She nestled into his good arm and for a while they stood motionless amid the path's shattered mosaic. The sun riding high in its smooth blue dome warmed their bodies.

'Shall we find a seat?'

His arm still around her, they walked together towards the ruins of the Roman temple. One of the largest columns had broken off at waist-height and its stump proved a perfect resting place.

'So what about Gilbert Fitzroy?' Jos asked after a while.

'It's not what you think. He's a friend, nothing more.'

His mouth formed itself into a grimace and she knew him unconvinced. 'He's been a good neighbour.' She struggled to explain. 'When I first arrived, he helped me settle in—and he's helped me since. I've started to teach Ralph again, too, so I suppose it's inevitable his father comes to Summerhayes. And of course he calls on Alice, which he's every right to.'

'Sounds cosy.' His voice was crisp.

'I can understand your suspicions,' she confessed. 'I have them, too. I'm pretty sure he wants more than friendship, but ever since I realised that, I've tried to keep my distance.'

'And have you succeeded?'

'Not entirely.' She had to be honest again. 'He can be persistent, but if he sees we're together the message will be clear enough. He'll have to forget whatever plans he's been hatching.'

'Then we better make sure he gets the message.' He bent down and found her mouth again, this time teasing her lips open and kissing her with an intensity that for a moment shocked. Then she was returning his kisses with equal fervour, until suddenly he broke away.

'I can't, Beth. We can't.'

'Whatever's the matter?' The dream they'd only just started to build began as rapidly to crumble.

'I shouldn't be doing this.' He sprang to his feet and walked around the perimeter of the temple, marking out its fallen walls in a forceful stride. Then he turned and made his way back to her. 'I should have kept out of your way. I meant to, I promised myself I would. If you've been wrong in keeping things from me, I've been doubly wrong. I should have been honest with you from the outset.'

Beth reached out, pulling him down beside her, then ran her fingers along the tanned curve of his cheek. 'Be honest with me now. Don't you think we've wasted too much time already?'

'I have to tell you something that will alter things between us.'

She braced herself. 'Tell me. Let me be the judge.'

'It's my father.'

'Yes?'

'He's not a well man. In fact, he's very sick.'

She took a while to absorb the news, but then dismissed it. 'I'm sad to hear that, but I can't see how it's important to us.'

There was a long pause before he said, 'His sickness is in the mind. He's been in a mental hospital for years.'

She felt immediate relief and hugged his good arm tight. 'Is that all that's bothering you?'

'You haven't thought it through or you wouldn't dismiss it so easily.' Jos stared ahead at the broken marble. 'His illness could be hereditary. You're an exceptional woman, Beth, but not even you would want to shoulder that burden.'

'Why would you think his illness is hereditary? There could be all kinds of reasons for your father's state of mind. Didn't you once tell me that he was distraught when your mother died? That his reactions were extreme? Surely that was the start of his troubles.'

His expression remained bleak. 'I've always hoped so. On

good days I'm sure of it, but I can't be certain and it's the uncertainty that's killing. Even the medics won't give a definite opinion. A while back you said you were scared of getting close to anyone, but how much more scary when that anyone turns out to have relatives like my father. Even if the craziness doesn't affect me, it might manifest in any children I have. The truth is I should never have allowed myself to love you.'

'You didn't have a choice. And neither did I. And for my part, I'm glad of it. You have to stop torturing yourself. It must have been your mother's death that caused your father to fall ill.'

'Do you honestly believe that?'

'It seems obvious to me. Maybe you're too close to the situation to see it objectively.'

'But the doctors...'

'Doctors prefer not to commit themselves, you know that. Just look at the evidence. Your father was a well man until disaster struck. There was nothing to suggest otherwise, was there, until he lost his wife? A healthy man and a successful one. An architect, you said?'

'A good one, too. Niall—he's my father's cousin—told me that Dad built a strong reputation from the moment he arrived in Canada, but after my mother died his energy vanished. His enthusiasm went AWOL and there were fewer and fewer commissions. The stuffing was knocked out of him, I guess. Niall said he became like an automaton. He took on some work —he had to earn money to keep us going—but the quality was no longer there. His hands could draw simple plans, but his intellect was shot to pieces.'

'He must have loved your mother very much.' She was over-awed by this tale of tragedy.

'Great love doesn't pay the bills,' he said wryly. 'Eventually there wasn't enough money to keep our apartment going and we moved in with Niall and his family. They were good to us.'

'And it was Niall and his wife who brought you up?'

'More or less. They were first-rate. But it's not the same as having your own family, is it?'

'No, it isn't.' Beth had felt that truth as deeply as it was possible to feel, and still did.

'I was lucky to be part of a lively household, I guess. That was as normal as my life was ever going to be. My father was just a distant presence. He had so little to do with me over the years that I figured it was OK to sign up and leave home without telling him.' Jos gave a deep sigh. 'Turned out I was wrong. It sent him completely out of kilter. He'd been working behind the counter of a corner store—by then he'd given up any idea of working as an architect—but when I left, he lost his mind completely. It was as though with my going, he'd lost every-thing, so why hold on to the small piece of sanity he had left? I'd no idea he would react in that way.'

Beth kept silent. There was not a thing she could say that would make things better.

After a while he added, 'How could I know? I didn't think he'd even realise I'd left. I had no reason to believe he loved me.' And that, too, struck a painful chord with her.

'So how did he end up in hospital?'

'He got to be a real problem. Began to wander all over the place, not knowing where he was or what he was doing. His speech became more rambling, and apparently he'd accost perfect strangers and begin haranguing them. Then he started seeing visions of my mother and believing that she was still alive.'

'That's uncanny.'

'Isn't it? After I found that painting and realised who Eliza-beth was, I thought of the old lady's visions. It gave me a queer feeling to think my dead mother could provoke such a fanatical response in two such different people.'

'It's that great love again, and great loss.'

'Niall and his wife were worried sick and got him to a

doctor. It didn't take long for the guy to pronounce my father mentally impaired and consign him to the hospital. He'll finish his days there. It sounds dire, but he seems happy enough.'

'You visit him?' She bunched herself a little closer.

'Not often. But yes, I visit.'

'It's a sad story, but there's nothing we can do that will change what's happened, either for him or for Alice.'

'There's one thing I can do for her. Ever since I found out who my mother was, I've been thinking about it. Alice must wonder why my father never wrote to her, why he never told her what had happened to her daughter. I'm sure she's still plagued by it, even after all these years.'

'Do you know why he didn't write?'

'There was bad blood and no doubt he felt the Summers didn't wish him well, but I'm sure that wasn't what kept him from writing. At first I guess he was too dazed to put pen to paper—he had a week old baby to care for—but then I think he began to blame his father-in-law for my mother's death. Dad hardly ever spoke to me, but occasionally he'd say the odd thing that made me think my mother's father had been a bad man. That he was some kind of monster. I know his name now. Joshua Summer. He was the guy who'd harried them out of England, or that's how Dad must have reasoned. If they'd been allowed to marry here, there would have been money for proper medical care and my mother would still be alive. He had to have someone to blame, someone to punish. I think that's why he didn't write. He couldn't know the man had followed his daughter to the grave. I guess he blamed me, too. If I hadn't been born...'

'You can't think like that.'

'I can and I do. But I faced that truth a long time ago and it no longer hurts. At least, not so much. Alice must still be hurting though. She's been left in ignorance all these years when a simple letter could have helped her accept her daughter's death. I need to explain to her just what a mess my father was, and hope she'll understand.'

'That's it!' Beth's hand flew to her mouth. 'That's why she wants to see you. She's become very bothered over something lately and I think it's because now she knows that Elizabeth is dead, she can't understand why no one ever took pity and told her. She must have decided you're the one who can slay the dragon. It's why I came looking for you—and I said I wouldn't be long.'

'Then we'd better go.' He tucked her hand into the crook of his right arm and walked with her towards the laurel archway.

30

LATE JUNE, 1944

Beth had never felt so happy. The threads of her life were weaving themselves into a pattern that was as near perfect as she could hope. It was a pattern that had always been there, but one she'd fought against every step of the way, fearing it a threat to the cool, impassive world she'd built. For months, though, she'd sensed at some deep level that it was a fight she couldn't win, no matter how many fences she erected. Those fences were down now and with them, her fear of commitment. The man she loved loved her back, and there was no more she could want.

The day they'd walked together to Alice's room, so that Jos might soften the blow of his father's long silence, had marked a new beginning. Most days after that he would climb the stairs to the apartment. The convoys of wounded were intermittent and his workload, like Captain Salito's, was very light. Ralph was often there, too. Now the boy was alone at Amberley, he stayed most of the day, though it made little difference to his scholarly progress; Beth had to acknowledge their lessons had become less and less rigorous.

That was all to the good as far as Ralph was concerned.

What he enjoyed most was simply being at Summerhayes. Previously, Beth had restricted him to the kitchen, but once she saw that he was perfectly at ease with an eighty-year-old, she relaxed and he spent a good deal of time with Alice. The elderly woman seemed to benefit from his presence, and Ralph himself was fascinated to discover that she had been a child at Amberley, too, and eager to learn what her life there had been. The four of them—Jos, Beth, Ralph and Alice—formed a tight little circle, exchanging news, passing on village chatter and generally enjoying each other's company.

It hadn't been easy for Jos to speak of his father's illness. His grandmother had heard him out in silence, but it seemed to Beth that she'd understood something of why Aiden Kellaway had cut himself off so irrevocably, and that understanding had brought her comfort. The last morsel of a painful mystery was now hers and happiness at having found a grandson seemed more important. Perhaps over the years she had suffered so greatly from not knowing, from expecting the letter that never came, that she could suffer no more. Or perhaps it was all too far in the past and, with Jos at Summerhayes, she had begun to look forward.

Whatever the reason, she appeared content, happy to be part of this unusual little band. When the rain arrived the four of them played board games, or gathered around the wireless to hear the latest news. The plan, it seemed, was for the Allies to take Caen in a pincer movement, but all was not going well. The Queens' Own Rifles had advanced to the south west of Caen, but had been ambushed by an SS Panzer Division and suffered heavy casualties. It was fortunate that when the news came through, Ralph was not in the room.

The boy remained unperturbed by his father's long absence. It was Eddie who filled his mind, Eddie who was on the tip of his tongue whenever the talk turned to the Allies' advance across France. He tried and failed to drag from Jos every snippet he could. Jos was adamant that he knew no more of his friend's whereabouts than Ralph. Whether it was true or not, Beth couldn't say. He had remained as tight-lipped with her as he had with the boy, and she didn't push him to know more. The days passed in a delightful blur and she was happy to let them.

It was only when Mrs Summer made casual mention of her nephew that she remembered Gilbert had not returned to Amberley. The last time she'd spoken to him had been the fractious call when she'd cried off dinner. He'd said then that he was staying overnight in London and would return the following day. She was startled to realise that over a week had passed and he was still not home, but she was far too happy to care.

His absence suited her fine, and suited Jos, too. While Gilbert was away there was no chance that she or Alice, or Jos himself, might be tempted into revealing Jos's true identity. That would have to wait until the war was finally over. *Why kick up a fuss?* he'd asked. *Right now, Fitzroy doesn't need to know a thing.* What he'd meant was why stir the waters when soon he would be joining the fighting again and might never return to Summerhayes? Neither of them spoke of that possibility, and Beth refused to think of it.

When the weather was good, she went to the Italian Garden with him and worked diligently on clearing another of the overgrown flower beds. Ralph would join them whenever he could escape his school work. She felt guilty that he wasn't making greater strides in his studies, but consoled herself that working in the fresh air was good for a growing boy. Ralph, himself, loved being outdoors. He'd found a slim volume in the Amberley library that catalogued a large variety of plants and showed a real aptitude for recognising the few that had survived the general devastation. In between trawling the book's pages, he could sometimes be persuaded to pick up a trowel. He was doing that this morning, having once more begged off lessons.

'Please, Miss Merston. I've done a whole page of sums and I'd rather be here. I'll work hard in the garden, I promise. Once Daddy's back, I won't get the chance. He'll be here tomorrow and nagging me to study.'

'Which is what you should be doing. I left you another three pages to complete.'

'But this is work, too, isn't it? And I like it much better. I think I want to be a gardener when I grow up.'

Bethany kept her counsel about how acceptable that might be to Gilbert Fitzroy, but she had to admit that Ralph already had some skill with plants. Jos had bought a tray of late pansies from the village the previous day and was keen to fill out the bed they had cleared, where only one or two of the original plants remained. It would be wholly unlike the garden that Joshua Summer had planned all those years ago, but its battered space would be filled with new colour.

'I don't think that's a good idea,' Ralph said, picking up the tray of plants and moving them into shadow. 'The sun is hot today and that flower bed,' he pointed to the tilled earth, 'is baking. I think we should plant them over there in the shade.'

'Over there is a mass of weeds,' Jos said.

'It is at the moment, but we could make it better.'

Beth and Jos looked at each other. The boy was right. If they planted where they'd thought to, the pansies would shrivel in the midday sun. They moved together to where Ralph was standing.

'OK, master gardener, where do you want us to dig?'

'Just here. But I'm thirsty. Would you mind if I went back to the house to get a drink?'

'Sneaking off as soon as there's work to be done,' Jos teased. Ralph hung his head and Jos tousled his hair. 'Go on, go and get your drink. But don't be long.'

Ralph beamed at him and then whisked himself through the laurel hedge almost before they'd had time to realise he'd gone.

'He must be very thirsty,' Beth remarked.

'Or very needy. He's desperate to see Eddie and this is the time of day when the convoy arrives. I've told him already that it won't be coming today, but he can't take my word for it. He has to check for himself.'

'He seems hugely attached to Eddie—too attached, maybe.'

'Eddie was kind to him. No, not just kind. He actually liked the kid a lot and he showed it. Somehow I don't think his father has the same approach.'

She paused, trowel in hand, and looked thoughtful. 'Ralph is his son and heir. I think that's what's most important for Gilbert.'

'Depressing for the boy.'

'Even more depressing for Gilbert if Ralph becomes a gardener!'

Jos laughed aloud and dropped to his knees, attacking the soil with his one good hand. 'This earth is iron. I doubt you'll be able to shift a handful.'

'Because I'm a weak woman?'

'Got it in one!'

She gave him a playful push and he teetered to one side. When he'd righted himself, he grabbed her by the waist and kissed her firmly on the lips. 'Miss Merston, you are messing with a soldier of the Toronto Queen's Own Rifles.'

'And why wouldn't I be?' She was quiet for a moment. 'I wonder if things are going better with them now?'

'Caen will be a tough nut to crack.'

'And Eddie's there cracking it.'

He paused in his digging and sat back on his haunches. 'That's what he won't be doing. Eddie was injured.'

She was stunned. 'You never told me.'

'That's because I've been hoping he'll turn up here, or somewhere in England. Until I know something definite, I thought it best not to worry you.' He passed a hand across his forehead and took a while before he spoke again. 'It was more than that, I guess. I thought that as long as I didn't speak about it, it would work out. Eddie would survive. Crazy, I know.'

She shook her head. 'No more crazy than crossing your fingers or avoiding the cracks in paving stones. But how do you know about his injury? Where was he? Where is he?'

'Hey, I'm as worried about him as you, but right now I've no answers. I won't allow myself to lose hope but, until we have news, I don't want Ralph to know.'

'I'll say nothing, I promise. You're sure he was injured?'

'I saw him go down. Or heard him rather—I'd know that yell anywhere. I'd been hit. My arm was pulverised and I was face down on the sand playing dead. When I heard his voice, I lifted my head just a fraction and saw the house overlooking the beach at Juno— then I saw Eddie silhouetted against the sky, then he fell.'

'How awful. Was he, did he...?'

'I saw his helmet roll down the beach. The bullet must have pierced it, but I can't be sure how badly he was hurt. He was carrying a good luck charm—my mother's earring—so perhaps he's still alive. All I can do is hope.'

'You gave him your mother's earring? Why?'

'I don't know. It just felt the right thing to do. It's always been a kind of talisman for me.'

'So why give it away?'

'I figured after all these years of keeping me safe, it might go on doing that—at a distance. I know that's crazy, too, but I like to think it brought me home to Summerhayes. I reckoned if Eddie carried the earring, it might bring him home, too.'

She didn't need to point out his mistake. He did it himself. 'I could be wrong,' he said. 'We were both hit, but I'm the one who seems to have survived. I was on that beach for hours, but by nightfall I'd been taken to the Chateau de Beaussy. They'd set up a field hospital there and taken in well over two hundred soldiers. More were being brought in all the time. Bullet and shrapnel wounds mostly, a lot of the guys in agony. They had a new drug, though—penicillin—I reckon that was a life saver for many.'

'But Eddie wasn't at the Chateau?'

'He wasn't. When I was able to walk, I went on a tour of the building, but I couldn't find him and he wasn't brought in later.'

She began digging again, but hardly made a dent in the rock-like surface. 'Was the chateau the only hospital? Were there others he might have gone to?'

Jos was digging alongside her. 'There were other centres, maybe not as extensive as Beaussy. I was there only a short while, but I got friendly with one of the Queen Alexandra's nurses and asked her to telephone as many as she could. Eddie wasn't listed at any of them. And he wasn't on the list of those who'd been brought back immediately after the first assault. He wasn't on the landing craft I came back on either. And his name isn't on the list of fatalities.'

'How strange.'

'Maybe, but in war anything can happen. Combat troops can go missing and turn up weeks later. If he wasn't too badly injured, he may have crawled up the beach and found help. There were combat sites all along the coast and the action was shifting from place to place. He could have ended up anywhere. Until I can be sure what's happened to him, we should keep from talking.' He turned his head and nodded towards the small figure pushing his way through the laurel arch.

'Come on, Ralph,' he called. 'If we're to get these plants in today, we need every pair of hands going.'

'Sorry I've been so long,' the boy said awkwardly, and took up his trowel. It was tough going, and after a quarter of an hour he sat back on his knees and wiped a grubby hand across a damp forehead. 'We could always finish this tomorrow.'

"We won't be planting pansies tomorrow,' Beth told him.

'You're expecting your father back, aren't you? And you'll have to make up for the study time you've lost today. We'll need at least a morning to finish the work.'

'But after the lesson...?'

'There won't be time. I have to go down to the village and buy some food. After today the cupboard is bare.'

'You can go to the village, Miss Merston.' He flashed a smile at them both. 'And Jos and I can come here.'

'And how is Miss Merston to carry all the shopping?' Jos asked him. 'It's a long walk from the village.'

'*You* can't carry it,' the boy said with certainty. 'You've only one hand.'

'If he can dig with one hand, he can carry with one,' Beth said just as certainly.

31

By nine o'clock the next morning, she was waiting for Ralph to arrive and hoping to fly through the lessons she'd prepared and spend the whole afternoon with Jos. It hardly mattered that their time together involved a mundane shopping trip. Every hour with him was precious and May had volunteered to sit with Alice.

She was surprised when there was a knock at the door since Ralph rarely announced his arrival. Usually he bound into the apartment before she'd had time to tell him to come in. Her surprise increased when she saw Gilbert Fitzroy at the top of the stairs.

'Caught the first train down this morning,' he said, by way of explanation. 'I've had more than enough of the Smoke.'

'I can imagine and welcome home. Have you brought Ralph with you?'

'He's downstairs. I left him in the office with that soldier who was here the other day. I wanted to speak to you alone.'

Another surprise, and one that verged on the worrisome.

'Things were a little more difficult in London than I expect-ed,' he continued. 'It's why I've been so long. The money issue turned out to be a tad complicated. But it's all arranged now and, with a bit of jiggery pokery, in a few months I'll be a free man. That's the reason I wanted to see you as soon as I got back.'

'It must be a relief for you to have it settled.'

Her disquiet was growing, but she led the way into the kitchen, hoping he'd say no more.

'A relief for you, too, I imagine. I know you've held back because of my wife, and I don't blame you. You're a nice girl and you wouldn't want to get mixed up in anything murky. But now the way is clear—there's nothing to stop us.'

Beth stared at him unbelievingly. He must live in a parallel world. How else could he say such a thing?

Her lack of response had no noticeable effect on him and he went on cheerfully, 'I've worked it all out. Alice trusts you and, as long as you're with her, she'll be happy to move to Amberley. I think we agreed that it would be a good deal more comfortable for her than this place. I perfectly understand why you've been unwilling to contemplate the move before—village gossip is pernicious—but once we're married, there'll be no problem.'

'Gilbert, I... You've misunderstood. I don't want to marry,' she said in a panic. 'I'm happy as I am, living here and working for Mrs Summer.'

'You can still work for her at Amberley, in a manner of speaking. You can look after her just as you do here. She'll be back in her old home, but with a companion she trusts. And if you're worrying about Ralph, I've explained to him what's happening and he's perfectly happy. You'll be happy, too. I'll make sure of that.'

'I won't.' The words came out more starkly than she intended. 'When I marry... *if* I marry,' she said more mildly, 'it will be to someone I love.' There was a long pause. 'I don't love you, Gilbert, and you must forget this idea.'

He was taken aback, but only slightly. 'I've sprung it on you,

I can see. That was a bad move. But you'll change your mind, I know.'

'You must believe me when I say that I won't.'

'You may not think it now,' he boasted, 'but you'll learn to love me. I'll make sure of it.'

She shook her head and was about to try once more to convince him how wrong he was when he lunged forward and pinned her against the kitchen cabinet. She found herself caged by two strong arms. Uselessly, she struggled to free herself and then his mouth came down hard on hers and, for a moment, sucked the breath from her body.

'I'll show you what you're missing,' he gasped. One hand reached in and tore open the buttons on her blouse while the other lifted the hem of her skirt. Frantically, she tried to push him away, but his hard, hot body thrust her back against the cabinet, leaving her not an inch to move. His mouth was nuzzling at her bare breast, and she thought she might be sick.

A sudden noise and the front door of the apartment swung open. Her terrified gaze saw Jos striding towards them and in an instant he had yanked Gilbert back so roughly that the man tottered and almost fell. She clasped hold of the cabinet for support. Her legs were trembling uncontrollably and her hands shaking so badly that when she rebuttoned her blouse, it sat askew.

'You're interrupting a private moment, soldier.' Gilbert was scarlet-faced and fuming.

'Is that what you call rape in this country?'

'How dare you suggest such a thing! It was nothing of the sort.'

'I'm not arguing. I don't argue with vermin. Your son's downstairs waiting for his lesson. You better join him before I send you there.'

Gilbert shrugged his jacket into place, a sneer on his face.

'Says a one-armed wonder. How do you think you'll manage that?'

'Stay much longer and you'll find out.'

'I'll leave when I'm ready.'

Before Beth realised what was happening, Jos had seized her attacker by the collar and dragged him through the open doorway to the top of the stairs. His boot found the man's backside and Gilbert tumbled halfway down the staircase. He managed to right himself and when he looked up, his face was murderous.

'You'll pay for this! Don't think you won't.'

Jos's expression was one of utter disgust. He shut the door with a bang and turned to Beth. She was still clasping hold of the dresser and tears were tumbling down her cheeks. He enfolded her in his arms as best he could, rocking her to and fro as though she were a small child.

Eventually she pulled away and patted his chest. 'I've soaked your shirt,' she snuffled.

'All in a good cause.' He hugged her again. 'But what the hell was going on?'

'He's mad, Jos. I'm convinced he's mad. Or at least, he lives in a different world to everyone else.'

She should have trusted her instincts from weeks ago. She'd felt uneasy the minute Gilbert had veered from business to friendship, but she'd allowed his geniality to fool her into a false security.

'He's a bully,' she added. 'As well as being insane.'

'I guessed that.'

She stroked his arm and rested her head against his shoulder. 'Thank you for rescuing me.'

'My pleasure—and believe me, it *was* a pleasure. He won't come calling again.'

Her face showed the doubts she felt. 'I'm not so sure. He

seems convinced I have feelings for him and won't accept that I haven't.'

'Forget him, Beth. I'm telling you, he won't bother you again.'

'Not while you're here at least,' she said shakily, and slipped from his hold. She walked over to the kitchen table and sat down with a thump. 'You won't always be here, though. You'll go back to France and then what do I do? I can't call the police. I wouldn't be believed for one thing, and even if they thought there was a smidgen of truth in my allegations, they'd be reluctant to intervene. Gilbert is an important person in these parts.'

'No one's so important they're above the law.'

'I suppose by the time you leave, he might have forgotten me,' she said hopefully. 'I seem to have become an obsession with him, but obsessions can die, can't they?'

He walked over to the table and pulled her to her feet, then held her at arms' length. 'There's a way of making sure he never bothers you, whether I'm here or in France.'

'Tell me,' she said eagerly.

'Marry me.'

She broke away from his hold. 'You're not serious?'

'Never more so. Let's do it, and soon. I guess you'd prefer a church.'

'No, yes, I don't mind.' Her head was scrambled.

'Then I'll ask the vicar how we can marry quickly. Good idea?'

'Yes, but—'

'I love you, Bethany. You love me. What's to stop us?'

He'd made the decision on the spur of the moment. The sight of Gilbert's hands on her had his fists clench, and he'd positively enjoyed kicking the guy down the stairs. But soon he'd be gone, leaving her without protection. She was right when she said the man would play the grand seigneur and she'd be at his mercy. Fitzroy would harry her, wear her down. She would be constantly on the watch, waiting for him to strike, and if she made a complaint against him, he would say that he was the one being pestered. That she was a poor girl, a paid companion to his aunt, and she'd been bothering him for months. He would turn the tables on her and Bethany was in no position to fight back. She needed the job, needed a home. Fitzroy could make her life so difficult that she would have to move from Summerhayes, find another job miles away, if indeed she could. And that would mean Jos's grandmother left alone.

Marriage was the perfect solution. Gilbert Fitzroy wouldn't risk his reputation by plaguing a married woman, particularly the wife of a serving soldier at a time of national crisis. It was the one thing he could do to help Beth. But Jos wasn't doing it to help. He was doing it because it felt right. It had always felt right, though he'd refused to admit it. From the first time he'd seen Beth, he'd known that whatever feelings he'd had for other women had been empty.

Sylvie had been beautiful and he'd been flattered by her interest in a man who had little to offer—except a good body and uncertain prospects. He'd been seduced by her glamour and, when the affair had ended in dreary recrimination, he'd been incensed that he'd never asked the right questions, never realised he was just one of a string of lovers. It had hurt when he'd discovered the truth, but it was damaged pride and not lost love that had pained him so badly.

Since then he'd kept clear of entanglement, concentrating every scrap of energy into soldiering. The army had been a crutch for his emotions when he was adrift, but that was no longer the case. He knew what he wanted, and he wanted Bethany for his wife. If they married very soon, they would have several weeks together before he returned to the Front. They would be weeks to treasure. And if the worst should happen, he would at least be leaving her something, a widow's pension that would help her find her feet in a bleak post-war world.

But the worst wasn't going to happen, he decided, tucking her arm in his and walking with her to the village that afternoon. She hadn't spoken of the morning's wretched events and he thought it best not to mention them. They had other priorities.

Tomorrow he would go to the vicar and ask how to arrange a church wedding as soon as possible. He didn't give a fig where they married, but he sensed that Beth would want an aisle to walk down. If he could get an early date—the vicar would know the drill—and then find help for Alice, they might manage a short vacation. They'd find a small hotel and spend the hours wandering and talking and loving.

He pulled her close, walking as tight to her as he could. Her warmth pervaded his body and he allowed the feeling to wash over him. When he looked down, he saw her face turned towards the sun. It was a lovely face, fresh and clear, and he was one lucky man. She must have sensed his gaze because she looked up at him then. He saw the tender curve of her lips, the light in her eyes, and rejoiced.

What he didn't see, as they walked together down the Summerhayes drive, was the figure of a man standing in the shadow of the house.

32

Another figure, dressed in khaki fatigues, pushed his way between crumbling masonry. Once on the other side, he tramped with some difficulty through the dense undergrowth, aiming for the belt of trees ahead. It was a nuisance that he'd been dropped at the rear entrance of Summerhayes, but he was lucky to have found a lift and the walk up through the garden could be taken at an easy pace.

His head still throbbed badly. He reached up and felt the bandages wrapped tightly around hair that had once been golden. The dressings seemed dry enough, but he would have to get them changed tomorrow. There was bound to be a medic returned to camp who could do the job. He shifted his backpack to one side; it weighed heavier than ever, but that was because he wasn't fit. He'd need to improve on that—he and Jos together. He'd heard his friend had been injured during the landings: a crew member on the craft back to Southampton remembered him from a previous journey.

Jos must have been at Summerhayes for several weeks now. If the military had picked him up from the beach as well, he'd have returned at the same time as Jos, but it was a French family that had taken him in. Not that Eddie wasn't mightily grateful. They had been kindness itself and the daughter had been a real looker. She'd held his hand while some French doctor extracted the bullet lodged in his forehead; luckily it hadn't gone deep enough to do real damage, though it hurt like hell. The family had cared for him like a son, but it meant weeks had gone by before he could get word to the authorities of where he was. Weeks when nobody knew he was alive.

He hoped that Jos hadn't believed the worst. Probably hadn't given him a thought, he smiled to himself. They would have some time together now before they were posted back to France. And Ralph. He wanted to spend time with him, too. He'd been surprised at how much he'd missed the kid. It would be good to see him again.

He jostled his way through the trees, the backpack catching on stray branches, and the vegetation underfoot tangling around his boots in a distracting fashion so that he was constantly in danger of falling. He still suffered from giddiness as well as from blinding headaches—the medics called it vertigo—well, what did you expect if you caught a bullet in the head?

It took immense effort to thrust his way through, but somehow he managed and was past the trees and out onto the temple platform. From here it was only a step down to the pathway, or what was left of it, that ran around the fetid lake.

His eyes opened in surprise. Someone had been at work since he'd last seen this place. An entire flower bed had been cleared and at least half of another. The sun was at its highest and he had to squint to see across the garden. They were new plants, he decided. Someone *had* been busy. Jos, he was pretty sure. His friend had seemed to love this part of Summerhayes.

Eddie was halfway along the pathway now and walking around the silted lake towards the archway, when a figure pushed its way through the laurel hedge. Both men stopped and looked at each other.

'Well, if it isn't my old friend, Gilbert,' he drawled.

'Rich?' Gilbert Fitzroy's face was a study of disbelief, closely followed by fear and then by anger. His complexion had turned a queasy yellow. 'But you're dead,' he stuttered.

'Not yet, pal. We Riches are survivors.'

Gilbert seemed incapable of saying more and stood like a stone column in the middle of the pathway, as though he were a permanent feature of the garden.

'I guess you'd rather not be seeing me,' Eddie goaded him. 'Not after our last little talk.'

There was a long, long silence, then Gilbert found his tongue. 'I'm sorry, I don't recall any such talk.'

Eddie shrugged his shoulders, causing the backpack to slide to one side. 'Fine, if that's the way you want to play it. I'm too tired to argue right now.'

Gilbert's face assumed a contorted expression, every muscle stretched to present an image of indifference. Eddie watched him mockingly, but he *was* tired, far too tired to tangle with the idiot in front of him. He'd keep it friendly.

'Have you seen my buddy on your travels, by any chance?'

'I believe he may be working in the duty office. At least, one of the officers there looks like the man you mean.' Gilbert's voice came out tight and a trifle shrill. He cleared his throat and when he spoke again, it was in a lower tone. 'He appears to have broken his arm.'

'A broken arm, huh? Not so bad then. I better get moving. I need to find the lucky son of a bitch and tell him Uncle Eddie is back.'

His antagonist's shoulders relaxed so suddenly they appeared almost to fly down his back. The conversation was evidently turning out far better than Gilbert could have hoped.

'I won't keep you. I imagine you'll have plenty to talk about.' Eddie adjusted his backpack and made ready to move on. 'I

think he made it to the beaches,' Gilbert added conversationally. 'Your friend. Did you?'

'Sure did, and got this for my trouble.' He raised his hand
and pointed to the stained bandage cradling his head.

Gilbert flinched at the sight of sour brown blood. 'It looks a
trifle nasty,' he said heartily. 'You'll need to get that checked as
soon as you can. I think there's one or two doctors returned to
camp.'

'I'm on my way, but nice meeting you.' Eddie trudged past
his enemy, the backpack thumping into Gilbert's body.

He'd reached the yew hedge and dropped the pack to the
ground before squeezing himself through, but halfway into
the opening, he stopped. Something had clicked in his mind,
and he was seeing smoke. A haze of smoke, winding a sinuous
path towards him. The smoke from a genie's lamp, he thought.
His bad genie. Suddenly he felt invigorated. He was tired, yes
—exhausted, yes—but the guy was a numbskull, no matter
how much politeness he was faking. So why not have
some fun?

He turned to face Gilbert, anchored to the path a short
distance away. 'Before I go, I oughta tell you something. See, I
don't want you shocked when you hear. Heart attack, and all
that. But now I'm back from defending your freedom, my
lawyers will be going full steam ahead. You'll get their letter
very soon—almost before you can rev the Bentley.'

Inch by inch, Gilbert's form grew alarmingly stiff. Only his
face was left moving, working itself to an explosion.

'You're not starting that nonsense again! I told you what I
thought of your ridiculous claim the last time you made it and I
haven't changed my mind.'

Eddie wagged an admonishing finger. 'No kidding, my
friend. I mean business and you should know it.' He walked
back along the pathway a few paces. 'You're looking kinda
rattled all of a sudden, and that's wise. Remember the painting?'

'I remember some fool thing about a portrait in one of the attics.'

'And did you check it out?'

'I did as a matter of fact, but not because I believed a word of your idiotic suggestion.'

'And you saw the earrings?'

'That's how idiotic it is. What the hell have earrings to do with anything?'

'Well now, let's see.' Eddie strolled further back along the pathway to face a man bristling with frustration. 'They were very special pieces of jewellery, designed and paid for by my grandfather, no less. They were worn, so I'm told, by Elizabeth Summer at her court presentation. Not sure what that means exactly, but I guess it doesn't matter. What's important is that they're the only pair in the world. Unique. You can ask my grandmother—sorry, your aunt—she'll tell you. So if I have one half of that pair, where did I get it from?'

'You could have got it anywhere.' Gilbert's face wore an ugly sneer.

'You're not thinking straight, fella. The earrings were the only piece of jewellery my mother took with her when she escaped from this place. They were precious, they meant something to her. She'd keep them safe, wouldn't she? And when she died, my daddy would have kept them safe, too. They'd have stayed in the family, is what I'm saying.'

'You heard the tale from somewhere. A complete fiction and you've swallowed it. You thought it might be a clever way to cheat me, I suppose, or is it blackmail you're fixed on?'

Eddie laughed aloud. 'Why would I stoop to blackmail when I've got this?'

He fished inside the breast pocket of his shirt and brought out a small velvet pouch. Tipping the earring onto the palm of his hand, he held it out for his antagonist to see. 'This will win me everything I want.'

Gilbert refused to look at the small object, but his fingers flexed nervously, curling and uncurling, until he clasped his hands tight together.

'See,' Eddie said teasingly. 'I don't lie.' He tipped the earring back into its pouch and replaced it in his shirt pocket. 'And I'm not lying about the lawyers either. You'll be getting that letter soon.'

'I don't believe you,' Gilbert almost shouted. And the sound of his voice echoed around the enclosed space.

'We'll see, won't we? But hey, relax. I'm not a mean guy. When this place is mine, you can visit any time you want. And I've a mind to make it famous again. Then if it brings in the money and you're a very good boy, I might even get you out of that great big ditch I hear you're in. I'll buy Amberley from you.'

Gilbert's fury was written on every feature. His face, his neck, his very hands had turned a violent red, so that it seemed his whole body was on fire. There was fire, too, in the roar he emitted, leaping across the few feet between them.

33

Since Jos's astonishing proposal, Beth had had little time to think. But now, as she mixed flour and water and dried egg to make a semblance of pastry, there was almost too much time. She'd said yes, she would marry him, but it had been on impulse. Why hadn't she listened to her head? Instead, she was doing what her heart decreed and it was frightening. A leap into the dark when she'd always been so cautious. Jos was a man she'd known for a matter of weeks and, in as many weeks again, he would be swallowed up by the conflict and she might lose him for ever.

But it was a risk she had to take. He had become her world and if she were only to know him for the briefest of times, that was how it had to be. Decisively, she wielded the rolling pin, turning the pastry mix into a cover for that evening's pie. She must believe he would return and they would make a life together.

There was another cloud hovering, though, less dramatic but more immediate: the need to tell Alice of their plans. She had no idea how the old lady would react—Jos was her grandson and Beth effectively the hired help. A marriage between them might find no favour with a woman still wrapped in the patrician world from which she'd sprung.

Over supper that evening, Beth tentatively broached the subject, but once the old lady understood what was happening, she grabbed Beth's hand and squeezed it hard between bony fingers.

'That is the best news I could hear. I've been hoping it might happen.'

'You have?' She was pleased but taken aback. She hadn't expected such unqualified approval.

'But of course. There was never any doubt in my mind the moment I met Jos and knew him. The moment I saw the two of you together.'

'You never mentioned it.'

'Society may have changed, Beth. I realise it has, but I still adhere to the principle that one doesn't intrude into other people's affairs.'

She took the reprimand meekly. Alice was from a generation when so much of life wasn't spoken of.

'I am glad it's settled,' the old lady went on. 'I did wonder this morning... there were raised voices. I was concerned that the two of you were quarrelling.'

'Nothing like that,' she assured her. The raised voices must remain a mystery; she had no intention of divulging Gilbert's vile behaviour, increasing the dislike Alice already felt for her nephew. 'We're very happy together. But I can hardly believe I'm to marry.'

'And why not, a lovely young girl like yourself?'

'To tell the truth, I've never wanted to,' she confessed.

Alice's face registered incomprehension. For a woman to remain single was for her a personal tragedy.

Beth tried to explain. 'My father died when I was a young child and when my mother remarried, well... it wasn't the happiest experience.'

'Marriages can be miserable, I don't deny, but when they work I'm sure they are the greatest comfort.'

'And when they don't? But even if they do, there's always the chance of loss.'

'When you care deeply for someone, that will always be a possibility. Love brings pain, but a life without love is nothing.'

Beth knew Alice was speaking from her own difficult past and she hurried to say, 'Jos is calling on the vicar tomorrow. I think Reverend Sallis will direct him to Chichester—I'm sure that's where he'll get a special licence. Then we can marry in the village church.'

The old lady gave a satisfied grunt. 'Exactly as it should be. I must get you to look out a nice dress for me. There used to be an entire rack stored in the attic furthest from Ripley's room.'

The dresses there were at least thirty years old, but she knew that Alice would only be happy wearing something with which she was familiar. Maybe she could bring it up to date a little, or perhaps May could. May was far more adept with a needle.

'It's a sensible idea to have the wedding as soon as possible,' Alice continued. 'It will give you time together before Jos is sent back to France.' She looked closely at Beth's worried countenance. 'I know he must go, my dear. But he'll return again, you can be sure, and then we can make plans.'

Alice seemed more excited than concerned, and Beth struggled to see why. 'Plans?'

'Yes, plans, and Jos will be in charge. You mustn't look so downcast. He'll come back. The Allies have almost taken Caen. They will be in Paris by August and when the city is liberated, the war will be over—at least in Europe. He'll come back and then we can begin to put this place to rights. It will be wonderful to have him make Summerhayes his own.'

'It will be some undertaking.' Beth couldn't share her

employer's certainty of either the Allies' progress or the rebirth of Summerhayes.

'Don't you think I know that? I've not ventured beyond these four walls for years, but I can imagine the mess the army has made of my house. And when war broke out the estate was already in a parlous condition.' She pursed her lips and stared gloomily ahead. But then the optimism returned. 'There will be compensation, you know. The Government will compensate us for the damage done, and with that money we can begin to put the old house together again.'

'I suppose so.' Beth was still dubious. 'But the money won't stretch to the whole estate, will it?'

'It won't, but we still own one of the farms. William sold the other to pay death duties. That was after Joshua died. Henry found him a buyer, but I was always concerned that it might be a trick. My brother never did anyone a good turn and some he did very bad turns. Sure enough we were robbed of an honest price. The purchaser turned out to be a crony of Henry's and they shared the spoils between them. William was too young to manage the estate and he wasn't a businessman like his father. And there was no wife to help him—and never would be.' She looked meaningfully at her companion.

For all kinds of reasons Summerhayes had a bleak history, Beth thought. And Alice's life had been filled with sadness, though right now sadness wasn't uppermost.

The old lady's voice held a note of fierce determination. 'After that episode, I was on my guard. I stopped William from selling the second farm and made him find a tenant instead. It was a good decision. Jos could take that farm back again, once the current lease has run its course, and make it pay.'

The supposition had Beth blinking in astonishment. 'Jos has been a soldier since he was seventeen, Mrs Summer. He's no farmer.'

'He could learn. He won't want to be a soldier all his life,' she said comfortably. 'And then there's the timber and the hives. Joshua had all of them working, all of them making money. He was good at making money.'

It left a lingering suspicion in her mind that Alice's husband had not been much good at anything else. 'You really think Jos could do that?'

'He'd have to hire people, of course. But he's managed men for years so organising staff won't be a problem. And if just one part of the estate can be made profitable, it will help fund a much wider restoration. We might even restore the gardens. At the very least, we could grow our own fruit and vegetables. That would save money—and taste a good deal better. I know the villagers grow plenty, but their produce is on the poor side. Mr Harris had the trick.'

She was amazed at how clearly Alice was thinking, now that she was focussed on a goal and resolute in achieving it. There had been several occasions in the past when Beth had been surprised at the older woman's acuity, but tonight a new spirit was animating the frail figure. And all because a man whom she'd not even known existed a few months ago had come into her life.

'I'm tired now, my dear. I need to rest.' Alice's energy had faded. 'Today has been almost too exciting—the Allies at the gates of Caen, an unexpected wedding to think of, and then that quarrel this morning—that was upsetting. I'm sure I heard Gilbert's voice.'

She kept silent, hoping the moment would pass, but it didn't. 'Gilbert Fitzroy is not a man you should have dealings with,' Alice warned.

It was beyond Beth how she should answer, and all she could do was hope her employer hadn't realised the reason for the brawl. She rowed back onto safer territory. 'I'll warm some milk and get your pills.'

But opening the bathroom cabinet, she noticed that the

bottle of pills had been moved slightly to the centre when she was convinced she'd left them to one side. Had Alice come into the bathroom and helped herself to tablets while she and Jos were walking to the village? The old lady had been upset by the morning's events, it was clear, and if she'd heard more of Gilbert's rantings than she should, she might have tried to calm herself by swallowing pills. Beth wasn't sure just how strong the tablets were, but she never varied from the doctor's instructions and dared not risk Alice taking a double dose.

'Mrs Summer,' she called from the bathroom. 'Have you already taken your pills?'

'No, I haven't and I don't want to.'

She wasn't sure she'd heard aright and came back into the sitting room, the brown bottle of tablets in her hand. Alice waved them away.

'I shan't take any more pills,' she said decidedly. 'They've done me no good and they may have done me harm.'

'But you've taken them for years.'

'Then it's time I stopped. It's right that I make a break from the past—it's controlled the way I live for too long. The years have drifted by while all I've done is wait.' The lines carved so deeply into the old face disappeared in the brilliance of her smile. 'There's to be no more waiting. I have Elizabeth with me at last. Jos has brought her back and it's made me content. The pills should go.'

Beth turned to walk back to the bathroom. She would keep the tablets just in case, but she applauded Alice's decision.

'If you are to marry my grandson,' the old lady called after her, 'you must stop calling me Mrs Summer. I shall be Alice from now on.' It was a lordly command.

'I'll fetch your milk then, Alice,' she called back, an amused smile on her face.

. . .

There had been no sign of Gilbert for days, though according to Ralph his father was still at Amberley. The teaching had fallen by the wayside, but it hadn't stopped the boy coming to Summerhayes every day. It seemed that Ralph was now at liberty to do what he wished. Whenever Beth had a free hour, the two of them worked in the garden together. She still felt uneasy if she were left alone there, but Ralph's chatter in her ear banished any dark shadow. Jos would join them in the afternoon when the office was at its quietest.

After his interview with the vicar, he'd taken the trip to Chichester and secured a special licence from the bishop. Their wedding was fixed for ten days' time and Ralph appeared even more excited than they. For a while they'd pondered whether they should say nothing of their plans, in case he relayed the news to Gilbert and that angry man tried to intervene. But Ralph, it seemed, hardly spoke to his father these days and whatever Gilbert had told him of his own plans for Beth—if indeed he'd spoken of them—had clearly made no impression on the boy.

'Will you have a holiday after the wedding? People who get married have a holiday, so where will you go?' Ralph had bounced into the office before Jos had time to finish his lunchtime sandwich.

'We're working on the holiday bit,' he told him. 'Mrs Prendergast has promised to stay at Summerhayes for a few days, but we haven't decided yet where we'll go.'

'You could always stay here,' the boy said hopefully. 'You don't have to go away. We could all do the garden together.'

'That's not quite the idea, but I promise we'll work on the garden when we get back. In the meantime, there's plenty to do. Have a look at these.'

Two open boxes lay on his desk, both filled with new plants. He'd studied old photographs of the garden and with the help of Ralph's book had managed to identify a handful of the original plants. 'They'll make the pansies we've grown look a bit sick, but it can't be helped. It's a first step in getting the Italian Garden back to what it used to be.'

'They look super,' Ralph enthused.

'They certainly do.' Beth had walked into the office while they were bent over the packages. 'However did you get hold of them?'

'I spoke to one of the guys in the pub the other day—when I went to order the wedding feast. He was pretty knowledgeable and had a contact up country.'

'There's going to be a feast!' Ralph interrupted.

'That was a joke. It will be as good as the Horse and Groom can manage, but you eat better at Amberley every day so don't get too excited.'

The boy's head drooped. 'I won't. It will be fun whatever it is. Much more fun than eating in the kitchen. Cook just makes me eggs or beans or something.'

'You don't eat with your father?' Beth felt the stirrings of anxiety.

'He doesn't eat. He stays in his study all the time.'

'When do you see him then?' She was now seriously concerned.

'I don't. I'm not allowed to bother him.'

That was the reason Ralph was always here, she thought. What was going on with Gilbert? Surely his last ignominious visit to Summerhayes couldn't be affecting him this badly? And how dreadful to treat his son in such a fashion. For all his quirky ways, Ralph was still very young.

Jos's eyes signalled a warning and she took the hint and said no more. 'If we could get these in this afternoon, it would be good.' He closed each of the box lids.

'Yes, let's do it now.' The boy perked up. He grabbed hold of one of the packages, but then stopped before he'd gone a few paces towards the door. 'I'm not sure there'll be enough room, not since we planted the pansies.'

'We'll have to make room,' Jos said. 'Clear another flower bed, or at least part of one. It rained last night, and the earth will be damp and much easier to dig. If you begin on the patch to the right of the temple and Beth on the left, the two of you should meet in the middle.'

'Oh, really. And what are you going to be doing?' she questioned.

'Need you ask? Supervising, of course.' He grinned. 'I'll be down to help, I promise, after I've made these few phone calls. Are you OK with that box, Ralph? Miss Merston should be able to manage the other.'

As soon as they'd pushed their way through the laurel hedge, she could see that Jos was right about the earth. She'd heard the rain in the early hours, a cascade of water tumbling down the roof tiles and spouting from the gutters. Rain had been scarce these past few weeks and the plants were looking grateful for their dousing. Beth was equally grateful when her trowel slid easily into the earth.

'Jos was right, Miss Merston. It's like slicing butter.'

'Almost. But we could still do with his help.'

'Not if we get a move on. We'll get this cleared in no time. There won't be anything for him to do.' Ralph evidently saw gardening as a competition, part of the afternoon's enjoyment.

'Won't he be sorry!' she said laughingly.

But the boy was as good as his word, working his way through the soft earth far longer than usual. He'd been busy for at least a quarter of an hour by Beth's calculation before he stopped. Then it was to exclaim, 'Gosh, look at this.'

34

'What is it?' Beth looked across from the other side of the flowerbed.

'I don't know—it's covered in dirt, but it looks like it might have been pretty once.'

She got up from where she was kneeling and walked over to him. He held out his hand to her and she took the small object nestling in his palm and rubbed away the encrusted dirt. Peering down, she couldn't believe what she was seeing; her stomach gave a fierce, painful jolt. Jos's earring. Or rather his mother's. There was no doubt of it, the design was too individual to mistake. But what was it doing here?

The sun had freed itself from cloud and was beating hotly down on her shoulders. In the trees behind the temple a family of crows was quarrelling over a nest. The laurel hedge in the distance seemed to blur in front of her eyes. The earring—Jos had given it to Eddie to keep him from harm. But how had it come to be buried in the earth of the Italian Garden?

'Is everything all right, Miss Merston?'

Ralph's anxious voice woke her from a daze. 'Yes, it's fine. I must have stood up too quickly.'

She would have to tell Jos. There must be a simple explanation for the earring, and he would know it. Her mind was travelling in a bad direction, and she must shake herself free of such thoughts.

'Let's keep going.'

The boy bent down once more and rippled his trowel through the loose earth. 'There's this, too,' he said, holding up what looked like a small piece of metal.

The dreadful premonition returned. She took the disc from him and turned it over. It was a dog tag. There was a number, then the word OFFICER. And below that a name—E. RICH, followed by INF and PRES. Infantry? Presbyterian? What did it matter? This was Eddie's dog tag and a dog tag never left a soldier's body, everyone knew that. She felt herself swaying dangerously towards the marble edge of the temple platform.

'What is it?' Ralph looked up, innocently curious.

'It's an old tag. Nothing to worry about. But maybe I should take over the digging for a while. Why don't you run up to the house and see if Jos is coming?'

'I'd rather stay and see what else turns up. It's buried treasure, just like the Famous Five.'

It wasn't going to be an Enid Blyton ending, of that Beth was certain. But she had to keep digging. She had to know the worst. She knelt where Ralph had been kneeling and carefully moved a small handful of earth to one side. That was all that was needed for the nightmare to come true. A fingernail. Her stomach churned, bile filled her throat, but she couldn't stop. Frantically, she scraped away soil and small stones; she longed to avert her eyes but knew she must look. This was horrible, horrible. The fingernail was attached to a finger, the finger to a hand and the hand to an arm. She knew the owner of that arm. Eddie had died not on a French beach, but here in the Italian Garden.

'Ralph, run to the house. Get Jos.'

'What have you found? Can I look?'

'No,' and her voice came out as a small scream. 'Just go. Now!'

But another voice had joined hers. 'You're not to do that, Ralph.'

Beth staggered to her feet and stood beside the young boy, both of them staring in amazement. She was too bewildered to feel fear, which surely she should have done. Gilbert Fitzroy was walking through the trees towards them and he held a rifle in his hand. It was levelled somewhere around her eyes.

'Daddy!' Ralph went to run to him when Gilbert made a violent gesture that he should stay back. The boy stopped in his tracks.

'Why have you got a gun? What are you doing?' His young voice broke in terror.

'You are to go home, Ralph, and stay there.'

'But Daddy—'

'This minute!' And he tipped his head towards the trees to signal the path the boy was to take. 'Miss Merston and I are going to have a little chat.'

Ashen faced, his limbs visibly shaking, Ralph skirted his father and disappeared into the trees. Bethany was left facing the gun.

'You know you are a most interfering young lady.' Gilbert's smile was horribly genial.

'What have you done?'

It was a foolish question but her mind was scrabbling to make sense of what had happened, of what was happening. She was finding it difficult to breathe, difficult even to stay upright. Gilbert Fitzroy was almost certainly the reason poor Eddie lay close by in his shallow grave.

'I did what had to be done.'

'You killed Eddie.'

'Not a great loss to the world, I'd say.'

'How could you do that?'

She hardly noticed the raised gun. She was thinking of Eddie. Somehow he'd survived the battle. All the time they'd feared him dead, he'd been alive and making his way back to Summerhayes. Only to be killed by a man who had lost his senses.

'How could I kill Eddie Rich? Easily, as it turned out. It was stupid of him to come back here, and really stupid of him to act so cockily. He took his eye off the ball and what do you know, a piece of terracotta did the trick. Made a bit of a mess of his head, but then it was a mess already.'

Beth felt nauseous. He was proud of killing a man who had done no more than mock him. Proud of cold-bloodedly shattering his skull. She looked directly into his eyes. They were as dead as Eddie's.

'Why would you do such a terrible thing?'

He moved towards her and the barrel of the gun, glinting in the sun, seemed larger than ever. 'I'll tell you why. He was a threat. He stood in my way and no one does that.' She was bewildered. How on earth had Eddie ever been a threat to this man?

'You're a little stupid, Bethany dear, though you don't realise it. You don't see what's beneath your nose. The man was a menace and had to go. I found the painting he told me about. Did you know that? The one with my cousin Elizabeth wearing those earrings. I found it the day I left the wine and I realised then that I might have a bigger problem than I'd expected.'

Beth was side-tracked. 'It was you who left the wine?'

'Who else? And it would have worked, knocked the old dear off her perch for good.' He looked up at the sky imploringly. 'Why do I have to suffer such fools? A glass of that would have done the business, but no, you had to pour it down the drain. The pills will be different, though. They'll do the trick—they should be working their magic at this very moment.'

'Pills?'

'You're a perpetual echo, my dear. Do stop. The pills that Aunt Alice takes to settle her nerves. Some nerves!'

'It was you who moved them?'

'Ah, not so stupid after all. Not only moved them but mixed them with a few of my own, once you and soldier boy had left. And by the way, I don't admire your choice. That was very short-sighted of you. You should have stuck with me.'

Beth's eyes had grown larger at each revelation. 'I don't understand why you would do such things.'

'Of course you don't. Unlike me, you've no notion of seizing an opportunity. When I met you, I saw mine. Ida wasn't coming back and you were someone who could be useful. You could deliver Alice to me. And be a pleasant addition to my household as well. But you didn't play ball. You were too protective of the old lady by far. I had to think of another way.'

'And that was?'

'I can't expect you to understand genius. The letters from Elizabeth, the ghost at the window. What did you really think?'

'That Molly Dumbrell was behind them. That for some reason she disliked Mrs Summer and was taking her revenge.'

'Molly Dumbrell!' His voice shook with anger. 'A girl with nothing in her head but sex and money. You think an idiot like that could plan such a brilliant campaign?'

'It wasn't that brilliant,' she retorted. 'It didn't succeed.' Beth knew it was unwise to taunt him, but she'd lost interest in being prudent. She was going to die so why not go out blazing?

'Only because you meddled,' he snarled. 'And the letters *had* begun to work. The old girl was beginning to lose her mind. It was only a matter of time before she was certified and I assumed power of attorney.'

The man's evil was sickening. It explained all the 'bad things', as Alice called them, that had happened this summer. Beth had thought him a decent man, a little pushy perhaps, but honourable. How stupid she'd been. How very naïve. He was right about that, at least.

'And it wasn't enough for you to send her mad, was it? You had to hurt her physically.' It was so clear to her now that she could speak without her voice shaking.

'The old girl wouldn't have known a thing. The ghost was a master stroke—Molly looked quite the part in my gardener's apron and felt hat. She swore that Alice was about to pitch herself from the window.'

His body relaxed as he considered how clever he'd been, and Beth saw the gun lower slightly. She wondered if she could rush him while his attention was elsewhere but, just as she'd tensed herself to go, his figure stiffened and he brought the gun upwards once more, its barrel pointing at the space between her eyes.

'And before you ask, the twine was my idea, too. If it had been done properly, no one would have been any the wiser. But Molly's talents stop at the bedroom door.' His mouth had become a thin slash. 'Another fool I've been blessed with. Ultimately she turned out to be useless—she had to go.'

Beth let out a small gasp. Was there another body buried in this garden?

'Forget the concern.' He smirked. 'Molly enjoyed the fun while it lasted, but she was a girl who could be bought. She's in Ireland now, flaunting her new-found wealth, and she won't be coming back. But neither will Mr Rich. Two threats eliminated and only one to go. You, my dear. Can't have you telling tales about dead bodies.'

She must keep him talking; she had no real idea why, except to live a little longer. It was just possible that Ralph had not returned home as he'd been ordered but had run to find help.

'Molly may have been a threat to you, but not Eddie.'

'That's where you're wrong. He was an idiot, I grant you, but a dangerous one. I had to get rid of him. He showed me the

earring, and then I knew. This place is mine. It always has been.
How dare anyone come between a man and his property?'

'Summerhayes isn't yours,' she said boldly. 'It belongs to
your aunt.'

'Who will shortly be following Lieutenant Rich. And once
she does, Amberley will recover the land that belongs to it.'

'All very grand, but Summerhayes is little more than a
wreck. Why would you want it?'

'I'll sell. What else?' Gilbert's mood had changed. The
grandiose speech had turned surly. 'I wanted this land for
Amberley, wanted what my father never managed. But I don't
have the luxury. I'll have to sell. The land alone should fetch a
tidy sum and the house, too—I'm told it has architectural value.'

'Why would you sell? Amberley's future is secure.'

'Secure?' His laugh was bitter. 'The divorce has left me high
and dry. My esteemed wife has made sure I haven't a feather to
fly with. Well and truly plucked.'

'But you said—'

'That Ida was settling money on Amberley? That will be
the day. The bitch will take her last dollar with her. But you
believed me, didn't you? As I said, a little stupid.'

'There was a time when you didn't think so, but no doubt
being kicked down the stairs changed your mind.' It was a small
enjoyment to remind him of his humiliation.

'You were a tool, that's all. A way of getting what I wanted. I
was lucky you were attractive—it wasn't hard to flirt with you—
and, if you'd come to see things my way, I'd have given you a
comfortable home without the need to dance attention on old
ladies. But dancing attention will be the least of your worries
now.'

'I was stupid to trust you, but I'm not the only fool. You
killed Eddie because you thought him a threat. But you were
wrong. Eddie was no heir to Summerhayes, he was merely
teasing you. That's what he did, tease. You got the wrong man.'

Gilbert's gun hand wavered. 'I did not.' He was riled, but a small doubt had been sown. 'It wasn't just the earring,' he blustered. 'It all fitted—my silly cousin eloping to Canada, having a child that no one knew of.'

'Eddie isn't the only soldier from Canada who might have a link to Summerhayes. You killed the wrong man, Gilbert. How does that feel?'

She was spinning out the time. Then—a sudden realisation that she must cavil no longer. She must give up and let this madman shoot her and disappear. Before Jos could arrive. Why hadn't she thought of that before? If Jos should finish his phone calls early and walk through the archway, he would have a rifle pointed at his heart, and she couldn't let that happen.

Gilbert jerked the rifle upwards and with narrowed eyes peered down the sight. 'I have no idea what you're talking about. And, frankly, I think you've talked enough.' He drew back the bolt on the rifle.

'She's telling you that you killed my best friend for nothing.'

Jos had come and how she wished he hadn't. He had pushed through the laurel with scarcely a sound and was standing just feet away. 'Here's the man you should have killed —you're looking at him right now.'

He was as unprotected as her and no matter how athletic he might be, with one arm in a sling, there was no way he could grab that rifle.

Gilbert was shaking his head as though trying to rid himself of a particularly painful idea, but when he spoke it was to say calmly, 'If I've made a mistake, I must rectify it. I'll kill you both. That way, I can be sure.'

She tried to edge closer to Jos. If they were to die, she wanted it to be together. But their adversary saw the movement out of the corner of his eye and stopped her before she'd moved an inch. 'Stay where you are, Bethany. One at a time. Then I can be sure that neither of you will live to tell tales.'

He *was* completely mad, she thought. Utterly insane. Did he think he could get away with blasting two people out of existence and somehow escape justice? He raised the rifle again, ready to take aim at Jos. She closed her eyes—she couldn't bear to watch the man she loved crumple and fall.

There was a loud report and she stayed frozen into position, eyes still tightly closed, waiting for the second shot to reach her.

A hand on her arm, an arm around her shoulder. 'It's OK, Beth. It's OK.'

Jos was there by her side and Gilbert lay sprawled across the path, his head dangling close to the filthy water of the lake. A service revolver lay on the earth. Jos walked across and picked it up.

'Difficult to control with one arm out of action,' he said laconically. 'But it can be done.'

35

1 JULY, 1944

'That frock is some pretty.' May Prendergast stood back and admired the emerald silk tea dress hanging from the wardrobe door.

'Do you think it smart enough?'

'It will knock the socks off people,' her friend assured her. '*You'll* knock the socks off 'em. Now, let's get going. I've saved some of the make-up I bought before the war.' She pulled from her handbag various pots and tubes and arranged them in martial fashion across the top of the dressing table. 'This'll make you the belle of any ball.'

'It's only a simple church service, May. I don't think we should go over the top.'

'Everyone will be there and you'll want to look your best.'

'For Jos certainly, but everyone?'

'Everyone,' May said firmly. 'The whole village is turning out to see you married. Turning out to see the old lady, too—it's years since they caught a glimpse of her. And what a blessed day for a wedding. Just look at that sun.'

Of late the weather had been temperamental but, when this morning Beth had flung up the blackout blinds, it was to see the sun had returned with only a wisp of cloud to mar the bluest of skies. It was an omen, she'd decided. After the heartache of recent days, it was an omen of happiness.

'Was Mrs Summer all right when you left her?' Beth couldn't suppress her anxiety for the old lady, though Alice appeared to have weathered the recent drama in good shape.

May sat her down at the mirror. 'Happy as a grig, my dear. Mr Ripley saw her into the jeep. She took to it straightaway and he's sitting alongside her. He'll look after her in church, you can be sure.'

'Captain Salito was so kind in offering a lift. I love the idea of walking to my wedding—it's the old way, I believe—but Alice certainly couldn't do it and Mr Ripley would have found it hard.'

'You'll find a lot of folks will be kind. You've had a bad experience, very bad—and they know it,' she finished fiercely.

It was only now, ten days later, that Beth could bear to visualise that dreadful scene. Then the aftermath of an ambulance, the police, the identification in the mortuary. That had seemed unnecessarily dreadful. And Ralph, poor dear little Ralph, who had done exactly as his father ordered. She had been the one to tell him the dreadful news. Jos had said it had to be her and she'd agreed. Ralph cared for her opinion, he'd grown to like her, to trust her, and he had no one else in the world. It had to be her, but the words had stuck in her throat.

'It's going to be a wonderful day.' May had sensed the sadness filling the room and her voice was deliberately cheerful. 'You're going to forget the goings-on at Amberley. We're all going to forget.'

'Does everyone know what happened?'

'Of course they do, my dear. This is a village. It's the most exciting thing that's happened for years. Not even the war can match it.'

The village would be craning its communal neck to see the

man who had killed Gilbert Fitzroy. Beth pushed the thought away. It was an open and shut case, the police had said, and Jos was a local hero, but it wasn't something she wanted to remember.

'We're all sorry for the youngster, but we're sorrier for you,' May went on. 'We know the Fitzroy family. We know what Gilbert's capable of and he's not missed, you can be sure.'

'I wonder what will happen to Amberley now?'

May swooshed her fingertips in Pan-Cake and dotted it around Beth's face, then picked up a little cardboard pot of coral powder. 'See, actual rouge! The boy will inherit the place, I suppose. Along with its debts. He'd be wise to sell up as soon as he can.'

'He won't be able to for years. Twenty-one is a long way off.'

'Then his trustees can rent it out and he can decide when the time comes. Have they been in touch with you? Here, spit on this mascara.'

'Yes. It's the same legal firm that was dealing with the divorce. A nice older man called a few days ago. He came all the way from London to speak to Ralph. Apparently his mother has offered the boy a home in New York, but Ralph doesn't want to go. He's asked to stay here and, considering the trauma he's been through, Mr Parsons—the solicitor—feels he should be allowed to. He wanted to meet me to ask if it were possible.'

'Hmm.' May studiously applied a coat of red lipstick.

'What do you mean, *hmm*?'

'Who's he going to live with, that's what I mean? He could go back to that school—'

'He doesn't want to do that either,' Beth interposed. For nights, she'd cuddled the small body as Ralph had sobbed himself to sleep. She would do nothing that would make the child's life less bearable.

'Well, then, I can guess who's going to be looking after him.'

May had finished her ministrations and stood with arms crossed, looking stern.

'Mr Parsons said the trustees would be very grateful if I could have him here.'

'I bet they would. Wriggling out of their responsibilities.'

'Oh, May, it's not like that. And they'll pay a generous allowance.'

'You deserve to begin married life on your own, not burdened with someone else's child.'

'I don't feel at all burdened.' She stood up only to find May's hand pressing her back into the chair. 'We've not finished yet, my love. We've hair to do.'

She settled again while her friend gathered together brush and comb and hairpins. 'Ralph gets along with Alice brilliantly, you know, and soon there'll be just the three of us—when Jos returns to France.'

The shadow was always there, but it looked as though Alice's prediction that the Allies would be in Paris by August might be fulfilled. Beth would believe it. She must believe it.

'I thought I might tidy out one of the attics, the one next to Mr Ripley's, and make it into a bedroom for Ralph.'

Her friend pulled the brush through a tangled mane, at the same time twisting small strands of hair around her hand.

'It won't be nearly as comfortable as Amberley, but I don't think he'll mind. The last two nights, he's slept alongside Jos in his billet, but it's no real solution. When Jos moves in here, the boy will be alone in the garden and I don't want that.'

'There. What do you think?' Her long dark hair had been swept into a pretty topknot, small tendrils curling around her ears and softening her forehead.

'How did you do that? It looks amazing.'

'Used to do my Ma's hair all those years ago and I trained for a while as a hairdresser—until Mr Prendergast came along. Then that was it. No more working, though I'd like to have carried on. But I haven't lost my touch, have I?' She stood behind Beth, surveying her protégée's image with pride.

'You certainly haven't.' Beth jumped up and went to embrace her friend.

'Hush, you'll mess your make up.' May looked at the small bedside clock. 'And it's nearly time. He'll be here any minute. C'mon, we need to get you dressed.'

It took a few seconds only to slip into the frock and for May to lace the back fastenings. The mirror was small and here and there spotted with brown, but it was clear enough for Beth to see that the dress fitted her slim figure to perfection, the gathered bust beneath a sweetheart neckline flowing into a clinched waist. The silk's intense green was a dazzling frame for dark hair and eyes. She slipped her feet into her sole pair of sandals, golden and chunky heeled. Somehow, she'd managed through the war years to keep the pair safe.

'You know, you could always live at Amberley.' May gathered up the pots and tubes from the dressing table and carefully stored the cherished goods away in her handbag. 'Ralph could keep his own room and you'd be a whole lot more comfortable. All of you. For Alice, it would be going home.'

Beth turned a little pale beneath her make up. 'I don't think I could. Not after...'

'Think about it,' May advised. 'Amberley isn't Gilbert and it's a fine old house.'

'But it's a house with a bad history.'

'It is that. But it's time to change it, don't you think? You could live there and put this place to rights at the same time.'

She had to agree that it was a sensible idea. 'I'll talk it over with Jos—in time.'

There was a lot to talk over with Jos, a lot she hadn't yet been able to broach. Discussing whether or not she should live in a house that had belonged to the man who'd killed his best friend was probably not top of the list.

Eddie's funeral had taken place only a few days previously and it had hit Jos hard. When he'd been unsure of Eddie's fate, he'd kept the hope alive that one day he would see his friend again. Now that hope was destroyed.

I'd have liked to have had him by my side when we marry, Jos had said, as they'd made their way back to Summerhayes after the funeral. The burial had been heart-breaking, only a few mourners at the graveside, and the vicar's solemn words still ringing in their ears.

I know, she'd replied, and put her arm through his and hugged him close. *But in spirit he'll be with us.* She'd hoped she was right.

May opened the bedroom door and shooed her across the landing into the kitchen. 'Yes, speak to your young man about Amberley. I reckon it would work fine. And I daresay he'll be up to talking a lot more once the honeymoon's over. Till then, he'll have plenty else to distract him.' She gave a small wink.

Beth was startled. The wink seemed so out of place, at odds with the sorrow she felt for Eddie, yet she knew May was right to be cheerful. Fretting did no one any good. She and Jos must put recent events behind them and, in the short time they had together, think instead of the future.

'It will be a massive undertaking to put Summerhayes to rights.' Beth was following her train of thought. 'Not that it can't be done. Alice already has plans. But we'll need this war to end first.'

'And it will. Very soon.' It was Jos.

He'd walked up the staircase unheard. He was wearing a dark dress uniform: slim trousers and a high collared jacket open at the front to reveal a scarlet undershirt. Silver buttons shone from each sleeve and a row of medals marched proudly across his chest.

May was looking at him open-mouthed. 'Handsome,' she breathed, 'some handsome.'

Beth looked across at Jos standing in the kitchen doorway. It was nearly their undoing—at any moment they might burst into laughter, and she would not offend May for the world. Dashing across to the sink, she grabbed her bouquet of freesias and cream roses, then tucked her arm in his.

'I think it might be time to go.'

Jos's eyes shone with amusement.

He bent his head and brushed her cheek with his lips. 'I think it might,' he said.

A LETTER FROM MERRYN

Dear Reader,

I want to say a huge thank you for choosing to read *The Secrets of Summerhayes*. If you enjoyed it and want to keep up to date with all my latest releases, just sign up at the following link. Your email address will never be shared and you can unsubscribe at any time.

www.bookouture.com/merryn-allingham

The Secrets of Summerhayes is a sequel, and thirty long years divide it from *The Girl from Summerhayes,* but each novel marks an enormous turning point in the fortunes of the country, the Summerhayes estate and of my characters themselves. *The Girl from Summerhayes* is set in the year that World War I was declared, when the Edwardian life it depicts was forever shattered, while *The Secrets of Summerhayes* sees the world once more in conflict, on the eve of another momentous event—D-Day and the forthcoming liberation of Europe.

If you enjoyed *The Secrets of Summerhayes*, I would love a short review. Getting feedback from readers is amazing and it helps new readers to discover my books for the first time.

Do get in touch on my Facebook page, through Twitter, Goodreads or my website—it will make this author's day!

Thank you for reading,

Merryn x

www.merrynallingham.com

 facebook.com/MerrynWrites
twitter.com/merrynwrites

Printed in Great Britain
by Amazon

44536446R00179